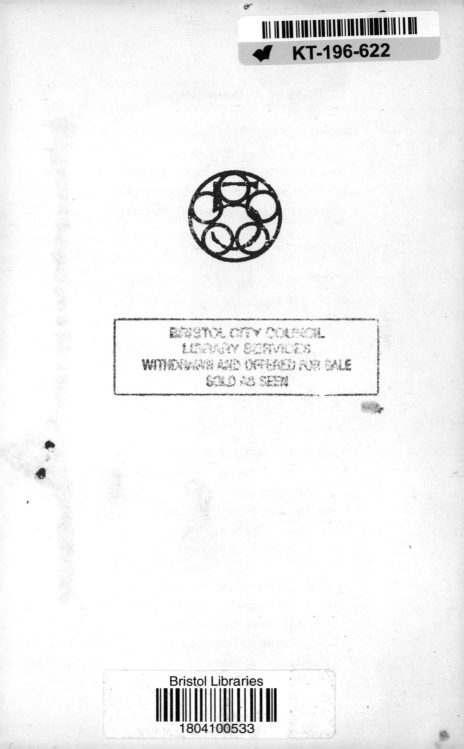

KT-196-622

BRISTOL CITY COUNCIL
LIBRARY SERVICES
WITHDRAWN AND OFFERED FOR SALE
SOLD AS SEEN

Bristol Libraries

1804100533

NIGHT RISE

WALKER
BOOKS

This is a work of fiction. Names, characters, places and incidents
are either the product of the author's imagination or, if real, used
fictitiously. All statements, activities, stunts, descriptions, information
and material of any other kind contained herein are included for
entertainment purposes only and should not be relied on for
accuracy or replicated as they may result in injury.

Based on an idea first published in 1986 as *The Silver Citadel*

First published as *Nightrise* 2007 by Walker Books Ltd
87 Vauxhall Walk, London SE11 5HJ

This edition with new cover published 2013

2 4 6 8 10 9 7 5 3 1

Text © 1986, 2007 Stormbreaker Productions Ltd
Cover illustration and design © 2013 Walker Books Ltd
Power of 5 logo™ © 2007 Walker Books Ltd

The right of Anthony Horowitz to be identified as author of this
work has been asserted by him in accordance with the
Copyright, Designs and Patents Act 1988

This book has been typeset in Frutiger Light and Alternate Gothic

Printed and bound in Great Britain by Clays Ltd, St Ives plc

All rights reserved. No part of this book may be reproduced,
transmitted or stored in an information retrieval system in any
form or by any means, graphic, electronic or mechanical,
including photocopying, taping and recording, without prior
written permission from the publisher.

British Library Cataloguing in Publication Data:
a catalogue record for this book is available from the British Library

ISBN 978-1-4063-3887-4

www.walker.co.uk

www.powerof5.co.uk

THE STORY SO FAR...

In *Evil Star*, Matt and Pedro failed to close the second gate that they had found in the Nazca Desert, and the Old Ones – ancient forces of evil – finally entered the world.

Having lost this battle, Matt learnt that his only hope was to find the three other Gatekeepers: two boys and a girl. By coming together, they would finally have the strength to defeat the Old Ones and save the world from chaos and destruction.

Nightrise, the third book in the series, begins in June, a few weeks before the end of *Evil Star*. The Old Ones know the power of the Five – and their servants are already searching for them, determined to keep them apart.

There are three worlds in this book. The world now. The world as it was before the Dark Ages, approximately ten thousand years ago. And a strange dream world that connects the two.

CONTENTS

THE CIRCUS OF THE MIND

The two men in the black limousine had already circled the theatre once. Now they pulled in on the other side of the road, opposite the main door. Outside, the temperature was well into the eighties. But they had turned the air-conditioning on full and the car was like a refrigerator. They sat in silence. The two of them had worked together for many years and despised each other. They had nothing to say.

The theatre was at the northern end of Reno, Nevada. It was a square red-brick building with a single door and no windows and could have been a bank or possibly a chapel but for the neon sign over the front door. It was supposed to read THE RENO PLAYHOUSE, but half the letters had fused so that, as the two men watched it from where they were parked in Virginia Street, just two words flashed at them through the fading light: HERE LOSE.

It wasn't exactly the most attractive invitation in a city that was dedicated to gambling, where every other building seemed to be a casino and where the hotels, the bars, even the launderettes, were stuffed with slot machines. Despite its name, the Reno Playhouse hadn't actually put on a play from the day it had been built. Instead, it provided a temporary home to a long line of second-rate performers: singers and dancers, conjurors and comedians who had all been famous, briefly, a very long time ago but who had never really been heard of since. These were the sort of people who performed night after night, trying to entertain audiences who were only thinking of the money they had come to win or, worse, the money they had already lost.

The next performance was due to begin in an hour's time. The two men had already bought their tickets – but there was something they wanted to see before they went in. They only had to wait a few minutes to be rewarded. The man in the driving seat suddenly stiffened.

"Here they are," he said.

Two boys had just got off a bus. They were walking down the pavement, dressed casually in baggy jeans and T-shirts, one of them carrying a backpack. It was obvious immediately that they were twins, about fourteen years old. They were both very slim – in fact they looked malnourished. Their hair was black and dead straight, hanging down to the neck, and both had dark brown eyes. One was a couple of centimetres taller and a few kilos heavier than the other. He said something and the other boy laughed. Then they turned the corner and a moment later were gone.

"That was them?" the passenger asked.

"That was them," the driver confirmed.

The first man shrugged. "They don't look that special to me."

"That's what you always say, Mr Hovey. But you never know. Maybe these kids will be the ones…"

"Let's get a drink."

The men had an hour to kill but there were plenty of bars in Reno and they might throw a few coins into a machine too. It had been a long day. The driver glanced one last time at the theatre and nodded. He had a good feeling. This time they were going to find what they were looking for.

He shoved the car into gear and they moved off.

The show that was currently at the Reno Playhouse – it had been there for the past six months – was called *The Circus of the Mind*. There was a glass panel next to the front door, and behind it a black and white poster showing the eyes and forehead of what might have been a hypnotist or a magician. His hands, disembodied, floated above him, the fingers pointing towards the viewer. It read:

DON WHITE PRESENTS
THE CIRCUS of THE MIND

There are many things in life that cannot be explained. Powers that exist on the edge of our consciousness.
Do you dare journey into the world of the paranormal?
Be amazed! Be mystified!
This is a show you will never forget.

∾ FEATURING ∾
Swami Louvishni – world-famous Indian fakir
Bobby Bruce – hypnotist to the stars
Mr Marvano – master illusionist
Zorro – escapologist
Scott & Jamie Tyler – telepathic twins

Performance times: 7.30 p.m. & 9.30 p.m.
Tickets: $35 – $55 (Senior citizens half price)

By twenty past seven that evening, a small crowd had gathered on the pavement, waiting for the door to open. There were about fifty people. Most of them had been attracted to the theatre by leaflets given to them by the receptionists in the hotels where they were staying. The leaflets promised "Five dollars off – this week only." In fact, there was five dollars off every week. The same leaflets had been handed out for the entire time that *The Circus of the Mind* had been playing. And the receptionists were only recommending it because they had been paid to do so. They would receive five dollars for every ticket they sold.

The audience was already beginning to wonder if the show really was going to amaze or mystify them in the slightest. The dusty brickwork, the broken sign and the single, amateurish poster were hardly promising. On the other hand, there wasn't much else in Reno that they could do for thirty dollars and it was probably too late to ask for a refund. There was a loud rattle and the doors swung open, pushed from inside. As one, the crowd moved forward. There were a few drinks and boxes of sweets on sale in the foyer but they were overpriced and no one bought anything. Almost unwillingly, they produced their tickets and passed through a narrow archway into the main auditorium.

The theatre contained two hundred seats and was shaped like a horseshoe around an elevated wooden stage. A red curtain – tatty and faded – hung down. At exactly half past seven, the sound system blasted out a burst of pop music and the curtain rose to reveal a dark, bearded man wearing sunglasses and a turban.

"Good evening, ladies and gentlemen," he announced. "My name is Swami Louvishni and it is my great pleasure to be here all the way from Calcutta."

None of this was true. It was just the first of many lies.

The Indian fakir was, of course, a fake. His real name was Frank Kirby and he hadn't been further east than New York.

13

He had taken his stage name from a Tintin story and his tricks from a library book he had stolen when he was nineteen. Bobby Bruce was an out-of-work actor and had never been anywhere near the stars. Mr Marvano, the illusionist, was Frank Kirby again but without the beard and the glasses and using another voice. Zorro was a drunk.

The audience tonight was hardly enthusiastic. The summer had already arrived in full force, the hot breezes rolling in across the desert, and the air-conditioning in the building was only working at half-strength. They were falling asleep in their seats. They clapped politely when the fakir lay down on his bed of nails and when the escapologist leapt out of a locked-up chest. But they barely acknowledged the illusionist, even when he suddenly produced – in an empty cage – a large, panting dog. Perhaps they knew that in Las Vegas, only a few hundred miles away, there were magicians who had done the same thing with elephants and white tigers.

By the time the last act walked onto the stage, the audience had clearly had enough. Some of them had already left. But as the music changed and the lights dimmed and then rose for the last time, something changed inside the Reno Playhouse. It happened every night. It was as if people sensed, without being told, that they were finally going to be given a little of what the poster had promised.

The twins had appeared, now dressed in dark trousers and black shirts, open at the neck. The taller one was gazing out into the glare of lights with undisguised hostility. He had the look of a street fighter and, indeed, there was a large bruise on one of his cheekbones. His brother was somehow friendlier, more welcoming. It was just possible that he enjoyed being here. He was the one who spoke.

"Good evening," he began. "My name is Jamie Tyler." He gestured at the other boy, who didn't move. "And this is my brother, Scott. For as long as I can remember, we've known what's been going on inside each other's heads. That doesn't make it easy when one of us is trying to pick up girls..."

They weren't his words. They were the words he had been taught to say and he didn't think the joke was even slightly funny. But he forced himself to smile. The audience was listening to him with a bit more attention. They had seen the poster. Telepathic twins. But nobody had said they were going to be so young.

"It was only recently that we discovered the truth," Jamie went on. "It's not just that we know what we're both thinking. We're true telepaths, connected to each other in a way that science cannot understand or explain. And that's what we're going to demonstrate for you tonight. Starting with this."

While he had been talking, a stage hand had carried in a table with a pile of newspapers. There were twenty different papers from all around America. There were other props too. He would come to those later.

Jamie scooped up the newspapers and walked down to the front row. He stopped in front of a large, frizzy-haired woman who was wearing pink leggings and an "I ♥ Reno" T-shirt.

15

"Would you like to pick one of these newspapers?" he asked. "You can choose any one."

The woman was with her husband. He nudged her and she pulled one out of the middle of the pile. It was a copy of the *Los Angeles Times*.

"Thank you," Jamie said. "Now this paper has several sections. Will you please choose any one of them and pass it to your husband."

The woman did as she was asked. She chose the Calendar section. Her husband took it.

"Will you please tear one page out of the section and pass it to the person behind you," Jamie instructed.

He was fortunate that there *was* someone in the row behind. On bad nights, he knew, he might have to travel three or four rows to find a third spectator.

The page was being held by a Korean tourist who had come with his wife and daughter. Jamie hoped that he would be able to understand English. He took out a pen. "You have a page with more than a thousand words on each side," he said. "That means you have at least two thousand words to choose from. Could you please circle one of those words. It can be a headline or an advertisement. It doesn't matter. The choice is entirely yours."

The Korean man smiled and muttered something to his wife. He took the pen and ringed something, then handed the newspaper back to Jamie. Jamie looked down. Without speaking the words, he read:

16

> The latest trend in Los Angeles is the eco-friendly funeral. Celebs are lining up to make sure they go green when they go.

One word had a ring around it. He looked at it. On the stage, Scott spoke for the first time.

"Funeral," he said.

Jamie held the newspaper in front of the Korean man. "Is that the word?" he asked.

"Yes... Yes!" The man was astonished.

For the first time that evening, the applause was loud and genuine. It had to be a trick, of course. Everything that the audience had seen had been a trick. But how had it been done? Both the frizzy-haired woman and her husband had been given a free choice. The man behind her could have chosen any word. Perhaps the two boys had secret microphones. They could be in radio contact. But how would that help? Jamie hadn't said anything. He'd barely glanced at the page.

Jamie had already returned to the stage by the time the applause died down.

"I'd like to invite someone to join me," he said. He pointed to the husband who had already taken part. "Would you mind, sir?"

The man climbed onto the stage. Scott didn't move. Apart from the moment when he had spoken, he could have been a statue. A boy carved out of wood. But Jamie was moving around, collecting the next prop, welcoming the man.

17

"I'm going to blindfold my brother," he explained. "And I want you to make sure that he really can't see. While you're here, I'd also like you to check that there are no hidden microphones. Nothing in either of his ears."

The man went over to Scott and ran a finger behind each of his ears. For just a second, something flared in the boy's eyes. It was a humiliation he had to endure twice a night, every night – and he could never forgive it. But the man didn't notice.

"He's clean!" he announced.

A few people laughed. They were enjoying this. They wanted to see what would happen next.

Under Jamie's guidance, the man placed two coins against Scott's eyes. They were old English pennies, larger than modern coins. Next, he was blindfolded, and then, to finish, a black hood was placed over his head. It was like an executioner's hood. It completely covered his eyes, his nose and his hair, but it left his mouth free.

Jamie went into the audience. He stopped beside a blonde woman in a tight-fitting dress. Her boyfriend was sitting next to her. He had his hand on her thigh.

"Can you give me something from your handbag?" Jamie asked.

"You want something from my handbag?" The woman giggled, then glanced at her boyfriend. He nodded, giving her permission, and she pulled out a small silver object. Jamie took it and held it in the palm of his hand.

18

"It's a key ring," Scott said.

Jamie held the key ring up so that everyone could see. The audience applauded again. Several of them were talking now, whispering to each other, shaking their heads in disbelief.

"Let's make this more difficult," Jamie called out. "I wonder if anyone here has a business card. How about you, sir?"

He had stopped in front of two men sitting next to each other. All he had noticed so far was that they were both wearing brown linen suits, which in itself was strange because nobody in Reno ever dressed very smartly. On the other hand, he always tried to look for someone in a jacket when he reached this part of the act. From his experience, a man was more likely to have a wallet and, in the wallet, a business card. Women took longer, searching in their handbags. The act was supposed to last eighteen minutes. If he went over, he'd get slapped. Or worse.

Jamie waited for the man to reach into his jacket pocket, and when that didn't happen, he looked down. That was when he knew he had made a mistake. At that moment he wished he had gone to any row but this. Jamie had been struggling to get through the act in the damp, sluggish heat of the theatre. The air-conditioning was failing as usual. But the very sight of this man was like cold water thrown into his face.

It wasn't just that he was ugly. Jamie had met many unpleasant-looking people when he was doing his act –

indeed he sometimes wondered if there wasn't something about the Reno Playhouse that actually attracted them. But this man was beyond ugly. There was something almost inhuman about him, about the way he was gazing at Jamie with eyes that were a very faint shade of blue: so faint as to be almost colourless. The man was quite bald but he hadn't lost his hair with age – nor had he decided to shave it off. The polished skull was unblemished, as if there had never been anything there to begin with. His face was the same. He had no eyebrows. There was no stubble on his cheeks or chin. His whole face looked like a mask stretched tight over a bone structure that kept it in shape but allowed it to express no emotion at all. He had very small, very white teeth. They looked false.

"He wants your card," the man next to him said. He spoke with a soft, rasping voice and a Southern accent.

This man had hair, tangled and black, tied in a ponytail, as well as a wispy little beard, sprouting in a triangle just under his lower lip. He was wearing plastic sunglasses that offered mirror reflections instead of his eyes. He smelled of cheap aftershave, which was failing to hide the truth. He needed to change his clothes more. He needed to wash. It was impossible to say if he was younger or older than his companion. Both of them were ageless.

Jamie realized that several seconds had gone by and nothing had happened. He swallowed. "A business card," he repeated.

The silence stretched on. Jamie was about to move away. Surely he could find someone else who would co-operate? But then the bald man shrugged and reached into his jacket. "Sure," he said. "I've got a card."

He took out a wallet, opened it and removed a white card, balancing it for a moment between soiled, cracked fingernails, as if considering. Then he handed it to Jamie. Jamie held it in front of him. There was a name and, below it, a company:

Colton Banes
NIGHTRISE CORPORATION

Beneath that was an address and a telephone number. The letters were too small for Jamie to see in the half-light.

The man was looking at him curiously, almost as if he were trying to see into him. With difficulty, Jamie turned back to the stage. He tried to speak but his mouth was too dry. He swallowed, then tried again.

"Scott, can you tell me who this man works for?" he called out.

Silence from the stage. What was happening now?

Then Scott spoke. "Sure, Jamie. He works for the Nightrise Corporation."

The man smiled. "That's absolutely right," he said loudly, so the whole theatre could hear. But his voice was almost taunting Jamie, as if he didn't care one way or another if the trick had worked. "The boy got it in one."

21

There was even more applause this time. There were only forty-five people left in the theatre but they were genuinely absorbed. It was the only real mystery they had seen all evening. Days later, they would still be wondering how it was done.

And none of them had guessed the simple truth, even though it was the only possible explanation and was staring them in the face. There were no microphones. There were no hidden signals. There were no codes or messages being sent from off-stage. The trick was that there was no trick. The two boys could genuinely read each other's minds.

But the Nightrise Corporation knew. That was why they had sent these men here tonight. To see for themselves.

It was time for Scott and Jamie Tyler to disappear.

BACKSTAGE

The performance was over. Scott and Jamie had half an hour until the next one began, so the two of them went back to their dressing room. A narrow, L-shaped corridor, lit by harsh neon tubes, ran all the way round the back of the stage with an exit door at the end. As usual, they had to pick their way past the costumes, baskets and props which were already set out for the next performance. Swami Louvishni's bed of nails was propped up next to Zorro's chains and straitjacket. A papier-mâché cow came next and then a broken piano missing most of its keys – these last two were left over from some other show. On one side, a bare brick wall rose ten metres up to the ceiling – this was in fact the back of the stage. On the other, a series of doors opened into small, square rooms. The entire area smelled of fried food. The theatre backed onto a motel with its kitchen directly opposite. Often when the boys left they would see the Filipino staff in their striped aprons and white paper hats, hanging around smoking.

As they made their way backstage, there was a sudden whining and a dog bounded out of one of the doors. It was a

23

German shepherd, ten years old and blind in one eye. It belonged to Frank Kirby, who used it when he was pretending to be Mr Marvano, master illusionist. Twice a night, the dog sat behind a secret mirror, waiting to appear in the cage.

Jamie leant down and patted its head. "Good boy, Jagger," he said. The dog had been named after the lead singer of the Rolling Stones. Jamie didn't know why.

"Hey – Jamie!"

Frank Kirby was in his dressing room. Zorro was with him, sitting at a table with a glass and a half-bottle of whisky in front of him. Jamie hoped the escapologist hadn't drunk too much of it yet. One night Zorro had been handcuffed on stage, tied up and locked into his chest where he had promptly fallen asleep. He'd lost a week's wages for that. He and Kirby often hung out together. They were both divorced. They were both in their fifties. And – Jamie couldn't avoid the thought – they were both losers.

"What is it, Frank?" Jamie asked. He leant against the door and felt his brother brush past behind him. Scott hadn't stopped.

"There's a rumour we may be moving." Kirby's voice was always hoarse. Smoking thirty cigarettes a day probably didn't help. "I hear maybe we're getting out of Reno. You know anything about that?"

"I haven't heard anything," Jamie said.

"Maybe you can ask your Uncle Don. He never tells us nothing!"

Jamie was tempted to say that Don White never told him anything either. But there was no point. Frank knew that anyway. So Jamie just shrugged and went into the room next door.

Scott was already there, lying on the single bed with its dirty mattress and striped blanket. There was another table and two chairs. All the rooms were the same: completely square with a window looking out onto the parking lot with the motel on the other side. Each one had a washbasin and a mirror surrounded by light bulbs. In some of the rooms, the light bulbs actually worked. Jamie glanced at his brother, who was staring up at the ceiling. There were a couple of old Marvel comics on the table and a half-empty bottle of Coke. That was it. The two of them never did anything between shows. Sometimes they talked, but recently it seemed to Jamie that Scott had begun to retreat into himself.

"Frank thinks we may be moving," Jamie said.

"Moving where?"

"He didn't say." Jamie sat down. "It would be great to get out of here. Away from Reno."

Scott thought for a moment. He was still gazing at the ceiling. "I don't see it makes much difference," he said at last. "Wherever we go, it'll only be the same … or worse."

Jamie took a sip from the Coke bottle. The liquid was warm and flat. It was like drinking syrup. He turned his head and examined his brother, lying there on the bed. Scott had unbuttoned his shirt. It hung loose at the sides, exposing his stomach and chest. The shirts looked good on the stage but they were cheap black nylon and made Scott and Jamie sweat. Scott's hands were loosely curled by his sides. At that moment he didn't look fourteen. He could have been twenty-four.

Jamie often had to remind himself that the two of them were exactly the same age. They were twins. That much at least was certain. And yet he couldn't help thinking of Scott as his older brother. It wasn't just the physical difference between them. For as long as he could remember, Scott had looked after him. Somehow it had never been the other way around. When Jamie had his nightmares, lying in some run-down hotel or trailer in the middle of nowhere, Scott would be there to comfort him. When he was hungry, Scott would find food. When Don White or his wife, Marcie, turned nasty, Scott would put himself between them and his brother.

That was how it had always been. Other kids had parents. Other kids went to school and hung out with their friends. They had TVs and computer games and went to summer camp. But Jamie had never had any of that. It was as if real life went on somewhere else, and he had been dumped outside.

Sometimes Jamie thought back to life before Uncle Don had come and introduced him and Scott to *The Circus of the Mind*. After all, it hadn't been that long ago. But the days added up into weeks and then months, and now it was as if a single, long road had smashed through all his other memories and all that was left were shabby theatres and circus tents, hotels, motels, trailers and camper vans. Hours spent on the dusty highways criss-crossing Nevada, always on the move, often in the middle of the night, chasing the next dollar, wherever it might be.

He wondered how he had managed to survive the last few years without going mad. But he knew the answer. It was stretched out on the bed in front of him. Scott had been the one constant in his life, his only true friend and protector. They had always been together. They always would be. After all, it was only when the adults had tried to separate them that The Accident had happened – the beginning of this whole bad dream in which they were now trapped. Jamie examined his brother. Scott seemed to have fallen asleep. His bare chest was rising and falling slowly and there was a sheen of sweat on his skin. Jamie thought back to what Scott had told him, that night in the big tent where they were performing – just outside Las Vegas. It had been the end of the first week. The first public showing of the telepathic twins.

"Don't worry, Jamie. We're going to come though this. Five more years and we'll be sixteen. They can't keep us then. They can't make us do anything we don't want to."

"What will we do?"

"We'll find something. Maybe we'll go to California. We can go to Los Angeles."

"We could work in TV."

"No. They'd turn us into freaks." Scott smiled. "Maybe we

could set up some sort of business ... you and me."

"At least we'd know what the competition was thinking."

"That's right." Scott warmed to the subject. "We could be like Bill Gates. Make millions of dollars and then retire. You wait and see. Once we're sixteen, we'll be unstoppable."

They still had two more years. But Jamie was aware of a growing anxiety. It seemed to him that with every day that passed, the dream was fading. Scott was becoming more silent, more remote. He could lie still for hours at a time, not quite asleep but not awake either. It was as if something was slowly being drained out of him and Jamie was afraid. Scott was the strong one. Scott knew what to do. Jamie could go on performing. He could put up with Uncle Don and the casual brutality of his life. There was just one thing that scared him.

He knew he couldn't do it on his own.

At the far end of the corridor, in a corner office with views in two directions, Don White was sitting behind a desk that he couldn't possibly hope to reach. His stomach was too large. He was an immensely fat man with flesh that seemed to fold over itself as if searching for somewhere else to go. It was ice cold in the room – this was the one place in the theatre where the air-conditioning worked – but there were wet patches on the front of his shirt and under his armpits. Don sweated all the time. For a man his size, even walking ten paces was an effort – he looked permanently exhausted. There were dark rings under his eyes and he had lips like a fish, always gulping for air. He was eating a hamburger. Tomato ketchup was dribbling between his fingers, dripping down onto the surface of the desk.

There were two men sitting opposite him, waiting for him to finish. If they were disgusted by the spectacle in front of them, they didn't show it. One was bald. The other had dark hair. They were both wearing suits. They both waited silently while Don finished his meal, licked his fingers, then wiped them on his trousers.

"So what did you think?" he demanded at last.

"The boys are very impressive," the bald man – Colton Banes – replied.

"I told you. They can really do it. There's no trick. It gives you the creeps, if you ask me. But it's like they can get inside each other's head." Don reached out for a half-smoked cigar and lit it. The bitter smell of old tobacco rose into the air. "The other acts in the show … they're nothing. But those kids are special."

"I'd be interested to know how they first came to your attention."

"I'll tell you. I picked them up three years ago. They were about eleven then. Nobody has any idea where they came from. They were dumped when they were just a few months old. They were picked up by the child protection people some place near Lake Tahoe. No mum. No dad. Probably got Indian blood in them … you know, Native American. Paiute or Washoe or something. Anyway, they were fostered a few

29

times but it never worked out for long. I'm not surprised. Would you want to have someone hanging around with you who could see into your mind?"

"They read other people's minds as well as each other's?"

"They can do it. Sure. But they pretend they can't and I can't make them. I mean ... all right, on the stage. Party tricks. But never outside. Never in real life." Don sucked on his cigar, then blew out smoke. "So they get bounced around a bit and they finally end up with my wife's sister and her husband in Carson City. But that didn't work out too well, I can tell you."

"What happened?"

"They were there for about a year and then Ed – he was the husband – did himself in ... committed suicide. Maybe it was something to do with the kids. I don't know. They were on their way out anyway. He'd had enough of them." He leant forward conspiratorially. "Ed always said there was something weird about them. Like, if you belted one, the other would feel the pain. Can you believe that? You whack Scott and it's little Jamie who gets the bruise on his face. One of them always knew what was happening to the other one, even when they were miles apart. Ed couldn't live with it. He used to say it was like being in an episode of *The X-Files*. So he was going to get rid of them, and the next thing I know, he's dead, my wife's sister is freaking out and nobody wants the boys."

A lump of ash fell off the end of the cigar. It landed on Don's sleeve but he didn't notice.

30

"That was when I decided to take them in," he went on. "I was running this show. At the time it was called *Don White's World of Illusion*. But when I saw the boys, when I realized what they could do, I changed all that. I called it *The Circus of the Mind* and put them in as the final act. The strange thing is, everyone thinks there must be some trick. Hidden signals and codes – that sort of thing. It isn't just the audience. Even the other performers don't know how the boys do it. Isn't that funny? Marcie and me, we think that's hysterical."

Banes had introduced the other man as Kyle Hovey. Now Hovey spoke for the first time. "Why haven't you put them on television?" he asked. "You could have made more money that way."

"Yeah. I thought about that. Marcie and me talked about it. But they get too well known, someone's going to take them away." He hesitated, not sure how much he should tell the two men. "You know how it is," he went on. "We only got them in the first place because the foster care system is so overstretched. Too many files, not enough case workers. That's what Marcie says. Right now it seems like everyone's forgotten about them … and maybe it's best to keep it that way." He examined the cigar for a moment, gazing into the burning ash. "Anyway, it's like I told you, they won't do it. It was hard enough getting them to perform on the stage. I took a belt to them. Then I starved them. I told them, If you don't work, you don't eat. And even then they still refused."

"So what did you do?" Banes asked.

Don White smiled. "I used one of them against the other. I told Scott that if he didn't do what I asked, I'd beat Jamie till he bled. I told him I'd do worse than that. And so he agreed – to protect his brother. And Jamie did it because Scott told him to. That was the end of it. Now we get along just fine. I'm their Uncle Don. They do the shows and I look after them."

"What about school?"

"They went to school in Carson City when they were with Ed, but it didn't work out. So now they're home-schooled. The state's happy enough about that. They even pay us money to look after them. Marcie's smart. She teaches them all they need to know." There was about a centimetre of the cigar left. Don took one last puff, then ground it out on the plate which had held his hamburger. "Maybe you're right," he admitted. "Maybe I should have put them on TV. I'm fed up with the theatre. Nobody's interested. Nobody comes. Look at this place! We get more cockroaches than we get paying customers. I want out.

"So I was in a bar and I heard somebody talking about this corporation that was prepared to pay good money for information about 'special' kids. I went over to them and they gave me a name. I made a call and now … here you are. You've seen Scott and Jamie. You know they're on the level. So what do you say?"

The man called Kyle Hovey glanced at his partner, who had been watching Don with empty eyes. Colton Banes nodded. "We want to take them," Banes said.

"Take them? Just like that?"

"Children disappear all the time, Mr White. As you yourself have just told us, these children have no family and no friends. The state of Nevada has lost interest in them. We will look after them from now on and no one will be any the wiser."

"What about the money?"

"We'll pay you seventy-five thousand dollars."

Don White licked his lips. That was more money than he had ever expected. But it still wasn't enough. "Seventy-five thousand dollars ... each?" he asked.

Colton Banes paused for a moment. But he had already decided. "Of course. One hundred and fifty thousand dollars for the two boys. But there is one thing you must understand. This figure is final. You will make no further enquiries about them, or about us. If you inform anyone about this transaction, you and your wife will also disappear. There is a great deal of sand in the desert, Mr White. You would not wish to find yourself underneath it."

"When will you take them?"

"Tonight. Mr Hovey and myself will be inside the theatre. We will have two more colleagues outside. It would help us if you would ask the boys to remain behind when the show has finished, until the other performers have left. We will then remove them and pay you the money in cash. Is that acceptable?"

"Yeah. Sure it's acceptable." Don's mouth was dry. But there were still some questions he had to ask. "Who exactly are you? I mean, I know who you work for. But what are you going to do with them? What do you want them for?"

"I don't think you heard what I said," Banes replied. "We are nobody. You've never met us. The boys no longer exist."

"Sure. Fine. Whatever you say…"

From outside the office came the sound of pop music, blaring from the speakers inside the theatre. A single bell rang once, warning the performers.

The second show of the evening was about to begin.

THE NEON PRISON

"For as long as I can remember, we've known what's been going on inside each other's heads. That doesn't make it easy when one of us is trying to pick up girls…"

How many times had he spoken those same lines? As Jamie began his second performance of the evening, he was suddenly overwhelmed with tiredness. He hated Reno. It was his prison. It was the island where he had been shipwrecked. But it would never be his home.

It felt empty. The streets were somehow too wide for the number of vehicles that went up and down them, stretching in a straight line for as far as the eye could see. The shops and offices were too far apart, separated by blank spaces that could have been building sites except that no building ever seemed to be going on. And there was never anyone around. They came every Friday – the tourists and the stag parties – but they were sucked into the casinos the moment they stepped out of their cars or planes only to emerge, bleary-eyed and broke, on Sunday night.

There was nothing else to do in Reno. Even the Truckee

River, which cut through the centre, was as grey and uninteresting as it was possible for a river to be: trapped between two cement walls, the water flowing rapidly as if it were trying to get out of the city as quickly as it could.

Often Jamie would look at the mountain ranges on the far horizon, thirty or forty miles away. Even when the summer sun was burning, they were still tipped with snow. Sometimes he imagined that they were whispering promises of some other life to come. If he could just get across the mountains, over to the other side... But he knew it would never happen. He was stuck here. Drive ten minutes in any direction and you came to desert, scrubland and sand-covered hills. Scott had got it exactly right, just a few days after they had come here.

"We're in the middle of nowhere, Jamie. And that's exactly where we're going."

There were fewer people at the Reno Playhouse than there had been at the earlier performance that night – no more than forty. So far it hadn't been a good show. Bobby Bruce had forgotten his lines. Zorro had got stuck in a pair of handcuffs. Even Jagger had been late appearing in the cage. Jamie could feel the bad temper of the crowd. They hadn't even smiled at his opening joke.

He continued on autopilot, allowing the spotlights to dazzle him, not even looking at the audience. This time, the volunteer picked the *Houston Chronicle* out of the newspaper pile and the word that got ringed was "and". That was always a bad sign. Small, ordinary words always made the trick seem less impressive. As Jamie returned to the stage, he remembered the word "funeral" that had come up earlier in the evening. It might not have been the most pleasant of words but at least it had had an effect on the audience.

Briefly, he swept his eyes round, looking for someone to come up and help him blindfold his brother for the next part of the act. And that was when he saw them. The bald man who had lent him his business card was sitting five rows back from the stage. The dark-haired man was next to him. Jamie had been talking but now he shuddered in mid-sentence and came to a halt. He felt Scott stop and look at him. Jamie knew what his brother was doing, even without turning round. Why had the two men come back? Sometimes people did return for a second perform-ance. More often than not they were magicians themselves: mentalists and mind-readers who were trying to work out how the two brothers' tricks were done. But these men in their identical, dark brown suits clearly weren't entertainers. Nor had they come here to be entertained. The way they were watching him … they could have been two scientists in front of a specimen tray. Jamie remembered his unease the first time he'd seen them. He felt it again, only doubly so, now that they were here again.

"I … um … need someone to help me on the stage." The words were forcing themselves from his lips almost despite himself. "Will you help me, please, sir?" Jamie had stopped in front of a man in his twenties. He was sitting with his arm around a girl. He had an Elvis Presley haircut.

"Forget it!" The man shook his head and sneered. He didn't want to leave his seat.

That happened often enough. There were plenty of people who preferred not to volunteer – because they were embarrassed or because the whole thing was beneath them. Normally, Jamie would handle the situation easily and move on. But tonight he didn't feel in control. He was afraid that one of the two men – the men in brown suits – was going to volunteer, and whatever happened he didn't want them to come close. What now? He struggled to find the right words.

"I'll help you!"

A woman had stood up, a few seats away. She was black, slim and attractive: in her thirties, Jamie would have said. Once again, he couldn't help feeling that something didn't quite add up. The woman was smartly dressed in jeans with a white silk shirt and a thin gold necklace. He could imagine that she was probably an executive in some sort of business. But what was she doing here – and on her own?

Still, she had given Jamie no choice. He waited for her to follow him up onto the stage and a few seconds later they were standing in the spotlights. Scott was slightly to the side, not looking at them, waiting for Jamie to begin.

"I'm going to blindfold my brother—" Jamie began.

"How did you do that just now?" the woman interrupted.

"That trick with the newspaper. I've never seen anything like that."

"Well…" Jamie didn't know what to say. Volunteers hardly ever spoke to him and they never asked him questions like that, not when they were up on the stage. Why was everything going so wrong tonight? He turned away and, without meaning to, found himself looking once again at the two men in row five. They were staring at him. Of course they were. Everyone was staring at him. He was the reason they were there. But he still couldn't shake off the idea that they were different from the rest of the audience, that they were interested in him for another reason.

Jamie forced himself to calm down. The two men were surrounded by a lot of empty seats. That was the only reason they seemed out of place. They were here for the same reason as everyone else: to be entertained.

"I'd like you to help me," Jamie said.

"Sure!" The woman nodded.

Jamie picked up the blindfold, the hood and the English pennies. "I want you to make sure there are no hidden microphones."

"How did you do it?" the woman asked again. "Can you really read each other's minds?"

The audience was getting restless. They hadn't come here to listen to an explanation of how the tricks worked. And it was late – almost half past ten. They were ready to leave. Without waiting any longer, Jamie pressed the coins against his brother's eyes. For a moment, he felt Scott's breath, warm against his knuckles. Later on, much later, he would remember it. But now he was moving briskly on. He secured the coins with the blindfold, remembering too late that he hadn't invited the woman to examine it. Never mind. What did it matter anyway? He placed the hood over his brother's head.

"What now?" the woman asked.

"I'd like something from your handbag," Jamie said. It was another mistake. Normally at this point he went back into the audience. He wished this woman hadn't forced herself onto him.

"I don't have a handbag," the woman said.

That got a few laughs from the audience. But it was hostile. They were laughing *at* him, not *with* him.

"Then give me something else," Jamie said. "Just don't say what it is."

"How about this?" The woman reached into her back pocket and took out a photograph, the size of a postcard. Jamie took it. He found himself looking at a black and white picture of a nine- or ten-year-old boy. It was obvious this was the woman's son. Jamie could see the resemblance. The boy's hair was much shorter but he had the same thoughtful eyes and slightly feminine mouth.

Jamie held it. He realized he was waiting for Scott to speak. Normally Scott identified the object the moment Jamie had it in his hand. Then it would be on to the wallet, the deck of playing cards, the driving licence and out before the final curtain. But Scott hadn't spoken.

"Scott – what am I holding?" Jamie asked. He had broken the rules that Don White had taught him. If he said anything, the audience would always assume he was using some sort of code. It was better to remain silent.

"I … don't know." Scott turned his head as if he was trying to look through the blindfold and the hood.

Jamie felt the floor opening up beneath him. Something had gone wrong. He glanced at his brother and felt the tension. Scott's arms were pressed against his sides, his fists clenched.

"It's a picture." Desperately, Jamie tried to help him. "What's it a picture of?"

And then Scott cried out. He raised a hand and touched his fingers against his forehead as if in pain. "His name is Daniel," he said. "And he's gone. It's your fault. You're still blaming yourself for letting them take him."

It was Scott's voice but it didn't sound like him. Nothing like this had ever happened before.

And then the woman stepped forward and snatched the photograph back, and when Jamie looked up at her he saw real anger flaring in her eyes. "Where is he?" she demanded. "What do you know?"

"I don't know anything!" The whole theatre seemed to be spinning. The lights were burning into him. Jamie just wanted to get off the stage.

"Tell me what you know."

"I've told you—"

"Ladies and gentlemen … Scott and Jamie Tyler, the tele-pathic twins!" Frank Kirby had been watching from the wings, still in the costume of Mr Marvano, master illusionist. He had decided to come to the rescue, walking on and clapping his hands at the same time. About half the audience joined in. They had seen something but they weren't sure what. Certainly the trick with the newspapers had been quite effec-tive. But the trick with the photograph had failed. Or had it? The woman in the white shirt certainly looked shaken. Had the twins correctly identified the boy in the photograph, and if so, where was he?

The show was over. Jamie took hold of Scott and dragged him into the wings, at the same time pulling off the blindfold. Frank showed the woman off the stage and went into the final speech that always brought down the curtain.

"Thank you, ladies and gentlemen. Tonight you have trav-elled with us to some of the furthest corners of the human mind…"

But nobody was listening. The woman was back in her seat, deep in thought. Banes and Hovey were a few rows behind her, unmoving, detached. Quite a few people in the audience were already gathering up their jackets and bags, on their way out. The music was playing again, drowning out Frank's words. Even when the show went well, it was disappointing. Tonight it had been a complete failure.

Don White was waiting off-stage.

As Jamie walked out of the spotlights, the scowling face of "Uncle Don" was the first thing he saw. He realized that Don must have been there throughout the entire act and he flinched, waiting for the backhand across his face or perhaps the fat fingers grabbing at his throat. Don certainly didn't look pleased. "What happened out there?" he demanded. His thick lips were turned down in an angry scowl.

"I don't know," Jamie answered. "It went wrong."

"It was your brother. He screwed it up."

"Yeah. That's right. It was me." Scott took a step forward. Instinctively, he had put himself between Don White and his brother. Like he always did.

Jamie waited to see what would happen. But tonight there was to be no violence. Don shrugged, his huge shoulders and arms rising and falling, his palms facing out. "All right. Let's just forget it," he said. "I'll see you two later. Go and wait for me in your room." He turned to the other performers, who had gathered round, wondering what had gone wrong. "The rest of you, I want you out of here. Let's close up for the night."

Jamie followed his brother back to the dressing room. It looked as if there wasn't going to be any trouble after all. If Don was going to hit them, he'd have done it then and there. Together, they went into the room, not even bothering to close the door. They took their time getting changed. The house where they were living – with Don and Marcie – was a twenty-minute drive away, and most nights they went there with Don. It was only when he decided to stay for a drink, or to throw away some money in one of the casinos, that they took the number 11 bus to Victorian Square and walked the rest of the way.

Frank Kirby passed the door, on his way out. They had worked with him for two years but they hardly knew anything about him. He didn't speak much and he never smiled. He smoked too much. He was usually the last to leave.

"Goodnight, kids," he rasped.

They heard him make his way down the corridor. The stage door groaned open and then clanged shut. Don White would be in his office, having a last drink, talking on the phone to Marcie. Otherwise they were on their own.

Jamie leant down and tied up his laces. There was a hole in his trainer. He could see through to his bare foot inside. "What happened?" he asked. "What did you see ... out on the stage?"

"I don't know." Scott bit his lip.

"You said you saw someone called Daniel. You said he was being hurt."

"Jamie, I don't want to talk about it. OK?"

"Sure…" Jamie looked at his brother in dismay.

Scott let out a deep breath. "I'm sorry. I didn't mean to yell at you." He shook his head. "Something's happening. I don't know what it is. But something's wrong…"

"What do you mean?"

"Tonight. That woman. Everything." Scott ran a hand

through his hair. It was thick with sweat. "Listen, Jamie. I've got a bad feeling. Maybe you're going to have to look out for yourself..."

"Why? Scott? What is it?"

It was the dog that warned them.

The theatre should have been empty. The theatre *was* empty in that all the other performers had gone, leaving only the twins behind. But what Don White had forgotten was that Frank Kirby was staying in a boarding house that didn't allow dogs, so every night he left Jagger in his dressing room. The German shepherd slept on a mat and normally no one would notice that it was there.

But something had disturbed it. Scott heard a low growling that suddenly rose, loud and threatening. It was coming from the corridor. Jamie looked up. He had never heard Jagger like that before. Scott raised a hand, signalling his brother to stay where he was, then stepped out of the door. And that was when he saw them.

Two men. One bald, one dark. Both in brown suits. Scott registered with a shock of disbelief that the bald man was holding a strange-looking gun.

Scott stared at them. They had seen him the moment he had appeared in the corridor but they couldn't reach him. The dog was between them, hackles raised and teeth bared. Jagger was ten years old. It slept most of the time. But now, suddenly, it had changed. It was as if it had discovered the savage animal it might once have been. It was about to attack.

There could be no doubt of it.

Scott realized instantly that he and his brother were in danger. He didn't know who the men were or why they were here, but he knew he had to get away and had only seconds in which to do it.

Jamie! Come here!

He didn't shout the words. He thought them. But it had the same effect. Jamie burst out of the room and saw the two men just as Jagger let out a final snarl and leapt into the air. He recognized them instantly. Banes fired the gun – not a bullet but some sort of dart. It hit Jagger in the neck. The dog screamed. Scott pushed Jamie ahead of him and the two of them began to run. Behind them, Jagger was still arcing towards the two attackers. The end of the dart – tufts of black feather – stuck out of the fur below its ear, but it was still conscious, snapping at the two men, snarling and barking. Kyle Hovey cried out as the dog sank its teeth into his arm and began to tear at his flesh. But then Banes got hold of it. His hands clamped down on the animal's head, holding it against the floor. Jagger tried to reach him, tried to get back onto its feet. But then the drug, whatever it was inside the dart, took effect. The dog's eyes glazed and it lay still.

The boys still hadn't reached the corner of the corridor. Banes had dropped the gun when he had dealt with the dog but now he snatched it up, aimed and fired. The dart missed Scott by an inch and bounced off the wall. Banes didn't have time to fire again. The boys had disappeared. White-faced, furious, he turned to Hovey, who was cradling his arm, half buried underneath the unconscious animal.

"After them!" he hissed.

Hovey stumbled to his feet. Banes reloaded his gun, pressing two more darts into the chamber. The two men set off even as the stage door clanged open ahead of them.

Jamie had reached the parking lot between the theatre and the motel. One end led onto Virginia Street with one of the casinos – Circus Circus – just opposite. The other tapered into a narrow alleyway leading to the quieter streets behind. There was nobody in sight. A few cars – belonging to the motel guests – had been left in the lot. The motel office, a box-like room looking out onto the main road, was closed with a NO VACANCIES sign in the window. Jamie came to a halt. The heavy night air seemed to fall onto him, instantly draining his strength. What was going on? Scott had called him – but he had done it telepathically. It had been like a knife going into his head. And then the two men from the audience. One of them with a gun. Jagger…

"Scott!" he cried out and at once he was angry with himself. He wasn't helping. He had no idea what to do. As always, he depended entirely on his brother.

Scott wasn't going to let him down. While Jamie had stood there doing nothing, he had snatched up a coil of electric flex that had been left on top of a rubbish bin. He had already slammed the stage door shut and was twisting the wire around the handles. Now the door wouldn't open from the

47

inside. He had bought them time. The two men – whoever they were – would have to go round the front.

"Who are they?" Jamie cried. "I saw them. They were in the theatre. They came twice."

"Not now," Scott rasped. "We have to move…"

It was already too late. Even as Jamie watched, a car appeared, a black Mustang, racing down the alleyway towards them. There was a driver and another man in the passenger seat and there could be no doubt that they had been waiting for the boys to come out. Two inside the theatre. Two sitting outside. How many of these people were there?

Jamie froze. Scott leant down and picked up one of the rubbish bins. It was full and must have weighed a ton, but maybe desperation had given him extra strength. As the car sped towards them, he threw it. The dustbin didn't travel far – but the speeding car did their work for them. The bin smashed into the windscreen. Glass shattered. Scott and Jamie threw themselves aside as the car rocketed towards them. Rotten vegetables and leftovers showered down as the dustbin rolled across the hood. They heard the metal door panels crumpling as the car slammed into the side of the theatre. Then it swerved away and smashed into the motel office on the other side. An alarm went off. The car came to a hissing, shuddering halt.

The two boys had hit the ground and rolled out of harm's way. Jamie was the first to his feet. He reached out for Scott and helped him up. For a brief moment, he wondered if the driver of the car and his passenger had been knocked out. But his hopes were dashed when the car doors opened and two men staggered out, one of them with blood oozing from a cut in his head, but both of them otherwise unhurt.

"Move!" Scott commanded, and Jamie set off, making for Virginia Street. They had to get out into the open where there would be other people, witnesses. But as they went, Jamie felt something streak past his ear and realized that one of the men had fired another dart at him. At least it wasn't a bullet. The plan was to take the two boys alive. But what then? What had brought these people to the theatre in Reno? For years, nobody had cared about him and Scott. Why was all this happening now?

The boys reached the main road and suddenly the darkness of the parking lot gave way to the brilliance of the Reno night. The casinos were illuminated by a thousand lights: flashing, spinning, rotating, cascading, doing anything they could to draw people in. There was the casino called Circus Circus with its huge clown, pink and blue plastic, ten metres high. It was holding a lollipop that rotated in its hand, advertising the games inside. The Eldorado was further down the street on a corner, its entrance illuminated by a neverending firework display of multicoloured lights. Jamie couldn't see anyone on the pavements, but there were a few cars, their headlights pushing back what little night remained. Which way? Jamie looked around him desperately. He had no idea. He didn't know how many people

49

were chasing him and there was nowhere to hide.

Scott cried out. The front doors of the theatre had burst open and the two men who had started it all had emerged into the street. Jamie was prepared to run but then he saw that his brother was standing quite still, one hand against his chin as if he had bad toothache. His face was completely white. Slowly, the hand fell and Jamie saw the black tufts of a dart, sticking out of his cheek.

"Oh no…" Jamie whispered.

"Run, Jamie," Scott said.

"No. I'm not leaving you."

"Just do it! You can't help me if they get you…"

Of course it was true. There was nothing else he could do. If he stood there, they would simply grab both of them. Jamie hesitated just one second more, then turned and was about to run when he felt something like a wasp sting, high up on his right shoulder. Instantly he knew that he, too, had been hit. The two men were twenty metres away. It was the bald one who had fired the shot. Jamie saw him lower the gun. He had stopped moving, knowing the chase was over. Jamie heard another man shouting something in the parking lot. The motel alarm was still screaming. There was the thud of rubber shoes against concrete. Scott fell to his knees. Dully, Jamie looked at him, knowing he would be next. In a way he was glad. Whatever was going to happen, he'd stay with his brother after all.

And then there was the screech of tyres and a second car

came out of nowhere, veering across the path of the on-coming traffic. Jamie heard the blast of horns. The neon lights were blurring and the whole night seemed to be folding in on itself. He thought the car was going to run him over and he wondered what would be the point of that. Drug him and then kill him? It didn't make any sense.

The car shuddered to a halt. One of its tyres had mounted the pavement. The car was between him and the two men – just as the German shepherd had been earlier. A door swung open and a voice called out to him.

"Get in!"

The dark-haired man had produced a second gun. But this one didn't fire darts. There was a sharp crack and one of the car windows shattered, the glass frosting before it collapsed out of the frame. A second shot and the mirror disintegrated.

"Get in!" the voice urged again.

Jamie took one last look at his brother. Scott was lying face down on the pavement, one hand outstretched, the other folded beneath him. The dart was still hanging out of his cheek. His eyes were closed. There was nothing Jamie could do for him. He fell forward into the car.

He wanted to know who was driving but he didn't have the strength to look up. He was half in the car, half out, but already they were moving. He felt his feet being dragged along the road and reached out with one hand, searching for something to hold onto, something to help pull him in.

A hand reached down and grabbed his arm.

"Hold on!" the voice commanded.

They were reversing. Jamie heard a third shot then a howl of an engine and more blaring horns as other cars swerved all around them. But the traffic had lost its shape. To Jamie the other cars were just blurs of colour, ricocheting off each other, firing off in every direction. The neon lights spun round and round. He thought he saw four huge playing cards – the aces of hearts, clubs, spades and diamonds – light up, one after the other. The giant lollipop turned in the hand of the clown. A bright red shop sign flashed on and off. EZ CASH SUPER PAWN. Somehow he was in the car. He could feel soft leather pressing against his face but his feet seemed to be clear of the road.

After that, he remembered nothing more. As he drifted into blackness, all he knew was that, somehow, he had got away.

Don White was waiting in his office when Mr Banes got back. Kyle Hovey was with him. His jacket was torn and blood had spread all the way up his arm.

"Did you get them?" Don asked.

"We got one of them," Banes replied.

"That's too bad." Don had a half-bottle of Bourbon. He poured himself a glass. "You're still going to have to pay me for two." Neither of the two men said anything. Don White assumed that meant they agreed. He lifted the glass and drank. "What happened?" he asked.

"You never told us about the dog," Banes murmured.

"I didn't know about the dog."

"It doesn't matter," Banes said, slowly. "We have one of them. And the police will be looking for the other."

"Oh yeah? And why is that?"

"He'll be wanted for murder."

Don White looked surprised – or tried to. It was always difficult to read emotion in his face. There was too much flesh. "Whose murder?" he asked.

Banes smiled. "You shouldn't have asked."

The sound of the bullet was very loud in the confined space of the office. Banes had shot Don White through the heart. For a few seconds, the man that Jamie and Scott had known as Uncle Don inspected his whisky as if acknowledging the fact that, sadly, he would never now drink it. Then his hand fell. The liquid spilled. He sat back, unmoving, in his chair.

Colton Banes took one last look at the corpse. Then he slipped the gun back into his pocket and the two men left the room.

TENTH STREET

Jamie opened his eyes and saw that he was no longer in Reno. He wasn't even in America. Somehow, impossibly, he had been transported to a deserted beach that stretched out along the edge of a black, lifeless sea. Was it day or night? He looked up but the sky seemed to be caught somewhere between the two. Jamie gulped for breath. He was still in the grip of his first panic, the knowledge that he was some-where far away and utterly strange, that he was on his own. There was nobody in sight. Nothing. Just the beach and the sea and, in the distance, what might be an island, rising up to a needlepoint high above the waves.

"Scott!"

He called out the name but the single word seemed to die on his lips. That was more frightening than anything. He could shout as loud as he liked but there was no one to hear him. He wasn't just lost. He was completely abandoned. Where was he? Even the deserts of Nevada had offered more life and colour than the place where he now found himself.

And yet...

He had been here before. He *knew* where he was. Jamie drew his legs towards himself, wrapping his hands around his shoulders: not so much to keep himself warm but to create a sort of protective cocoon. He forced himself to take a deep breath, to relax. Yes. It had been a long time ago, maybe years, but he knew this place. The island... The last time he had come here, there had been two boys making their way towards him in a boat made out of straw. He had wanted to meet them – he didn't know why – but he had woken up before they arrived. And he hadn't been alone: Scott had been here with him.

And, standing next to them, there had been a girl.

"This is a dream," Jamie muttered to himself. His voice still sounded very small but it was reassuring to hear anything at all. The waves were hitting the shore right in front of him, but they were sluggish and hardly made any sound, as if someone had turned down the volume.

A shaft of light flashed in the sky, far away. A storm. Jamie got to his feet. He was shivering. It wasn't cold – like everything else here, the temperature seemed to be fixed in some sort of neutral – but there was something about the lightning that set his teeth on edge. There it was again. He watched it flicker twice more – white forks of electricity so brilliant that they seemed to tear into the world as if determined to smash it. Somehow he knew that this was no ordinary storm. It was an announcement. Something was happening. It was still far away but soon it would be closer. There was a very slight breeze now. He could feel it, clammy and dead, batting against his face.

"Scott!" he called out again. At the same time he wished, miserably, that he could wake up right away.

He heard something on the shingle, over to one side.

He glanced round, expecting to see his brother, but instead there was a man kneeling beside the edge of the sea, holding a large, flat bowl which he seemed to be filling with water. Jamie had no idea where he had come from. He certainly hadn't been there the moment before. The man was huge – and he was completely grey. His face, his hands, his clothes, even his eyes were the colour of stone, and if he hadn't been moving, Jamie would have assumed he was a statue. He was wearing old-fashioned shapeless trousers tied with a leather belt and an open-necked shirt with rolled-up sleeves. He also had a hat – not a cowboy hat but something similar – and boots that came up to his calves. He was completely focused on what he was doing.

Jamie stood up and went over to him. He was about to speak but his feet, crunching on the shingle, gave him away. The man twisted around and straightened up. At that moment Jamie saw that he really was huge – at least seven feet tall with hair curling down to his neck and a face that was hard and craggy and full of anger. He had dropped his bowl. Now there was a large knife in his hand.

"I'm sorry…" Jamie didn't know why he was apologizing.

The man looked down at him but said nothing.

"Can you help me?" Jamie asked.

"He's gonna kill him," the man said. He had a peculiar accent. It was American yet strangely old-fashioned, like something in a black and white film.

"Who are you talking about?"

"You know that. You know who I'm talking about."

"You mean … Scott?"

The man nodded. "He's gonna kill him. And it's your job to stop him."

"But who's going to kill him? You have to help me find him—"

That was all Jamie had time to say. The man suddenly lashed out with the knife. Jamie heard it as it came sweeping through the damp air. Something slammed into the side of his head and he thought he'd been stabbed. But the man had struck with the hilt, not the blade. With a single cry of pain, Jamie was thrown off his feet and went crashing down onto his back. He could feel blood oozing out of his hair and wondered if his skull had been broken. The man stepped forward and loomed over him. He was holding the knife in both hands, as if about to make a sacrifice. Lightning shimmered one last time.

"Stop him!" the man commanded.

His hands came plummeting down.

Jamie woke up.

His head was throbbing and for a moment he thought he really had been attacked. He raised a hand and touched it to the side of his skull. There was nothing. No blood. No sign of a wound. He was lying, fully dressed, on a bed. For a moment he lay completely still, allowing his thoughts to swirl around him, separating what was real from what he had dreamed, trying to work out what had happened to him, where he was now and how he had got here. The attack at the theatre. That was real. He remembered the blare of the traffic, the neon lights, the car cutting across the street to pick him up.

Scott. They had taken him. Jamie sat bolt upright, instantly searching for his brother even though there was little chance that he was anywhere near. But it didn't matter. It was instinctive. He sent out his thoughts, first into this room, then into whatever room might be next door, then further. He was shouting his brother's name but without uttering a word.

There was nothing. Jamie felt a sense of blankness that told him exactly what he feared. He was on his own.

He slumped against the pillow, feeling the stiffness in his shoulder where the dart had hit him, and knew that he had been drugged. How long had he been asleep? The sun was shining. A blind had been drawn across the window but he could see the light streaming in along the sides.

His mouth was dry and he felt sick. He looked around him and saw that he was in some sort of hotel room. He could tell from the emptiness of the place, the cheap furniture, the prints on the walls – black and white photographs of Reno as it had been fifty years ago. There was a glass of water beside the bed. He picked it up and drank. It was still cool. A few lumps of half-melted ice floated on the top. He was thirsty. He emptied the glass, then swung his legs over the side of the bed, preparing to stand up.

The door of the room opened and someone came in, morning sunlight streaming over her shoulders. At first he couldn't make out who it was. Then the person closed the door and Jamie saw a young black woman, dressed in jeans and a white T-shirt with a brightly coloured cotton shirt hanging loose on the outside. She was carrying two supermarket shopping bags.

"When did you wake up?" she asked.

Jamie didn't answer her question. "Who are you?" he demanded. "How long have I been here?"

"It's after ten. I was getting worried about you. I thought I was going to have to call a doctor." The woman paused. "You're going to have to help me out here. Are you Scott or Jamie? The two of you are so alike."

Jamie tried to stand up but he still didn't have the strength. He felt as if he had been lying down for a week. "Where am I?"

"You're in a motel," the woman replied. "We're still in Reno, right next door to the airport. The Bluebird Inn. Do you know it?" She put the shopping bags down on a table. They were full of food. A couple of apples spilled out and she scooped them up. "I thought you might be hungry so I went out shopping. I'm glad I timed it right. I didn't want you to wake up on your own."

59

"You were in the theatre." Jamie recognized her. She had been the woman with the photograph at the last performance. She had volunteered to come up onto the stage.

"Yeah." The woman nodded. "Actually, I saw you three times. I was there at the seven-thirty show. And the night before."

"Why?"

"I wanted to see how you did it. Your act..."

Jamie forced himself to his feet. He was weak and his head was still throbbing, but he didn't want to stay here, on his own, in the room with this strange woman. Scott had gone. Someone had taken him. That was all that mattered.

"Where are you going?" the woman asked. She placed herself between Jamie and the door.

"I have to find Scott."

"I know how you're feeling." She shook her head. "But you can't just walk out of here. It's too late."

"What do you mean?" Without knowing it, Jamie had clenched his fists. His eyes were fierce and bloodshot. "You were there. Why? Did you know what was going to happen? Were you part of it?"

Now it was the woman's turn to become angry. "I think you're forgetting what happened," she replied. Her voice was still soft but Jamie could see that she was having to control herself. "I saved you. If it wasn't for me, they'd have taken you too."

Of course. She had been in the car. Jamie hadn't seen her –

he'd only heard her voice before he'd passed out. But there could be no doubt. He recognized it again now. "Do you know where he is?" he asked. "Do you know who they were?"

"No."

"I have to look for him."

"I know how you're feeling, Jamie. Can I call you that? You said you were looking for Scott so I guess that answers my question." Again he didn't answer, so she went on. "Just try to think straight for a minute. You want to find your brother. But where are you going to start?" She walked over to a table and picked up a small, silver object, shaped like a bullet but with a needle jutting out at one end and a black tuft at the other. "Do you know what this is?"

Jamie felt his blood run cold.

"I dug this out of your shoulder," the woman said. "God knows what was in it but you've been asleep for eleven hours. Your brother was hit too, and right now he could be any-where. You can look all over Reno if you want. You can look all over Nevada. But you're not going to find him."

She was right. Jamie knew it. But it didn't matter. He could-n't stay here, not without Scott. "I have to see Uncle Don," he said.

"Don? The woman blinked. "You mean Don White? The man on the posters? Is he your uncle?"

"No. He's nothing – but he made us call him that. He'll be wondering where we are. He was there at the theatre last night. Maybe he can help."

61

"I'm not so sure…"

"I don't care what you think." Jamie took a deep breath. "We were renting a house. It's over in Sparks. There's him and Marcie. I have to tell them what happened. They'll contact the cops."

The woman thought for a moment. Then she nodded. "Why don't you call them?"

There was a telephone on a table beside the bed. Jamie picked it up and dialled the number. He waited, listening as it rang at the other end. There was no reply. He let it ring a dozen times. Then he hung up.

"If they cared about you, they'd have called the police already," the woman said.

"How do you know they haven't?"

The woman sighed. "Fair enough. I haven't seen the papers yet…"

"You knew what happened." Jamie couldn't keep the hostility out of his voice. "Why didn't you call them?"

"I wanted to talk to you first."

"Great. Well now you've talked to me. How long did you say I've been here? Eleven hours. That means you've given them eleven hours to get away with Scott. I don't even know your name but you're nothing to do with me. I just want to go home."

"I'm not stopping you!" The woman raised her hands in a gesture of surrender. "You want to go home? That's fine! In fact I'll drive you there myself. OK?"

Jamie nodded.

"Then let's go."

The woman went over to the door and the two of them stepped outside. Jamie screwed up his eyes as the sun hit him. The door opened onto a parking lot and he could feel the heat bouncing off the tarmac, roasting his forehead and cheeks. The air smelled of burning rubber and gasoline. The Bluebird Inn was an old-fashioned building, two storeys high, mainly white-painted wood. It had been named after the state bird of Nevada but if anything with wings came close to the place it was more likely to be a plane. The motel had been constructed exactly opposite the runway and even as Jamie stood there, he heard the roar of a jet – though whether it was taking off or landing he couldn't see.

"You always stay here?" he asked.

The woman glanced at him. "I always stay near airports," she replied. Why? What did she mean? But Jamie didn't ask her. Whatever her problems were, they had nothing to do with him.

She had rented a car, a silver four-door Ford Focus, and Jamie saw that she had called someone out early that morning. The window had been repaired. But one of the wing mirrors was missing. That would cost her plenty when she took the car back. He got into the front seat and closed the door.

"Alicia McGuire," the woman said.

"I'm sorry?"

"You didn't ask me my name, but I thought you'd like to know it anyway." She started the engine. "So where are we heading?"

"It's just off the 80. I can show you."

They drove together in silence. Jamie looked out of the window as the offices and hotels of Reno slipped past. He knew them all. They had become as familiar to him as the features on his own face. And yet now, somehow, they seemed a long way away. As they drove up the ramp and onto the freeway heading east, he felt a sense of dislocation. It was as if someone had taken a giant pair of scissors the night before and cut a straight line through his life.

The air-conditioning was on full and he let the air current wash over him, separating his clothes from his skin. He hoped it would wake him up. He was still groggy, perhaps from the drug, perhaps from the shock of what had happened. He tried to make sense of the events at the theatre but he couldn't. At least four men, perhaps more, had come for him and Scott. Two of them had been in the audience. The others had appeared from nowhere. But the whole thing had been carefully planned. That much was obvious. And if it hadn't been for Jagger, the two of them wouldn't even have made it out of the theatre.

Frank Kirby's dog. Jamie remembered the struggle and hoped the animal was all right. Frank was always worrying about the dog ... it was old and had a weak heart. Jamie knew that the men in the theatre would have quite happily killed

Jagger without so much as a second thought, and these were the same people who had taken Scott. Well Jamie would find them, with or without his uncle's help. They didn't know him. They didn't know what they were up against.

"It's the next exit," he said.

Don White and his wife had rented a house in Sparks, a suburb of Reno, just a few miles to the east. Alicia turned off and they descended into a grid system of pretty, tree-lined streets that seemed a world apart from the main city. And yet the poker tables and slot machines had spread out even here. Two huge towers, bookends that didn't quite match, rose up on the other side of the freeway. This was the Nugget, another enormous casino and hotel complex. Many of the people who lived in Sparks worked there as waiters, croupiers, cleaners or security guards. There was no escaping it. It seemed to look down and sneer at the little community as if to say, I am your master. You owe your livelihood to me.

Every house in Sparks was different and each one stood on its own little plot of land. There were cottages made of brick, wooden bungalows with painted shutters and verandas, villas built in the Spanish style with wrought-iron gates and white stucco walls. Some of the houses had been decorated with wind chimes, dolls and flowerpots. Others had been allowed to fall into dis-repair. It just depended who was living there – and it seemed that all sorts of people had chosen this neigh-bourhood for their home.

Number 402 Tenth Street was at the top end, close to the

casino. It stood out at once because it was the most dilapi-
dated building in the street, with a garden that had been
allowed to run wild and a rusting barbecue on its side in the
grass. It had a porch with a net screen running all the way
round, but it was full of holes, as if it had been stabbed. The
paint was flaking. The window frames were rusting. A single
air-conditioning unit clung to one wall as if by its fingernails.
The house was two storeys high with a garage to one side.
There was a caravan parked in the driveway and from the look
of it, it hadn't been moved in a long time.

"This is it," Jamie said.

"I sort of guessed." Alicia didn't stop outside. She drove a
few doors further down and pulled up beneath an acacia tree.
"Park in the shade," she explained.

Jamie nodded. "Thanks," he said. He reached for the door
handle.

"Wait a minute!" Alicia stared at him. "What do you think
you're doing?"

"It's OK. This is where I live. You don't need to come in."

"It's not OK! I can't just leave you here. I want to see you're
safe."

"Then wait in the car—"

"No!" Alicia turned off the engine. "I'm coming in with
you." Jamie opened his mouth to argue but she stopped him.
"You've been away all night," she went on. "Maybe it would
help you if you had someone to explain what happened – to
back up your story."

66

Jamie thought for a moment, then nodded. The two of them got out of the car and walked back along the pavement, passing the house next to the one where he lived. It belonged to a family with two children – girls – about ten and twelve years old. Jamie often saw them playing on the front lawn and their bicycles were there now, parked next to a swing. But he had never spoken to them, not in all the time he had been at Sparks. The girls had probably been told to avoid him and Scott. Nobody ever went near number 402. It was as if the whole neighbourhood knew that these weren't people you wanted to meet.

He climbed three concrete steps and crossed the porch to the front door. He was glad now that this woman was with him. There was no way that Don or Marcie could blame him for what had happened the night before, but the trouble was that the two of them were likely to strike out first and ask questions later. He had disappeared for more than twelve hours. At least Alicia would give him time to explain why. They wouldn't dare hurt him while she was there.

At the last minute he stopped and rang the doorbell. It had suddenly occurred to him that he couldn't just walk in, not with a complete stranger. It wasn't midday yet. Marcie probably wouldn't be dressed. He listened for any sound of life, a door slamming open or the tramp of feet coming down the stairs, but there was nothing. As usual, the television was turned on in the front room. That didn't mean anything. Marcie switched it on first thing in the morning and sometimes left it on all day, even when she was playing music on the radio in the same room. He could hear a man's voice reading a news bulletin. He rang a second time. There was no answer.

"They're not in," Jamie said.

"Do you want to wait for them?"

"Yes." Jamie nodded. "You don't have to worry about me. You can leave me here if you want to."

"No. I'll come in too."

She was determined. Jamie shrugged and opened the door. He had known it wouldn't be locked. It never was. There was nothing worth stealing in the house and none of the furniture belonged to them anyway. Don had rented the place through an agency. The owners were in another state, and whoever they were, they certainly hadn't been house-proud. The carpets were thin, the wallpaper peeling and the light bulbs hung without any shades. The two boys had mattresses on the floor in one of the rooms upstairs. Don and Marcie had a sagging bed next door. In the kitchen, there was a table and four chairs. That was about it. The house was little more than a shell. If it had been abandoned altogether, nobody would have noticed any difference.

"...with less than five months until election day and still no lead opening up between the two candidates, the pressure is most definitely on. Who will be the next president of the United States? It seems that only time will tell. This is Ed Radway reporting from Phoenix, Arizona..."

There was no audience in the room for the television

presenter who chatted on regardless, searching for eye contact with two empty seats.

"This is where you live?" Alicia couldn't keep the dismay out of her voice.

"We just rent it," Jamie explained. He was feeling ashamed although he had no reason to. "You don't have to stay," he added.

"Excuse me! Are you still trying to get rid of me?"

"No."

But he was. He didn't like anyone seeing him here. He didn't like admitting that this was where he lived. Alicia was looking at him and Jamie realized that he had barely spoken to her since they had left Reno – and when he had, it was only to be rude. And yet what she had said back at the hotel was true. She had rescued him. She had risked her life, driving through gunfire. And he hadn't even thanked her. "I'm sorry," he said.

"Forget it." Alicia looked around her. "You're right. It doesn't look like there's anyone at home," she said. "What does this woman – Marcie – do for a living?"

"She doesn't really do anything."

"So how did you—"

But Alicia never finished the question. They both saw it at the same time. The image on the television had changed. A thin boy with long, dark hair and pale skin was facing them. With a strange jolt, a sense of unreality, Jamie realized he was looking at himself.

"...wanted in connection with the murder of his legal guardian, Don White," the reporter was saying.

The picture divided into two. Jamie and Scott side by side. They were obviously twins, but on the television screen they didn't look so identical.

"Scott and Jamie Tyler are identical twins. Although they are only fourteen years old, they are said to be armed and dangerous. The public is urged not to approach them."

"This is crazy..." Jamie whispered.

"Sssh!" Alicia was staring at the screen.

The picture changed to the Reno Playhouse. There must have been four or five reporters standing outside, each one with their own personal microphone and cameraman, clamouring for attention. Their voices could be heard in the background as the local reporter – a blonde, excited-looking woman – told the story.

"Scott and Jamie Tyler were performing here, at this theatre in downtown Reno," she was saying. "They were part of a so-called mind-reading act that used simple trickery to fool their audience. According to witnesses, both boys were heavily involved in substance abuse and last night it seems they lost control, stealing the gun from their guardian, Don White, and turning it against him..."

"It's all lies!" Jamie exclaimed. He turned to Alicia, suddenly afraid that she wouldn't believe him. "What she's saying. None of it's true!"

"Jamie..."

"He didn't even have a gun!"

"Listen to me, Jamie—"

But at that moment there was a blast of sirens outside the house that could mean only one thing. The police had arrived.

As far as Jamie was concerned, it was all just another bad dream, worse even than the one he'd had the night before. It seemed to him that one impossibility after another was piling up on him and he almost expected the grey cowboy from his dream to jump out at him from behind the sofa, just for good measure. He heard the screech of tyres, the sound of cars pulling up in the street. At the same time, the squawk of radio transmitters filled the air. Doors opened and slammed shut. Somebody somewhere called out an order. "This way!"

It was Alicia who took control of the situation. As Jamie stood, rooted to the spot, she grabbed hold of him and suddenly she was very close.

"We have to move," she said urgently. "You can't be found here."

"But…"

"You heard what they said on the news. That's what they all think. You've been set up! If the police get you, you're finished. We have to go."

"Go where?"

Jamie turned towards the front door but it was already far too late. He heard footsteps coming up the drive. The front patio had been laid with gravel and the boots crunched against it. Alicia understood. That way was blocked. "Into the kitchen!" she commanded.

Jamie was angry with himself. The situation was completely out of control. If Scott had been here, he would have known what to do. Once again Jamie was weak and helpless, allowing himself to be pushed around ... this time by a woman he had only met a few hours before. Fortunately Alicia had taken charge. A door led into the kitchen. She pulled it open and they went through. And that was when they realized that they hadn't been on their own in the house after all.

Marcie was lying on the floor and it was obvious – even without the pool of blood – that she was dead. Her arms and legs were spread-eagled almost comically and her cheek was pressed against the linoleum as if she was trying to listen to something in the cellar below. In life, she had been a short, stocky woman. Death had somehow compressed her even more so that she didn't look quite human. A fat, stuffed doll. But somebody had shot her twice and let the stuffing out.

Jamie tried to say something but the words wouldn't come. He heard the front door open on the other side of the living room and realized that the police were already in the house. They hadn't bothered to ring the bell. Somebody muttered something but it was impossible to make out the words against the noise of the TV. Meanwhile, Alicia was looking around. A pair of French windows led into the back garden but she didn't know if they were locked or not and she didn't have time to find out. There was another door right next to her. Grabbing Jamie, she pulled him out of the kitchen and into a narrow utility room. There was a washing machine, a drier, a couple of shelves of canned food. She stopped and held up a hand, warning Jamie not to move. At the same moment, the police entered the kitchen.

"Oh, Jesus!" Jamie heard one of the policeman gagging.

"That sure is a beauty." A second voice.

"Looks like the kids came home last night."

There was a way out of the utility room. Another door at the far end. Alicia signalled and she and Jamie tiptoed over to it. There had to be at least three policemen in the kitchen, separated from them only by a thin partition wall. The door was locked but the key was there. She reached out and turned it…

Just as a policeman walked into the room behind them. He stood, staring at them, like something straight out of a Hollywood film, with his black, short-sleeved shirt and black shades that completely hid his eyes. He was young and white and he worked out. The ugly tools of his trade dangled from his belt: gun, CS gas canister, handcuffs and baton. For a moment he didn't say anything. Then his hand dropped down to the gun.

Jamie had been standing behind Alicia. Suddenly he stepped forward so that he stood directly opposite the police-man. She saw him look up and there was something in the boy's face that she couldn't recognize, a sort of intensity that seemed almost unworldly.

"There's nobody here," he said quietly. "The room's empty."

The policeman stared at him, as if puzzled by what he had just been told. Alicia waited for him to say something. But he didn't. His eyes were vacant. He nodded slowly and walked out again.

Jamie and Alicia heard voices in the kitchen as the officer rejoined the other men.

"Anything?"

"No. There's nobody there. It's just an empty room."

"Hey – Josh. Why don't you tell the paramedics to get in here? They can start clearing up."

Jamie glanced at Alicia, as if challenging her to ask questions. But this wasn't the time. Alicia opened the back door and the two of them passed through into the garage. It was empty apart from a rusty lawnmower and a deep-freeze cabinet. Don had taken his car to the Reno Playhouse and, of course, it had never been driven back. The two doors were closed but there was a window at the back. Jamie opened it and they climbed out. Now the garage was between them and any police officers who might be standing guard at the front. Jamie made sure there was nobody around, then slipped behind the neighbouring house, making his way through the garden where the two girls had played. Only when he was on the other side of the house did he cut back to the street. Alicia's car was parked right in front of him.

He took one last look at the house where he had lived for the past six months. The entrance was already taped off. There were police officers everywhere: in the porch, on the front lawn, carrying equipment in and out. Three police cars were parked in the street. Distant sirens announced that more were on the way.

Nobody noticed as Jamie and Alicia crossed the pavement and got into the car. And if anyone had turned round, they would assume that the two of them were neighbours. It was only when they were inside the car – and before she had started the engine – that Alicia turned to him.

"What *was* that?" she demanded. "What did you do to that policeman? How did you make him...?" Her voice trailed away.

"I can't tell you," Jamie replied. "I don't know what I did. And it doesn't matter. Because I'm never going to do it again."

Alicia nodded and turned the ignition. One of the policemen glanced in their direction but did nothing to stop them.

Alicia put the car into gear and the two of them drove away.

MISSING

It was later that afternoon. Alicia had managed to book adjoining rooms at the Bluebird Inn and had opened the connecting doors. Jamie was sitting at the table in his half, staring at a selection of food that she had spread out on paper plates: lunch or dinner or something in between. But he wasn't hungry. He wasn't even sure how much time had passed since he and Alicia had left Sparks. He felt hollowed out. Somewhere inside him, a voice was telling him that by now he should have been on his way to the theatre, preparing for the first evening performance. But there was going to be no performance. That was all over, and nothing was ever going to be the same again.

The television was still on. A commercial break ended and yet another news bulletin began. They were reporting two murders now. Don White, shot at the theatre, and his partner, Marcie Kelsey, killed with the same weapon at her rented home. Kelsey. The name barely registered with Jamie. He had always known her as Marcie or Mars. And now she was dead and he was wanted for her murder. Jamie Tyler, twin brother of

Scott Tyler. Both boys missing. Delinquents. High on drugs.

"That's enough!" Alicia picked up the remote control and turned the television off. "It's none of it true, so what's the point of listening to it?"

Jamie said nothing.

"And you're not just going to sit there. You've got to eat something." She pushed a plastic tub of salad towards him. Jamie glanced at the label. AUNT MARY'S LO-CALORIE CAESAR SALAD. There was a picture of an old lady in an apron. She wasn't real, of course. The meal would have been prepared in a factory, chilled and trucked in. The lettuce leaves looked fake too.

"I'm not hungry," Jamie said.

"Of course you're hungry. You haven't eaten all day." Alicia sighed. "We have to get our heads together, Jamie," she said. "You've got the police looking for you. Your brother's gone. Two people are dead. Do you really think you can help anyone just sitting here like this? Have some food and let's talk about what we're going to do."

She was right. Jamie pronged some of the lettuce with a plastic fork, then took a slice of ham. There were no cooking facilities at the motel and Alicia had chosen food they could eat straight out of the packet. There were also cookies, fruit, cheese and bread rolls. She'd taken a beer out of the motel minibar. Jamie had a Sprite. He opened the ring pull and the hiss of escaping gas seemed to unlock something in him. He was hungry, after all. And thirsty too. He drank most of the

Sprite, then began to eat.

"We need to talk," Alicia continued. Despite what she'd said, she herself wasn't eating. "That trick you pulled back at your aunt's place. That was quite something. Are you going to tell me how you did it?"

Jamie shook his head. "I don't want to talk about that."

"Well, let me suggest something to you. The act that you and your brother were doing on the stage. It was no act. You could really do it ... read each other's thoughts. Am I right?" Jamie didn't answer so she went on, "And I guess what I saw back at the house was some sort of mind control."

Jamie had finished the Sprite. He was holding the can in his hand and suddenly he closed his fingers, crumpling it. "You don't understand," he said. "I never talk about this stuff. Not with anyone. Except Scott." He looked up at her and she saw that his eyes were filled with anger, challenging her to argue with him. "You don't know what it's like. You have no idea. And I'm not going to tell you."

"All right. I'm sorry." Alicia drank some beer straight out of the bottle. She thought for a moment. "Look, I know this is difficult for you. But we're not going to get anywhere fighting each other. Maybe it would help if I told you my story. Right now I'm a complete stranger to you. But it wasn't just a coincidence, my being in the theatre last night. I was there for a reason."

"Something to do with that photograph. Daniel..."

Alicia put down the beer. "Exactly," she said. "Daniel.

That's what this is all about."

She leant forward, resting her elbows on the table. Then she began.

"The boy in the photograph, Daniel, is my son. Last week should have been his birthday. He turned eleven on 9 June. But I don't know where he is. I don't even know if he's alive. He disappeared seven months ago and I've been looking for him ever since.

"You don't need to know very much about me, Jamie. I'm thirty-two. I have a sister. My parents are from New Jersey. A year ago, I was living in Washington DC, working for Senator John Trelawny. Maybe you've heard of him. You should have. Right now he's trying to become the next president of the United States and people say there's a good chance he's going to win. Anyway, I was with him for five years, sorting his mail, sorting his diary … that kind of thing. He's a good man and I liked my job.

"The other thing I need to tell you is that I was married for a time. My husband got sick and died two years after Danny was born so I had to bring him up on my own. But in a way I was lucky. I had a little house round the corner from a really nice school. And I had a wonderful home help – Maria – who looked after Danny every afternoon until I got home.

She drew a breath.

"And then, towards the end of last year – it was the first week in November – I got a call from Maria. It was about six o'clock in the evening and I was working late. Anyway, she said that Danny hadn't come home from school. She'd tried his cell phone but she wasn't getting any answer and she didn't know what to do. I remember telling her to call round some of his friends and to phone me if he hadn't shown up by seven. Looking back, I can't believe how calm I was. But Danny often went home with one or another of his friends – he was in a band and played drums. And he was rehearsing for a Christmas show. It never occurred to me that anything could be wrong.

"Well, Maria did call back at seven o'clock and Danny still hadn't shown up and nobody had any idea where he was. It was dark by then and that was when I really began to worry. I called the police. The fact that I was connected to Senator Trelawny helped. They were round in about ten seconds and they put him straight onto the NCIC Missing Persons File. They also put out an Amber Alert, which meant that all the local businesses and shops had his description and his picture and it was like they were building a network of people who would look out for him. And I still thought he was going to show up. I could actually hear myself scolding him for being late!"

She stopped. There was a long pause.

"He never did show up," she went on. "Nobody had seen anything. Nobody knew anything. It was as if he'd vanished into thin air. I searched all over the house, trying to find some clue as to where he might have gone. I drove out to all the places he used to hang out. I went on the TV and the radio. His picture was in store windows all over town and on the back of trucks too. But nothing…"

"I think Scott saw him," Jamie muttered. "When you showed him the photograph."

Alicia nodded. "I know." She swallowed hard. "It's the first news I've had of him since it happened."

She forced herself to go on.

"Two weeks before Christmas, I made a decision. The police didn't know where to look for him. Nobody knew where he was. But I wasn't going to give up. So I resigned my job and set out to find him myself. There are plenty of organizations that deal with missing children and I contacted them. I passed out leaflets. I trawled the Internet. Do you know how many children go missing every day? I began to put together names, faces, times, places. I noted all the cases that had been reported in the last year. I drew maps. I called the parents and spoke to them.

"To my surprise, a picture began to take shape. At first it didn't make any sense and I thought maybe I was imagining things. But very quickly I realized that it was true. There was a sort of pattern. A series of coincidences. And that's what led me to you.

"What I noticed was that in the past six months, a large number of the kids who had disappeared had been what you might call special. What do I mean by that? I'm talking about kids with special abilities. Jamie, I won't beat about the bush. These were kids with paranormal powers. I know it sounds crazy. You're not supposed to believe in these things any more

– not in the twenty-first century – but even so, there was a definite link…"

Alicia got up and went over to the sofa. She opened a briefcase and took out a sheaf of documents. She spread one of them in front of Jamie. It had been taken from a local newspaper and showed a photograph of a rather intense-looking boy with cropped hair. The headline read, JACK HAS A FLASH OF THE FUTURE.

The story didn't take itself too seriously. Apparently, there was an eleven-year-old boy called Jack Pugh who lived on his father's farm in Kentucky. He'd had a dream and had warned his parents that a local church was going to catch fire. Twelve hours later, the church had been hit by lightning and had burned to the ground. Fortunately, nobody had been hurt.

"Six weeks after the paper printed that story, Jack vanished," Alicia said. She took out a second sheet of paper.

This time it was a girl. Her name was Indigo Cotton and her story had been reported in the *Miami Herald*. It seemed that she could bend spoons and stop watches just by looking at them. There had been a picture of her in the back of a paper, leaning against a grandfather clock. The clock had stopped at exactly midday. According to the story, she had been responsible.

"She disappeared too," Alicia said. "Two months after the story ran."

She added more pages to the pile. There was a boy who had managed to predict the winner five times in a row at a local racecourse. Another boy who, without moving, had fused all the lights in his school. A girl who talked to ghosts. An autistic boy who knew the names of everyone he met before he was introduced to them. Another pair of twins who seemed to live in each other's minds.

"They all disappeared?" Jamie asked.

"A dozen of them in just six months. That may not sound like a lot to you, Jamie, but I know how statistics work and I can tell you it's completely incredible. Of course, loads of other kids went missing too. But this was something quite different. It seemed clear to me that someone was deliberately *targeting* these kids."

"So did you go to the police?"

"No." Alicia sat down again. "Read the articles. None of them are serious. I mean ... one kid who can bend spoons? Another who talks to dead people? 'TALES FROM THE DARK SIDE. Grave Business of Girl Who Gossips with Ghosts.' Read it for yourself. Of course, once these children had disappeared, everyone treated them very seriously. But the paranormal stuff was just forgotten. It wasn't important. In fact it was hardly even mentioned."

Jamie thought about it for a moment. Then something suddenly occurred to him. "What about Daniel?" he asked.

Alicia nodded. "There was a piece about him too," she said. "At the time, I didn't want it to appear and I was annoyed when it did. But the thing is, quite a few strange things happened with Danny too. He used to have these premonitions. They weren't dreams ... they were just feelings. He once stopped me going on a train. He was only six years old and he got quite hysterical about it. Like, he was throwing stuff around the room and in the end I gave in. I couldn't leave him with Maria, not like that. So I didn't go – and you know what happened? A few days later I learnt that there had been an incident on that train. Some guy out of his mind on drugs shot someone. If I'd been travelling that day, could it have been me? I don't know...

"Then he did it again, only this time at school. He warned a boy not to go home. That same afternoon, a bus skidded off the main road and went straight through one of the walls of the boy's house. Smashed into the kitchen and brought down most of the upper floor. Of course, everyone at the school was talking about it and a local paper picked it up."

"And you think someone may have read it," Jamie said.

"Yeah. I think someone read it. I think someone came for Danny because he was special. And for the last few months, I've been scouring the newspapers, looking for kids like you. Because, you see, if there really is someone out there searching for kids with powers, maybe I can get there ahead of them. Maybe I can find out who they are and discover what they've done with my boy.

"Now you know why I was in Reno. I happened to see this piece in a magazine. It was about two boys performing a mind-reading act. The writer said he'd seen them twice and he couldn't work out for love nor money how they did it. So I came over to see for myself…"

"And you arrived just in time," Jamie said.

"I couldn't believe it when those men came after you with stun darts and bullets." For a moment, Alicia's eyes lit up and she couldn't keep the excitement out of her voice. "But it proves what I'm saying. There is somebody out there who really is going after these special kids. They got your brother and wherever they've taken him, that's where Danny may be too."

"There's one thing I don't understand," Jamie said. "Suppose you're right and somebody is kidnapping kids with special powers. Why would they do that? What's the point?"

"It could be the government, the CIA or someone like that. Think about it for a minute. If you could really read someone's mind, you'd make a perfect weapon. You could be a spy. You could be anything!"

"You really think they'd believe in that sort of stuff?"

"Of course they believe in it, Jamie. They spend millions of dollars every year experimenting with the paranormal. And there are major corporations out there who run programs, working with special children and their families. I even got in contact with one. I thought they might be able to help."

"Who was that?"

Alicia put down her beer. "They're a huge multinational. They're into communications, healthcare, security, energy … just about everything. But they also have a division that specializes in paranormal research." She paused. "They were the people who came for you in the theatre. Their name," she said, "is Nightrise."

BUSINESS AS USUAL

The boardroom was on the sixty-sixth floor of The Nail – which was the name of the newest and most spectacular addition to the Hong Kong skyline. The Nail had been constructed at an angle so that it slanted towards Orchard Hill and away from the waterfront. It seemed to be made of solid steel, an illusion caused by the one-way glass in all of its windows. The top three floors, sixty-four to sixty-six, were circular, and wider than the rest of the building. Viewed from Kowloon, on the other side of Victoria Harbor, it really did look like a giant nail that had been hammered into the heart of the city.

There were just three men in the boardroom, although fifty could have fitted in easily. A conference table made of black, gleaming wood stretched the full length of the room with black leather chairs placed at exact intervals. Two of the men were already seated, going through papers, preparing themselves for the conference that was about to begin. The third was standing in front of the floor-to-ceiling windows that curved round in a great arc, enjoying the view.

The Nail was the worldwide headquarters of the Nightrise

Corporation. The man standing on his own was its chairman.

Unlike the office, he had no name – or if he did, he never used it. He was simply the chairman, or Mr Chairman when he was directly addressed. He was in his sixties, although he had done his best to disguise his age with extensive plastic surgery. This left him with a face that was younger than it should be and yet strangely unnatural, as if it belonged somewhere else. He had thick, white hair which could have been a wig but was actually his own, and silver, half-moon spectacles. As always, he was wearing a suit, made to measure by his own personal tailor.

It was seven o'clock in the morning and the sun had not yet fully risen. The great sprawl of Kowloon was still half asleep, the bars and electronics shops briefly shuttered before the start of another day. The sky was a blazing red. The chairman thought it appropriate. Kowloon means "nine dragons" and it seemed to him, looking out from the window, that they had all breathed at once.

Behind him, one of the other two men spoke.

"They're coming on-line now, Mr Chairman."

The chairman walked to his place at the head of the table and sat down. He rested his hands on the polished surface and composed himself. There were thirteen plasma screens mounted all around the room and one after another they flickered into life as the other executives, in different parts of the world, came on-line. A webcam, standing on the table, pointed at the chairman, carrying his own image out. In Los

Angeles, it was two o'clock in the afternoon. In London it was midnight. But the time of the day was unimportant. This was the monthly meeting of the senior executives of the Nightrise Corporation and none of them would have dared to have been even a minute late.

"My greetings to you, ladies and gentlemen." As ever, the chairman was the first to speak. He had an unpleasant, throaty voice, as if he were ill. He spoke very softly and his voice had to be amplified as it was transmitted. He had no obvious accent. This was an international businessman and he had managed to develop an international voice.

"I don't think I need to remind you that this is a critical time for us all," he went on. "It is a world-changing time. Everything we've been working for all these years is about to come to fruition. Business has never been better but right now there is so much more at stake than simple profit and loss. We have the Psi project. We have news from South America. And, of course, we have the upcoming election ... the race to become the most powerful man in the world." He paused and it was almost as if a thin mist had passed across his eyes. "I hardly need to tell you, ladies and gentlemen, that this is one time we cannot afford to make mistakes."

He stopped. Nobody moved. The images on the television screens were so still that they could have been accidentally frozen. Two thousand miles away, the private Nightrise Corporation satellite that was making this conference possible continued its orbit around the world, picking up the signals and beaming them into the different countries. And it was as if something of the black emptiness of outer space was being sent with them. The images were dead. The dozen offices with their dozen televisions seemed to contain no life at all.

"Let's start in New York. The election. What can you report?"

The New York executive's screen was about halfway down the room. He was a solid, square-shouldered man who had spent twenty years in the army before moving into business – and it showed. His name was Simms. "This is a hard nut to crack, sir," he reported. "And whatever happens, it's going to be close … maybe as close as one or two states. Our guy is doing better than expected, but so far we haven't been able to do serious damage to Trelawny."

"Advertising?"

"Sir, we've taken out advertisements that suggest that Trelawny is soft on crime and soft on immigration. We've said he's a coward and a liar. We've even managed to plant newspaper stories that hint he might be gay. But nothing seems to hurt him. For some reason people like him, and right now all the indications are that the two of them will be neck and neck by November."

"Baker must win. There can be no other result. Trelawny must not become president."

"Well, short of assassinating John Trelawny, I'm not sure what we can do."

"I think, Mr Simms, you should be considering every possibility."

"Yes, sir."

Next, the chairman turned his attention to a screen that was next to him, on his right-hand side. "Could you please make your report," he said.

"Certainly, Mr Chairman."

The woman on the plasma screen gazed directly into the room. She looked more like a school teacher than a businesswoman, with glasses that were too big for her face, very cropped grey hair and a long, thin neck. She was dressed in black. She was speaking from an office in Los Angeles and although outside the sun was brilliant, none of it had been allowed to reach her. There was a shadow across her face. Her skin was pale. She could have been lit by the moon.

Her name was Susan Mortlake.

"I have good news to report and also bad news," she began. "It has now been almost a year and a half since we began the Psi project but we may have had a breakthrough. It seems that we have finally managed to track down two of the Gatekeepers."

This caused a stir around the room. The disembodied heads in the television sets turned, even though they couldn't actually see each other. The two men making notes scribbled furiously. One of them turned a page.

"It's still too early to be absolutely sure that they are who we think they are," the woman went on. "The fact of the matter is that we've looked at hundreds of children who have demonstrated any measure of psychic power. Telepaths, fire starters, clairvoyants ... anything out of the ordinary. Half of them, of course, have turned out to be a waste of time. A few of them have moved away before we were able to track them down. But as for the rest ... we've managed to take possession of seventeen of the most promising subjects and we've been experimenting with them in our facility at Silent Creek. However, it now looks as if all our efforts may have been a waste of time. We have one of the Gatekeepers in our power, I'm sure of it. So far, we've only been able to begin a brief examination, but it's already obvious that his powers are far greater than anything we've yet encountered."

"Why do you only have one of them?" the chairman asked.

"That's the bad news, Mr Chairman." Susan Mortlake paused. "The two boys – Scott and Jamie Tyler – were performing a telepathy act at a theatre in Reno. It was their guardian, who was also the producer of the show, who first brought them to our attention. He was quite happy for us to take them in return for a sum of cash – although, of course, it was always our intention to kill him. This we have done. I arranged a fairly simple operation to pick the boys up but unfortunately something went wrong. It may be that their power is even greater than we had imagined. At any event, they knew we were coming and one of them – Jamie – managed to get away."

"Where is he now?"

"We have no idea. My agents tell me that he was helped in his escape by a woman, but they were unable to get her registration number. It all happened too quickly and it was dark. However, I believe the situation is now under control."

"Go on."

"We shot the producer, a man called Don White. He was living with a woman, Marcie Kelsey. We shot her with the same gun and then used our contacts within the Nevada police to set up a false trail. Jamie Tyler is now wanted for both murders and it can only be a matter of time before he's tracked down. At which point, we will have him."

Susan Mortlake sounded confident, but the chairman was unimpressed. "Your agents allowed one of these boys to slip through their fingers. They also failed to track down the car. Have you taken any disciplinary procedures, Mrs Mortlake?"

"No, sir." The woman looked up defiantly. "It did occur to me that you might be asking for my own resignation."

The chairman considered, then shook his head. "If you have one of the Gatekeepers, that will be enough," he said. "We only have to break the circle and we will have won. However, you still need to make redundancies, Mrs Mortlake. We cannot have people letting us down."

"Of course, Mr Chairman. I thought as much myself."

"And I want you to deal with Scott Tyler personally. You understand that, generally speaking, it would be better if he were not allowed to die."

"I understand. But as a matter of fact, we may be able to use him. I'm hoping to bring him round to our point of view."

"Good."

The single word was praise indeed. The chairman never complimented his staff on anything. At the Nightrise Corporation, excellence was taken for granted. He spoke again, this time addressing all the executives.

"As I began by saying, this is a critical time. It's also a very positive time and before we part company, I want to introduce you to an associate whose name will be familiar to you. We have worked together on many occasions and he has very kindly agreed to say a few words to you today."

There was a fourteenth screen at the far end of the table, opposite the chairman. Until now it had been blank, but it suddenly flickered into life. At first it seemed that there was something wrong with the picture. The head that had appeared simply looked too big for the screen, too heavy for the neck that supported it. Its eyes were very high up, above a nose that seemed to travel a long way to the small and rather babyish mouth below. It was as if the image had been stretched – but in fact there was nothing wrong with the transmission. The man was Diego Salamanda, head of Salamanda News International. He was beaming the signal from his research centre in the town of Ica in Peru. And this was how he really looked.

"Good evening," he began. The local time was just after seven o'clock. "It is a great pleasure to be able to speak with

94

you. I would like to thank your chairman for inviting me. And I have some excellent news to share with you.

"I have now had a chance to decipher the diary of the mad monk of Cordoba which was unearthed very recently in Spain and passed into my hands. I don't need to remind you that this is the only written history of the Old Ones and their fight against the five children who came to be known as the Gatekeepers. The Old Ones ruled the Earth about ten thousand years ago. They were all-powerful but they were defeated – according to the diary – by a trick. Sadly, we have no more details. There was a great battle, which the Old Ones lost, and they were banished. Two gates were built to keep them out of our world. Many of us have been working for their return ever since.

"Further examination of the diary has provided me with the answers that I have been looking for and I can tell you that, without a shadow of a doubt, very soon we will have achieved our aims and a new millennium will have begun. Yes, my friends, the Old Ones are about to return to take control of a world that should, in truth, have been theirs all along."

He stopped to catch his breath, his nostrils flaring. It hurt him to speak. It hurt him to do almost anything, a result of his head having been deliberately mutilated at birth.

"We are now in mid-June," he went on. "And the twenty-fourth of this month is a sacred day in my country. We call it Inti Raymi, the summer solstice. On that day, the second great gate, built in the desert in Nazca, will open. By carefully examining the

95

diary, I have discovered the means to unlock it and nothing can now prevent me."

He lifted a hand. Next to his head it looked ridiculous, out of proportion.

"But we have enemies," he said. "Incredible though it may sound, the five children who defeated us all those years ago have somehow returned. You may have found two of them in America. One of them is on his way here to Peru. My agent encountered him in a church in London.

"This much I can tell you. There have to be five of them. It's only when they come together that they have the strength to be a danger to us. On their own, they are powerless. And nothing can stop us. On June twenty-fourth, the Old Ones will take what is theirs and all of us will share in the rewards."

Around the boardroom table the executives began to applaud. They were thousands of miles apart: in London, Los Angeles, Tokyo, Beijing … all over the world. It was as if someone had turned up the volume. The noise echoed around the room.

The fourteenth screen went black. Salamanda had broken contact.

"Now you know the stakes," the chairman said. "Just a few days stand between us and the end of the old world. But let's not fool ourselves that our work is over. It's just begin-ning. A war is coming and our job is to prepare the way. We need a president of the United States who is sympathetic to our aims. Mr Simms, I am relying on you. Mrs Mortlake, see to the child. Make him one of ours. Then find his brother and deal with him too."

The chairman signalled to one of his two assistants. One of them reached out and flicked a switch. The remaining thirteen screens went black.

In her office in Los Angeles, Susan Mortlake watched the red light on her own webcam blink out and knew that she was no longer transmitting. She also knew that she was very fortunate to be alive. The chairman had briefly considered asking her for her resignation. She had seen it in his eyes.

Even so, he had told her to make redundancies. She leant forward and reached out with a long finger, the nail sharpened to a point. There was an intercom in front of her and she pressed a button. "You can send them in now," she said.

A few seconds later, the door opened and Colton Banes and Kyle Hovey walked in. There were two chairs opposite her desk and they sat down without being asked. The room was ice cold, the air-conditioning turned up to its highest level, but Susan Mortlake noticed that beads of sweat had broken out on Hovey's forehead. Banes was looking more relaxed. He didn't even flinch when she turned and looked at him. Both men knew why they were here. It was inevitable that they would be called to account.

"Well?" Mrs Mortlake snapped out the single word. She really was like a teacher now, a headmistress about to select the punishment.

"It was his fault!" Hovey chipped in at once, eager to get over his version of events. He glanced at Banes. "He made serious mistakes. He should have known about the dog." He raised an arm, wincing at the same time as if to prove his point. Underneath his suit jacket he was covered in bandages where he had been bitten. He'd had to be injected against tetanus and rabies. "And he should have had more men waiting at the stage door."

"Mr Banes?" Mrs Mortlake turned her head back to him. She was wearing long earrings that jangled as she moved.

Banes shrugged. "It's true," he said. "I didn't know about the dog. The kids were lucky. Sometimes it happens like that."

Mrs Mortlake considered. She already knew what she was going to do. She hadn't risen to a position of power in the Nightrise Corporation without being able to make fast decisions.

"It seems to me that you half succeeded," she began. "Which is to say, you half failed. One boy got away but we still have the other one. If both boys had escaped, I would have no choice but to make you both redundant. As it is, one of you can be spared." She smiled sweetly. "Mr Banes, I'm very sorry…"

In the chair next to him, Mr Hovey relaxed.

"But I'm going to have to ask you to strangle Mr Hovey. I know you're friends. I know you've worked together for a long time. But the corporation really cannot allow failure and the fact that Mr Hovey is a bit of a whiner, I personally find most displeasing."

"Do you want me to do it now, Mrs Mortlake?" Banes asked.

"Yes. Please go ahead."

Colton Banes stood up and walked behind the other man. Kyle Hovey sat where he was. His entire body had slumped in on itself. He was carrying a gun – it was in a holster under his jacket – but he didn't even try to reach for it. At least this would be quick. Fairly quick, anyway.

Banes's hands rested briefly on the other man's shoulders. "I'm sorry, Kyle," he said, "but for what it's worth, you always were a loser." His outstretched fingers reached underneath the black ponytail and closed on the other man's throat. He began to squeeze. From the other side of the desk, Susan Mortlake watched with interest. It took just a minute. Then Colton Banes went back to his chair and sat down. Next to him, Kyle Hovey remained where he was as if nothing had happened.

"Will there be anything else, Mrs Mortlake?" Colton Banes asked.

"No, thank you, Mr Banes. You can wait for me here in Los Angeles."

Kyle Hovey slid gently to one side, then toppled to the floor.

"You'd better get your friend cremated," she continued. "And send flowers if he has a family. As for me, I'll be heading out to Silent Creek. I can't wait to meet this boy, Scott Tyler. I think we need to begin his treatment right away."

JAMIE'S STORY

They saw her come out of the office building, the woman dressed in black with the closely cut grey hair. There was a limousine waiting for her and they watched her as she was driven away, up West 4th Street towards the Harbor Freeway. But they didn't know who she was or where she was going. They would find that out later.

Jamie and Alicia were sitting in a car in the business district of Los Angeles. It was the same car that Alicia had rented in Reno – the two of them had driven out the day before.

Jamie had slept for much of the journey although he had been awake at the start. An hour after they had left Reno, the highway had sloped upwards and suddenly he had found himself passing through forests of fir trees that rose steeply on both sides. If he looked up far enough he could see clumps of snow still refusing to melt and he had realized that he was finally going over the mountains. Beyond the snow. He had once dreamt that he would make the crossing and this was where he would find a new life. Now he wasn't so sure. All he knew was that his old life had been shattered

100

and he was leaving the pieces far behind.

Alicia would have preferred to take a plane. But Jamie had no picture ID. He couldn't fly. And with the police still actively searching for him, it wouldn't have been safe to go near an airport. So she had driven, stopping overnight in another motel in Fresno before arriving in Los Angeles the following afternoon, grimy and bleary-eyed from so much driving.

As they came down over the valley, Jamie had caught sight of the famous Hollywood sign, the white letters reflecting the rays of the sun. He'd seen it often enough on TV. This was the city of angels, the dream factory, home to the stars and the beautiful people. All sorts of clichés tumbled through his mind. But he felt nothing. He had come here because he had to. Los Angeles meant nothing to him. And as for the sign – what was it? Just some big letters on a hillside.

He was exhausted, hollowed out. Don and Marcie had been killed and the police thought he'd done it! The story had been reported all over America. After all, he was only fourteen. A juvenile, on the run, guilty of two homicides. The newspapers had lapped it up. But worse than all this, worse than anything he had ever experienced, was the knowledge that Scott had been taken. Driving into this new city, he once again reached out for Scott's thoughts, wondering if – against all odds – he might get some tiny sense of his brother's presence. But there was nothing. In fact, Scott felt further away than ever.

Jamie had wanted to stay in Reno but Alicia had persuaded him that it would be too dangerous. They had one clue: a name on a small white card. Nightrise Corporation. Alicia had checked on the Internet. Nightrise was based in Hong Kong but had offices all over the world. Two addresses were listed in the USA: one in New York, one in Los Angeles. Driving all the way to the East Coast was out of the question. Coming here was their only option.

And so here they were, parked opposite a skyscraper that was nothing more than a rectangular block, fifty storeys high, its identically sized windows punched in with mathematical precision. The top six floors belonged to Nightrise, with banks, insurance companies, law firms and dozens of other businesses below. Jamie and Alicia had been here for an hour, watching people come and go. Right now it was five o'clock and the rotating doors were never still as workers hurried out, eager to get home.

But there had been no sign of Colton Banes or the dark-haired man with the ponytail who had been sitting next to him at the theatre. Perhaps they weren't here at all.

They waited another hour, then Alicia sighed and started the engine. "This is a waste of time," she said. "Are you hungry?"

Jamie nodded. He had no real appetite, but he hadn't eaten anything since the morning and he could feel his energy levels falling. Alicia pulled out and they drove back towards where they were staying in West Hollywood. Alicia had mentioned she had a sister. It now turned out that she was a flight attendant and lived in Los Angeles. She would be away for a week and had gladly lent them her house. Alicia had telephoned her from Fresno. She hadn't mentioned Jamie.

They stopped at a restaurant on Melrose Avenue, a shabby, colourful street full of shops mainly selling antiques or clothes. They sat in the open air under a giant pink umbrella. A waitress came with the menu. Alicia chose a salad. Jamie hesitated. He looked awkward.

"What is it?" Alicia asked.

"I've never eaten in a smart restaurant like this," Jamie said.

Alicia smiled. "It's not all that smart," she said. "It's just a café really."

"I can't afford to pay for this."

"I've already explained. You don't have to pay for anything."

Alicia had bought Jamie a set of fresh clothes in Fresno. He was wearing a brightly coloured Hawaiian shirt. It wasn't his style, but the more striking the shirt, the less likely people would be to look at his face. At least, that was what Alicia had said. She had also bought him sunglasses and a baseball cap, the uniform of teenagers all over America. Even if the police were looking for him in California, they would never spot him now.

Jamie ordered a hamburger and the two of them sat in silence sipping freshly squeezed orange juice until their meal arrived. It was only when Jamie began to eat that he realized how hungry he was and wolfed the food down. Alicia ate more delicately. Jamie had already noticed that she did everything very carefully. Even making the coffee in the morning, she handled the cups as if they were made of expensive porcelain.

"We need to work out what we're going to do," Alicia said.

"Nightrise." Jamie muttered the single word with a sense of dread.

"Think back to Reno, Jamie. You said there were four men at the theatre. How many of them do you think you'd recognize?"

Jamie thought for a moment. "The bald man. I'd know him anywhere. He looked creepy. And his friend – the one who got bitten. I'd know him too." He tried to remember the sequence of events. Everything had happened so quickly. "One of the men, the driver of the car, got hurt. He cut his head. He'd have a wound."

"The men in the car may have been local. Was there anyone else?"

"I didn't see anyone." Jamie had finished eating. Everything had gone, right down to the last salad leaf. He pushed his plate away. "What difference does it make, Alicia? Even if we catch sight of one of them, we can't go to the police. They'll just arrest me and that will be the end of it."

"That wasn't what I had in mind."

"Then what are we going to do?"

"I've got an idea – but I'm afraid I'm not going to do anything, Jamie. This is down to you."

"What do you mean?"

Alicia put down her knife and fork. She thought for a moment, searching for the right words. "Look, I know you don't want to talk about this," she said, "but we can't avoid it any more. You're very special. You have a power. I know you don't like it. But you can use it to find Scott."

"How?" Jamie asked. But he could already see where she was going.

"We find one of these men – Banes or the other one – and you go up to him and you ask him where your brother is. Just like that. Of course he won't tell you. But that doesn't matter, does it? Because you can read his mind. You can find out the answer without him saying a word."

"No!" Jamie clenched his fists. He had shouted his refusal and two people at the next table turned briefly to look at him.

But Alicia wasn't giving up. "Why not?" she insisted. "What's the matter with you? Have you got any better ideas? Why don't you want to help?"

"I'm not going to do it," Jamie said. All the colour had drained out of his face and his shoulders were rising and falling as he caught his breath. "I've already told you. I don't even want to talk about it."

"But what about Scott?"

"You don't care about Scott. You don't care about either of us. You're just using me because you want me to help you find Daniel."

As soon as he had said the words, he regretted them. But it

was too late. Alicia looked at him as if he had just slapped her across the face. "That's not fair," she said in a quiet voice. "Daniel is my son, it's true. Of course I want to find him. I want it more than anything in the world. But do you really think I'm just using you? Do you think I'll just forget you if I find my boy?" She paused, then continued more slowly. "I can't even be sure that the same people have taken them both. We know people from Nightrise were there in Reno. But there's nothing to say they were in Washington eight months ago. Maybe I'm just clutching at straws and Danny was murdered the day he disappeared. But that won't stop me searching for Scott. We're in this together now."

"I still can't do what you're asking," Jamie said.

"Fine." Alicia sat there, rigid. "Then let's go home."

They drove back in virtual silence. In fact, Alicia only spoke once. As they reached the main intersection at Santa Monica Boulevard, she noticed a huge billboard. It showed a man in an open-necked shirt, leaning against what might have been a gate or a fence. The photograph looked casual, almost like a family snap. There was a headline: AN HONEST CHANGE. And, at the bottom, a straightforward announcement in black letters:

SENATOR JOHN TRELAWNY TALKS AT THE LOS ANGELES CONVENTION CENTER. 8.00 P.M. JUNE 22

"That's the day after tomorrow," Alicia said. "I didn't know he was coming to Los Angeles."

Jamie wondered why she cared.

"I used to work for him," she reminded him. "In fact, I still do."

"I thought you said you resigned."

"I tried to, but he put me on indefinite sick leave … until I found Danny. I still get a pay cheque every month. That's how I can afford to go on."

Alicia's sister owned a pretty studio house – one of five that stood in a row, all of them designed in the Spanish style. At the front there was a courtyard with flowers spilling out of terracotta urns and twisted vines climbing the walls. A pair of cats stretched out in the sun and the air smelled of perfume. The house itself was very simple. A living room and a kitchen, two bedrooms and a bathroom, all of them furnished simply. Fans circulated and cooled the air. Two framed travel posters and, on the coffee table, a model of an old biplane, were the only clues that the place might belong to a flight attendant.

"Can I get you a drink?" Alicia asked.

"No, thank you."

"Do you want to lie down? You can watch TV if you like…"

Jamie looked around. "What's your sister called?"

"Caroline."

"Are you close?"

"We see each other when we can."

Jamie and Alicia were standing in the living room. They

both looked awkward. This wasn't their house. And they still hadn't quite absorbed the chain of events that had brought them together. "Look, I'm sorry. All right?" Jamie muttered the words. "What I said, back at the restaurant, that was wrong. You're trying to help me. I know that. But what you want me to do – you don't understand…"

"I'll make some coffee," Alicia said. "Why don't we go outside?"

Ten minutes later, they were sitting together on the patio at the back of the house. Night had fallen but a full moon had come out, illuminating a stretch of decking, a tangle of plants. They were surrounded by other houses but there was nobody else in sight. It felt very private. Even the noise of the Los Angeles traffic couldn't reach them here.

"I don't like talking about myself," Jamie said.

Alicia said nothing. She wanted him to relax, to begin in his own time.

"Me and Scott. We've always been…" Jamie held up a finger and thumb, almost touching, to show what he meant. "He's the smart one. He's the one who gets us out of trouble. He always knows what to do. I think of him as my big brother although I guess we're twins."

"You don't know?"

Jamie shook his head. "We were found dumped near a place called Glenbrook, near Lake Tahoe. We were, like, babies in a basket, left by the side of the road. Except it wasn't a basket, it was a cardboard box. We had no names. Nothing.

108

Oh yes – this was really funny. Someone had given us a tattoo. Both of us, the same tattoo."

"Where is it?" Alicia hadn't meant to ask but she couldn't stop herself.

"Here." Jamie flicked a thumb over his shoulder. "On my shoulder. It's a sort of circle with a line through it. It doesn't mean anything."

"So how did you get your names?"

"They called him Scott because the box we were found in was for Scott's grass seed. I got called Jamie after the local doctor who examined us. They thought we had Native American blood. They asked about us on the reservations."

"You do have that look," Alicia agreed.

"I won't tell you too much about our life – what happened to us. I don't suppose you care a whole lot. Because what you want to know about is The Accident. That's what we called it. But we never talked about it. I never said anything to anyone about it except Scott and I don't want to talk about it now."

Alicia sighed. "Maybe if you start at the beginning, it'll make it all easier."

"Whatever. There's not much to tell you anyway."

Jamie had a cup of coffee in front of him, but he hadn't drunk any of it. For a few moments he stared into the black surface of the liquid as if it were a mirror, showing him the past.

"OK. We were just left by the roadside. We never had a mum or a dad or anything like that. There was a newspaper story about when we were found. We were called the Seed Box Babies. And after that we were taken into protective custody. I guess they kept us in hospital for a while but then we were fostered. They put us in this foster home somewhere in Carson City. There were another half dozen kids there, all with Indian blood. I can't even remember where it was any more. The people who ran it were called Tyler and we took their name while the police and the social services tried to find out where we'd come from.

"Except they couldn't. Everyone was interested in the tattoos. They thought the tattoos had to mean something. After all, who'd go to the trouble of putting a tattoo on a baby? They went onto the reservations and asked questions and they offered a reward. But it didn't work. And in the end they closed the file and just let us get on with it.

"But things never stopped going wrong for us. We were always blowing out of different foster homes. We used to get into fights with other kids. We didn't pick these fights – they just sort of happened. By the time we were about six years old we knew that it was always going to be the same … Scott looked out for me and I looked out for him. And as for the rest of them … we didn't give a damn.

"I lost count of the number of homes we were in and out of. The one thing was, they never separated us. We had this case worker. Her name was Derry and she said that it was important they keep us together. Like it was the law. When we were nine, they tried fostering us out-of-state in Salt Lake

City and that worked for a time. I think we were happy. We were with a couple who couldn't have kids of their own. They had a nice place and they were kind to us, but about twelve months after we'd been there, they decided they'd had enough. Derry flew out to see us, and by now she knew what was going on and that was when she tried to tell us. We were different. We were special. But we made people uneasy. That's what she tried to tell us, but she didn't exactly put it into words. Maybe she thought we'd laugh at her.

"It didn't matter, though. We'd already worked it out for ourselves. We knew we had this … ability. Maybe you'd call it a power, only that would make it sound as if we could put on costumes and turn into Spider-Man or something and it was never like that. Even while Derry was talking to us, trying to explain it, we knew we could have looked into her mind and seen what she was thinking. Telepathy. That's the word for it. But we weren't superheroes. We were freaks. We weren't like anyone else. And that was why we'd never been able to fit in."

"Did you ever use your ability?" Alicia asked. She felt she hadn't breathed the whole time Jamie had been speaking. He was so skinny and vulnerable, sitting out here on the patio with his black hair falling to his neck. Only now was she beginning to understand all he had been through.

"How do you mean?" Jamie asked.

"I don't know. To cheat in exams. Or to find out about stuff you weren't supposed to know."

"No!" Jamie shook his head. "You don't understand how it

111

feels to be able to read people's minds, Alicia. It isn't fun. It was like there was this whispering all the time. All the time! We'd be walking down the streets and it would be everywhere, all around us, never stopping. Can you imagine what it would be like going to a movie if the audience never stopped talking? Well, that's how it was for us. Sometimes it could drive us mad.

"What most people are thinking, most of the time, isn't very nice. They're thinking about their husbands or their wives and the arguments they've had. They're thinking about the people they want to hurt and how angry they are and how miserable they are and why it's never their fault. Or maybe they're worrying about money or about losing their jobs or it can be even worse. They can be thinking horrible, foul thoughts. So, no, we didn't use our ability. We did the exact opposite. It was like putting our hands permanently over our ears. We managed to close all the doors.

"We kept just one of them open. I could hear what Scott was thinking and he could hear me. It worked even when we were a mile apart, although it got fainter … you know … like a whisper. But we were never scared to go into each other's heads because we always knew there would be no bad surprises. We knew it would be safe. And that's how we became the telepathic twins. That's what Don White made us."

"Were you sent to him next?" Alicia asked.

Jamie shook his head. "Can I have another drink?"

"Coffee?"

"Coke."

"Wait there…"

Alicia went into the kitchen. Fortunately, her sister kept the place well stocked. She came back with a can of Coke and a glass filled with ice. She waited while Jamie drank. Then he put the glass down.

"Reading minds wasn't the only thing we could do," he said.

The Accident. Alicia remembered he had mentioned it when he began talking. She guessed that he was coming to it now.

"After Salt Lake, we were moved back to Nevada, to Carson City. We were fostered by a couple called Ed and Leanne. Ed worked in a local hospital. He did maintenance. Leanne didn't do anything.

"We were still going to school at that time. We were ten years old. And we still didn't fit in. We were flunking most of our classes. Anyway, there was a big kid at the school. His name was Ray Cavalli and he used to pick on us all the time. Everyone was scared of him because he threw his weight around and nobody would go to the teachers because they didn't want to rat. Anyway, I got into a fight with Cavalli and he was really beating me; of course Scott knew what was happening as soon as it started and suddenly he was there. And he came between us and I'll never forget the look in his eyes. He just looked straight at Cavalli and told him to get lost.

"And you know what happened? Cavalli stepped back like he was dazed and didn't understand what was going on. Then

113

he just sort of walked … stumbled … out of the school and kept going.

"It took the police two days to find him and he nearly died. He'd walked into the desert and he'd got lost. This was the summer and it can easily get into the hundreds out there and he had no water. When they found him, he had no idea where he was or how he'd got there. Anyway, that was about it. I heard he got better in the end and the family moved to another state. I never saw him again."

"You think the two of you were responsible?"

"I know we were. You want to hear the rest of it?"

Alicia nodded. Jamie took another sip of Coke.

"Ed and Leanne weren't too bad. We liked Carson City. We used to see bald eagles and hawks in the summer. It was OK. But trouble always followed us around. And this time it was my fault. There was this teacher, Mr Dempster, and he used to pick on us. Maybe Scott and me knew a bit too much about him. Maybe he guessed that somehow. Anyway, he was always putting us in detention and stuff like that and one day I decided to get my own back on him and I slashed the tyres on his car. He had this Beetle and he was so proud of it. It was a dumb thing to do but I took a knife to his tyres and the worst thing was … I got caught.

"I never thought the whole thing would get so out of hand, but the next thing I knew, I was under arrest and I had a probation officer. Suddenly I was in front of a judge – and the upshot of it was, what Ed had always been saying came true."

"You were sent to jail?"

"I was sent to a juvenile hall – just for a couple of weeks. The judge said it would be a wake-up call. I ended up in a place just outside Reno. I was also told I'd have to work after school hours to pay back the cost of the tyres."

He drank again. A cloud slid across the moon. It was like a knife, cutting it in half. Somewhere in the distance, an ambulance screamed its way along the boulevards.

"Juvie wasn't too bad," Jamie went on. "It was clean and the food was OK and I actually got on with the other kids. It was just boring, mainly. The worst thing was when I got home again. Scott was waiting for me; I thought he'd be pleased to see me – but he wasn't. He was furious. He said what I'd done was stupid. He said things were bad for us already and I'd just made them worse.

"He was right. After I got back, things were never the same with Ed and Leanne. They were having problems anyway. They were always fighting … shouting at each other. But now they decided that Scott and me were just in the way and that they should never have taken us in to begin with. Ed had started drinking. Vodka, mainly. He'd get through half a bottle a night, easily. About a month after I got back, he had an argument with Scott and he hit him. That was the first time he ever did that. And the power was still working – the link between us – because I was the one who got the bruise even though I wasn't even in the room at the time.

"At the same time, Derry – my case worker – got sick. She'd

115

been looking out for us right from the start, but now she couldn't work any more and all her files were farmed out. She wrote to us, but I never saw her again and I never saw anyone else either. They had overload. They couldn't handle the number of cases they were already dealing with and they figured Scott and me were OK, so they just let us go. They probably think we're still with Ed and Leanne even now. I don't know...

"We weren't OK. Ed's temper was getting worse and worse. He lost his job and that was when he told us we were going to be moving on again. I remember it so well. Leanne was out, and we were alone with Ed. He'd been drinking again and, maybe just for the fun of it, he started taunting Scott. He said that he'd already spoken to Child and Family Services and the two of us were finally going to be separated. Scott was staying in Carson City. But I'd be in another state.

"I don't know if he was lying or not. But he made it sound so real, like it was going to happen any time. He and Scott were yelling at each other and he was drinking, straight out of the bottle, and laughing at us. That was when it happened. Scott looked him in the eyes and I'll never forget what he said. I can tell you the exact words. *'Nobody's going to separate us. You can go hang yourself.'"*

Jamie fell silent.

"Oh my God!" Alicia whispered.

Jamie nodded. "That's right. Ed got up and there was this weird look on his face. As if he'd been shocked ... told something worse than anything he'd heard in his life. He just got up and walked out of the room and into the kitchen and then into the garage. We heard the door open and close. I thought about running after him but I was so fazed by what had happened, and you have to remember I was only eleven years old.

"Leanne was the one who found him when she came back. He'd gone into the garage. He'd climbed a stepladder. And he'd hanged himself with a cord tied to a metal bracket. Of course, nobody was surprised – what with the drinking and the arguments and losing his job and everything. He'd just had enough. That's what they all said.

"Only Scott and me knew the truth. We spoke about it only once: Scott said it was an accident and that's how we always thought about it afterwards. The Accident. Because Scott hadn't known what he was saying. He hadn't meant for anything to happen. It was just words."

"It wasn't Scott's fault," Alicia said. "Neither of you should blame yourselves."

Jamie shrugged. "The next few weeks were a mess. There was the funeral, of course, and that was where we met Don and Marcie. She was Leanne's sister. It turned out that Ed had been talking to Don and the two of them must have known more about us than we thought, because they were already planning to put us into some sort of show…"

"We moved in with Don and Marcie. They were living in a trailer park just outside Reno then. They took us out of school … Marcie said she'd home-school us from now on and after the business with the tyres the school wasn't going to complain. But she never taught us anything. Don persuaded us to perform for him. He hurt me because he knew that was the only way to get at Scott and in the end we agreed. We worked out a half dozen tricks – but that was all we did. You remember the policeman at Marcie's house?"

"Yes. Of course."

"What I did to him … that was the first time I ever did it. Scott made me swear that I would never try it with anyone. He was scared for me. Because if I started doing that, who knows what would happen? What if I got angry with you and said something and the next thing I knew you were injured or dead? Don't you see? I can kill you just by thinking! That's my wonderful power. I can hurt you just with the blink of an eye."

"But you won't," Alicia said. "I trust you, Jamie."

"I won't because I won't let myself. And now you know why I reacted the way I did. Why I didn't want to do what you asked and read that man's mind. You think being a telepath means being able to reach into someone's head like picking an ace out of a deck of cards. But it's not like that. Even with Scott it isn't, and he's my brother. These men … if I go into one of their heads, I'll see everything bad they've ever done. I'll be part of it. The people they've killed. The kids they've hurt. Everything! It'll be like diving into a sewer and I still might not find out what he's done with Scott."

"We'll just have to find another way," Alicia said.

"No." Jamie shook his head miserably. "There is no other way. What else can we do?"

"Find Colton Banes. Follow him wherever he goes."

"That could take weeks. We don't have the time." Jamie looked exhausted. He had never talked as much as this. "I'll go in there first thing tomorrow. I'll find Banes and I'll ask him what he's done with Scott." Jamie smiled grimly. "And even if he doesn't open his mouth, I think he'll tell me what I want to know."

BAD THOUGHTS

"I wish I hadn't talked you into this," Alicia said. "I'm going to be worried sick about you."

Jamie shrugged. "You don't need to worry. I can look after myself."

"I just don't like the thought of you going in there alone."

"It's broad daylight. We're in LA. Nothing bad is going to happen."

Jamie looked through the windscreen at the office building across the road. It seemed very ordinary in the morning light with the sunshine bouncing off the windows. There weren't so many people around now. The traffic had died down and the pavements were virtually empty. Jamie had quickly learned that in Los Angeles, nobody ever walked anywhere.

And yet there were at least a thousand people inside. Jamie tried to imagine what it must be like to work on the twentieth floor of a skyscraper with your own office and a personal assistant and a pay cheque at the end of each month. Ordinary life. There had been a time when this had been his dream, all that he wanted. To have a job. Holidays. Promotion. He had looked at the office buildings in Reno with a sort of envy. This sort of life would always be beyond his reach.

Once, he had said as much to Scott. But Scott had laughed at him.

"I don't want to work in one of those places, Jamie. You go in young, you come out old. And you don't notice what's happened in between."

"I thought you wanted to be Bill Gates."

"That's right. I don't want to work for anyone. Just like him."

Scott. Where was he now? Jamie quickly scanned the building, trying to feel for any sign of his brother's presence behind the monotonous rows of windows. There was nothing.

He opened the car door and felt the warm, heavy air rush into him. "Don't worry about me," he said. "I'll be fine."

"I'd much rather come in with you," Alicia said.

"Then we'd have twice as much chance of being stopped." He got out of the car, then turned round and leant back in. "Give me ten minutes. Then make the call."

"Make sure you're there, Jamie. The timing has to be exactly right."

He tapped his wrist. He was wearing a cheap watch. Scott had bought it for him on his thirteenth birthday. "I'll be there."

He took a large envelope off the dashboard. One last glance at Alicia and he closed the door behind him.

As he crossed the road, he was suddenly nervous. The

revolving doors ahead of him looked like a trap. When they turned round, they would swallow him. Was he so sure that they would let him out again? What exactly was he walking into? He knew almost nothing about the Nightrise Corporation but even its name gave him pause for thought. It employed a man called Colton Banes and Banes had been there when Scott was taken. They were looking for kids like him. And now he was just walking in, delivering himself to them.

It's the middle of the day. We're in LA. Nothing bad can happen.

But why not? Who really knew what went on in every street, or even in the building next door? It suddenly struck Jamie that even the brightest sunlight could hide many dark and ugly secrets.

He had reached the other side of the road. Briefly, he glanced back, just checking that Alicia was still there, that she hadn't driven off. He saw her raise a hand, reassuring him. He felt a spurt of annoyance. Why was he being so cowardly? He was the one who had thought up this plan. It was the only way to find Scott and if it had been the other way round, if he had been the one who had been kidnapped, Scott wouldn't even have hesitated.

He slapped his hand against the revolving door and pushed. The door turned. He was in.

The lobby was a black box that stretched the entire length of the building. The walls were black granite, the floor black

122

marble. The furniture – there was a low glass table and four chairs – was black too. One wall had a water feature. Streams of water trickled down endlessly, disappearing into a sort of trough. Otherwise there was no decoration. Two burly black men in black suits stood guard, watching anyone who came in. One of them walked over to him.

"Yeah?"

Jamie lifted the envelope. "I've got a package for Colton Banes. He's with Nightrise."

The guard looked at him quizzically. "You're a bit young to be working in despatch."

"I'm doing a week's work experience."

The guard nodded. If it had been anyone older he would have been more suspicious. But it was just a kid. And the envelope was clearly labelled. "It's the forty-fifth floor," he said – and swiped his own security card to activate the lift.

Jamie stepped in and waited for the doors to close. He felt his stomach shrink as the elevator moved silently up. He glanced at his watch. Only a couple of minutes had passed since he left the car and he was sure he still had plenty of time. However, the elevator stopped a couple of times before it reached his floor. People got in and got out. Another whole minute had ticked away before he finally arrived.

The forty-fifth floor. He stepped out.

It was all very ordinary, after all. What had he been expecting? A wide corridor ran left and right with the words NIGHTRISE CORPORATION in raised silver letters. There was a floor-to-ceiling window at one end, looking across to the building opposite, and a pair of modern glass doors at the other. He could see a reception desk and two women in smart suits, wearing headphones and throat mikes.

"Good morning. Nightrise Corporation. How may I help you?"

"Good morning. Nightrise Corporation. How may I direct your call?"

A second lift door opened and a FedEx delivery man stepped out, holding a parcel. Jamie waited while he went ahead, through the glass doors. The package would have to be signed for. That was good. It would distract their attention. That would give him his chance.

One of the women was talking on the phone. The other was dealing with the delivery. Now! Quickly, Jamie passed through the glass doors, walking as if it was his right, as if he had visited the building a dozen times before. He found himself in a smart, carpeted area with leather seats and a water cooler. There were pictures on the wall: modern art. A wide, glass door stood on each side, leading to corridors and more offices. Which way? He had to make an immediate decision. If he hesitated, he would be noticed. And then he would be stopped.

He turned right and went through the door, expecting at any moment to hear one of the receptionists call out after him. But they hadn't seen him. Now it would be easier. He was inside. Anyone seeing him would assume that he had been allowed through.

But where was he to begin? Jamie glanced at his watch again. Everything depended on exact timing and somehow another two minutes had gone by. That just left him five minutes to find Colton Banes. He looked around. The forty-fifth floor had been expensively decorated in different shades of blue, with more paintings between the doors. On the left-hand side of the corridor all the outer rooms, the ones with a view, had been given over to senior executives and their assistants. Their names and the office numbers were printed in small letters beside each entrance. On the other side, the central part of the office was open-plan. Jamie could see a maze of desks divided by partitions. There were perhaps twenty or thirty men and women, most of them young, bent over computer screens or talking on the phone. The carpets were thick and seemed to absorb any sound. Was that how business was done here? With the same hush as a laboratory … or perhaps a church.

He came to an open door and looked inside. There was a photocopying machine and a young man in jeans and an open-necked shirt, only five or six years older than Jamie, sorting through a stack of documents. Jamie was about to move on but the young man suddenly looked up.

"You OK?" he asked.

"Sure."

"You looking for someone?"

"Yeah…" Jamie lifted the envelope, showing the name on the front. "I've got to give this to a Colton Banes."

"Banes? Do you know his department?"

"No. It doesn't say."

"Well, let's take a look…" The young man went over to a table and picked up a plastic ring binder. He flicked through it. "Banes…" he muttered. He turned a page. "Here he is. You're on the wrong floor. He's up on forty-nine. Room four nine two five. Must be a big shot! That's the way it is here. The bigger you are, the higher you go."

"Thanks." Jamie backed out the door.

He thought he would have to go back to the lift, but as he came out of the photocopying room, he noticed a sign: FIRE EXIT. Of course, in the event of a fire, the lifts would shut down. There had to be stairs.

He continued down the corridor. A woman holding a bundle of files hurried past him but nobody stopped him. Nobody even looked in his direction. He came to the fire exit, pushed it open and found a flight of metal and concrete stairs on the other side. He climbed up, taking two steps at a time. He had Banes's office number but time was running out. Alicia would make her call in just a couple of minutes. And all of this was easy compared to what had to happen next. Jamie dreaded it even as he quickened his pace. He could feel his heart beating and knew it wasn't just the exertion of the climb.

The forty-ninth floor was exactly the same as the one he had left, with the senior offices and conference rooms on the outside and the common pool at the centre. There were more people moving between the different work stations but they were still talking in low voices as if afraid of being overheard.

126

But there was no art here. The walls were covered with posters: the same poster. It showed a serious-looking, grey-haired man. He had been caught half smiling, as if he wanted to be friendly but had too much on his mind. VOTE CHARLES BAKER. Jamie recognized the name of the senator running for president against John Trelawny. From the look of things, the entire floor had been turned into a campaign office on his behalf.

Jamie felt more exposed here. It could only be a matter of time before he was noticed. But at least he knew where he was going. 4907, 4908... He followed the office doors round. Another quick look at his watch. He had two minutes left.

Colton Banes had an office suite at the far corner and the door was half open. Jamie edged forward and looked through. There was an outer room with a desk for an assistant but it was empty. A second door, also open, led into another, larger space. And there he was, sitting in a high-backed leather chair behind an antique, highly polished desk. Jamie drew a breath. He had come here looking for Banes, but even so it was a shock to see him again: the cold, watery eyes, the bald head that could have been the result of some disease. This was a world away from the Reno Playhouse and Jamie found it almost impossible to make the connection. Had Nightrise sent this man to kidnap him and his brother? Had Banes really killed two people – Don and Marcie – when the plan had gone wrong?

He looked at his watch. Thirty seconds left.

"Who are you? What are you doing there?"

The voice had come from behind him. A man was moving down the corridor and Jamie could see at once that he wasn't anything like the younger man he had met in the photocopying room. He was plump and bearded, wearing a suit, and he had a radio transmitter in his hand. He must be part of security. And he was suspicious.

The telephone rang. Jamie heard it. Out of the corner of his eye, he saw Banes pick it up.

"Who are you?" the security man demanded.

"Hello?" Jamie heard Banes answer the telephone and knew he had to get into the office. There were just seconds left.

Sitting outside the office building, speaking on her cell phone from the car, Alicia asked, "Is this Colton Banes?" She had been passed through to his office by the switchboard.

"Yes." Banes was already puzzled. He didn't know the voice. Why was this woman calling him?

The security man was waiting for Jamie to answer. When Jamie said nothing, he took a step forward. "I think you'd better come with me," the man said.

"I'm with him." Jamie jerked a thumb in the direction of the office. He knew it sounded feeble but he couldn't think of anything to say. He stepped inside, closing the door behind him.

On her cell phone, Alicia knew the moment had come. "Where is Scott Tyler?" she asked.

Banes looked up and saw a scrawny boy in a brightly coloured shirt and baseball cap standing in his office and knew he had been tricked. The woman on the phone had asked him a question and although he had no intention of saying anything more, he couldn't stop himself thinking of the answer. That was why Jamie was here. This was what the two of them had arranged. He had arrived just as Alicia had opened a window in the man's mind.

Jamie jumped through it.

He did exactly what he had done a thousand times on the stage. He jumped – not physically, but as if he were throwing a miniature replica of himself out of his head. But this time it wasn't Scott at the other end. This time it wasn't his brother with his warm and familiar thoughts.

It was Colton Banes.

Jamie felt himself plunge into utter darkness. It was like diving into a pool of freezing oil. And at that moment, he shared everything that Banes had ever felt or thought. There were pictures – millions of them – but there were also experiences and emotions: fear, arrogance, lust, anger, cruelty, hatred and much, much more. Jamie had tried to explain it to Alicia but he could never have found the words. A man's brain is a world. That's what he should have said. And the world in which he now found himself was beyond any imagining.

He saw the death of Kyle Hovey. Worse than that, it was *his* hands that were around the other man's neck. He could feel the warm flesh and the pulsing vein under his own fingers as he squeezed. This had been the most recent killing and it was uppermost in Banes's mind. He saw a woman watching him. She had very short grey hair, a long neck, glasses. Banes was afraid of her. Jamie felt the fear. He saw the cruelty in her eyes and for a moment she was looking straight at him, smiling while he committed murder.

But then the image folded away and he was inside a trailer. There was a young girl lying on a bed with a dazed expression on her face and long hair straggling over the pillows. She moved her arm and Jamie saw that the flesh was bruised and mauve and that there were puncture marks, some of them covered with scabs. There were clothes everywhere, crumpled beer cans and ashtrays spilling out their contents, a dirty calendar on the wall. Colton Banes at home. It was there and then it was gone. Jamie had seen it only for a second. But it felt like an hour or even a day.

And then he saw other murders; a gun fired endlessly in front of him, a whole line of people, young and old, being shot down as if in an obscene fairground gallery. Some had died quietly. Some had cried for mercy. Jamie heard them and watched them fall. Mainly men. A few women. The bullets spat out, one after another, and blood splattered a dozen different walls.

And then he came to Don White.

"Whose murder?"

"You shouldn't have asked."

He heard the words and saw Don White jerk backwards as

the bullet hit him. Then it was Marcie's turn. She had been taken by surprise in the kitchen. She hadn't even heard the door open. She had just turned round and that was it.

So many deaths. A chamber of horrors.

He saw himself, chased out of the theatre. The dog – Jagger – forced to the ground. And the man who was running for president, Charles Baker. That was crazy. What was he doing in Banes's head? But it was definitely him, raising a hand and smiling, saying something to a journalist.

Another flicker, a hundred different places, flashing past like a falling deck of cards. He had arrived in a city, maybe somewhere in China. A strange boat with dark, wrinkled sails making its way across a stretch of water. Gone. Now he was back in Los Angeles, seeing himself as he entered the office. He felt the moment of recognition, his own name whispered in anger and surprise. Jamie fought against the torrent of words, images and emotions, searching for the one thing he needed.

"Where is Scott Tyler?"

Alicia had asked the question and the answer had to be there, ricocheting through Banes's mind. Jamie wasn't sure how much longer he could stay there. He was going to be sick. He felt as if he was drowning.

And then he saw him. His brother. Scott.

He was lying on his back in an enclosed room, stripped to the waist. He was ill. There was a tube running into his nose, the sort of thing you get in a hospital, and another in his wrist.

131

Some sort of transparent liquid was dripping down. Scott was covered in sweat. His hair was soaked through. There was a trickle of dried blood at the corner of his mouth. His eyes were open and filled with pain. Jamie wanted to know what Scott was thinking but that was impossible. He was seeing him as Banes had seen him. When? Not yesterday. The day before, maybe. Recently...

"Where is Scott Tyler?"

Banes didn't want anyone to know. He was fighting it. But still the images came, one after another. Jamie saw desert. A cactus shaped like the letter Y. He saw mountains with the moon suspended eerily between two peaks. There was a loud electronic buzz as a gate opened automatically, then an echoing crash as a second one closed. Faces. Other boys, some the same age as Scott, but all of them lifeless, vacant. A security camera swivelling round. Showers, the steam rolling out. More boys, their outlines just visible behind plastic curtains. Another gate smashed shut. And there it was at last, the sign that Banes didn't want him to see.

SILENT CREEK.

Jamie saw it and began to back out from inside the man's head. He couldn't stay here any longer, surrounded by so much poison and pain. He felt himself pulling away, as if flying up through a great tunnel. More images swept past, but so fast that he couldn't see them.

And then he was back where he had started, in the office, with Banes staring at him, open-mouthed, from behind the desk.

132

For a few moments, neither of them moved. Jamie couldn't have if he'd wanted to. He was exhausted. He felt drained. Then Banes smiled. "Jamie," he muttered.

Jamie could only watch as Banes reached into his desk and took out a gun. It was the dart gun that he had used on Scott. The man seemed to know that Jamie was helpless, that he had nowhere to go. His movements were careful and unhurried. He didn't even stand up. He took careful aim.

And then the outer door crashed open and the security man blundered in.

"Excuse me, sir..." he said, and stopped dead in his tracks. He had come through the outer office only to find a Nightrise executive pointing a gun at a child.

Jamie saw the look on his face and realized that, although he might work here, the security man had no idea what went on behind the closed doors of the different suites. What would he do now? Jamie decided not to find out. He reached behind him and grabbed hold of the man, pulling him forward between Banes and himself. It was at that exact moment that Banes pulled the trigger. The dart flew its short distance and buried itself in the man's arm. The security man shouted out in pain and alarm. Jamie let go of him and ran out. He heard a second dart slam into the door frame as he ran through. Then he was back out in the corridor, running as fast as he could.

He already knew that he couldn't take the lifts. Even if one happened to be waiting for him with the doors open, they would deactivate it before it reached the ground floor. But he was heading in the opposite direction. The fire escape. Forty-nine storeys led to the street but he only had to get below the forty-fifth and he would be out of Nightrise: he would be safe.

One of the managers tried to stop him. Jamie saw a man in a suit standing in the corridor, his arms apart as if he wanted an embrace. Jamie lashed out, punching the man full in the stomach, then leapt past him as he crumpled, gasping, onto the floor. The fire exit was ahead. Suddenly there were people everywhere but none of them were moving, hoping someone else would take the responsibility. In the corridor behind him, he heard Banes shouting orders. Jamie hit the fire exit and plunged through.

And at exactly that moment, every alarm in the building went off. The air exploded in a chaos of howling sirens and bells. Jamie wondered if the door was wired up and he had triggered the alarm himself. But that wasn't possible. He had already opened it once. It was Alicia. It had to be. She must have dialled 911 the moment after she made the call to Mr Banes.

Jamie hurtled down the emergency stairs. Below him, he heard doors bang open. Nightrise shared the building with at least a dozen other businesses and they were all being evacuated. The stairway ahead of him was already crowded. Jamie pushed and twisted his way through the crowds but, even so, it took an age to reach street level. As he broke into the sunlight, firefighters and police officers were making their way in, looking for any sign of smoke. There were two or three hundred people out on the pavement. Already, word was beginning to spread that the whole thing had been a hoax.

Jamie hurried across the road. Alicia was waiting for him in the car.

"Did you get it?" she asked.

"Let's go…" Jamie was breathless. His heart was pounding. And he felt dirty, with Banes's memories still clinging to him. He wanted to get them out of his system. He needed to go far away.

They drove off, looping round the block and then heading back towards West Hollywood and the house. Alicia looked briefly at Jamie but said nothing. Perhaps she understood that he needed to be left alone.

Then her cell phone rang.

She looked at it for a moment. Nobody knew that she was in Los Angeles apart from her sister – and she was probably somewhere in the air. So who…? A number showed in the screen and, with a sense of dread, she recognized it. She had no choice. She answered the phone.

"You called me a few minutes ago," Colton Banes said. "I believe I am speaking to Mrs Alicia McGuire."

Alicia pulled over and stopped.

His own telephone system would have stored her number, of course. How had he got her name? It wouldn't have been difficult. The Nightrise Corporation was a huge business. It would have its own resources.

"What do you want?" Alicia demanded.

Next to her, Jamie heard the voice and knew at once who she was speaking to. But he couldn't make out the words.

"You have a son," Banes replied.

Alicia stiffened. Pain flared in her eyes.

"We want Jamie Tyler. He's nothing to you. You know that. If you ever want to see your son again, give him to us. It's a very simple proposition, Mrs McGuire. You give us this boy, we'll give you yours. But this is a once-only offer. If you refuse me, you'll never see Daniel again."

Alicia wasn't breathing. Jamie knew that something terrible had happened. She was holding her phone as if she were trying to crush it. About ten seconds went past. At last she spoke.

"You go to hell, you bastard," she whispered.

She ended the call. Then she turned off the phone. Finally, she threw it onto the back seat as if it had bitten her.

"What did he want?" Jamie asked.

"He offered to swap Danny for you," Alicia said.

Jamie didn't know what to say. He knew what she must be thinking. He didn't have any need to read her mind.

But when she turned to him again, she was smiling even though her eyes were bleak. "He's told me what I wanted to know," she said. "Nightrise have got Danny. Before it was a suspicion. Now it's a fact. And that means I know what to do."

She slammed the car into gear and once again they drove

off. Jamie looked back. The sun was still shining. The office of the Nightrise Corporation looked no different from any of the others that surrounded it as they joined the freeway, leaving it far behind.

FRIENDS IN HIGH PLACES

The police had thrown a tight security ring all around the Carlton Hotel in Wilshire Boulevard, just south of Beverly Hills. It seemed to Jamie that Los Angeles had no real centre. It sprawled carelessly from district to district … but if the city had a wallet it would surely keep it here. Jamie had never seen so many expensive shops and boutiques standing shoulder to shoulder, the windows dripping with watches and jewellery and five-thousand-dollar suits.

The Carlton was an old-fashioned building, fifteen storeys high and stretching an entire block. As Alicia and Jamie drove into the front courtyard, a dozen valets in matching grey waistcoats hurried forward to help them out of the car and then to park it below. But even the valets were outnumbered by the secret service personnel, who had their own uniform: black suits, white shirts, sunglasses and earpieces. To Jamie they looked almost ridiculous, like something out of a cartoon. But perhaps that was the idea. They were advertising the fact that the hotel was protected.

Senator John Trelawny was staying here for twenty-four

hours before he gave his speech at the LA Convention Center and he had taken over the entire twelfth floor for the night. There were less than five months until the general election and his campaign team numbered almost a hundred people, including media advisors, political consultants, speech writers, pollsters, personal aides and more security men. All of them had rooms, and for one night all the lifts to the twelfth floor had been blocked. To visit the senator, guests would need to show ID and then receive a pass key – provided by the secret service. Callers were accompanied all the way. If they didn't have an invitation, they didn't get in.

"Will he see us?" Jamie asked as he and Alicia followed a winding corridor into the hotel.

Alicia nodded. "I just have to let him know we're here…"

They entered a cavernous lobby with a huge chandelier hanging over a round, polished table. Jamie found himself staring open-mouthed at the wealth on display. There was too much of everything. Too many electric candlelights, too many vases of flowers – at least ten of them – on the table, too many antique clocks and mirrors and display cases packed with handbags, scarves and shoes. And too many people. There was a concierge desk and a reception desk and porters and guests everywhere. Rush hour for the rich, Jamie thought. He had never been anywhere like this.

Alicia stopped and looked around, searching for someone she knew. A few moments later, she found him. "There!" she exclaimed, and moved forward.

A man was standing next to a table close to the lifts. He was dressed in the same dark suit and white shirt as the other security men, but he had a brightly coloured tie as if to announce that he wasn't actually one of them. Even so, there was a telltale wire curling behind his ear and he was obviously doing the same job: scanning the lobby with suspicious eyes. He was at least six and a half feet tall with blond, close-cropped hair, blue eyes that were constantly on the move and the body of a weightlifter. His shoulders were huge. Either he was ex-army or a retired basketball player … or both.

The man saw Alicia and recognized her before she was nearer than ten paces.

"Alicia!" He greeted her by name but he seemed more surprised than pleased to see her.

"How are you, Warren?"

"I'm good." He drawled the words. "I didn't know you were in LA."

"I didn't know I was coming until a couple of days ago."

Warren had noticed Jamie, who was standing a few steps behind her, trying to keep out of the way. The man frowned briefly, and Jamie was suddenly nervous that he might have been recognized.

"This is a friend of mine," Alicia said. "His name is David." There was a showcase against the wall, advertising Davidoff cigars. Jamie knew that she had plucked the false name from there and hoped that the security man hadn't noticed it too. She turned to him. "David, this is Warren Cornfield."

Warren nodded slowly at Jamie, then turned back to Alicia. "What can I do for you?" he asked.

"I want to see the senator."

"You want to see the senator?" A slow smile spread across Cornfield's lips. But he wasn't amused. "You know that's not possible, Alicia. Tomorrow he's talking to ten thousand people. Somehow, I don't think he's got time to see you right now."

But Alicia stood her ground. "When I left, he said his door would always be open to me."

"That's not what he told me."

"Why don't you ask him?"

"I'm not his assistant, Alicia. You know that. I think maybe you should ring back another time and get an appointment."

Jamie could see that Alicia was struggling to keep her temper. "I'm here right now, asking for an appointment, Warren," she growled. "And you're right. You're not his assistant. So why don't you call up to Elizabeth, who *is* – and she can ask John if he'll see me."

"You're wasting your time."

"We'll see, shall we?"

Alicia smiled pleasantly but Warren scowled. He didn't like being talked to in this way but it was clear that Alicia wouldn't be argued with. Warren held up a single finger and walked away, his head cocked, talking into a concealed microphone. To anyone else looking, he could have been arguing with himself.

"Warren is John's personal security officer," Alicia explained. "He's supposed to liaise with the secret service but half the time he thinks he actually runs it. We never did get along."

"I can see that."

"They say he was with the CIA a while ago but he got thrown out. Personally, I think..."

But Alicia didn't finish the sentence. Warren Cornfield was walking back towards her and his whole demeanour had changed. He was like a sulky child. "He says he'll see you," he muttered.

"Thank you, Warren."

"Why don't we make that Mr Cornfield? You're not part of the team any more..."

He snapped his fingers like an angry diner demanding a drink. One of the younger secret service men came running over. "Show these people up to twelve," he said.

"Yes, Mr Cornfield."

Alicia smiled at him and she and Jamie went over to the lift. The security man inserted a key into the lock and pressed the button for the twelfth floor. The doors closed. "You friends of the senator?" he asked.

"I used to work for him," Alicia said.

"He's a good guy," the security man went on. "I might even vote for him myself. Charles Baker is a jerk."

There was a silver-haired man in a suit but no tie waiting for them when the lift arrived. Warren must have radioed up from below. The man knew Alicia at once. "My dear, it's very good to see you. How have you been keeping?" He had an Irish accent.

"It's great to see you, Patrick. Still playing the horses?"

"Still losing."

"This is a friend of mine." She indicated Jamie but was careful not to say his name. "Patrick is John's campaign chairman for the state of California."

"Good to meet you." Patrick smiled and Jamie warmed to him at once. He was obviously puzzled by Jamie's appearance but had decided to ask no questions. "He can't see you for very long, Alicia," he said, as he led them down a corridor. "Right now the pressure's on."

"How is he?" Alicia asked.

"He's doing a grand job. I just wish the contest wasn't going to be so damned close…"

There was a set of double doors at the end of the corridor with yet another secret service man on guard. Patrick showed a pass and led Alicia and Jamie into a large conference room with a single table scattered with notepads and pens, computers, printouts, files, trays of sandwiches and bottles of mineral water. There were a dozen people sitting round and from the look of them none had slept very much in recent days. They were busy talking, arguing over a graph of some sort, but as Alicia came in, one of them stood up and with a shock Jamie recognized the man he had seen on posters all over Los Angeles.

John Trelawny didn't look like a politician. That was Jamie's first thought. He was a handsome man, taller than Jamie had expected from his picture and younger too, perhaps in his late forties. He had hair which had once been fair but had since faded, on its way to going grey. But he looked fit and healthy. He was wearing cords, a loose-fitting blue sweater and trainers. He was obviously tired but his light brown eyes were full of life.

"Alicia, this is a very unexpected surprise. How are you?" He embraced her. "Is there any news of Daniel?"

"Yes, there is, Senator. That's why I wanted to see you." She turned and introduced Jamie. "This is Jamie." This time, she used his name.

Trelawny reached out and they shook hands. "How do you do."

"Sir..." Jamie found it hard to believe that he could be shaking hands with the next president of the United States.

"I'm sorry to come here like this," Alicia went on. "I know how busy you are and how important this time is for you. But I urgently need to talk to you."

"You've found your boy?"

"I think I may have. Yes. But I can't reach him."

"Senator..." A woman sitting at the table held up a cell phone. "I have the mayor of Auburn on the phone for you. He wants to talk about the birthday parade."

Trelawny looked bemused. "Not right now, Beth," he said. "Can you tell him I'll call him back?" He turned to Alicia. "I'm

144

afraid I can't give you too much time," he explained. "There's a lot going on right now. But, you know, a break might be good for me. In fact, it might be good for all of us. OK, everyone!" He raised his voice. "Go out and get some fresh air or have a snack or do something that approximates to real life. We'll get back together in ten minutes." He turned to Alicia. "Why don't you and I go next door where we can talk undisturbed?"

Alicia glanced at Jamie. He nodded back. The senator and his former assistant walked off together. There was a sitting room next to the conference centre. Jamie watched the two of them go in. They shut the door behind them. None of the campaign workers left the table. They just went on working as they had before. The Irish man came over. "Can I get you a drink, young man?" he asked.

"Do you have a Coke?"

"Sure. Why don't you sit down on the couch and make yourself at home."

Jamie did as he was told, glad to be out of the way. There was a plasma TV turned on in the corner but it had the sound turned down and was tuned into a news station. Patrick returned with a Coke and Jamie drank it slowly, wondering how long Alicia would be. John Trelawny had said ten minutes but it seemed to him that much time had already passed.

At last the door opened and Trelawny appeared again. "Michael," he said, addressing one of the men in the room. "Can you get me the file on Nightrise?" He turned to Jamie.

"I'd like to have a word."

Jamie got up and went in. He was aware of the campaign workers glancing at him with curiosity. They were working on a major speech. Why was this teenager taking up so much of their boss's time? The man called Michael had snatched up a thick folder and handed it to Trelawny, who nodded his thanks. Jamie followed Trelawny into the second room, closing the door behind him.

Alicia was sitting on a sofa but Jamie was directed to an empty chair as if the senator wanted to keep them apart. Trelawny stood by the door, gathering his thoughts, then he put down the folder and moved into the room.

"Alicia has just told me the strangest story I've ever heard in my life," he began. "If I didn't know her well, I'd have already told her to leave. In fact, even now I have to ask myself if she isn't in some way disturbed. I don't mean that cruelly. After everything that's happened to her, the loss of her son, I'd understand. But she tells me that you have also lost someone … a brother. Scott. That he was taken from a theatre in Reno – is that right?"

Jamie nodded. He knew what was coming.

"According to Alicia, the people who took Scott may be the same people who took Daniel. And the reason they're interested in you, she says, is because you have an extraordinary ability. You can read people's thoughts. My thoughts, for example."

"I'm sorry, Jamie," Alicia muttered.

146

"That's OK." Jamie had guessed what he was going to have to do, but this time he wasn't worried. Everything about Senator Trelawny, even the way he spoke, made him feel comfortable. He wouldn't be the same as Colton Banes. He didn't live in the same world.

"I try to keep an open mind," Trelawny went on, "and I'd be the first to admit that there are plenty of things in this world that can't be explained. But this..." He shook his head doubtfully. "Anyway, this should be fairly simple. Alicia suggested to me that I put you to the test. Do you mind?"

"No, sir." Jamie was ready.

"Very well." Trelawny gestured at a low table in front of the sofa. There was a plain wooden box, about the size of a cigarette packet, placed in the middle. "My wife gave me that," he said. "I carry it with me wherever I go. Alicia doesn't know what's in it. I haven't told her. But she says you can tell me."

Jamie concentrated for a moment. Then he looked Trelawny straight in the eyes. "There's nothing inside the box," he said. "It's empty."

Trelawny didn't give anything away. But Alicia could feel a sudden tension in the room.

"Your wife made it," Jamie went on. "She likes working with wood. Her name is Grace. You keep things in it when you go to bed. Cuff links and stuff like that. Right now it's difficult to tell you more because all you're thinking about is the election. It's weird..."

"Go on."

"Well, I was going to say, you're really scared of losing. But what's strange is, you're even more scared of winning."

There was a silence. Trelawny stood where he was, so still that he was barely breathing. At last he let out a long breath. "You have an extraordinary talent," he said. "I won't call it a gift – because perhaps it isn't. I can't imagine what it must be like for you – to have this ability."

"I don't use it," Jamie said. "I don't want it."

"Nobody but me has ever looked inside this box," Trelawny said. "It travels with me when I'm on the road. I've never told anyone who made it." He went over to the table and picked it up, opened it and showed it to Alicia. There was nothing inside.

"Alicia has suggested that I should launch a full-scale investigation into the Nightrise Corporation," he said. "But as it happens, I've already started." He went over to the folder and opened it. "This is just the tip of the iceberg. Let me tell you a little bit about them. And then I'll tell you why, right now, there's nothing I can do."

He sat down.

"I don't believe all big business is bad," he began. "But Nightrise are very big and they seem to take pride in being as bad as they can get away with. The trouble with this country is that we're all too ready to turn a blind eye to crimes committed in the name of business. A factory burns down and twenty workers are killed. A tank leaks and a whole river system gets polluted. A weapons system is sold abroad and ends up being used against American soldiers. Nobody notices – and you know why? Because profit is all that matters. Profit is king. These companies are making huge profits and employing tens of thousands of people. So we let them get away with murder.

"I first heard about Nightrise about six months ago." He produced a clipping, cut out of a newspaper. "This was sent to me by a friend. He thought I might be interested in the story of a twelve-year-old child working in a toy factory in Indonesia who got burned by one of the machines and died. The kid had been working ten hours a day for twenty cents an hour and he was exhausted. I call that murder. He was making parts for a shooting game and the company that employed him just happened to be fully owned by Nightrise. But did they pay any compensation? Did they care? Of course not. And you could buy that toy in any mall in America…"

"You said there's nothing you can do," Jamie cut in.

"Here's why." Trelawny frowned. "The current vice president and the chief of staff both used to work for Nightrise before they went into politics. When they leave the White House, whoever wins the next election, they'll go back on the board. Nightrise has about three hundred companies all around the world and many of them do work for the US government. There's one that manufactures bombs. The bombs are dropped. Then another one that's hired to rebuild the cities that the bombs destroyed. You see what I mean? Business and politics go hand in hand.

"And just to make matters worse, Nightrise is supporting Charles Baker in the presidential election. In fact, they're one of his main sponsors. They've channelled millions of dollars in his direction. They have to be clever how they do it: there are laws about donating money to political causes. But there are dozens of independent organizations and little groups fighting against me and, although they don't seem to be connected, we're pretty sure that Nightrise is bankrolling the whole lot of them. But I've got no proof, Jamie. They've been too careful. And if I start making accusations, it'll just make me look like a sore loser – at least, I'll look as if I'm afraid of losing, and that won't help anyone."

"So what can you do?"

"I have to wait and hope I win. If I become president of this country – and I believe that there's a very good chance of that happening – I want to make it my first priority to fight corruption in business and I mean to make a start with Nightrise."

"We can't wait," Jamie said. "They're hurting Scott."

"How do you know?"

"I just know."

"Hold on," Alicia said. She reached into her handbag and took out a sheet of paper. "Thanks to Jamie, we managed to find out that Scott may be being held in a place called Silent Creek. I checked it out on the Internet. Silent Creek is a prison, a Youth Correctional Facility, out in the Mojave Desert. It's the only privately run prison in Nevada. And it's owned by Nightrise."

"Scott's there," Jamie said.

"We think Scott is there. And, we think, Daniel could be there too." Alicia sighed. "It makes sense. If you wanted to hold a bunch of kids somewhere nobody could find them, somewhere out of the way, a prison in the desert would be perfect. Can you go in there, Senator? Could you get the police to raid it?"

"I could try." Trelawny thought for a moment, then shook his head. "But it wouldn't be easy. First of all, I've got no real proof that there's anything wrong going on there. I haven't even heard of Silent Creek – and if it's in Nevada it isn't even in my jurisdiction. And finally, if I did make enough noise to get an investigation started, the prison supervisor would hear about it before we got anywhere near. If those two boys were there, there'd be all the time in the world to move them some place else. Or worse…"

Alicia nodded. She had been expecting this. "You may be right," she said. "But we have another thought."

"I could go in there," Jamie said.

"Go in there … how?"

"You must know people," Alicia said. "Suppose Jamie were to become one of the inmates. With a false name. A judge could send him there with another bunch of juveniles. Once he was inside Silent Creek, he could find out if Scott and Daniel were there and get a message to me. Maybe he could even help get them out."

"How would he do that?"

"There are things I can do," Jamie explained. "Things you don't know about."

"I know you want to take these people on in your own time, Senator," Alicia said. "But we don't have any time. We have to do something now."

There was a knock at the door and, without waiting for an answer, Warren Cornfield burst in. Trelawny's security man was looking furious. He stood framed in the doorway, which was almost his own size.

"Excuse me, sir," he said. "I'm sorry to butt in..."

"What is it, Warren?" Trelawny asked. He didn't seem concerned.

"Sir, that woman has lied to me." His finger jabbed in Alicia's direction. "That boy she's brought to see you, I think you should know that his name is not David. I thought I recognized him and now I know who he is. His name is Jamie Tyler and he is a wanted felon."

"Alicia has already told me who he is," Trelawny replied.

"She has?" Cornfield was taken aback. "Sir, the Nevada police are actively looking for this child. He's wanted for first degree murder. If you let him leave here, if anyone finds out that he's even been in the same room as you, he could destroy your entire campaign."

"Come in, Warren. Shut the door behind you."

The security man did as he was told. Trelawny waited until he had calmed down.

"Have you called the police?" Trelawny asked.

"No, sir. Not yet."

"That's good. Let's leave it that way." Trelawny turned to Alicia. "You'd better go," he said. "But I have your cell number and I'll get in touch. It should be possible to arrange what you've asked. I have friends..." He went over to Jamie and laid a hand on his shoulder. "I won't forget meeting you," he said. "And what you said, about winning the election – you're absolutely right." He smiled. "I hope you find your brother."

"Sir..." Warren Cornfield couldn't believe what he was seeing. "These two people should be in jail."

"It's OK, Warren. I think I know what I'm doing. I want you to show my guests out. Don't arrest them. Don't call the police. Make sure nobody gets in their way."

"Whatever you say, sir."

Cornfield was still scowling as he showed them to the door. At the last moment, Jamie turned round and took one last look at the man who might become president. He had picked up the little box and was holding it with a sort of wonderment, as if he too could somehow look through the wooden surface and uncover the secrets locked inside. Then the door closed. He didn't think he would see him again.

Pain.

Scott Tyler didn't know how long he had been here. Nor

153

did he know where "here" was or how he had got there.

He was lying on a bed. To begin with, there had been chains around his wrists and handcuffs, but now they had no further need of them. He was too weak to move. If he had been able to examine himself, he would have seen he was still in the same clothes that he had been wearing at the theatre, although the shirt had been ripped open and the trousers were crumpled and torn. Not that he remembered the theatre any more or anything that had happened on the night he was seized. A very large part of his memory had been taken away from him. The drugs dripping into his right arm had done that. The doses had been carefully monitored, the injections exactly timed. They didn't want to kill him or to drive him mad. Their aim was more complicated than that. They wanted to tear him away from the life he had been living and leave him floating helplessly until he was ready to be made theirs.

He hadn't eaten for days and they had barely brought him enough water to keep him alive. Nor had he slept. Every time his eyes closed, they would bombard the room with a barrage of sound, drum beats, music, machinegun fire. The lights were kept on all the time. Right now it could have been the middle of the day or the night. It made no difference. Scott was barely conscious. And he was ready for the next stage.

The door opened. Scott didn't even try to look up to see who had come in. He was afraid to do anything without being told. There was a rustle of fabric as someone sat down. He smelled a scent, some sort of flower. Trembling, he turned his head and saw that a woman had come in and sat down in the chair next to him. She was looking at him as if unsure what to make of him. Or maybe she was deciding what to do next.

She lifted a hand. Scott saw that she wore several rings. For a moment, two of her fingers rested on his arm. "What have they done to you?" She spoke for the first time. Her voice was soft and almost musical. "You poor boy," she went on. "I'd have come sooner if only I'd known but, you see, it's so difficult for me. I want to be your friend. But I have to know that you trust me. You have to be on my side."

Her fingers moved to his forehead, moving a lock of hair out of his eyes.

"Jamie left you," she went on. "Do you remember – at the theatre? That's when they came for you and your brother just abandoned you. All your life you looked after him but he didn't care. The first chance he got, he was away, leaving you to all this. Right now, he's laughing at you. Because he's all right. He's having a fine old time. And you're stretched out on your back, connected up to all these nasty tubes, and you could die here and nobody would think twice.

"But that's the mistake you've made since you were little, Scott. Do you remember Ed and Leanne in Carson City? You thought they'd look after you but they let you down. And then there were Don and Marcie and they were even worse. But that's the thing about life, isn't it? It's always the good people who get pushed around. The little people. Do you want to be a little person, Scott, or do you want to be with me? Because, you see, in the world that's coming, I'm going to be in charge, and you're going to have to start asking yourself, which end of the whip do you want to be?

"I'll leave you to think about it, my dear. There are some people I work for … well, not exactly people. They'll be with us very soon and they'll be so glad to know that you've joined us, that you've decided to become their servant. Jamie, unfortunately, is not sensible enough to make that choice. But maybe one day you'll be able to get your own back on him. Maybe one day we'll let you take that little swine and put a knife through his heart.

"But right now, I must go. You think about what I've said and maybe tomorrow we'll have another little chat."

The door opened a second time. Somebody else had come into the room. The woman stood up.

"Mr Banes has come to see you now," she explained. "I wish I could stay with you and keep him away. But until you're ready for me, until you're mine, I can't. I'm so sorry, my dear. But I will come back. I promise."

The bald man sat down in her place. Scott squeezed his eyes shut and groaned, deep inside himself.

He heard the door close softly and the two of them were left alone.

SILENT CREEK

Jamie had been in court once before so there were no surprises here: not the smallness of the room, the few people in it, the speed at which everything took place. There were two tables facing the judge, and a middle-aged woman dressed in black sat between the flag of Nevada and the Stars and Stripes. Jamie was at one table with his lawyer. His probation officer and a woman from the district attorney's office were at the other. A clerk took notes and a security man stood by with a seen-it-all-before look on his face. There were two rows of chairs at the back of the room. No press or public were allowed into a juvenile court but Alicia was sitting there on her own, an anxious look on her face. She had come as a family friend.

Jamie's hands and feet were shackled. That had alarmed him because it hadn't happened the last time he had been taken into custody. But this time the offence was more serious. He had been arrested, supposedly, for selling drugs at school – a crime which would guarantee him jail time. It was all fake, of course. The probation officer and the lawyer were both part of the set-up, somehow connected to John Trelawny, who had arranged the whole thing. They had even given Jamie a false name – Jeremy Rabb: case number J83157. Somehow they had slotted him into the Nevada juvenile justice system and, as far as Jamie knew, the judge was the only person in the room who didn't know what was really going on.

It was all fake – and yet the plastic strips binding his wrists and the chains around his ankles were horribly real. Free movement, the most basic of all human rights, had been taken from him. He felt the horror of having his identity stripped away, of belonging to a system that would now do with him as it pleased. Worse still, he remembered what the senator, John Trelawny, had told Alicia on the telephone.

"I can get him in, Alicia, but there's something you have to appreciate: I can't get him out again, not once he's been sent to Silent Creek. Too many people would know. What we're doing here is necessary and I can justify it in my own mind, but it's borderline illegal. Do you understand what I'm saying? Once Jamie's inside the system, I cannot intervene."

Alicia had explained it to Jamie, who understood. The senator was already sticking his neck out for him and couldn't risk a scandal if it all went wrong. At the same time, Jamie wasn't too concerned. He had his power and he could use it to walk out of prison at any time. He thought about Scott. Finding his brother was all that mattered to him and there was no other way. It was only now, unable to separate his hands, unable to walk without shuffling, that he had second thoughts. He was about to be sentenced, processed, swallowed up. When that happened, he would be completely on his own.

His hair had been cut short and he had been given a pair of thick black plastic glasses to wear. He was surprised how much his appearance had changed. The danger was that anyone who had met Scott would recognize him as an almost identical twin, but there seemed little chance of that now. Looking in the mirror, he could barely recognize himself.

"...the sentence set down by this court is twelve months in a detention facility..." The judge was talking. Jamie had missed the first part of what she was saying. She turned to the probation officer. "I've looked through the case files and I think Summit View would be appropriate."

Jamie had heard of Summit View. It was a Youth Correctional Centre on the edge of Las Vegas. But the probation officer was shaking his head. "With respect, your honour, I was going to recommend Silent Creek."

The judge was surprised. "It's pretty tough out there," she remarked. "The boy is only fourteen and this is a first offence."

"Yes, your honour. But he was selling crystal meth to kids as young as twelve. Some of them are now in rehab programmes, out of school. Rabb has shown no remorse. In fact, he's been pretty pleased with himself."

Rabb. Jamie had to remind himself that they were talking about him.

The judge thought for a moment, then nodded. "Very well. It'll be a hard lesson, but maybe that's what he needs." There was a file in front of her. She closed it. "Twelve months in Silent Creek."

The security guard stepped forward and Jamie was led out through a side door, his feet moving only inches at a time. The last thing he saw was Alicia watching him. Her eyes were wide and full of dread.

They took him by minibus, still shackled, with a bottle of water wedged between his knees. He was going to need it. The temperature would rise quickly as soon as the sun rose and they planned to drive all night. There was nobody else on the bus: just the driver – an old, weather-beaten man – and a guard who had briefly checked Jamie's wrist and ankle restraints and then ignored him.

It had been eight o'clock in the evening when they left. Jamie had watched the darkness fall before he had nodded off, sitting uncomfortably upright, asleep but still aware of the shuddering movement of the bus. When he opened his eyes, the light dazzled him. They had left the highway and were following a track, kicking up a cloud of dust all around them. Jamie could see only sand and scrubland with a few Jericho trees dotted around the landscape. A mountain range, burned red by the sun, stretched out across the horizon.

Then the road dipped. They had come to a miniature valley. And now he saw his new home, Silent Creek. The two words were written on a sign – unnecessarily. The inmates surely knew where they were and there was nobody else to read it for miles around. Despite everything, Jamie felt a shiver of excitement. He had seen the sign before – inside the head of Colton Banes. Scott was here, somewhere inside this complex. Jamie felt sure of it. He would find his brother and the two of them would bust out. The nightmare was almost over.

A long rectangular compound stood in front of him. The buildings were low-rise but they were surrounded by a razor-wire fence at least ten metres high. There were two satellite dishes pointing up towards the sky and on the other side Jamie saw a playing field with two goals – but of course there was no grass, not in this heat. The surface was yellow-grey sand. At the far end of the pitch, there was a wall – like all the other buildings, made out of cinder blocks and topped with more razor wire. As they bounced down towards the main gate, Jamie caught a glimpse of more buildings on the other side of the wall but realized he would be unable to see them again without the advantage of height. For some reason, Silent Creek had been divided into two: one third on one side, two thirds on the other.

The minibus passed between a number of outlying houses. These must be where the guards and maintenance staff lived. Jamie was annoyed with himself. He had only woken up at the last minute and he had no idea how near they were to any town or community. Scott would have been better prepared. But it was too late to worry about that now. They had stopped in front of the gate. This was the entrance to the prison, known as the sallyport. There was a buzz and the gate slid open electronically, allowing them into a narrow corridor between two lines of razor wire. The minibus jolted forward and stopped in front of a second gate. This only opened when the first one had closed. Now, at last, they were inside the prison. Jamie looked around him, searching for security cameras. There were no guard towers. Nor was there anybody in sight.

The minibus stopped one last time. The door hissed open.

"All right! Out!" They were the only words the guard had spoken since they had left.

Jamie shuffled out of his seat, along the aisle and out of the door. At once the heat hit him. It was like being physically battered. He was forced to squeeze his eyes shut, then opened them more carefully, fighting against the glare. He was already sweating. The temperature had to be in the nineties. Even the air was scorched. He looked around. The sun had sucked the colour out of almost everything. The silver of the fence, the grey sand, the ash-coloured cinder blocks – they all seemed to seep into each other like an over-exposed photograph. An electric generator and a fuel tank stood next to each other, locked in a cage. They were bright yellow. There was nothing else to catch the eye.

"This way!"

The guard led him to a door set in a wall, which opened as they approached. Jamie noticed a camera, mounted high above. It swivelled to follow him when he moved. The door led into a large, shabby room with a second officer sitting behind a desk with a computer. There were a couple of holding cells, some chairs – none of them matching – and a shower with a plastic curtain drawn half across. There were no windows. The room was lit by strip lighting. Mercifully, after the furnace of the courtyard, it was air-conditioned.

"Sit down!" It was the second guard who had spoken. He was casually dressed in jeans and a short-sleeved shirt. Jamie saw that he carried no weapon. He was a man in his forties, with black hair tied behind his neck. He obviously had Native American blood and Jamie wondered if that might make him more sympathetic. But his manner was brisk and formal.

"My name is Joe Feather," the man said. "But you call me Mr Feather or sir. I'm the Intake Officer and I'm going to process you and then show you into Orientation. Do you understand?"

Jamie nodded.

"You're going to find it tough here. You've had a spell in juvie – is that right?"

"Yeah."

"Well then you know the basics. Keep your head down. Do as you're told. It'll make it easier on you." He nodded at the other guard. "You can take off the shackles."

Jamie's hands and feet were unfastened and gratefully he moved his legs apart. There were red marks across his wrists and he rubbed them. In the next twenty minutes, his details were entered into the computer ... or at least, the details of Jeremy Rabb, the boy he was supposed to be. He had been up half the previous night with Alicia, memorizing them before he had been handed over to the police.

"Go into the shower and strip," the Intake Officer told him. "I want all your clothes, including your shorts. You have any piercings?"

Jamie shook his head.

"OK. I'll pass you your new kit..."

Jamie went into the shower and drew the curtain. But it seemed he wasn't going to be given any privacy. The side wall of the shower contained a window looking into a storeroom and, as Jamie stood under the running water, he was aware of Joe Feather examining him from the other side. Jamie had been through strip searches when he was in juvenile hall, but even so he was embarrassed and turned away. That was when the officer saw the tattoo on his shoulder.

"Mr Rabb..." Joe Feather spoke the words softly. "Turn off the shower."

Jamie did as he was told. He stood with drops of water trickling down his shoulders and back.

"Where did you get that tattoo?" the Intake Officer demanded.

"I've always had it. It was done when I was born."

"You have a brother?"

Jamie froze. Had he been recognized already? "I don't have a brother," he said.

"No brother?"

"No, sir."

Joe Feather handed him a bundle of prison-issue clothes. It fitted through a slot beneath the window. "Put these on," he said. "I'll take you in."

Jamie was the ninety-sixth boy to arrive at Silent Creek. The prison could hold one hundred in total with ten full-time guards – or supervisors, as they called themselves – to watch over them. There were four living units – North, South, East and West – and life was arranged so that the inmates were kept apart as much as possible. That way, rival gang members barely saw each other and never spoke. Each unit ate at a different time – there were four sittings for every meal – and there were four exercise times in the prison gym. The age range went from thirteen to eighteen.

There were rules for everything. The boys had to walk with their hands clasped behind their backs. They weren't allowed to talk while they moved and they couldn't go anywhere, not even the toilet, without adult supervision. They were watched constantly, either by supervisors or security cameras. They were patted down after every meal and if a single plastic fork went missing, they were all strip-searched. There were six hours of school every morning, two hours of recreation (in the gym – it was too hot outside) and two hours of TV. Only sport was allowed – never movies or news. The prison uniform consisted of blue tracksuit trousers, grey T-shirts and trainers. All the colours had been chosen carefully. Nothing was black or bright red. Those were gang colours and might be enough to provoke a fight.

Life at the prison was not brutal, but it was boring. There were library books for the boys who could read, but otherwise every day was the same, the hours measured out with deadly precision, stretching out endlessly in the desert sun. There was solitary confinement or loss of privileges for anyone who stepped out of line and even an untied shoelace could bring instant punishment if the supervisors were in a bad mood.

And there was the medicine wing. Boys who were violent or unco-operative went to see the doctor in a small compound set right against the cinder-block wall. They were given pills and when they came back they were quiet and empty-eyed. One way or another, the prison would control you. The boys accepted that. They didn't even hate Silent Creek. They simply suffered it as if it were a long illness that had happened to them and that wasn't their fault.

It didn't take Jamie long to find out what he needed to know. None of the other boys had met Scott. There was no record of his ever having been here. But he knew that what he had so far seen of Silent Creek was only half the story. There were two parts to the prison: he had seen that much for himself when he arrived on the bus. There was a whole area of the prison, on the other side of the wall, which stood quite alone. Nobody communicated with it. It had its own gymnasium, its own classrooms, kitchens and cells, as if it were a slightly smaller reflection of the main compound. And there were rumours.

On the other side of the wall. That, it was said, was where the specials were kept.

"They're the real hard acts. The killers. The psychos."

"They're sick. That's what I heard. They've got something wrong with their heads."

"Yeah. They're vegetables. Cretins. They just sit in their cells and stare at the walls…"

Jamie was having lunch with four other boys. The chair he was sitting on was made of metal, welded into the table, which was in turn bolted to the floor. The canteen was a small, square room with bare white walls. No decoration was allowed anywhere in Silent Creek, not even in the cells. The food wasn't too bad though – even if it was served up in a compartmentalized plastic tray. Jamie had been surprised by most of the boys he had met. Nobody had given him a hard time – in fact they'd been glad to see a new face. Perhaps his experience at juvenile hall had helped. From the start he was one of them. So far, he hadn't needed to use his false name. The other boys at the table called him Indian. He knew them as Green Eyes, Baltimore, DV and Tunes.

"The story I heard is that nobody wants them," DV said. He was seventeen, Latino, arrested following a drive-by shooting in Las Vegas. The boys weren't meant to ask one another about their crimes but of course they did. DV was a member of the Playboy Gansta Crips. He had tattoos on both arms and planned to go back to the gang as soon as he got out. He had never known his father and his mother ignored him. The gang was the only family he had. "They got no parents," he went on, "so now they're using them for experiments. Testing stuff on them. That sort of thing."

"How many of them are there?" Jamie asked.

"I heard twenty," Green Eyes said. Jamie wasn't sure how he'd got his nickname. He was fifteen years old, arrested for possession of a deadly weapon – meaning a gun. His eyes were blue.

"There are fifty at least," Tunes growled. He was the youngest boy in the prison, barely fourteen. He turned to Jamie and lowered his voice. "You don't want to ask too many questions about them, Indian. Not unless you want to join them."

Jamie wondered where all these rumours began. But that was the thing about prisons. There were never any secrets. Somehow the whispers would travel from cell to cell and you had as much chance of keeping them out as you had of stopping the desert breeze.

As usual, they were being supervised while they ate. This was one of the few times when they were allowed to speak freely, but they still couldn't even stand up without asking permission first. This was what had most struck Jamie about life at Silent Creek. They were no longer people. They were objects. At no point in the day could they do anything for themselves.

The man watching them was the most senior – and the toughest – supervisor. He was a bulky, round-shouldered man with thinning hair and a moustache. His name was Max Koring. If anyone was looking for trouble, it would be him. He seemed to enjoy humiliating the inmates, carrying out strip searches for no reason at all, taking away a month's privileges simply because it amused him.

Baltimore leant across the table. He had been named after the city where he'd been born. He was a tall, handsome black boy who never spoke about the crime that had brought him here. "You want to know about the other side, you need to talk to Koring," he whispered. "He works both sides of the wall."

"How do you know?" Jamie asked.

"I've seen him come in through the medicine wing."

The medicine wing stood right up against the wall. Everyone knew that it served both sides of the prison. At least, that was what they said.

"He's one of the only ones who's allowed," Baltimore went on. "They've got guards working the whole time on the other side. Armed guards. They don't have nothing to do with us."

"You want to visit the other side, just ask Max," DV said. He smiled briefly. "The only trouble is, he'll have your brain wired up to a computer and the next time anyone sees you, you'll be a vegetable like all the others."

The meal came to an end. The boys handed in their trays and plastic forks, then turned out their pockets and stood with their legs apart for the pat-down before they were returned to their cells for an hour's rest. As they left the room, walking slowly through the blinding sunlight, Jamie noticed Joe Feather standing on the edge of the football field, examining him. It seemed to him that the Intake Officer had been watching him from the moment he had arrived. Did he suspect something? If so, Jamie would have to move quickly. He might be running out of time.

He remembered what Feather had said when he was processed, almost a week before. He had seen the tattoo on Jamie's shoulder and he had asked, "You have a brother?" There was only one way he could have known that. He had seen Scott. And that meant that Scott had to be here, at Silent Creek.

Jamie was sure of it. After all, it made sense. Silent Creek was the only privately run prison in Nevada and it was part of the Nightrise Corporation. According to Alicia, Nightrise had been responsible for the disappearance of not one but many boys with paranormal abilities. What better place to keep them than within a maximum security prison, miles from anywhere, surrounded by the Mojave Desert? He had seen the name in Colton Banes's thoughts. And what else could there be, concealed on the other side of the wall?

Jamie took off his trainers (it was rule number 118 or 119: no shoes inside the cell) and left them neatly in the corridor. The other boys had done the same. He went into the cell and a few seconds later there was a buzz and the doors slid shut

170

electronically. His room, painted white, measured ten steps by five. There was a bunk that was actually part of the floor, moulded out of it. The cement simply rose up to form a narrow shelf with a thin, plastic mattress on the top. Opposite the bed he had a metal shelf which acted as a desk, with a chair bolted into the floor. A stainless-steel unit stood beside the door – a toilet and a basin combined. There was a mirror made of polished steel. And that was it. The room had a single window: a long strip no more than a few centimetres wide. There were no bars. Even if he had been able to smash through the industrial-strength glass, he could never have slipped out.

The other boys had told him that the door was electronically sealed and whenever he was alone, locked into the cell, Jamie had to fight back a growing sense of panic. Alicia knew he was here. At the end of his second week, he would be allowed to telephone her. But she was his only link with the outside world. What if something happened to her? Then he would be stuck here as Jeremy Rabb – or Indian. How long would it be before he went crazy and either had to be locked up in isolation or drugged?

But that wasn't going to happen. Jamie still had his power and tonight he was going to use it. There would be a guard on duty in his unit and that guard would take him to the other side of the prison. He would find Scott and together the two of them would walk out.

Except…

It was only now, when it was much too late, that the first

171

whispers of doubt came. Scott had the same powers as him – so why hadn't he used them to break out himself? Was there something Jamie didn't know? Why was he so certain that Scott was even there? A sickening thought occurred to him. Scott could be dead. He could have escaped and got lost in the desert. Anything could have happened.

Sitting alone on his bunk, Jamie opened his mind as he had done every night since he had arrived. He was sending his thoughts along the corridors, into the different blocks, trying to feel for any sense of his brother being near by. He concentrated on the other side of the wall. But there was nothing. Why was that? Jamie refused to accept that Scott wasn't here. He had to be somewhere. Inside the secret compound. And if he wasn't responding there must be a reason. Maybe it was simply that he was asleep.

Somehow the next hour crawled past. Then there were more lessons, an hour in the gym, dinner. The day finished with a wrap-up session in the unit's living area – an open space with four circular tables where they were allowed to play cards or board games. The boys were supposed to talk about the day and how it had gone, but of course there was never very much to say. A guard sat watching them from behind a bank of television screens which showed different views of the corridors. There were no cameras in the cells. Tonight, Max Koring was on duty, which meant that the lights would snap out at exactly ten o'clock – or perhaps fifteen minutes earlier if he felt like it.

They were sent back to their cells at nine o'clock. They were given nothing to wear in bed – it was too hot anyway – so the boys just slept in their shorts. Each of them was given a toothbrush to use but it was collected and locked away again before the doors were shut. The handle of a toothbrush, sharpened, could make a lethal weapon, and the supervisors weren't taking any chances. Jamie had no watch. It had been taken away from him along with anything else that might give him any sense of identity or independence. Eventually the lights in the cell blinked out. Although it still wasn't truly dark, there were arc lamps all around the prison perimeter and they would stay on all night, the white glare seeping in through the window. Jamie lay on his bunk for about half an hour. Then he got up and dressed. It was time.

He pressed the call button next to his cell door.

A few minutes later, there was the rattle of a key and the door slid open. Max Koring stood there, his stomach rising and falling, his face half hidden in shadow. He had opened the door manually, overriding the electronic control. And he wasn't pleased to be here. None of the supervisors enjoyed the graveyard shift, but being bothered by the kids just made it worse.

"Yes?" he demanded.

"I want you to take me to the units on the other side of the wall," Jamie said.

The supervisor stared at him. He looked puzzled.

"You will do it now," Jamie continued – and pushed, projecting his thoughts into the man's head. He knew what he was doing. He had done exactly the same thing when he had come face to face with the policeman at Marcie's house in Sparks.

Max Koring didn't move.

"We're leaving now," Jamie said. And pushed again.

"You think you're being funny?" Koring muttered. "What the hell d'you think you're doing?"

Jamie felt a shiver of bewilderment – followed by panic. It wasn't working! But it had to. "Take me to my brother!" he demanded. He was still pushing, burning a hole in the man's brain.

Now Koring was examining him as if seeing him in a completely new light. He smiled – but there was nothing warm or pleasant in it. "You have a brother?" he asked.

Desperately, Jamie changed tack. He couldn't make the man obey him – but he could still use the moment to get information from him. He no longer cared about the consequences. He had to know about Scott and so he concentrated and jumped into Koring's mind, just as he had with Colton Banes.

Nothing happened. His power wasn't working. Jamie just had time to absorb the shock before Koring grabbed hold of him and backhanded him – hard – across the face. The room spun. Jamie tasted blood. Then he was thrown backwards, crashing into the bunk.

"I don't like my time being wasted," Koring said. "And you don't give *me* orders. You may be new here, but you should know that. So maybe it's time you had your first taste of CRR."

CRR. Corrective Room Restriction. Another way of saying solitary confinement.

Ten minutes later, Koring returned with another supervisor. Neither of them said a word. They simply jerked Jamie out of his cell and dragged him down the corridor. The other boys must have heard what had happened. Suddenly they were all awake and shouting encouragement.

"Good luck, Indian!"

"Don't let them grind you down!"

"See you soon, Indian. You take care!"

The isolation cells were in a separate area, a pair of heavy steel doors separating them from the main unit. Jamie didn't even try to resist. He was flung into a cell half the size of the one he had left. This room had no mattress, and although there was a narrow window, the glass was frosted so there was no view.

"Let's see how you feel after a week in here," Koring said. "And in future, you call me *sir*."

The door slammed shut.

Jamie stayed where he was, curled in a ball on the floor. He had hit his head against the bunk when he fell and his nose was bleeding. He was utterly alone. And his power had let him down. Had it gone, or was there something about the prison that he didn't know? Maybe it had been built in this part of the desert purposefully. There could be something in the water or even in the soil that was playing with his mind. It made sense. If they were locking up kids with powers, they would have to be certain that those powers were under control.

Eventually, almost reluctantly, he crawled onto the bunk and fell asleep, his knees close to his chin, his arms loosely folded around his legs. And that was when he had the second dream.

He knew where he was immediately, and he was almost grateful for it even though this world – this dream world or whatever it was – was as alien to him as Silent Creek. There was the sea in front of him, the island once again, the sky as empty and as dead as ever. Jamie didn't know what it all meant or why he should find himself here again, but somehow he understood that it was important. He remembered the two boys in the straw boat and searched for them, hoping they would come into sight. Maybe, at the very least, they could tell him where he could find Scott.

Something moved close to the water's edge and Jamie's heart sank. It was the man he had encountered the last time he had been here. He was already straightening up – all seven feet of him – moving across the shingle, the hollow eyes staring out of the grey, putty-like face. The man was holding his bowl. This time there was no sign of the knife.

"He's gonna kill him," the man said.

Despite everything, Jamie felt a spurt of anger. "That's what you said last time," he called out. "But I can't stop them killing Scott unless you tell me where he is."

"No, boy. You don't understand—"

The man was about to go on but he never got the chance. There was a lightning strike. No – it was more than that. It was as if two giant hands had seized hold of the universe and ripped it apart like paper. The whole world – the sea and the sky – was torn in two. Jamie felt the ground convulse underneath him – an earthquake more powerful than anything the world had ever known. Everything was shuddering. He could feel his teeth rattling in his head. He was thrown off his feet and as he fell he tried to catch sight of the man … but he had already gone. At the same time, an ear-splitting scream echoed all around him. He would have said it was a shout of triumph, except that there was nothing remotely human about it. Jamie was deafened. He was clinging to the ground, which was twisting in turmoil beneath him.

In the next few seconds, a series of shapes suddenly appeared, plummeting through the sky – flying or falling … he couldn't tell. It was as if a great hole had opened up on the other side of the universe and flames were bursting out. The whole sky was on fire. He thought he saw a gigantic spider, another animal like an ape or a monkey, something that looked like a huge bird… Thousands of tiny specks followed them: a great dark swarm of them, twisting and cartwheeling in the air.

And there was something else. Jamie was aware only of an approaching blackness, a sense of something so terrifying that he could no longer bear to look. He closed his eyes and hugged the ground. The sea had gone, the water rushing away from the coastline. The wind was howling all around him.

It seemed to go on for ever. But there was no real time here and it could have been all over in a minute. As the storm died down and the waves returned, he lay where he was, completely exhausted.

Jamie knew nothing of the Old Ones, the five Gatekeepers, the struggle that had been going on for thousands of years and the part that he had been chosen to play. He knew nothing about a stone circle called Raven's Gate or the second gate that had been built in the Nazca Desert in Peru. Nor did he know that it was now midnight on 24 June – the day known as Inti Raymi.

The second gate had just opened.

25 JUNE

Nazca, Peru

The jeep seemed to be on fire. As it tore across the plain, it trailed a cloud of dust and sand which, in the moonlight, could have been smoke. The headlights were on but they were almost ineffectual in the great emptiness of the Nazca Desert and the moon itself was a better guide. It was three o'clock in the morning on the twenty-fifth of June, the day after Inti Raymi. The night was unusually cold, even in a desert where the temperature could drop ten degrees with the setting of the sun. And there was something strange about the light. It had a hard, almost unnatural quality – as if there had just been a terrible storm.

A woman was driving. Her name was Joanna Chambers and she was a professor of anthropology, a world expert on the wonder known as the Nazca Lines. She was large and slightly eccentric in appearance. She enjoyed playing the mad professor and she could be outspoken, even rude at times. But right now she was tight-lipped, her hands clutching the steering wheel. She was gazing ahead with a real dread of what she might find.

She was not alone. There was an Englishman in the passenger seat next to her. He was Richard Cole, the journalist who had been with Matt Freeman – the first of the Five – when he had discovered the secret of Raven's Gate in Yorkshire and who had then chosen to travel with Matt to Peru. He was looking exhausted, more gaunt and bedraggled than ever. Richard had come a long way – in more than one sense – since he and Matt had met in a rundown newspaper office in Greater Malling. At the time, Richard's work had mainly involved writing about weddings and funerals … and he wasn't sure which he found more depressing. But Matt had introduced him to a world of impossibilities: dinosaur skeletons that came to life, witches and demons, lost civilizations and cities hidden in the mountains of Peru. And now this. It seemed that their adventures had come to a sudden and sour end. Matt might be dead. This time, they hadn't won.

"We're almost there," Professor Chambers said. She glanced briefly at Richard, who didn't even seem to have heard her. "I feel this is my fault," she went on. "If only I'd been able to work it all out sooner, maybe we'd have had more time…"

"It's not your fault. It's mine." Richard took a deep breath. "I should never have let them go into the desert alone. Matt and Pedro. They're just kids, for heaven's sake!"

"It was a two-seater helicopter and there were three of them in it anyway. There wasn't room for anyone else."

"I shouldn't have let them go. The Incas warned us. They said that one of them would be killed…"

"They said one of them *might* be killed. And you know that Matt is no ordinary child. He's one of the Five. Pedro too. I think you should have more faith in them."

But as they drove on, it became clear that something terrible had happened. The ground had been torn up, the entire landscape broken apart. An earthquake had already been reported on Peruvian radio, but both Richard Cole and Professor Chambers knew that was only part of the truth. Matt had taken off to intercept Diego Salamanda at his mobile laboratory in the desert, but it seemed that he hadn't arrived in time. The second gate had opened. Richard would have known it even without looking at the upturned desert floor. He could sense it in the air. There was a sheet of lightning pulsating in the far distance, behind the mountains. It burned into his eyes. He was beginning to feel sick.

"There!" Professor Chambers exclaimed and swung the wheel.

The jeep's headlights had picked up the wreckage of a helicopter, half buried in the desert floor. Two of the rotors were missing and the other two were buckled and broken. The tail had snapped in half and the cockpit was a mess of shattered glass and dangling wires. Now that they were closer, they could smell fuel in the air. Professor Chambers slammed on the brake but Richard was already out and running before the jeep had come to a halt. He had seen a boy, lying with his back against the wreckage, his legs stretched out in front of him. One of them was bent at an impossible angle.

It was Pedro.

"What happened? Where's Matt?" Richard shouted out the questions before he remembered that Pedro didn't speak a word of English. Pedro looked at him quizzically and Richard felt ashamed of himself. He had been so worried about his friend, he hadn't stopped to consider how the other boy must be feeling. He crouched down and laid a hand on Pedro's shoulder. "Are you OK?" he asked.

A moment later, Professor Chambers arrived. She had thought to bring a bottle of water with her and she handed it to Pedro, who drank. "*¿Como estás*?" she asked. "How are you?"

Quickly, Pedro explained what had happened. The helicopter had been hit by a bullet. They had lost control and crashed. Richard looked into the cockpit and saw the young pilot – Atoc. He was belted into his seat, his hands resting on the controls. He was obviously dead. Pedro was still talking. His leg had been broken and he was unable to move. Matt had gone on his own to find Salamanda.

"You must leave me," he said, speaking in Spanish. "You have to find Matteo. The gate opened. I saw…"

He faltered and stopped.

"What did you see?" Professor Chambers asked.

"I can't talk about it. Just find Matteo."

Richard had understood the gist of what Pedro was saying.

He reached out and touched Professor Chambers on the arm. "You stay here. I'll go on," he said.

The professor nodded. Pedro pointed. *"Allá..."* Over there.

Richard didn't take the jeep. He was afraid he would miss Matt if he drove too quickly. He was sure that he couldn't be far from the helicopter, but even so it took him twenty minutes to find him, and when he did it looked as if he had arrived too late. Matt was lying on his back and Richard had never seen anyone more broken or more still. The boy had wept blood. His face was completely white.

He was dead. He had to be. There was no sign of any breathing, not the slightest movement in his chest. Richard had to blink back tears – not just of sadness but of anger. What had been the point? Had they come all the way from Britain just for this? The gate had opened. Pedro was wounded. And Matt was dead. Briefly, he wondered what had happened to Salamanda. He could see the wreckage of the mobile laboratory in the distance, but there was no sign of the man himself. Had he been responsible for this? But, examining Matt, he could see no sign of any external injury. He hadn't been shot. It was more as if the life force had somehow been sucked out of him.

Richard reached forward and took Matt's wrist in his hands. Matt's flesh was cold. But that was when he felt it – tiny, irregular, but definitely there. His pulse. Richard wondered if he was imagining it. Quickly, he rested his fingers against Matt's neck. There was a pulse there too. And although it was so faint as to be almost imperceptible, there was still some breath reaching his lips.

But he needed help. He had to get to hospital – fast.

Richard straightened up and set off, running back to get the jeep.

Hong Kong

The chairman of Nightrise was standing in his office on the sixty-sixth floor of The Nail, just down the corridor from the conference room where he regularly addressed his executives. He was watching the boats in the harbour and holding a glass of the most expensive Cognac in the world. It was almost a hundred years old and came in a crystal bottle. It had cost five thousand American dollars. How much of the golden-coloured liquid was he cradling in his palm? It seemed to him a strange thought, and a very satisfying one, that outside the window – in Kowloon – there were people who could barely afford to eat, women and children stuck in factories all day and much of the night, working for pennies simply to survive; while he could enjoy this vintage brandy at perhaps two hundred dollars a sip. That was how the world should be, he reflected. And very soon the gap between those who had and those who had not was going to be greater than ever. How fortunate he was to be on the right side.

A sleek cruise liner slid past far below and the chairman turned away. He didn't like boats. More than that, he had a fear of them – and with good cause. He went back to his desk and sat down. It was time to consider the events of the night before.

The Old Ones were back. That was all that really mattered. His agents in Peru had reported that the stars had aligned exactly as predicted ten thousand years before, and that the great gate, hidden in the Nazca Desert, had unlocked. He wished he could have been there. He had heard it said that you could be struck blind looking into the eyes of the King of the Old Ones – but even so it would have been worthwhile.

Not all the news was good. At their last telephone conference his colleague, the South American industrialist Diego Salamanda, had said that one of the children who called themselves the Gatekeepers was coming to Peru. He had said he would have no trouble tracking him down. But now it seemed that Salamanda himself had been killed, and as for the boy, he was still at liberty. The chairman didn't care about Salamanda. That was one less pair of hands to share in the rewards. But the fact that the boy might have survived … that was unsatisfactory. That was a loose end. In his part of the organization, it wouldn't have been allowed.

The private telephone on his desk suddenly rang. Very few people in the world had the number that connected to it. Any call that came through on this line had to be worth taking. He set the brandy glass down on his desk and picked up the phone.

"Good evening, Mr Chairman." It was Susan Mortlake. She

was calling him from Los Angeles.

"Mrs Mortlake." As ever, the chairman sounded neither happy nor sad to be hearing from her.

"My congratulations, sir." Of course she had heard what had happened in Peru. "It's wonderful news."

"What have you got to report, Mrs Mortlake?" Even at a time like this, business came first. The executives of Nightrise didn't telephone each other simply to scratch each other's backs.

"I've been thinking about Charles Baker," Susan Mortlake replied. "The presidential campaign. In view of what's happened, it's even more critical that he should win."

"Yes." The single word showed that the Chairman was getting impatient.

"You've seen the latest figures…"

John Trelawny was edging further ahead in the polls.

"Of course I've seen them, Mrs Mortlake."

"And our agent in New York has been unable to come up with a strategy?"

"I'm afraid Mr Simms has resigned."

Two days before, Mr Simms, the New York executive, had plunged head first into the Hudson River. In fact, his head had entered the water several minutes before his body. The two of them had later been found washed up, fifty metres apart.

"I believe I may have a solution to the problem, Mr Chairman. As a matter of fact, it was something that Mr Simms suggested himself … while he was still with us. He

186

said that the only answer might be to assassinate Trelawny."

"I don't think he was serious."

"But I am, Mr Chairman."

The chairman considered. Killing a presidential candidate was possible but it would not be easy. Quite apart from the fact that Trelawny was continually surrounded by secret-service men and that nobody with a gun could get close, the real problem would come later, if the attempt succeeded. There would be a public outcry and the police investigation would be huge and never-ending. It might even lead them to Nightrise. You pay someone who pays someone who pays a madman to fire the fatal bullet – but still the line can be traced back. Assassination was messy and full of danger. It was always a last resort.

But Susan Mortlake was confident.

"Suppose Trelawny was shot by someone who was close to him," she said. "Someone who had absolutely no link with us. Suppose the killer was caught immediately and was unable to explain his actions but seemed to have suffered some sort of massive nervous breakdown. There would be no doubt about his guilt. He would be tried, sentenced and executed. There would be no further investigation. Trelawny would be dead and that would be the end of it. Of course, someone would take his place, but it would be too late. He'd never catch up. Meanwhile, Charles Baker would look sad and sombre. He might even attend the funeral. In fact, that would help his poll ratings. Nothing would stop him becoming the next president of the United States."

"Can you do this?" the chairman asked.

"Yes, Mr Chairman. I can."

The chairman thought for a few seconds. But he knew Susan Mortlake well. He recognized the confidence in her voice.

"Then do it," he said. And hung up.

He reached out again and lifted up the precious brandy, contemplating its colour swirling in the glass. The Old Ones needed time. More than that, they needed a world that was ready to do things their way. He had no doubt that Charles Baker would be the right man in the right job at the right time. He smiled to himself and lifted the glass to his lips. At the last second he changed his mind and up-ended it, pouring the last inch into a potted plant.

Expensive fertilizer.

Then he got up and walked quietly out of the room.

New York

The car carrying John Trelawny pulled up outside the great tower at the southern end of Broadway in Lower Manhattan. There were two men with him. The driver, as always, was a secret service man. Trelawny knew that he was armed and in constant contact with his back-up team who would be in a second car, probably just a hundred metres behind. Warren Cornfield was sitting next to him. He was such a large man that

188

he barely left enough room for the senator but, over the past few months, Trelawny had got used to it. From the day he'd started his run for president there had been many things he'd had to get used to – and never being alone was the first of them.

"I'll be one hour," he said, and reached for the door handle.

"I'm coming in with you, sir," Cornfield announced.

Trelawny hesitated. This was an argument he'd had a hundred times. He appreciated what Cornfield was doing. Essentially, it was his job. He just wished he liked him more. "It's all right, Warren," he said. "This apartment building has its own security and nobody knows I'm here. I'm having lunch with an old friend and you're not going to tell me she's a security risk."

In the end, they compromised. Cornfield came with him through the lobby but allowed him to enter the lift on his own. There were times when Trelawny wondered if all this security was really necessary – but he supposed it only took one crazy person with a gun to prove that it was. And, of course, it was so easy to buy a gun in America. That was one thing he planned to look into one day, if...

He barely felt any motion as he was whisked up to the seventieth floor. The owner of the penthouse knew that he was coming and had programmed the lift to take him there. Trelawny thought about the woman he had come to see. The two of them had known each other for most of their lives – although he sometimes thought that what the two of them

189

didn't know about each other probably outweighed what they did. She was very wealthy. She had made a fortune creating and selling low-cost computers to inner-city schools, hospitals and youth clubs. She had supported his campaign from the start, holding a series of fund-raising dinners on both the East and West Coasts. The strange thing was, he probably trusted Nathalie Johnson more than any woman on the planet, even including his own wife. And she knew things. She had connections all over the world and seemed to be in tune with the stories that never made the news. He thought of her as a keeper of mysteries. That was why he had come to see her now.

The lift doors opened directly into a fan-shaped living room with windows giving extraordinary views over the Hudson River on one side and the East River, with the Brooklyn Bridge cutting across, on the other. His eye was instantly drawn to the panorama. There was the Statue of Liberty, looking very small and distant at the entrance to New York harbour. And there was Ellis Island, where the great waves of immigrants in the nineteenth and twentieth centuries had first arrived. The floor-to-ceiling windows were like a picture postcard on a gigantic scale and captured one of the most famous views in the world.

"John! How are you?"

Nathalie Johnson had come out of the kitchen carrying a tray with two glasses and a bottle of wine. She set the tray down and the two of them embraced. She was about fifty years old, slim and serious-looking, with dark reddish-brown hair that came down to her shoulders. She was wearing a simple black dress. In all the time that Trelawny had known her, he had never seen her in jeans.

"It's good to see you," she went on. "How long are you in New York?"

"Just a few days." Trelawny sighed. He was never in one place for very long. "I have to go back to Washington, then Virginia and then next week I'm heading back to California. My home town is giving me a parade."

"Auburn?"

"It's my birthday. They're closing the whole place in my honour."

"That's very sweet! Maybe I should come."

"You'd be very welcome."

The two of them sat down. Nathalie poured the wine and for a few minutes they talked about the campaign, the speech in Los Angeles, the latest negative advertisements that had been playing on TV. But after a while, Trelawny fell silent.

"There was something you wanted to ask me about," Nathalie said.

"Yes." He rubbed a hand over his mouth, trying to work out where to begin. "Something happened when I was in Los Angeles," he explained. "It's like nothing I've ever experienced and I can't get it out of my mind. I have to talk about it with someone and you're the only person I could think of who wouldn't think I was going mad."

"I'll take that as a compliment."

"Well, I had a visit from an old assistant of mine, Alicia McGuire. You remember her?"

"Wasn't she the one who lost her child?"

"Her son, Daniel. Yes. He vanished into thin air at the end of last year."

"How awful for her." Nathalie Johnson had never married and had no children of her own. She couldn't imagine what the other woman must have been through.

"When I was in LA, Alicia turned up at my hotel. She hadn't found Daniel but she had another kid with her, a fourteen-year-old boy. A Native American from the look of him. She told me this incredible story. I wouldn't have believed a word of it. I'd have thought she was out of her mind. But then she showed me something which was completely impossible and which could only have happened if everything she had been saying had been true."

"Tell me…"

Choosing his words carefully, Trelawny described everything that had taken place at the Carlton Hotel, his meeting with Jamie Tyler and the business with the little wooden box. If he had expected Nathalie to react with amazement or disbelief, he was disappointed. She showed no emotion when he talked, but she flinched at the mention of Nightrise and nodded in understanding when Trelawny mentioned their interest in children with paranormal abilities.

"Where is Jamie Tyler now?" she asked, when Trelawny had finished speaking.

"Maybe I acted against my better judgement," Trelawny replied. "But he was so desperate to find his brother. And I believed it was the right thing to do." He made a gesture with his hands. "I arranged for him to be sent to Silent Creek."

"He's in jail?"

"Not under his own name. We changed his appearance too. Don't forget, the Nevada authorities are still looking for him for the death of his two guardians."

"Let me just ask. Did this boy ever mention anything about England or Peru?" There was no answer, so she went on. "Did he say anything about the Old Ones? Or the Gatekeepers?"

"No." Trelawny shook his head. "I don't know what you're talking about, Nathalie. The Old Ones? What are they? What have they got to do with a bunch of disappearing kids?"

"If I'm not mistaken, they have everything to do with it," Nathalie replied. "And these two boys – Scott and Jamie Tyler – you have no idea how important they may be. They're both at Silent Creek?"

"I can't tell you. Jamie's there … probably. He was sent there several days ago. As for his brother, he was going to find out when he got there. That was the plan."

Nathalie put down her glass and leant forward.

"Listen to me," she said. "You came to me for advice. You chose me because I'm an old friend. But – don't deny it – you also came here because you know that I'm a member of … an organization."

"The Nexus." Trelawny spoke the two words and smiled as Nathalie sat back, alarmed. "I've heard that name," he admitted. "I know it's some sort of secret society and I've always suspected it might have something to do with you."

Nathalie nodded slowly. "You've been touched by something you know nothing about," she said. "But I know a great deal about it. For half my life I've been involved with it. So you must believe me when I say that it is absolutely vital that we find Jamie Tyler and get him out of Silent Creek immediately – and his brother too, if he's still there."

"That may not be so easy."

"John, you could be the next president of this country. But there may not even be a country to be president of – unless you do what I say."

"What are you talking about? Who *are* these two boys?"

Nathalie Johnson took a deep breath. "This is what you have to do…"

Los Angeles

Colton Banes was sitting at his desk when the telephone rang.

He didn't like being in the office. It felt too much like the prison where he had spent the eleven years before the Nightrise Corporation had employed him. True, he could leave when he wanted to. He was well paid. But being stuck indoors, dressed in a suit, waiting to be told what to do … it made him uneasy.

And yet he had to admit that he'd never had a better job. In fact no job could possibly exist that was better suited to his talents. Colton Banes liked hurting people. He liked killing them too – but hurting them was better because they were still around to talk about it afterwards, to tell him how it felt. From school bully to delinquent to armed robber to prisoner and finally to this... His whole life had been leading him in only one direction. He knew that one day he would slip up and Mrs Mortlake would get rid of him with the same carelessness with which she had got rid of Kyle Hovey. But he didn't really think about it. People like him never had long lives. It went with the territory.

He picked up the telephone on the third ring. "Yes?" He didn't have to announce his name. The switchboard wouldn't have put the call through unless the caller had asked for him.

"This is Max Koring."

"What is it?" Banes recognized the name of the senior supervisor at Silent Creek. He was calling from there now. It was easy to tell. There were no landlines in that part of the Mojave Desert and the satellite reception was poor. The prison had been built in a dead zone, in the middle of a natural magnetic field, making communication almost impossible. The field had other side-effects too. The location had been chosen with great care.

"There's something you should know," Koring continued. "We had something weird happen last night. One of the kids

– a new arrival – tried to get me to take him over to the Block."

"What do you mean?"

"He asked me to take him to the other side of the wall. In fact, he didn't ask – he *told* me, like he expected me to do what he wanted. And he said he wanted to see his brother."

Banes's eyes narrowed. "What is the boy's name?"

"The name on his face sheet is Jeremy Rabb."

That meant nothing to Banes. "Tell me what he looks like," he said.

"I don't need to. I thought the moment I saw him that he looked familiar. He's cut his hair short and he's got these thick glasses, but thinking about it, I figured out who he is."

"Jamie Tyler?"

"No doubt about it. I checked with the guy on Intake. He has the same tattoo on his shoulder. A sort of swirly thing with a line through. It's the twin. No doubt about it."

Colton Banes smiled. First the news last night from Peru – now this. Things couldn't be going better. So Jamie Tyler had decided to track down his brother. And he'd gone to the right place. The trouble was, he'd chosen the wrong time. "Where is he now?" he asked.

"I've got him in solitary. Do you want me to move him across to the Block?"

"No." Banes thought for a moment. Once the boy arrived at the Block, he would know he was too late. It would be more fun to keep his hopes alive for the moment. And Jamie

196

Tyler had escaped from him twice. Banes had a personal score to settle. He would let the boy sit there and stew for a few hours, then he would walk in and see the look on his face when he knew that he had failed, that pain and death were all that remained. "Turn off the air-conditioning in his cell," he said.

"Are you sure?" Even Koring was surprised. "It's a hundred degrees out here. The kid'll fry..."

"He'll be OK for twelve hours. I'll fly out tonight. I want him softened up before I arrive."

"He won't be soft – he'll have melted by then. But all right. Whatever you say, Mr Banes."

"That's right, Mr Koring. Whatever I say."

Colton Banes hung up, then settled back in his leather chair. Suddenly the office didn't seem so bad after all. Outside, the sun was shining. It was going to be a lovely day.

THE BLOCK

The heat.

Jamie had never felt anything like it. Even the theatre in Reno had never been as bad as this. He hadn't heard the air-conditioning unit in his cell switch off, but he had felt the result only moments later. The cool air had evaporated instantly. The heat had hit him from every side. He would have said it was like being in an oven except there was no "like" about it. He *was* in an oven. Baking, slowly, to death.

He had waited for what felt like an eternity, then gone over to the door and pressed the call button to summon help. The temperature was a hundred degrees and rising. The sunlight was pounding the outer walls and the roof, and sweat was pouring out of him. His clothes were sodden. He didn't dare breathe too deeply for fear of scorching his lungs. Nobody came. He hit the call button again and then again but he soon realized that it had either been disconnected or he was being deliberately ignored. Was this part of the punishment for what had happened the night before? He doubted it. Although he couldn't be sure, he suspected that this new treatment might signal something much worse.

He went over to the metal sink – it was already too hot to touch – and turned on the tap. A dribble of cold water came out. So far he had only been given bottled water to drink at Silent Creek. Indeed, he had been warned that the tap water was unfiltered. But there was no helping it. If he didn't drink, he would die. He cupped his hand and scooped some of the water into his mouth. It tasted stale and metallic. He took off his T-shirt and held it under the tickle, then pressed it against himself. Rivulets of water ran under his armpits and down his chest, cooling him for just a few seconds. He squeezed the shirt against the back of his neck. He would have to do this constantly until someone came or until the air-conditioning was turned back on. But somehow Jamie knew that neither of those things were going to happen soon.

Time crept past mercilessly. The window was a narrow slit with glass the colour of milk. He couldn't see out so there was no way of knowing what time of day it was, except that – as midday approached – the glare became even stronger, the heat ever more unbearable. He had nothing to read, nothing to do. He wanted to scream and pound his fists against the door but he knew that nobody would hear him and it would do no good. Besides, he wasn't even sure he had the strength. He was finding it more and more difficult to breathe. As each hour passed, he drifted between consciousness and a sleep that he feared might be his death. He had to force himself to get up every few minutes and return to the tap. The trickle of water was the only thing keeping him alive.

He knew now that he had failed. He should have guessed from the way Joe Feather had looked at him at the end of the meal only the day before. The Intake Officer had somehow recognized him and he must have passed on his knowledge to the supervisor, Max Koring. This was the result. They would leave him here until he died and then tell the authorities that it had been an accident. Apart from his bloody nose, there would be no signs of violence on his body. They would bury him in the desert and that would be the end of it.

Had they done the same thing to Scott? That was what he didn't understand. Why go to all the trouble of the kidnap, the dart guns, the double murder of Don and Marcie – just to bring him here to die? Nightrise was supposed to be looking for kids with paranormal powers. Scott, Jamie himself, Daniel McGuire and many others. But he still had no idea why they wanted them.

And then the door opened.

Jamie felt a cool breeze that danced on his skin. He was lying on his back, naked down to the waist, his trousers soaked and the crumpled ball of his T-shirt pressed against his head. His chest was rising and falling as his lungs fought desperately for air. Somehow he managed to turn his head and he saw a man standing there, silhouetted in the doorway. Jamie couldn't make out who it was but then the man stepped inside and his heart sank as he recognized Joe Feather.

Feather stood where he was. He swore quietly to himself,

then muttered, "What are they doing?"

He backed out again and Jamie was afraid that he was going to abandon him – but instead Feather found a switch and turned the air-conditioning back on. Almost at once the temperature in the cell began to fall. And then Jamie must have blacked out for a brief moment because suddenly Feather was there, kneeling down beside the bunk. He had a bottle of cold water.

"Drink this," he said. "Not too much. It'll make you sick…"

He held the bottle against Jamie's lips and Jamie swallowed gratefully. He had never felt anything quite as wonderful as the sensation of cold water trickling down his throat.

For a while, neither of them spoke. As Jamie recovered his strength, he once again examined the man who had introduced him to Silent Creek. Joe Feather was perhaps older than he had first thought. It was difficult to be sure, as his face was so sunburned, so lived in. His eyes were very dark. He was looking at Jamie with a mixture of dismay and … something else. For the first time, Jamie wondered if this man might not be his enemy after all. They were both Native Americans. Didn't that put them on the same side?

"Can you get up?" Feather asked. He glanced nervously at the door, making sure there was nobody outside. "We don't have much time."

"Why?" Jamie asked.

"You have to get out of here. They want to hurt you. But I have friends. I've called them. Very soon, they will come.

They will help you escape."

"Escape…?" This was all happening too fast. Jamie struggled to sit up. He took the bottle and drank some more water, then poured the rest of it over his head. It felt ice cold, trickling down his neck and over his shoulders, and revived him instantly. "What are you talking about?" Jamie demanded. "Why do you want to help me?"

"Later," Feather replied. "We can't talk now."

"No." Jamie shook his head. "I don't know you. I don't know what you want. Why should I trust you?"

The older man sighed in frustration. "I know you," he said. "I know who you are."

"Who am I?"

"You are one of the Five."

It wasn't the answer that Jamie had been expecting. It made no sense to him at all. He tried another approach. "When I came here, you asked me if I had a brother," he said. "Have you seen him?"

"You said you had no brother but I knew you were lying to me. And last night, Mr Koring told me your real name. You have a twin."

Jamie ran a hand through his hair, squeezing out more of the water. "That's right," he admitted. "My name is Jamie Tyler."

Joe Feather nodded. "There was a Scott Tyler here. He was sent to the Block … on the other side of the wall. But I wasn't here when he arrived. I didn't see him."

"You're lying! You knew about the tattoo. He's got the same tattoo in the same place. You must have seen it!"

"It was because of the tattoo that I knew who you were. There is much that I have to explain to you. But not now. Not here. I have friends who are already on their way here to help you. Tonight, when it is dark, you will leave—"

"I'm not leaving without Scott!"

Jamie had raised his voice and the Intake Officer turned anxiously towards the door, afraid that he might have been overheard. "Your brother was brought here a week ago," he whispered, the words tumbling over each other. "I don't go into the Block. I'm not allowed there. But sometimes I hear them talking and I know the names. He was here but he has gone again. They took him away."

"When?"

"Just before you arrived."

"Where? Where did they take him?"

Joe Feather cast his eyes down. "I don't know. They wouldn't tell me. All I can tell you is – he has gone."

It was almost the worst news that Jamie could have heard. To have come so close! Scott had been here! If Jamie had arrived earlier, everything might have been different. But his brother had already gone. Nightrise could have taken him anywhere in the world. His search was about to begin all over again.

"If you want to find your brother, you must get out of this place," Feather urged him. "You must do what I say. If you stay here, there is no hope."

"Wait a minute..." Jamie tried to collect his thoughts. Everything was still happening too quickly. "Tell me about the Block," he said. "That's what you call the units on the other side of the wall, but what's it for? How many kids are there locked up? What goes on over there?"

"Please." Feather looked pained. But he could see that Jamie was determined. "Listen to me," he whispered. "I've worked here only a few months. I don't know what goes on. There are the boys in the main prison and there are the specials. There is something they call the Psi project. I don't know what that means. And I don't work in the Block. Sometimes I see things. I see names on lists. And I hear the other supervisors talking. But it was just a job for me until I saw you. Then I knew I had to act..."

"Why?"

"Because of the tattoo!" Feather couldn't bear it any more. He went over to the door and looked out. But there was no one in the corridor. The other isolation cells were empty. The two of them were on their own. "I will tell you everything," he promised. "But only when we are far from here."

"All right." Jamie could see there was no point arguing. And he had no desire to spend a minute more at Silent Creek, not if Scott had already gone. "But there is one thing," he went on. "There's a boy called Daniel McGuire."

"McGuire..." Feather nodded. "Yes. I have seen that name."

"He's in the Block?"

"Yes."

"He's coming with me." Feather opened his mouth to argue but Jamie didn't give him time. "I'm only here because his mother helped me. I promised her. I can't leave him behind."

"But there is no way into the Block. There are cameras and guards..."

"You can help. You have to help me!"

The supervisor gritted his teeth, then nodded. "I'll see what I can do. There is no more time to talk now. Mr Koring will arrive very soon. I will come for you when it gets dark. Then we will see."

"I'm not going anywhere without Daniel."

"I will do what I can."

And then he was gone, leaving Jamie's head spinning. He heard a faint click and realized that Feather had turned off the air-conditioning again. That made sense. If Max Koring looked in, he would have to see that Jamie was still suffering. The heat returned, an unwelcome blanket that completely smothered him. But he had a whole bottle of water inside him and the worst of the day was over. Jamie wished he had asked Feather the time, but he could only lie there, gazing at the rectangle of white glass, watching as the light softened and faded away. Eventually the evening came and then the night. The single light bulb, in a steel cage over the sink, flickered on automatically. Nobody had brought Jamie any food. Perhaps that was part of the punishment too … or a way of weakening him up for whatever was to come. He was beginning to get nervous. Had Joe Feather been discovered? Had he had second thoughts? He'd said he would come back when it was dark, and surely more than an hour had passed since the sun had set.

But it was much later when the door finally opened and the Intake Officer hurried in. He had Jamie's trainers and a new T-shirt with him. He was also carrying another bottle of water. Jamie drank greedily while Joe talked. He wished the supervisor had thought to bring some food too.

"We must hurry," he said. "Mr Koring has gone…"

"Where?"

"There's a landing strip. A small plane. He's picking up Mr Banes."

Banes. It was the last name Jamie wanted to hear. He was instantly on his feet, pulling on the T-shirt, ready to go.

"My friends are close," Feather went on. He glanced at his watch. "It is ten o'clock. At half past ten they will come. We must be ready by then."

"What about Daniel?"

Feather took a small plastic bottle out of his pocket and unscrewed the cap. Jamie saw that it was filled with some sort of red syrup. "This contains chokecherry juice," he explained. "It won't harm you." Before Jamie could stop him, he had squeezed it all over the side of Jamie's face. Jamie put his hand to his skin and then examined his fingers. The juice looked exactly like blood. "I will take you to the medicine wing," Feather said. "You must pretend you are hurt." Jamie remembered what Baltimore had told him while they were having lunch. The medicine wing stood right up against the wall and served both sides of the prison. Now he understood what Feather was doing.

"The security cameras will see you," Feather continued. "But the guards will see the blood and they won't ask questions. There is nobody inside the medicine wing. In an emergency, they would expect me to call the nurses – but of course I won't. We will be alone."

"How do we get through to the Block?"

"Come now. I will tell you."

The two of them left together. The juice had streaked all the way down the side of Jamie's face and anyone watching him would assume that either he had been in a vicious fight or he had tried to kill himself. Joe Feather held onto him and, as they went down the empty corridor, Jamie staggered as if he could barely stand up. They came to a door which led out to the football pitch. Jamie already knew that none of the guards carried a key to this one. It could only be opened electronically from central control. He felt a camera high above, swivelling round to examine him. Would it work? Silence. Then a loud buzz and the lock clicked open. Joe helped him through. They were out!

It felt strange, crossing the football field in the artificial light of the arc lamps. The desert was pitch black. Tonight there was no moon. But the entire prison was a strange electric white, the razor-wire fence glittering all the way around the perimeter. Jamie could see the windows of the four units and thought of the boys he had met – Baltimore, Green Eyes, DV and the rest of them – and felt sorry that he was leaving them behind. They had made mistakes. They had done stupid things. But he had known them and he had thought none of them were really so bad.

The medicine wing rose up in front of them with the solid cinder-block wall stretching out behind. Joe Feather had a key to the door and he let Jamie in. They passed into a reception area with a desk and two small clinics leading off a narrow corridor behind. There was an eye chart on one wall, a couple of anti-drugs posters on the other. Jamie noticed another camera watching him from the corner. How could the two of them do anything when they were being followed all the time?

Joe Feather knelt down and pretended to examine his wound.

"The camera can see us but it can't hear," he whispered. "They will expect me to use the phone, to call the nurse. I will pretend to do that. You must take this…" Jamie felt something metallic being pressed into his hand. "This is the master key," Feather continued. "It opens the cells in all four units: North, South, East and West. It should also open the cells in the Block, but I can't be sure of that. If it doesn't, there's nothing more we can do."

"How do I get to the Block?"

"There is a door at the end of the corridor."

Jamie glanced round, at the same letting out a groan of pain for the sake of the camera. It was true. There was a single door just past the two clinics. And – of course – he should have been able to tell from the layout of the building that the corridor was a sort of tunnel, running directly through the outer wall.

Meanwhile, Joe Feather had gone over to the telephone and tapped out a number. Somewhere inside the prison complex, other supervisors would be watching his every move. The first rule of prison life was that there should be no surprises. Every minute of the day had to be exactly the same as the day before. The fact that a boy had been hurt and needed medical aid was a break from routine and the other guards would be on full alert. Feather was pretending to talk to the nurse at the end of the line but in fact he hadn't been connected. He was actually talking to Jamie.

"I've fixed the generator," Joe continued. "The electric generator in the yard. It has an override system. Sometimes we have to shut it down for repair. It will cut out very soon now and it will take them time to bring the emergency generator on-line. That will give us at least a minute with no cameras, no lights and all the prison doors automatically set to manual. That is when you will deal with your friend. He's in cell fourteen."

"Won't there be guards?"

"There's only one supervisor on duty during the graveyard shift. Leave him to me."

"Why are you doing all this?" Jamie asked.

Joe looked up from the telephone and allowed himself a brief smile. "I already told you. You're one of the Five."

"Yes. But one of the five what? What does it mean?"

Without any warning, the lights blinked out.

"Move!" Joe commanded.

He had a torch and flicked it on. Jamie followed him down the corridor and waited as he unlocked the door at the end with a key of his own. Everything was pitch black but the beam of the torch picked up a few details as Joe swung it from side to side: a unit almost identical to his own; a corridor lined with cell doors; a table bolted into the floor; a bank of monitors; a supervisor already rising to his feet, reaching for the canister of CS gas attached to his belt.

"What—?" the man began.

Joe hit him with his torch. The light beam threw crazy shadows across the far wall. Jamie heard the supervisor grunt. He folded forward and collapsed.

"Go!" Joe was already dragging the unconscious man back into his seat. There was a paperback book on the desk in front of him and Joe was arranging him so that when the lights came back on, it would look as if he was leaning forward, reading a page. Jamie looked around him, trying to find his way. Joe threw him the torch. He caught it and ran forward.

The cell numbers were clearly printed beside each door. He

had to move quickly. As soon as the emergency generator kicked in, he would be seen and – worse – the doors would be sealed electronically. He could hear shouting. It was coming from behind the locked doors. Some of the kids must have been awake and now found themselves in total darkness ... a new experience for them. They were pounding their fists against the doors. He wondered if the same thing was happening in the units on the other side of the wall.

He reached number fourteen and, using the torchlight, eased the key into the lock and turned it. With a sense of relief, he felt the lock open. He slid the door aside and stepped inside.

There was an eleven-year-old black boy lying on a bunk, wearing a T-shirt and shorts. He was small for his age but strong and wiry. He had short, curly hair and round, white eyes. There was a plaster on his wrist, just over the vein, and he was very thin. But otherwise he seemed unhurt. He was already awake and staring at the figure who had burst into his room. Jamie slid the door shut again – but not quite the whole way. He turned the torch on himself.

"Don't be scared," he said. "I'm a friend."

"Scott?" The boy on the bunk thought he'd recognized him and for a moment Jamie was thrown. But, of course, he wasn't wearing the glasses. And in the half-light it would have been easy to mistake him for his brother, even with his short hair.

"I'm not Scott. I'm his brother."

"Jamie!"

"Yes." Jamie felt a whirl of emotions. Scott had been here. This boy had met him. Perhaps he might know where he had gone. "You're Daniel ... is that right?" he asked.

"I'm Danny."

"I met your mother. She's been looking for you. She sent me to find you."

"You saw my mum?"

The lights came back on. Danny gasped, seeing the red stains all over Jamie's face. "You're hurt!" he said.

"No. Don't worry. It's fake..."

Jamie wasn't sure what was meant to happen next. He was inside the cell with Daniel McGuire, inside the Block. The other prisoners were still hammering at their doors, shouting for attention. The lights were back on. The security cameras were in operation. The entire prison was in a state of maximum alert. What exactly had they achieved?

Colton Banes had seen the lights come on too.

He was in a jeep, being driven from the airstrip where he had landed in the four-seater Cessna that had carried him from Las Vegas. Max Koring was behind the wheel. He had known at once that something was wrong. Silent Creek could usually be seen for miles around, and darkness in this part of the desert was simply impossible – it was like some sort of enormous magic trick. As the two of them drove along the track, the lights flickered on and the prison reappeared.

Koring turned to him. "A power failure," he muttered. "It

happens. Sometimes the generator cuts out."

"An accident?" Banes shook his head slowly. "Not tonight, I think..." He reached under his jacket and took out a gun. "Put your foot down," he snapped. "We need to raise the alarm."

But he was too late. The jeep was still a hundred metres from the main gates when the first shots were fired.

EAGLE CRY

They had come from nowhere, riding out of the desert in dusty pick-up trucks, open-top cars and jeeps. If this had been an old Western, Silent Creek would have been a fort and they would have been wearing war paint and feathers – for they were all American Indians, at least thirty of them from different tribes, firing with guns and rifles as they approached the perimeter fence.

They were aiming at the arc lamps. One after another the lamps shattered and darkness took hold once again. But more lights had come on inside the buildings. The supervisors knew they were under attack and they had weapons too. The alarm had been raised in the outlying houses and more guards were pouring out, some of them halfdressed, roused from their sleep.

One of the jeeps hurtled towards the fence then swerved away at the last minute. There was a man standing in the back, clinging onto the side bars, and as he drew near, he threw something: a home-made grenade. It landed on the sand, bounced, then exploded – a ball of flame that tore a gaping hole in the perimeter fence. At once, a siren went off, howling uselessly into the darkness. On the other side of the prison there was a second explosion as another part of the fence was ripped open. Now one of the cars roared into the inner compound, the last strands of razor wire ripping apart as it burst through. Four men, almost invisible in the shadows, tumbled out and took up positions around the football pitch. Another explosion. This time it was one of the satellite dishes behind the teaching wing. The attackers had made sure there would be no more communications tonight.

Not that they needed to have bothered. Colton Banes was watching the attack with amazement and already he had realized something that the attackers must have known from the start. Silent Creek was a maximum-security youth correctional centre: it had been built to remove the slightest chance of anyone breaking out. But nobody had considered the possibility of a well-armed force trying to break in. Worse than that, its position, in the middle of the Mojave Desert, had become its Achilles' heel. There was nobody for miles around. By the time anyone arrived to help, it would be far too late.

Banes's car drew level with one of the trucks, and for a moment he had one of the attackers in his sights ... another man with black hair and eyes that were alight with excitement. The man was wearing jeans and a tattered T-shirt and he'd painted streaks of red and white down the sides of his face. He couldn't have been more than twenty years old. Banes took careful aim and fired. But at the last minute, Koring jerked the wheel, avoiding a pot-hole in the track. The shot went wild. The car swerved off the track. Banes swore. The truck raced ahead.

"Who are they?" Koring rasped. His eyes were wide and he was sweating. Perspiration dripped from his moustache. It wasn't just the heat of the night: Colton Banes scared him. This situation was out of control. And that scared him more. "What do they want?"

"They're here for the boy!" Banes snarled. "Jamie Tyler. There can be no other reason."

"What do we do?"

"Kill him! Kill Tyler! It doesn't matter what else happens. He mustn't leave here alive."

Inside the Block, Jamie had heard the gunfire and the explosions. There was a loud bang and the lights failed again. His torch was still on and he swept it around him. All the other prisoners were awake now. He could hear them shouting and cheering in their cells. Daniel McGuire had already got dressed. Jamie had to admire him. He had been locked up for seven months and suddenly he had been woken in the middle of the night and in total darkness by a stranger who seemed to be covered in blood. A pitched battle was going on outside. But he was completely calm, waiting to be told what to do.

Joe approached, hurrying down the corridor behind the beam of a second torch. "My friends are here," he shouted. He no longer cared if the cameras saw him. It didn't take a great deal of imagination for Jamie to see that the Intake Officer wouldn't be coming back. "Now we go!"

216

"What about the others?" Jamie asked.

There were twenty cells in the corridor, ten on each side. Flashing his own torch over them, he saw faces through the glass windows set in the doors. Not just boys – girls too. He remembered what Alicia had once told him. The kidnappers had been interested in both sexes, girls and boys, provided they had some sort of paranormal ability. He had no doubt that this was where they had all ended up. It was incredible. A prison within a prison. And he still had no idea why they had been brought here.

Joe Feather was waiting for him to go. But Jamie wasn't moving. "We can't leave them," he said.

"We have to!" Joe exclaimed. "My friends came for you. Only for you. It's too dangerous to take them outside…"

"But they've done nothing wrong!" It was Daniel who was speaking. He had a high voice; obviously it hadn't broken yet. "They're like me. They were all snatched and brought here."

Joe shifted from one foot to the other as if he were standing on burning coals. "When you are out of here, then you can help them. You can speak with the authorities. But if we don't go now, we will never leave."

Jamie knew that he was right. It would take them too long to open all twenty doors – and what about his friends back in the unit? He couldn't get them out either. Scott wasn't here. His first job was to get Daniel back to his mother. Then Alicia would be able to go to John Trelawny. And the senator would see to the rest of it.

217

"Joe's right. We have to go." He turned to Daniel. "I promise you, we'll come back and help the others."

Daniel nodded, and just for a second Jamie had the weird sensation of being, for the first time in his life, the older brother. For so many years he had looked up to Scott – even though they were the same age. But Scott hadn't been around for a while and maybe in that time Jamie had changed. He'd had to start to think for himself.

There was another explosion and more shooting. The gunfire had intensified and Jamie guessed that the supervisors must be shooting back. Following Joe, they ran along the corridor into the medicine wing. As soon as they were there and could look out of the windows, they saw the truth. A fierce battle was taking place in the prison grounds. There were gaping holes in three different parts of the fence and the cage holding the generator had been blown apart. The generator itself was on fire. That explained the second power failure, and for some reason the emergency generator hadn't yet kicked in. Half a dozen different vehicles had come to a halt in front of the four units, the dining hall, the gymnasium. He saw figures, little more than silhouettes, popping up to take a shot at the prison windows. There were brief flashes of white as the supervisors returned fire.

The three of them pushed the door open and slipped out into the warmth of the night, crouching down in case anyone saw them. Daniel was next to Jamie, who put a hand on his shoulder, keeping him close. Joe Feather rose up and called out in a language that neither of the boys understood. It was almost a high-pitched war cry, his voice echoing across the compound above the noise of the shooting. A moment later, someone answered back. There was the sound of an engine starting and renewed firing as a pick-up truck came hurtling over the sand, making towards them.

"Now we go!" Joe said.

The truck slid to a halt. Jamie caught sight of a driver and a passenger leaning out of the window with a rifle balanced over his arm. They were both young – only a few years older than him. Quickly, Jamie helped Daniel into the back, then climbed in himself.

"Hold onto the back!" Joe told them. He was the last in. No sooner had his feet left the ground than they were on the move again.

There was a bar running across the back of the driver's cab. Jamie found himself standing up, clinging onto it for dear life. Daniel was lying down, being bounced around on the wooden floor as the truck lurched forward. The ground suddenly seemed to be pitted with holes – maybe it was a result of all the explosions. More bullets were fired. One of them smashed into the side of the cab, ricocheting off with a loud clang. Whether it was a lucky shot or deliberately aimed at them, Jamie couldn't say. They were heading for the fence, a few metres away from the gate that had been opened, less than a week ago, to allow Jamie in. The gate was still there but the fence had been blown apart. He could see the track and the

219

guards' houses on the other side.

They drove through. Jamie ducked down, afraid of being gashed by a piece of dangling razor wire. The driver fired a shot through a window and a guard spun backwards in the sand, wounded. The other vehicles were also leaving the prison. Looking back, Jamie saw half a dozen of them following not far behind.

The wind – warm and welcoming – rushed over his shoulders and through his hair. He almost wanted to laugh. He still didn't know who these people were but they were on his side and they were taking him and Daniel out. He would contact Alicia and the prison would be shut down. And surely someone there – one of the supervisors, a nurse or an administrator – would know what had happened to Scott. There would have to be a record somewhere in one of the files.

They passed a jeep parked next to the track. Jamie saw it and assumed it was empty. He didn't see the man rise up next to it. Nor did he see the gun aimed at his back.

Colton Banes had been waiting for him. He had realized that there was no point entering the battle inside the prison. Everything there was dark and confused. It would be better to wait just outside the compound. If they were going to bring out the boy, they would have to come this way. And he was right. He could see Jamie, standing up, holding onto the driver's cabin for support. He was a perfect target, almost like one of those paper cutouts Banes had used for practice at the range.

He fired.

Jamie heard the shot and felt the bullet smash into his back, high up, next to his shoulder. It was like being stabbed with a white-hot knife. All the strength went out of him. His legs folded under him and he fell, sprawling, on top of Daniel. He hadn't closed his eyes, but suddenly everything was black. He heard Joe call out, but before the Indian had reached the end of the sentence the words had faded away. He couldn't feel the floor of the truck. He couldn't feel anything.

Colton Banes hadn't finished yet. He had seen the boy go down but he still had time for a second shot. Although he was fairly sure that the first bullet would have done the job, this one would make certain. A smile spread across his lips as he brought the gun up, taking careful aim.

But he never pulled the trigger. He heard something come whistling out of the darkness and jerked back, wondering what had happened. He looked down and was surprised to see an arrow, complete with feathers, jutting out of his chest. Had it just been fired into him? Had one of these people really brought along one of their ancient weapons and used it against him? A car sped past. The young man with the war paint was leaning half out of the window, whooping. The bow was in his hands.

For a moment Banes stood there, unaware that his hand had dropped and that the gun was now pointing at the ground. He opened his mouth to speak but no words came. Hot blood flowed over his lower lip. His last thought was that he had never expected to die like this, and certainly not quite so soon. Then he fell onto his knees and crashed face down into the sand.

Max Koring stood up shakily. A few supervisors were still firing, but it was already over. The last of the vehicles had disappeared into the desert night.

Sunrise.

Daniel McGuire woke up and found himself lying on a thick woollen rug in a tent that was completely circular, tapering to a point high above him. The walls were made of some sort of leather and were wrapped around a framework of wooden poles. There was a flap for the door and he could see the sunlight filtering through the cracks. It was still early in the morning. The air inside the tent was cool and the light was tinged with red.

He had slept fully dressed. He blinked and stretched and then crawled forward, pushing his way through the flap. He saw at once that he was in the mountains. There were great boulders all around and although the tent had been erected on a flat shelf, the ground rose up steeply behind him. And it wasn't a tent. Looking round, Daniel saw that he had spent the night in an Indian tepee.

There was a figure sitting cross-legged in front of a small campfire, his eyes fixed on the smoke curling into the air. Daniel recognized the man who had helped rescue him the night before. What had Jamie called him? Joe. Now Daniel recalled what had happened. The sudden appearance of Jamie in his cell, the blackout, the gunshots, the race out of the prison. As he had awoken, he had thought it might all have been a dream – but with full wakefulness came the realization that it had actually happened. And Jamie…

"Where is he?" he asked.

Joe Feather turned. "You must have something to drink," he said. "And eat…"

"Is he all right?"

Joe gestured. Daniel had noticed a number of bundles spread out over the ground. Now he saw that one of them was Jamie, completely wrapped in blankets with only his face showing. The face was very white. His eyes were closed and he didn't seem to be breathing.

"Is he dead?" Daniel asked.

"He is very close to death." Joe's voice was low. "I have done what I can for him."

"We've got to get him to a hospital!"

"A hospital cannot help him now. And anyway, there is no hospital. Not for thirty miles. Even if we could carry him there, he would be dead before we arrived."

"Then what are we going to do?"

"You are going to eat and drink."

"I don't want anything."

Joe's eyes flared. "This boy risked his life to take you out of Silent Creek. You won't help him by sitting there dehydrating. He wanted to take you back to your mother and I will make

223

sure that happens. But for now you must trust me."

"Can you help him?"

"I have already helped him. I have called for the *shaman*. The *shaman* will be here soon."

Daniel nodded. There was a bottle of water and a basket containing fruit, bread and some sort of dried meat. He forced himself to eat. Joe was right. He could hardly believe it but the nightmare of Silent Creek was finally behind him – and it was all thanks to this boy he had never met but who somehow knew his mother. He glanced across at the silent figure. He remembered the moment when the bullet had hit him as they sped out of the compound. It seemed so unfair. One more minute and they would have been away.

The morning wore on. The sun rose, becoming ever hotter. Jamie had been placed in the shade, protected by a great boulder. Daniel was worried that someone would find them – the police must surely be looking for them by now – but Joe seemed unconcerned. Yet of course, Native Americans had spent years hiding in the mountains. Not being found had been the only way for many of them to survive.

A little before midday, there was a movement and a figure appeared, on horseback. At first it was difficult to see who it was. The sun was behind the person, who seemed to shimmer, out of focus, as the warm air rose up from the ground. Joe sprang to his feet, relief flooding into his face. Daniel understood.

It was the *shaman*. The medicine man.

The horse and its rider seemed to take for ever to reach them, struggling against both the steepness of the slope and the heat of the day. Daniel saw the *shaman* kicking at the horse, but not very hard and with little effect. At last the figure drew close and he was able to see the man in whom Joe had such faith. He wasn't impressed.

The *shaman* was one of the oldest men Daniel had ever seen. He had the sort of face one would have expected to see on a corpse, the skin withered and yet at the same time stretched tight over the skull. What few teeth he had left seemed to be on the edge of falling out. His arms were emaciated and there was a hollow in his throat you could have put your fist into. His hair was silver. It was long, hanging down to his shoulders, but tied with a piece of black ribbon. Only the *shaman*'s eyes were truly alive. They were grey in colour but seemed to shine with an inner strength.

Very slowly, he climbed down from the horse. Joe was still standing there, his hands clasped in front of him, his eyes turned down.

"Goddamn horse!" The *shaman* turned and spat. "I've only been on it a couple of hours and I swear I've been sitting on a cactus." He turned to Joe. "Don't just stand there, Joe Feather. Make me a cup of tea! And I wouldn't say no to a piece of pie if you happen to have one."

It was only now he heard the voice that Daniel realized the *shaman* was not a man but a woman. Her body had reached such a stage of decay that it was hard to tell the difference.

225

Suddenly he felt her eyes on him.

"You Danny?"

"Yes, ma'am." Danny wasn't sure what to call her.

"How long they keep you in that prison of theirs?"

"I was there for thirty weeks and three days."

"You counted every one of them." She shook her head. "There's evil people in this world. People who don't deserve to walk the land and that's the truth. Now, let's take a look at this boy."

Her manner changed as she approached the silent figure of Jamie. She knelt down beside him and rested a gnarled hand against his forehead. Joe was busying himself with a kettle but she called out to him. "Forget that, Joe. Come and help me turn him."

Joe hurried over and the two of them turned Jamie onto his side. The back of his T-shirt was saturated with blood. Daniel could see the hole where the bullet had gone in. The shaman examined the entrance wound, touching it gently with the tip of her finger.

"Is it bad?" Joe asked.

"It's bad. It couldn't be much worse. The first thing we're going to have to do is get that bullet out. Lucky you've got a fire burning. We're going to need that."

"Is he going to live?"

The *shaman* shook her head as if dismissing the question. She turned to Daniel. "I want you to go back into the tepee," she said. "I know you want to stay and help, but there's

226

nothing you can do and this is something no young child should have to see."

"Please…" Daniel wanted to argue, but one look at the old woman's eyes told him not to waste his time. He did as he was told.

The *shaman* nodded at Joe. "Take off his shirt."

Joe knelt down beside Jamie. He didn't try to pull the shirt over Jamie's head. Instead, he used a knife to cut the material, then ripped it apart, exposing the wound. The skin was bright red and puffed up around the bullet hole. Meanwhile, the *shaman* went back to the horse and untied a leather bag that had been strapped to the saddle. As she returned to the unconscious boy, she opened it and took out some muslin packets tied with strips of sinew, some bowls, two glass bottles and a wooden wand, about ten centimetres long, with an eagle carved at one end. Finally she produced a knife. Joe looked at it and winced. There was nothing ancient about the knife. It was a straightforward surgical scalpel.

She caught his eye. "The spirits will only do so much," she said. "To start with, we have to cut the bullet out."

Joe nodded.

"Tell me when my tea is ready," the *shaman* said.

She leant over Jamie and made the first cut.

Daniel waited for as long as he could. He tried to sleep, but now that the sun was up it was too hot, even in the shade of the tepee. He wished he could talk to his mother but he

227

doubted that the *shaman* carried a cell phone – and anyway it was the wrong time to ask. Perhaps he did manage to doze off in the end, because the next thing he knew, there were long shadows falling across the tepee and the heat seemed to have lessened. Once again, he crawled out through the flap not sure what he expected to find.

Joe was sitting next to Jamie, who looked no better than he had the last time Daniel had seen him. He was lying on his side with a dressing over the wound. The *shaman* had made some sort of poultice. Daniel could both smell it and see it, seeping through the bandages. The *shaman* herself was further down the slope, on her knees, facing the sun. It was late in the afternoon. The sky was already tinged with red. The campfire was still burning, sending a thin trickle of smoke up towards the clouds.

"How is Jamie?" Daniel asked.

Joe turned round angrily. "Stop!" he said. "You must not say his name."

"Why not?"

"It is our practice. When someone dies, you mustn't speak their name for four days."

"When someone…?"

The full impact of what Joe had just said hit Daniel. "You mean…" He forced himself to finish the sentence. "He's dead?"

There was a long silence. Then Joe spoke. "We took the bullet out," he said. "The *shaman* cleaned the wound with yarrow and other herbs. But there was nothing more she could do. He has crossed to the other side."

Daniel felt the tears well up in his eyes. He looked down at Jamie lying there, at peace. He couldn't believe that it had ended like this. He had met Scott, Jamie's twin brother. The two of them were so alike. When Jamie had come into the cell the night before, it had been like the beginning of a new friendship, the first chapter in a story that still had pages to run.

And now…

"I thought…" Daniel began. His voice choked. He turned away and looked at the old woman, who was muttering something, holding the little wand in her hand.

"What's she doing?" he asked.

"You mustn't ask questions," Joe replied. Then, more gently, he continued. "She is doing what she can. She is using powerful magic. Summoning up what we call *we ga lay u*. Her spirit power."

"What is that? I don't understand."

Joe's eyes narrowed. "The medicine men get their powers from helpers who give them guidance in their work. They take many forms – but always animals or birds. This woman may not look it but she is very strong. She is not from my tribe but she is famous. You saw her wand with the wooden carving. Her spirit power is the eagle."

"But if he's dead…"

"The eagle is the only spirit power that can cross over and

bring him back. It is so powerful that none of my people will even keep one eagle feather in their house. It can do too much harm. But she has summoned it to help her. Look…"

Joe pointed.

Daniel didn't see it at first, and when he did he wasn't sure if he was imagining it. A bird was swooping down, flying directly out of the sun as if it had just been born in the flames. As it descended, it cried out, a sound that echoed across the mountains. It didn't land, but flew over them in a circle.

The *shaman* raised her arms. Her spirit power had heard her call and it had come.

The eagle circled twice more, then soared back into the sky.

SCAR

This time it wasn't a dream. Jamie was sure of that much. There was no sea and no island, no seven foot tall man waiting to deliver a cryptic message. And anyway, the world he now found himself in was too real. He wasn't just seeing it: he could feel it and smell it too. And it was cold. He rubbed his hands together and found himself shivering. It wasn't possible to feel cold in dreams – was it?

He looked up. Wherever he was, it certainly wasn't Nevada. The desert sky had been an intense blue by day, the deepest black with a scattering of stars by night. The sky here was a strange mixture of colours, as if someone had spilled a dozen different pots of paint – but it was predominantly grey and red with dense, writhing clouds and no sign of any sun. Jamie took in the ancient trees, which could have been carved out of stone rather than wood; the wild, swaying grass; the twisted rock formations. Not only was he not in Nevada, he wasn't even in America. Even the breeze was wrong: slow and sluggish and smelling of cinders, wet mud and … something else.

Where was he?

He tried to remember what had happened. He had been standing in the back of a truck which had managed to break through the prison fence, but then he had been shot. He remembered the searing pain as the bullet entered his back, just next to his shoulder. He had felt his legs fail him and had collapsed onto the floor of the truck. That was all. He had thought he'd heard someone shouting, but then the darkness had closed in.

Until now.

He looked around and saw that he was surrounded by corpses. There were dozens of them, lying broken and twisted as if some unstoppable force had scythed through and killed them all in the same instant. With a growing sense of horror, Jamie stumbled to his feet and limped over to the nearest. They were all men, dressed in the same shades of brown and grey. Soldiers. He could see that now. But not modern ones, not like the soldiers he had seen on the TV news, waving and putting their thumbs up on their way to some faraway war.

These men were wearing strange clothes: long jackets that came down to their knees and loose-fitting trousers. Some were hooded, the dark material sweeping round their heads and over their shoulders. They didn't seem to have any guns. Instead they'd been armed with swords and shields, but even these were like nothing he had ever seen before. The shields were small and round with a single spike sticking out so they could be used either for defence or to stab anyone who came close. The swords were different shapes: some straight, some curving, some with multiple blades. There were arrows all around but they were made of metal, not wood, and with some sort of black leaves taking the place of feathers.

They had all been mutilated. Some were almost unrecognizable as human beings. As the smell of the freshly spilled blood rose in his nostrils, Jamie turned and threw up, then staggered away, desperate to hide himself, to try and make sense of what he was seeing.

He had woken up near a ruined building perched on a hill. It loomed high above him, built out of red bricks and shaped like a giant thumb with a curving terrace where the nail should have been. There was a wooden door hanging off its hinges and, inside, a spiral staircase leading up from what had once been a circular entrance hall. The fortress – for that was surely what it was – had recently been set on fire. Parts of it were still smouldering and it was obvious that the men in front of him had died trying to defend it.

Still nauseous and disorientated, Jamie stumbled over the rubble until he reached the entrance, resting his hand against the door frame. He winced. The wood was too hot to touch. Rubbing his palm, he continued round the back of the building, away from the dead bodies. He found a patch of grass and sat down, forcing himself to keep control. His heart was beating twice as fast as it should have been. There was a foul taste in his mouth and his head was spinning. He wanted to be sick again but there was nothing left in his stomach.

It was now that he realized he was no longer wearing his own clothes. Someone had re-dressed him in a coarsely woven grey shirt that was buttoned up to the neck without a collar. There was a leather belt outside the shirt, above his waist. His feet were bare. He looked very much like all the dead men around him.

Except he was alive.

Or was he? It suddenly occurred to him that he might have been killed trying to escape from Silent Creek and that this might be the result. Jamie had read bits of the Bible. He'd been to church a few times. Marcie had forced it all on him and Scott as part of their home-schooling. He knew about heaven and hell, although he'd never believed in either of them. Now he wondered if maybe he'd been wrong. Maybe this was hell. There were no flames and no devils with horns, but hellish was exactly the word to describe where he was right now. This could be the place where bad people went after Judgment Day.

But he knew it wasn't true.

He reached behind him and tried to find the place where the bullet had entered his back. But there was no sign of any wound, and even as he moved he knew he wouldn't find one. He wasn't in pain. It was as if the gunshot had never happened.

"I'm alive!" He whispered the words to himself as if hearing them could somehow prove them to be true. He turned his hands towards his face and flexed his fingers. They obeyed him. His stomach felt hollow and his throat was raw, but otherwise he was fine.

So if this wasn't a dream and he wasn't dead, could he be suffering some sort of hallucination? He'd seen that sort of thing on TV, in science-fiction programmes. A woman in a car accident hits her head and wakes up somewhere weird. She thinks it's real, but in fact she's just imagining it and she's really in a coma in a hospital bed. That was more likely. Jamie lowered his hands and gazed around him again. The great tower did not look like a hallucination. There was one way to make sure. He gritted his teeth, counted to three and slammed his fist into the brickwork. He yelled out loud. It hurt! He looked down and saw blood on his knuckles. Well, surely that had to prove something. He swore quietly to himself and licked the wound.

Was it possible that he had been knocked unconscious on the way out of the prison? Could it be that Colton Banes or Max Koring had captured him again and brought him here as a punishment? No. That didn't work either, because "here" was too different. The bullet wound had gone. And what about all these dead bodies, lying there in their strange clothes? Some sort of war had taken place. And he had just woken up on the losing side.

There was no simple explanation. Jamie realized that he had to accept the situation as it was and try to make the best of it. After all, his entire life had been completely insane, from the day he'd been abandoned in a cardboard box and left on the edge of Lake Tahoe to the time he'd found himself being chased across America for two crimes he hadn't committed. He was a freak. A mind-reader. He'd learned to live with all of that, so why not this? Somehow, in some impossible way, he had been transported to another place ... maybe even another planet. And it seemed that he was on his own, the only living person for perhaps miles around. He could stay here, cowering in the corner, or he could move on.

There was no choice really. It was time to go.

He wiped his mouth on his arm, then stood and began to make his way down the hill. The further he went, the more bodies littered his path, until he found himself stepping over them, doing his best to avoid treading on them while at the same time trying not to look too closely. The wounds were too horrible.

The battlefield stretched on all the way down to the bottom of the hill and beyond. Jamie saw more broken swords and shields. He came upon a young, fair-haired man pinned to a tree by a spear that had gone straight through him. The man was holding some sort of flag – a blue five-pointed star in a circle set against a white background. Jamie began to understand. This was like one of those battles he had seen at the movies. All these dead men could have been warriors. But who had they been fighting? Their enemies, whoever they were, had been utterly ruthless. It was possible that they had taken prisoners, but they had left nobody alive on the field.

Jamie looked further down the hill. The field stretched on towards the horizon, which formed an almost invisible line between the darkening sky and the grass. Even though he had moved away from the fortress, the smell of burning was growing stronger and he realized that the clouds were actually smoke, that something huge – a town or a city – had burned a short while ago and that although the fire might now be out, it had left a pall that had smothered the sky. If so, this battle was probably one of many. And the carnage might stretch on for miles.

He came to a muddy lane that gave him a choice of two directions, although neither of them had much to offer. Jamie was tempted to continue across open country. He might be safer away from the beaten track. After all, there was a victorious army somewhere in the area and he didn't want to go blundering into it until he knew which side he was meant to be on.

There was a movement. Jamie started, about to run away, then relaxed. A single figure was walking down the lane towards him, an old man supporting himself on a stick. He looked like a monk, dressed in a brown robe with a hood folded back over his shoulders. He was still a long way away, but as he drew closer, Jamie saw that he was at least sixty years old, almost bald, with sagging skin and weeping, bloodshot eyes. The old man could barely walk. All his weight was concentrated on the stick, which he placed carefully in front of him before he took each step.

Jamie felt a huge sense of relief. He was no longer alone! The man raised a hand and waved at him. It seemed that he was friendly. Now perhaps Jamie might learn where he was and what had happened here … assuming that the man spoke his language. Jamie waited as he made his way along the track. It took him a very long time before he finally arrived.

The man stopped and spoke.

"Rag dagger a marrad hag!"

That was what the words sounded like. Jamie heard them quite distinctly and they should have made no sense at all. The man was talking gibberish. But Jamie understood exactly what he meant. Somehow his brain had tuned itself in to a foreign language which he had learnt instantly. Impossible, of course. But that was how it was.

"Good day to you, my friend!" the man had said. He had called out the greeting in a trembling, high-pitched voice. He stopped to catch his breath, then went on, the words instantly translating themselves. "A living child among so many dead! That's very strange. Who are you, my boy? What are you doing here?"

Jamie hesitated, wondering if he could respond. "My name is Jamie," he replied, but although they were the words he thought, they weren't the ones that came from his lips. Without even trying, he was speaking the man's language. He paused, then went on, "I don't know what I'm doing here. I don't even know where I am. Can you help me?"

"Of course I can help you." The man laughed briefly. It was

a dry, unpleasant sound. "But as to where you are, there is nothing left here so why should it even have a name? And if it did have a name, it would soon be forgotten, like everywhere else. There are no countries now. No cities, no towns. All is but ashes." He ran an eye over Jamie and frowned. "Where have you come from?" he asked.

"I'm American," Jamie said. "From Nevada."

"America? Nevada? I don't know these places." Now he was suspicious. "How did you arrive here?"

"I don't know." Jamie shook his head. "I didn't mean to come here. It just happened."

"As if by magic?"

"Well … yes." Jamie wasn't sure that the old man was joking.

"Perhaps it *was* magic!" The old man's hand tightened on the walking stick. "Perhaps you were brought here by the Old Ones. They might have wanted you, although I can't think why." He cocked his head to one side. "Do you serve the Old Ones?" he asked.

Jamie shook his head. "I'm sorry. I don't know what you're talking about."

"You're not a servant of the Old Ones?"

"No! I'm not anybody's servant!"

"It is fortunate, then, that I came this way. It would seem that I've arrived just in time."

"To do what?" Jamie was suddenly uneasy.

"To kill you."

239

The old man lifted his walking stick and Jamie almost laughed out loud. The idea that this sixty-year-old could even hurt him was ridiculous. He half raised a hand to defend himself, then stepped back in horror, his eyes widening as the impossible happened in front of his eyes. The old man seemed to unpeel himself, the flesh falling away like pieces of discarded clothing. Another creature, some sort of giant insect, exploded out of him, ugly black scales taking the place of skin. Two huge claws, with pincers snapping open and shut, ripped through his sides and stretched out where his arms had just been. His eyes had turned yellow. His head and legs were still human, but now they were grafted onto the body of a scorpion, and as Jamie fell back a huge tail rose over its shoulders with a massive stinger pointing down at him from above. The walking stick had changed too. Now it was a spear of mouldering steel, like something recovered from a shipwreck. The end was twisted and bloodstained, shaped like a letter Y, with not one point but two.

The man-scorpion screamed at him and Jamie saw that its teeth had become silver needles and its mouth was full of blood. The yellow eyes were wide and furious. He heard something shudder through the air and fell back just as the steel rod, held in one of the claws, slashed through the air an inch from his face. If it had made contact, it would have smashed his skull – or taken his head clean off his shoulders. Jamie lost his balance and almost fell, then leapt back as the creature's tail lashed out at him, white poison splattering the ground.

A few tiny drops of the stuff sprayed onto his hand and he cried out. It was like acid. He could feel it burning through his skin. The tail lashed again and this time Jamie threw himself onto the ground, afraid of being burnt or blinded. The creature laughed and Jamie knew that he had no chance at all, that he really was going to die right now – and that he would never even find out what had happened, how he had arrived here to begin with.

The thing lumbered forward, its head twisting from side to side, its face distorted with anger and hatred, holding the two-headed spear high up above it. Jamie dragged himself backwards, looking for anything, a weapon he could use to defend himself. There was a soldier lying beside the lane, still clutching a sword that was curved like a sabre with a second, shorter blade jutting out just below the hilt. Jamie reached out and grabbed it, wrenching it out of the dead man's hand, then rolled over and over, aware that the creature had hurled the spear towards him. The spear stabbed into the ground so close to his stomach that he felt its edge against his shirt. The man-scorpion scrabbled towards him and, at the same time, Jamie leapt to his feet, holding out the sword. Just for a second, he felt himself gripped by a sense of unreality. It almost paralysed him. He was facing something that wasn't human. He had a sword. He was in a fight to the death.

And he wasn't afraid.

That was the strangest thing of all. Suddenly, he knew exactly what to do, and although he had never held a sword in his life, it felt almost a part of him. It had happened the moment he had picked it up. Without even thinking, he had been aware of its weight, the length of the blade, the balance of it in his hand. It was as if he had somehow absorbed it into himself so that he and the sword were one.

The man-scorpion attacked, its tail stabbing down. Jamie stepped aside and swung the sword, grinning as the sharp edge of the blade sliced through scales and skin, hacking into the stinger and cutting it clean off. The creature screamed. Poison sprayed the air. Jamie went in low, thrusting forward. This time he felt the point bury itself in the creature's body. Blood – dark red and sticky – gushed out of the wound. Jamie felt it splatter into his face and retched as he tasted it on his lips. But he had done it. He was still alive. He had won.

The man-scorpion reared back, taking the sword with it. Jamie could see that it was dying but, after all, it wasn't finished yet. With its last breath, it snatched up the spear, jerking it out of the ground, and aimed a second time.

"Die!" the creature screamed and stepped towards him.

Jamie was unarmed. He stood where he was, poised on the balls of his feet with all his instincts alert, trying to decide which way to throw himself to avoid the attack.

Then something whizzed through the air, and the next thing he knew there were three me al arrows jutting out of the man-scorpion's chest between its two claws. It was thrown back, barely able to stand up. Two more arrows hit it. One bounced off its shell but the other plunged into its throat.

It screamed one last time. The light in its eyes went out and it collapsed in on itself, a twitching heap of blood and poison. At last it was still.

Jamie turned round just in time to see a girl on a horse riding up to him, with three men on horseback a short way behind. All the riders were dressed similarly to Jamie and they reminded him of Bedouin tribesmen crossing the desert – except there was no sand and no sun. The girl was holding a bow already aimed at the corpse of the man-scorpion, but seeing she had no need of it, she lowered it and returned the arrow to a wooden quiver hanging behind her back. She had a belt with a short sword dangling down to her thigh, and a black wristband. There was a tattered red scarf around her neck.

A girl. She was obviously in charge. Jamie could tell that from the way the men held back, waiting for her command. And yet they were at least ten years older than her, because – Jamie was trying to take this all in one step at a time – she could only have been about fourteen or fifteen, the same age as him. She was very small with dark eyes that were somewhere between brown and green and, he would have guessed, mixed-race ... part European, part Chinese. It was quite a difficult face to work out because it was neither one thing nor another. It was also covered in grime and dirt. Her hair was black, cut short at the front, tied with another scrap of cloth at the back. She had a very slender neck. If he hadn't just seen it for himself, he wouldn't have said she'd have had the strength to fire an arrow with enough force to kill a creature at least twice her own size.

She was looking at him very strangely. She held up a hand, signalling to the three men to stay where they were, then swung herself down from the horse and walked towards him. She stopped a few feet away, gazing at him with a mixture of wonderment and disbelief.

"Sapling," she said.

Jamie waited.

"You *are* Sapling!" the girl exclaimed. She was speaking the same language as the man-scorpion and she sounded almost annoyed.

"No. I'm Jamie."

"Jamie?"

"Yes."

"No, you're not." The girl shook her head. "You're Sapling."

"I think I know my own name," Jamie said. It occurred to him that it was one of the very few things he did know.

The girl thought for a moment. Then she nodded. "Names change," she said. "It doesn't matter. All that matters is that you're alive. It really is you! I can't believe it..." And before Jamie could stop her, the girl threw her arms around him, kissed him on both cheeks and buried her face against his chest. Then, abruptly, she pushed him away and burst into tears.

"Scar..." One of the three men had climbed down from his

244

horse and came over to her. He was about thirty, a great bear of a man with a beard, a scar high up on his cheekbone and a broken nose. Standing next to her, he looked twice her size.

"Leave me alone, Finn," the girl said. She wiped her eyes with her sleeve. The tears had stopped as quickly as they had come. "So Matt was right," she went on. "Why did I have to argue with him? He told me you'd be here…"

"Who is Matt?" Jamie demanded. "Why don't you tell me what's going on? I don't know where I am. I don't get any of this. One minute I was … somewhere else. And now I'm here. Scar. Is that your name?"

The girl nodded. She looked at him again and now there was puzzlement in her eyes. "Do you really not know who I am?"

"No." But even as Jamie shook his head, he knew he was wrong. He had seen her before. It made no sense at all, but he was certain that she was the girl in his dream. Two boys in a boat. His brother, Scott. And her.

The other two men had also dismounted. They were younger than Finn, fair-haired, obviously brothers. One of them seemed to be wearing a metal glove. But then he moved his arm and Jamie realized, with a feeling of queasiness, that the entire hand was missing and had been replaced with a steel replica. All of them were staring at him. Jamie knew they were waiting for him to speak but he had nothing to say.

"My actual name is Scarlett," the girl explained. "But every-one calls me Scar. That's what you always call me."

"I'm sorry. I've just told you, I don't know you."

"Of course you know me. You've just forgotten. After everything that's happened, I'm not surprised." She stopped and examined him and suddenly she was sad again. "You know, I cried when I saw the flames. I thought it was all over. But it wasn't just that. I couldn't bear the thought that I'd never see you again."

"What flames? I don't know what you're talking about."

The man called Finn had been listening to this with growing impatience. Now he stepped forward between them. "We can't talk here," he said. He looked around him. "If there was one shape-changer, there'll be others. The fields are crawling with the enemy. We have to get back to the city before we lose the daylight."

Scar nodded. "You're right, Finn," she said. "You're always right. That's what's so annoying about you." She glanced at Jamie. "Are you hurt?" she asked.

"No." Jamie shook his head. "I don't think so."

"We have your horse."

Jamie looked past her and saw a fifth horse that had been led behind the others. It had no saddle, just a rough blanket folded in half. "I can't ride," he said.

The man with the metal hand had overheard him. "What madness is this?" he exclaimed. "Is this the boy or isn't it? Maybe this is some sort of trick."

"Be quiet, Erin," the girl snapped. "Matt sent us here and he surely knew what he was doing. Let's all hope so. Anyway,

246

we've been told what we have to do." She turned back to Jamie. "We have to travel about ten leagues," she said. "And if you don't know how to ride now, all I can say is, you will certainly have learned by the time you arrive. And since you claim not to know me, you may not know the others either. This is Finn. He's saved my life so often he has little time for anything else. And the other two are Erin Silverhand and his brother, Corian."

The two brothers nodded but Erin still didn't look convinced. Meanwhile, Corian had led Jamie's horse forward. It was a grey and from where Jamie was standing it looked enormous.

"Listen to me," Jamie said. He had already forgotten that he was speaking a language he had never learned. The words simply tumbled out naturally. "I'll come with you. It seems I don't have any choice. But there's something I want to know first. You seem to know who I am – so tell me this. Is Scott here?"

The two younger men exchanged a look but said nothing. Finn turned to Scar, once again waiting for her.

"Scott," she said. "Is that what you call your brother?"

"Yes."

"You are twins."

"Yes." Jamie was growing impatient. With every second that passed, he was becoming more confused.

"Scott is here," Scar said. "But that is not our name for him. We call him Flint. Sapling and Flint. When I first saw you

247

just now, I thought for a moment that you were him. I never was able to tell the two of you apart."

"Where is he?" For the first time in ages, Jamie felt a spurt of hope.

"Not too far. We will camp tonight in the City of Canals…"

"What city?"

"It has no other name – if it did, it would have been lost long ago." Scar glanced up at the sky. It hadn't been very bright to begin with but it was already getting darker. "We should listen to Finn. If we stay here talking, we're all going to end up with our innards on a stick. I suggest we move."

Jamie reached out and took the bridle of his horse.

"I'll help you." One of men – Corian – came up to him and cupped his hands, and while his brother held the horse steady, he hoisted Jamie up. Jamie had never sat on a horse in his life. The nearest he had been to one was at the Clark County Fair when he and Scott had been on the road. But it was exactly the same as with the sword. The moment he straightened up on the horse's back, he felt in control. He wasn't nervous. Even without knowing what to do, he thought he would probably be able to control the horse and make it move in the right direction.

But if he was pleased with himself, he was knocked back down to size a moment later. Scar sprang onto her own horse with a single movement and a look on her face that reminded him that *she* didn't need two men to help her up. Finn, Erin and Corian all mounted equally easily.

"To the city," Scar said.

The four of them set off with Jamie in the middle, just behind Scar. He had no idea where he was. He had no idea where he was going. But he was comforted by the fact that at least he was no longer alone.

IN THE RUINED CITY

Scar had said they would ride for ten leagues, but as Jamie had no idea exactly how far a league was, the journey seemed to drag on for ever.

Almost from the moment they set out, Jamie had realized that riding a horse – like everything else – had somehow been programmed into his mind. He had no difficulty getting the animal to do what he wanted: stopping, starting, turning left or right, falling back or keeping up with the others. He didn't feel even slightly nervous. He had found his balance and knew he wasn't going to fall off. It really was as if he'd been riding all his life.

Even so, he couldn't wait to arrive. He was still covered with the blood of the creature that had attacked him. He could feel it in his hair and taste it on his lips. How long had it been since he had eaten? He would have given anything for a rest, a meal and a hot shower, but it was becoming ever more apparent that he wasn't going to be offered any of them.

And then there was the landscape. How could he measure his progress when everything looked the same and it was all so bleak and miserable? There was nothing for him to aim for. They were following the track but it was barely visible, beaten down by footprints – animal and human – until it had almost disappeared into the churned-up mud and grass. They were moving steadily towards the hills that Jamie had noticed when they first set off but they never seemed to get any closer. A few clumps of ancient-looking trees broke up the countryside and now and then they came upon great chunks of granite, boulders that could have fallen there from outer space. But otherwise there were no features at all.

Jamie had no idea what time it was. His watch had been taken from him when he went into Silent Creek and it was unlikely that he would ever see it again. He looked up. The sky was getting darker but it would be difficult to tell when day became night: not when there had been no sign of the sun to begin with. He was still cold. The older of the two brothers – Corian – had seen him shivering and given him a jacket to wear. It was the same as theirs – reaching down to his knees. There were no pockets and no buttons. Jamie nodded his thanks and pulled the heavy fabric around him. He couldn't say it made a great difference.

They had been riding for about two hours and, apart from some of the trees bowing in the wind, Jamie had seen no movement at all. They had left the dead bodies behind but it seemed that there was nothing actually alive: no cows grazing in the fields, no birds even in the sky. There were a thousand questions that he wanted to ask but he knew this wasn't the time. Scar was still leading, with Finn next to her. Jamie wondered if he had disappointed her. She had come expecting to find someone who called himself Sapling and instead she had found him. And yet, at the same time, she had accepted him and taken him with her. She had said they were going to bring him to Scott, even if she knew him as Flint. Sapling and Flint. What did it all mean? He wished she had told him a little more before they set off.

The track dipped down. Now they were passing through a natural basin with a stream flowing sluggishly alongside. The water looked dirty and uninviting, but Jamie was suddenly thirsty.

"Scar…" he called out.

She twisted round on her horse. "What is it?" She didn't sound pleased.

"Can we stop for a drink?"

"The water's poisoned." She said it as if it was obvious and Jamie realized that Sapling would never have asked such a stupid question. Sapling would have known.

But next to her, Finn took pity on him. The big man had a water bottle attached to his belt and, glancing sourly at Scar, he unhooked it. "Take some of this," he said, holding it out. Jamie rode forward and took it. It was made out of animal skin.

He was just about to raise it to his lips when Finn froze. He had heard something, but his senses must have been tuned to the finest degree because as far as Jamie was concerned there were no sounds in any direction apart from the bubbling water and the faint whisper of the breeze. "Down!" he hissed. Then, to Jamie, "Don't say anything!"

Scar was already sliding down the side of her horse. She had begun moving even before Finn had spoken, showing that she was as alert as him. Finn and the two brothers followed her, pulling the horses down with them. Jamie was astonished to see that the animals had been trained to lie flat on their sides. He did the same, rolling off the horse and then tugging at the bridle to bring it down with him. The horse crumpled as if it had died. Finn stretched out and rested his hand on its flank, steadying it. All of them lay still.

Very slowly, Jamie turned his head, trying to see why all this was necessary. In front of him he saw Finn's eyes widen, warning him not to move, not to make any reaction. Nothing seemed to be moving. He could see no danger. He wondered what it was that had made them so afraid.

And then he saw it.

At first he thought he was looking at a column of smoke that might have been rising from a particularly dense bonfire, except that there was no fire and the cloud wasn't moving up but down, twisting from the sky to the surface of the earth. Then he realized what it was. A swarm. Insects of some sort ... beetles or flies. They were black and there must have been a million of them, pouring down as if tipped out of some giant glass container. At the same time he heard them buzzing as their tiny wings vibrated so fast that they were almost invisible.

What was it they wanted? What had attracted them here? A minute later, with a sense of utter horror and disbelief, he understood why Scar had needed to hide.

As the insects hit the ground, the column broke apart. For a few moments it was just a black fog. Then it re-formed and solidified. Now Jamie saw that it had taken a shape. Standing in front of him was a group of ten warriors on horseback – but the warriors and the horses were made up entirely of flies. He wondered what would happen if he took a sword to them. The blade would presumably pass right through. But what if they attacked him? Would a sword made up of flies be able to cut or would they separate again and sting him to death? He didn't want to know.

The leader of the fly-soldiers held up a hand, signalling the others to wait. He must have sensed something was wrong, that the enemy was near. His head turned slowly in their direction, his black eyes scanning the area. The other soldiers stayed where they were, shimmering a little but keeping their shape. Jamie felt his horse trembling and wondered if it was about to whinny. If so, it would kill them all. Finn stretched out his hand, stroking it, willing it to stay calm. The leader seemed to be staring right at them. Jamie wasn't even breathing. His nerves were screaming at him to get up and run away but he wouldn't have been able to move even if he had tried. Scar was lying on her stomach, her hand resting on her sword. She didn't look scared. She looked angry.

What was this place? First the man-scorpion, now this.

What sort of nightmare had he landed himself in?

And then it was as if a decision had been made. The leader kicked at his horse – a horse that was in fact a part of him, part of the swarm from which he had come – and they jolted forward. The rest of the troop followed. Jamie saw them ride for about ten paces before – at the same instant – they all came apart again, separating into their million tiny pieces and dissolving into the air. Once again they were nothing more than flies, a huge cloud of them hanging over the ground. Then they were swept away as if by the wind, and a moment later they were gone.

"Drink!" Finn nodded at Jamie, who was still holding the water bottle. He was squeezing it so hard, he was surprised it hadn't burst. He thought for a moment, then shook his head and handed it back. He was still thirsty but he doubted his ability to swallow anything. His entire body felt stretched. His heart was pounding and he had to concentrate to stop himself trembling in front of the others. Part of him knew that Sapling wouldn't have been afraid.

"The enemy is gathering for the last fight," Finn said. "The end of the war."

Scar nodded. "Will they attack tonight?"

"Who can say?" Finn thought for a moment as he clipped the water bottle back onto his belt. "They believe they have already won. They will be too busy congratulating themselves. They'll wait for the morning light."

"If we don't hurry it'll be morning before we even get

home." Scar pulled her horse up onto its feet. "Let's move."

The others allowed their own horses to stand up, then they mounted and set off once again, moving – much to Jamie's dismay – in the direction that the fly-soldiers had just taken. But by the time they reached the brow of the hill, there was no sign of them. If they were still flying over the vast landscape, there wasn't enough light left to see them.

But now there were buildings. Looking down into a valley, Jamie saw that they had come to a small town, hexagonal in shape, surrounded by walls with oddly shaped towers at the corners. It was impossible to say when the town had been built. It looked new. Most of the buildings were low-rise and there were no modern roads, no evidence of traffic or urban life. Everything seemed to have been constructed around an interlocking system of waterways with narrow footbridges leading from one side to another.

The City of Canals. But it was no city and the water had been drained out of the canals. As they rode down the hillside, Jamie realized that the place had been almost completely destroyed. The surrounding walls were breached. In places it had collapsed. There were scorch marks suggesting a recent fire. Perhaps this was the source of the smoke that had spread out across the sky, swallowing the sun.

They rode through the remains of an entrance shaped like a giant keyhole, and at once Jamie saw the scale of the devastation. Broken doorways, shattered walls, burnt grass and trees that had been reduced to stumps. The canals were full of

256

rubble. He tried to picture what this city might once have been like but it was simply beyond him. Most of the buildings had been made of red brick with roofs of terracotta tiles. The pathways had been brightly coloured, finished with mosaic. But the simple truth was that no city like this had ever existed in America and even at school, looking in picture books, he had never seen anything like it. It wasn't modern. It wasn't medieval. For the first time Jamie began to wonder if he was even on the planet Earth.

They followed a street between the remains of two matching pagodas and entered a wide empty area. Ahead of them stood a circular temple – it could surely be nothing else – with white columns placed evenly around it, supporting a dome-shaped roof. A series of arches stood at the left and the right in the square, part of a system of aqueducts. These had once brought water into the city, but now there was none left to bring. There were two fountains, one on either side of the temple, and a series of flower-beds that would have made this a pleasant place to walk. But everything had been destroyed. Some of the columns had been smashed, there were great holes in the temple roof, the fountains were dry and there were craters everywhere, suggesting that the whole place had been bombed from the air.

Scar lifted a hand, reining in her horse. The other four stopped. She turned to Jamie.

"Don't do anything," she warned him. "Don't say anything. Just play your part. It's important."

Jamie wanted to snap at her. He was worn out after the long journey. His throat was parched and he stank of his own sweat and the man-scorpion's blood. He was fed up with being pushed around. But he nodded, forcing himself to stay in control.

People had begun to appear, moving slowly towards them. At first there were just a handful of them – four or five here, another few on the other side. But as Jamie watched, more and more of them came forward, closing in from all sides. They were all dressed in the same manner with long jackets, head-dresses and leather belts, although some of the women wore wide-sleeved, embroidered gowns that came down to their feet. Many of them carried curving swords and round, pointed shields. They were every age, some as young as eleven and twelve. Soon there were more than a hundred of them, filing into the square, nobody making any sound. None of them looked even slightly welcoming. Their movements were heavy, their faces tired. It occurred to Jamie that they didn't need to prepare for battle. These people were already defeated.

But as they drew closer, an extraordinary change came over them. It was almost as if a magic wand had been waved. They had seen something and they couldn't believe it. A sense of excitement rippled through them. Jamie saw it in their faces. With every step they seemed to find new strength. They were gazing at something with a sense of shock and wonder, and now they were smiling. Some of them were raising their hands in salute. And then Jamie realized what they had seen.

Him.

Scar pulled herself up to her full height. "Do you believe me now?" she called out. "We told you the truth. He's here. We found him."

"Sapling!" someone shouted.

And at that, the entire crowd began to cheer. Swords were raised and banners appeared as if out of nowhere, the blue five-pointed stars fluttering as they were waved above their heads. All of the people were hurrying forward, wanting to be the first to reach him, the children at the front, the adults looking up at him with new hope alive in their eyes. At that moment, Jamie was grateful to Scar. He had no idea what was going on but she had warned him what he had to do. Play the part. Explanations would come later. He raised a hand, acknowledging the crowd, and the cheers grew louder, bouncing off the remaining walls so that it almost seemed as if the city had come alive once again, as if some of its old joy had returned to the streets.

Scar kicked her horse and they jolted slowly forward, the crowd parting – but only reluctantly – to let them pass. They dismounted at the circular temple and went in. The cheering crowd followed them as far as the columns but stopped here as if this was a line they were not allowed to cross. Jamie and his four companions were on their own once again, but he could still hear the people out in the square, calling out one name – his name – Sapling, their voices rising into the rapidly darkening sky.

"All I've ever known is war," Scar said.

They had lit a fire. There was plenty of wood to salvage in the ruined city and Finn, Erin and Corian had piled it up so that it looked almost like a funeral pyre. Jamie was afraid that it might attract the enemy. Perhaps the fly-soldiers might return. But Scar had assured him that they were safe. The outer walls would hide most of the light and the sky was dark enough to hide the smoke as it trickled out through a hole in the roof.

There was nothing inside the temple. They were in a round space – it reminded Jamie of a circus – protected by brick walls that rose up about fifteen metres all around them. There had been frescoes once: strange symbols and pictures of animals and birds. But they had worn away. Or perhaps they had been purposely erased.

Jamie had at last been able to wash – using water drawn from a well. Nobody had offered him any privacy and he had been reluctant to undress, especially with Scar around. Fortunately, she had disappeared for a time and none of the men had so much as glanced in his direction. The water was muddy before he even got in it, but even so he had been grateful for it, washing away the grime and the blood that covered him. There were no towels. He had pulled on his trousers and dried himself in front of the flames.

After that, he had been fed. Corian had cooked some sort of meat over the fire. It tasted like chicken but it was tougher, harder to chew. Jamie had no idea what it was and decided it might be better not to ask. It had been served with beans and solid slabs of bread. He had been given a bowl of steaming liquid to drink. It tasted bitter and sweet at the same time and Scar – who had returned in time for the meal – had told him that it was made with acorns and honey. Jamie was glad to have it. Just holding something warm between his hands made him feel better.

And now they were talking. The two brothers were resting against a wall, leaning against each other, shoulder to shoulder, with their legs stretched out in front of them. Finn was squatting on a broken piece of column, gnawing at a bone, his fingers covered in grease. Scar and Jamie were sitting cross-legged in front of the fire. As Scar spoke, Jamie could see the fire's reflection dancing in her eyes.

"Finn has often told me that the world wasn't always like this," she said. "A long time ago there were no shape-changers and death squads and overlords and fire riders and all the rest of them. But this is all I've ever known, so don't ask me for a history lesson. I never met my mother or my father. By the time I was born, most people never knew their parents. All I can remember is being carried around by different people. Someone would take me with them and just when I was getting to know them and think that they were kind, they'd be killed and someone else would take their place. And everything was always ruined, like this city. I don't think I ever spent more than a few days in a house before it was broken to pieces or burned down." She raised her bowl in mockery of a toast. "Welcome to the end of the world, Jamie. Because that's where you are."

"You called me Jamie." Jamie wasn't sure where to begin. It was all too much to take in. "But before you said I was Sapling." He glanced in the direction of the main square. "They called me Sapling."

"There is no point calling you Sapling," Scar replied. "Because you're not him, even if you do look exactly like him and all those people think you *are* him." She gestured in the direction of the square. "I imagine you're confused."

"You could say that."

"Well, so am I. I just hope Matt will explain it all eventually, although he can be very annoying at times and never gives you a straight answer to anything."

"You mentioned Matt before," Jamie said. "Who is he?"

"Matt's the one in charge. He's our leader. The first of the Five. He's the one who's supposed to understand what's going on."

The Five. When he was at the prison, Joe Feather had said he was one of the Five. Had Joe known something about this world and the events that had taken place here?

"Tell me about Matt," Jamie said. He pictured someone like Finn; grey-haired and battle-scarred. "Is he old?"

Scar laughed. "No. He's the same age as us. Do you really not know who we are? You and Flint and me and Inti and Matt?"

262

"Flint is my twin."

"Yes."

"Then he's Scott. I was looking for him when I was shot. That's how I ended up here." It still made no sense to Jamie, even as he tried to explain it. Then he remembered. "I have seen you before," he said. "But it wasn't real. It was in a dream."

He thought Scar would laugh at him, but she nodded, perfectly serious. "People used to think that dreams didn't mean anything," she said. "That they were just things that happened when you went to sleep. But we use them all the time. There's a dream world that we visit sometimes and that's how we found out who we were. That's how we found each other in the first place."

"You should start at the beginning," Finn called out. He had finished his food. He threw the bone onto the fire. The flames devoured it as if they were as hungry as he had been. "You're a rotten storyteller."

"There was no beginning for me," Scar retorted. "Or if there was, I don't remember it. Matt's the only one who knows the whole truth and he never tells us anything."

"Start with the Five!" Finn insisted.

"All right. All right." Scar sighed. "But don't interrupt me, Finn. You only make it more difficult."

"Adults taking second place to children!" Finn shook his head in despair. "That's what I *really* call the end of the world." He fell silent.

263

Scar turned to Jamie. "I've only been alive for about fifteen years," she said. "And this war has continued for more than fifty. So that's why I say that, for me, there's never been a beginning. I wasn't even in this country. I was far away, on the other side of the world, and when I was about nine years old, the village where I was living was burned down. All the old people were killed. The children were sent to the mines."

"Wait a minute." Jamie was already lost. "This world you live in … is this my world? What year is it? I don't even know where I am!"

"And I don't know where you've come from so I can't help you. You're just going to have to listen to my story. If you keep interrupting, we're not going to get anywhere."

Jamie sighed. "Go on."

"We were digging for precious stones. There were thousands of us … working deep underground. They used the children to burrow into the smaller tunnels. It was terrifying. There were cave-ins. We were always wondering when we were going to be buried alive."

"Who made you do it? Who were you working for?"

"We were working for the ruling classes. The overlords and the advisors. And behind them, of course, the Old Ones."

"Who are they?" Jamie remembered the old man talking to him before he had turned into a scorpion. He had asked if Jamie served the Old Ones.

"They're the enemy," Scar replied simply. "Matt says that

264

they are the first and the greatest evil, that they were born the day the world began. They want to destroy us. That's the only reason they exist. But they want to do it slowly, one step at a time. You see, they feed on human misery. It's what nourishes them. In the end, they'll kill all of us, but they'll make it last as long as they can."

"Where did they come from?" Jamie asked.

"I don't know," Scar replied. "You'll have to ask Matt."

Erin had fallen asleep, leaning against his brother. His long fair hair had fallen across his face and his metal hand was stretched out in front of him, the fingers curled and pointing up. Corian was lying still, careful not to wake him, listening to Scar tell her tale.

"I suppose it must have been about a year ago," she went on. "I don't know because time doesn't really mean very much any more. When you're a slave, being beaten and forced to work in the darkness, every day is the same. Anyway, about a year ago I found out that I was different. I was told that I was one of the Five."

"Matt told you?"

Scarlet nodded. "Yes. Well, he came to me in a dream. Or maybe I went to him. It's very difficult to explain. But you say you've had dreams too. You must know what I'm talking about."

"I think so." Jamie thought back. "There's a sea with black water. And the stars are shining but it's not exactly night…"

"There's an island."

"Yes." Jamie was excited. She knew what he was talking about. "And two boys in a straw boat."

"Matt and Inti." She looked at him curiously. "Have you been to the library?"

The question was so unexpected that Jamie was taken aback. "What library?" he asked.

"In the dream world."

"No. I never saw any buildings."

"Forget it." Scar had lost her train of thought. She gazed into the fire as if she might find it there, then went on. "Anyway, that's how I first met Matt. He came to me in a dream and he explained everything to me. There were five of us in different countries. He was here. I was where I was. You and Flint were on the other side of the world and Inti … I don't know where he came from and neither does he. But the point was, we'd all been chosen. We all had these powers and if we could just find each other and come together, we'd have the strength to beat the Old Ones and give the world a new start."

It hadn't occurred to Jamie that he might still have his power, that it might have returned to him after the shock at Silent Creek. Could he use it now? Could he reach out to Scott? He decided not to try. In this world, Scott was someone called Flint. He didn't want to reach him yet. He was afraid of what he might find.

"There were people fighting already," Scar went on. "People like Finn and Erin and Corian and all the others. There

266

were resistance groups. But they needed us. It's funny, isn't it, but it's like Finn said. They were all adults but they needed five children if they were going to survive. And we needed each other. So we set out to find each other. And that's how we got here."

"You're not making any sense!" Finn taunted her.

"I'm doing the best I can!" Scar snapped back.

She turned to Jamie. "Matt told me I had to escape from the mine, so I did. It was very close. I nearly got caught. But it's a long story and I'm not going to tell it tonight. All you need to know is that I got away. And at the same time, the others were doing the same thing. Flint and Sapling in one kingdom. Inti in another. We were all leagues away from each other. We'd never met. We hadn't even known that the others existed. But we used the dreams to speak with each other and Matt told us where to go and eventually four of us met close to a river not far from here, on the other side of the hills. Matt is waiting for us there now. Flint is with him."

"Where's the boy you call Inti?"

"He's not there yet. He had the furthest to travel. But he should arrive with the break of day."

"And then...?" Jamie asked the question but he already knew the answer. There was a queasy feeling in his stomach.

"There will be a battle. It's been predicted for ages. If the five of us can reach one another, we will win. If we can't, the world will come to an end."

She reached out and Finn threw her a water bottle. In that single movement, Jamie saw how well the two of them knew each other. She hadn't asked. He had known what she wanted. She hadn't looked round. Yet she knew he would have it ready for her.

"How did you find me?" Jamie asked. "The fortress or whatever it was. You came there ... and it was like you were expecting me."

"We weren't expecting you," Scar replied.

"Then why were you there?"

She took a long drink, then used the back of her hand to wipe her mouth. When she continued talking, her voice was low.

"It's because of what happened two days ago," she said.

"Tell me!"

"It was Matt." She paused. "I've already explained to you. We had to meet, the five of us, to win. And we were so close ... but there was a problem. The Old Ones knew that Inti was coming and they positioned their entire army between him and us. They were searching for him everywhere. You saw the fly-soldiers today. Well, there were hundreds more like them as well as shape-changers and fire riders. Inti was pinned down. He had to hide. He didn't dare move any nearer."

"How did Matt know?"

"Matt always knows! And two nights ago he called a meeting between the four of us. He said there was only one way to help Inti and that was to send out a small force to a place

268

called Scathack Hill. There was a fortress there and he said that we'd find something that would help us in the fight against the Old Ones. Of course, Finn offered to go. There isn't a single soldier who wouldn't gladly volunteer to do anything Matt wants. But he said it had to be one of us. One of the Five."

Scar paused a second time and when she began speaking again, Jamie was astonished to see that there were tears in her eyes.

"We believed him," she said. "Why shouldn't we? He had always been right before. But even so, it seemed crazy – when finally there were four of us there – to separate once again. But he insisted. He wouldn't let me go. It had to be either Sapling or Flint. He took them into his tent and spoke to them, and an hour later, Sapling came out, got onto his horse and rode off. A hundred men went with him. He didn't say anything to me, but I saw his face and I'll never forget his look. It was as if he knew what was going to happen. And none of the soldiers asked any questions. He ordered and they followed."

Her voice cracked.

"You know what happened next," she said. "Scathack Hill was where we found you. The Old Ones must have known about the expedition because they sent a huge force in pursuit. You saw the result. The moment Sapling arrived, they surrounded him and closed in. The battle lasted almost an entire day. Sapling was incredibly brave. But he was hopelessly outnumbered with nowhere to go. His soldiers died all around him ... all but two of them. The Old Ones let them live, not out of mercy, but so they could come back and tell the rest of us. Sapling was left almost to the end. He was badly wounded, but he kept fighting and the last time they saw him he was leading a charge, trying to break out, to get back to us.

"They cut him down. He took three arrows in his chest but he still kept fighting. But then the enemy soldiers closed in and hacked him to pieces, laughing as they did it. Even when he was dead they wouldn't leave him alone. Some of them cut off fingers for souvenirs. He had long black hair and they cut that off too. Then they built a fire and burnt the rest and sent just two men back to tell us what had happened."

"So it was all over." Jamie whispered the words.

"That's what we thought. Inti was still surrounded – but even if he did manage to reach us, it wouldn't matter. There never would be five of us. He was too late."

"But what was at Scathack Hill?" Jamie asked. "What was so important in the first place?"

"There was nothing there." Scar's voice was cold. "The two men told us that. Matt had been wrong from the start. The fortress was empty and abandoned. Sapling had died for nothing."

Scar fell silent. She'd had enough.

"Finish the story," Finn murmured. He reached out and touched her gently on the arm. "The boy needs to know. The next part matters too."

Scar nodded slowly.

"I never wanted to see Matt again," she said. "I thought he'd betrayed us. I thought he'd brought us all this way for nothing. To be honest, I hated him. I hated him almost as much as the Old Ones. But then, last night, he came to me – and what he said to me … I wanted to scream at him. But you don't scream at Matt. When you meet him, you'll understand.

"He told me to take part of the army and ride to the ruined city where we are now – but after that I was to go on alone to Scathack Hill, just with Finn, Erin and Corian. He said it was still important to bring back what I found there and, even though he knew I was angry about what had happened to Sapling, I'd understand why he'd died." Scar frowned. "At first I didn't believe him. I hated him and I didn't even want to listen. But Finn persuaded me and so we set off. We left everyone here and went on alone. And when we got to Scathack Hill, we found you. That's why I cried when I saw you. I thought you were Sapling."

"Maybe he is," Finn growled.

"Are you?" Scar turned to Jamie. She was almost pleading with him. "Because we need you to be. Tomorrow we fight the Old Ones for the last time. They're waiting for us, less than half a league from where we're sitting now. We need you to be one of us."

Jamie tried to collect his thoughts.

"I'm Jamie," he said. Suddenly, he was tired. "I'm sorry," he went on. "I wish I could be the person you want me to be, but I don't think I am."

"Then it's over," Scar replied. "Sapling is dead and the Old Ones have won."

She got up and walked off into the dark.

FROST

Jamie woke slowly the next morning and, before he had even opened his eyes, he sent out his thoughts, searching for his brother. It was instinctive, something he did automatically. He knew there would be no reply.

Scott. Where are you…?

But this time it was different.

Here!

The single word came back, very faint, from somewhere far away. Jamie sat bolt upright, fully awake in an instant. That was when he saw where he was. He was lying on the temple floor, dressed in the clothes he had worn the day before and wrapped in the same blanket that he had used as a saddle. One side of his body was numb and there was a crick in his neck. In fact most of his bones were aching; he was surprised he'd managed to sleep at all. He groaned quietly and raised himself up on an elbow. Erin was on the other side of the temple, relighting the fire, stirring the embers with his metal hand.

Had it been Scott who had replied? Jamie tried again, visualizing his brother.

Scott, are you there…?

But this time there was silence and Jamie wondered if he hadn't simply imagined his brother's voice while he was still half asleep. Scott wasn't here. As far as these people were concerned, Scott didn't even exist. Jamie looked around. Nobody had noticed that he had woken up. Erin was lifting a pot of water onto the flames. Corian was sitting near by, sharpening his sword between two stones. There was no sign of Scar or Finn.

So what had happened? How had he got here? Still lying on the hard ground, Jamie went back over everything that had happened, trying to make sense of it. All he knew for certain was that he had arrived at the end of a long war between mankind and creatures who called themselves the Old Ones. And the hopes of all humanity rested on five teenagers. Matt was their leader. Then there was Scar and a boy called Inti, who was near but who had yet to arrive. And finally two brothers … twins. Flint and Sapling.

That was the most difficult part. As far as everyone was concerned, Jamie *was* Sapling. And that meant he was expected to fight in the battle that was going to begin just a few hours from now. The thought of it made him tremble. He didn't know anything about swords or arrows. And now here he was in the middle of a war of his own and he was hopelessly out of his depth.

And yet…

That wasn't quite true. Only the day before he had

snatched up a sword from a dead soldier and fought hand-to-hand with a creature twice his size. He had known exactly what to do – and he had won. Admittedly Scar had arrived in time to finish off the man-scorpion, but only after Jamie had cut off its tail and stabbed it almost to the heart. And that wasn't the only thing. Although he had never sat on a horse in his life, he had ridden many miles, trotting, cantering, even galloping. And right now he wasn't even stiff. It was as if his body was used to spending long hours in the saddle.

What did it mean?

He wasn't Sapling. He was Jamie Tyler. But Sapling seemed to be part of him. The two of them were the same age. They looked the same and had the same skills, even if they had been born thousands of miles and perhaps thousands of years apart.

There was a movement at the entrance to the temple and Finn appeared, carrying a water bottle. He came over and handed it to Jamie.

"You're awake," Finn said. "Did you have any dreams?"

"I was too tired for dreams." Jamie sat up, took the water bottle and drank. "Where does the water come from if the rivers are poisoned?" he asked.

"We have wells, but they have to go deep."

Jamie was aware that Finn was examining him. In his own way, Finn was as beaten about as the city in which they had spent the night. His hair had turned grey too soon. The scar on his cheekbone had been left by a wound that had cut deep.

His eyes, soft grey and watchful, had seen too much pain.

Jamie handed back the water bottle. "Thank you," he said.

"Sapling…"

"I'm not him." Jamie shook his head. "I know you want me to be. I know he was your friend. But I'm not."

"Maybe not," Finn said. "But today you have to be."

"Then tell me about him. And tell me about Scar. How did the two of you meet?"

Finn sat down next to Jamie. There was obviously some sort of activity going on outside. Jamie could hear the clatter of hooves, the occasional whinny. The army was assembling in the main square just outside the temple. They were preparing themselves for the last march to war. But for the moment Finn seemed content to let them get ready on their own.

"I met Scar four seasons ago," he began. "Before the snow arrived. I had travelled far and I was resting with my back against a wall, wondering what to do next. There was a door in a wall and it opened and she appeared … just like that. She was lucky in a way. If my sword had been in my hand I might have killed her before I realized who she was, but I'd been careless and left it with the horse. She told me her name, but I didn't ask her where she had come from even though – and this is the strange thing – the door in the wall didn't lead anywhere. It was just a ruined wall. She knew where she was going. That was all that mattered. And I decided to go with her.

"She and I travelled together for a while and I looked after her. She was different then from how she is today. She was more scared – though it would be best not to tell her I said so. She said she was searching for someone called Matt, a boy she had seen in her dreams. I thought she was mad. But then we found him – or he found us – and suddenly I saw it was all true."

"And Sapling...?"

"I can't help you there. It's all beyond my understanding. You look like him. You sound like him. And if I didn't know for certain that he had been killed and his body burned, I'd say you *were* him."

"What year is this?"

Finn shrugged. "It's the year after the one before. I've heard it said there were numbers once but that was long ago and they've all been forgotten."

"The Old Ones..."

"That's right. They've made life miserable and painful but at least they've made it short." Finn thought for a moment, then got to his feet. "Come with me," he said. "I have something to show you."

Jamie rolled himself out of his blanket and followed Finn across the floor to the far wall, where there was a doorway he hadn't noticed before. It led into a small circular room with a ceiling that was vaulted and painted blue with gold stars. The walls had once been painted too but now there was nothing left, any images scratched out of existence.

Scar was there, kneeling in front of a stone slab that might once have been an altar, cradling across her thighs a parcel wrapped in cloth. Hearing Finn, she got up and turned round. She looked at him almost accusingly.

"What are you doing here, Finn?" she demanded.

"And good day to you, Scar," Finn replied.

"I was asleep."

"No you weren't." Finn glanced at the bundle she was holding. "I knew you'd be here," he said. "Give it to me."

"Why?"

"I want to prove a point."

Scar hesitated, then handed the bundle to him. Carefully, Finn unwrapped the cloth and took out a round shield made of dark and beaten metal with an intricate pattern of leaves around the side. It had no spike. Instead, there was a design right in the middle and Jamie gasped with surprise. He recognized it instantly. A spiral with a single straight line dividing it in two halves. It was exactly the same design that he'd been born with.

He was sure this was what Finn had wanted to show him. But Finn laid the shield aside.

Instead, he took out a sword and handed it to Jamie. The sword had a symbol too – a five-pointed star in the middle of the crosspiece, just above the blade. Jamie saw that it had been made out of some blue stone – lapis lazuli – set in silver. The blade was surprisingly thin and weighed almost nothing. He wouldn't have thought it could cut through anything, but at the same time he could see that it had been sharpened with amazing precision, like a surgical instrument. He swung it a couple of times and felt the very air being cut in half.

"It was his," Jamie said.

"Yes." Finn's gaze held his eyes. "Now tell me what is written on the blade. Don't read the words. Just tell me."

Standing next to the altar, Scar stiffened. But she said nothing.

"Frost," Jamie muttered.

"You see?" Finn was talking to Scar. "He knew."

Jamie looked down. There was a single word inscribed on the blade. The letters were foreign – like Hebrew or Greek – and should have meant nothing to him. But he understood them instantly.

FROST.

"It is the name of the sword," Finn told him. "Sapling called it that because although it is cold, it brings with it the first light of day. That was his hope for it. And he carried it with him to Scathack Hill. We found it moments before we came upon you. He must have lost it in the fight. But now do you see?" He glanced at Scar. "Don't you see, both of you? There's something happening – some sort of magic – and maybe none of us understands it. But this boy is Sapling, there's no doubt of it, even if he has forgotten." He looked away, suddenly gruff again. "Let's just hope he hasn't forgotten how to fight."

* * *

279

A few moments later, the five of them walked out onto the main square: Scar and Jamie first, then Erin and Corian with Finn behind. All of them were armed for battle with swords, daggers and shields. Jamie glanced at Erin and saw him touch the palm of his artificial hand. At once five blades sprang out of his fingers and thumb. At the same time, his left hand curled around a curved dagger that he had slipped into a belt around his waist.

Their army had assembled: a hundred men, women and children, waiting quietly for the order that would bring them to victory or death. Scar stepped forward. She also carried a shield with the same pattern of leaves as Sapling's but hers had the image of a lizard – with slanting eyes and a spiky tail – curled around the centre. Three steps separated her from the crowd outside the temple. She walked to the very edge and lifted her sword. Jamie wondered if he should do the same but felt too awkward and shy. He realized that everyone's eyes were on her. But they were watching him too.

"This is the day that we have been waiting for," she called out and, although she was young and small, her voice echoed easily across the square. "I cannot say what happened to the world to make it the way it is. I do not know where the Old Ones came from or how they were allowed to take control. All I can tell you is that it's over. After today, the world will belong once again to us and even if some of us must die, it will have been worth it. Matt and Flint are waiting for us. Inti will be riding in from the east. I am here and I am not alone. Sapling is with me. Yes! Sapling was not killed."

The beginnings of a cheer broke out among the soldiers closest to the front, but Scar raised a hand for silence.

"The Five are coming together at last!" she exclaimed. "The Old Ones thought they'd beaten us, but they were wrong. And now we're going to show them. We're going to show them the power of Five."

"Five!" The single word blasted out all around. Banners flew, swords were raised and from somewhere came the thunder of drums and a great fanfare. Jamie looked up and saw the musicians, three small boys, none of them older than ten, perched high up on one of the aqueducts. Their horns glittered in the daylight as they saluted the crowd below. Scar's horse had been led forward and she leapt onto it. The grey horse had been brought out for Jamie and he did the same. This time he didn't need help. A moment later, they were riding forward with Finn, Erin and Corian, leading their cheering army between the two pagodas and along the mosaic path that led to the city walls. There were people riding singly, others two to a horse. A few ran behind. With so many of them, it took several minutes simply to pass through the gate.

As they left the city and emerged onto the plain, Jamie turned to Scar. "That was quite a speech," he said.

"You have to make a speech before a battle," Scar said. She looked down guiltily, then back up again. "Actually, if you must know, Finn wrote it for me. He made me learn it last night."

"Well, I think it worked."

"I hope so."

They were circling the City of Canals, travelling in the opposite direction to Scathack Hill. Ahead of them the landscape was flat and open, a table top covered with wild grass and a few flowers. But the flowers were strange, unnatural colours and the grass was sharp and leathery. They rode under the branches of a fruit tree and Jamie reached up to pick what looked like a mauve-coloured peach but with a hard prickly skin. Scar stopped him. "Don't!" she called out. "It's poisonous."

They continued into the fields and for the first time Jamie saw animals – or their remains. A herd of cows had died here. They were lying, bloated and stiff, their tongues lolling out, their eye sockets buzzing with black flies. As he rode past, Jamie smelled the sweet decaying flesh and felt his stomach churn. He was glad he hadn't been offered breakfast.

Ahead of them, less than a mile away, the ground rose up, covered by a wood. The trees looked like pines, with branches that were so straight they could have been artificial. They had dark green needles like splinters of broken glass. Jamie could hear something now, a strange unnerving sound. It was a rhythmic hammering of metal against metal. Boom, boom … *boom*. Boom, boom … *boom*. Each time, the third beat was the loudest. It was as if there was some kind of huge machine still out of sight on the other side of the hill.

Scar was moving ahead of him so Jamie urged his own horse on. He didn't need to kick it or snap with the reins.

282

Somehow, the horse seemed to understand him. He jolted forward and caught up. They reached the first of the trees and began to weave their way through the trunks, climbing steeply towards the top of the hill. Jamie felt a growing nervousness in the pit of his stomach. Just a few weeks ago he had been walking onto the stage at the Reno Playhouse to perform a magic act with newspapers and playing cards. And here he was now, riding to war.

He should have been terrified. He should have been hollowed out by the horror of it all. But the strange thing was that he felt nothing but a sense of elation. They were still scrambling up the slope, surrounded by the soaring, hostile trees and he knew that there could be no going back. This was it. The drumbeat was still calling to him. Boom, boom … *boom*. Boom, boom … *boom*. And he was being carried forward willingly with the soft thunder of hooves all around and the smell of the horses' sweat in his nostrils. He had discovered the secret of war, the moment when soldiers cast aside their fear and become part of a machine that is so much bigger than themselves. For only then are they prepared to die.

They were moving faster and faster. As they arrived at the last reaches of the hill, the trees thinned out and they broke into a gallop. But then Scar raised a hand and they slowed down to a stop. They had arrived. The fighters who had hitched a lift with the riders were dismounting and preparing their weapons. The wagons were emptying and Jamie saw children as young as eleven and twelve flexing their bows, their faces set in grim concentration.

"How are you feeling?" Scar asked.

It took Jamie a moment to realize that she was talking to him. He nodded. "I'm all right."

"It'll be over very quickly," she said.

"How do you know?"

"Matt has a plan."

"Do you know what it is?"

Scar smiled. "He told me last night."

To his surprise, Jamie felt a little annoyed. Matt must have spoken to Scar in her dreams. Why had he been excluded? But there was no point in arguing about it now. "Are you scared?" he asked.

Scar shook her head. "Not really. What's the worst that can happen?"

Jamie could think of all sorts of things but decided not to answer.

Scar looked behind her. The rest of her forces had finally assembled and were looking upwards, awaiting her command. Finn was leaning forward on his horse as if he were listening for something. He looked even older than he had that morning and Jamie saw that he was close to exhaustion. Not just tired after a bad night's sleep but worn out from years of fighting. "Finn is scared," Scar muttered, making sure that Finn couldn't hear her. "He's trying not to show it but he always is. He's scared for me."

"You mean a lot to him."

"I suppose so. I'm the daughter he never had, although he tells me he has four sons." She turned to Jamie. "I've been hard on you and I'm sorry. I'll try to be kinder if either of us survives."

Jamie didn't know what to say, but it didn't matter because Scar didn't give him a chance. She signalled, and at once they began to move forward, covering the last few yards to the top of the hill. They were very quiet now. Jamie could just hear the horses' hooves as they padded through the carpet of dead needles but otherwise the animals made no sound. The rest of the attackers, tiptoeing with their weapons and shields, barely seemed to breathe. At the very top, a last line of trees provided shelter. Once again they stopped and at last Jamie saw what was awaiting him on the other side.

The battleground.

It was like nothing he had ever seen before. It was more terrible than anything he could have imagined.

He was standing above a strip of very dark, almost black grass about a quarter of a mile wide that flowed like a river between the hills on one side and a dense forest on the other. Below and in front of him, the last great army of humanity had been assembled, two thousand strong, united under the blue five-pointed star that he himself carried on his sword. It was on their banners and on their shields. It flew from the tents which slanted out of the bottom of the hill, tall and triangular, like the sails of a ship caught in the breeze. Had there been more light it would have shone out, but the sky was grey and threatening and the shadow of imminent death stretched across the entire scene.

The army was advancing in three blocks – a central phalanx and two wings – each one made up of so many people that, for Jamie high up on the hill, it was impossible to separate them. The horsemen were at the front, hundreds of them, leading the charge. Then came the foot soldiers. Behind them a long line of men stood waiting, each one holding onto what looked like a length of copper pipe almost the same height as themselves. Then came the archers and finally, just in front of the tents, a row of cannons with two soldiers kneeling beside each. Jamie was puzzled by the variety of weapons, for they seemed to belong to different times and different continents. But he realized that there was nothing uniform about the people either. They had assembled here having travelled from all over the world.

Two boys were preparing to lead them into battle. Jamie saw them, at the very front, both of them riding on dapple-grey horses. He didn't need to be told who they were. They were only fourteen years old and they commanded all these men; they had brought them here. Their strategy would either win or lose the day. Jamie couldn't see their faces. They were riding with their backs to him. But he knew he was looking at Matt and Flint and he wished that they would turn round, if only for a moment. He wanted to look at their faces. He wanted to see his brother, Scott.

But the two of them were continuing forward, and it was only when he looked past them and across to the other side of the field that Jamie understood the full horror of what they were about to face. The army of the blue star was hopelessly outnumbered. It was facing certain death. For every one of them, there were ten of the enemy. Human and non-human, they went on for as far as the eye could see. Sometimes it was hard for Jamie to work out which was which.

In the front line were the most wretched of all, the human slaves who had put their trust in the Old Ones and stayed with them to the bitter end. This was their reward. They had all been chained together, either naked or covered with a last few rags, their names branded into their flesh as if they were cattle. They had been given wooden clubs and axes with which to defend themselves. Many of them had been disfigured, missing eyes or ears. Even worse than that, some of them had had the lower part of their arms cut off and replaced with jagged blades so that they and their weapons were one.

Behind them were more humans: surely the ruling classes. These were the people who Scar had referred to as overlords and advisors. They had swords and shields and – some of them, at least – odd pieces of armour. They were pale and sickly, for although they had been happy enough in their positions of power, they had no stomach for the fight. Even from a distance the fear and cowardice could be seen in their faces.

Then came four lines of horsemen – Jamie could only think of them as knights, encased in black armour. The first two were identical to the fly-soldiers he had seen on the way to the City of Canals. But there were two more lines behind them and these were so ugly and grotesque that Jamie could barely bring himself to look at them.

Perhaps they were the officers. Perhaps they were human beneath the armour. It was impossible to know. They had blades jutting out of their shoulders, their elbows and their knees. Their helmets were also surrounded by vicious black spikes so that, from the neck up, they were like porcupines. Their horses had been mutilated with silver bayonets jutting out of their foreheads, screwed into place just above their eyes, turning each of them into a grotesque version of a unicorn. The knights were standing rigidly to attention. How many of them were there? It was impossible to say. Each was the same height as his neighbour. In fact, they could have been the same man, replicated a thousand times. They were holding shields – also surrounded by spikes – and striking them rhythmically with the flats of their swords. That was the booming that Jamie had heard. Seeing them now and hearing the sound froze his blood.

The worst was still to come.

It was an infestation. Jamie couldn't think of another word for it as it bled out of the forest, pouring into the field. Jamie had thought this would be a fight between two armies, but what he was seeing now was a horde with no shape or formation, just an oozing mess of nightmarish creatures desperate for the kill. They carried clubs studded with nails, huge axes, spears, nets and pitchforks. Some slithered. Some scuttled forward on three legs or more. They were half man, half animal, as if the two had been mixed up on purpose, to see what could produce the most hideous result. Some were part scorpion, like the creature that had attacked Jamie at Scathack Hill. But there were also man-dogs, man-crocodiles, man-eagles and even man-sharks, a crazy mixture of arms and teeth and beaks and scales and feathers and claws, all brought together to create unimaginable monsters.

And finally there were giant animals passing through the forest, high above the trees, looming up behind the army yet not quite part of it.

The first was a spider. It was about twenty metres high, standing on eight elongated legs, with a fat poison sac hanging beneath its stomach. It had two feelers that twitched in front of it as if testing the air, and great fangs dripping venom and saliva. As it turned its head, Jamie saw the army reflected many times in the glistening black mirrors that were its eyes. Once it attacked, it would be invincible. Swords and arrows would be useless against it. They might as well fight it with pins and needles.

A huge monkey had appeared next to it, jabbering and screaming with a hideous, high-pitched voice. It wasn't muscular like an ape but almost insect-like, with a long tail and filthy, matted hair. It had only four fingers on one of its hands. As it stood there, the trees suddenly parted and a gigantic hummingbird burst into the air, its wings beating so fast they were just a blur. The bird was creating a storm around itself, whipping up dust and dead branches. A moment later another bird appeared, soaring up into the sky. This one was a condor the size of a plane. It flew overhead, its own wings thundering as they made the air shudder and vibrate.

And then, just when he thought he couldn't take any more, Jamie saw a single figure making his way through the middle of his army, advancing to take his place at the front. This was the commander … it had to be. He was riding on an animal that at first glance looked like a horse, but which had horns, burning red eyes and steam rising like smoke from its mouth and nostrils. Thirteen more riders surrounded him but he seemed not to notice them. His eyes were fixed on the two boys directly ahead.

"Chaos," Scar whispered.

"What?" Jamie couldn't move. He could barely breathe.

"He has no name. But that's what we call him. He is the King of the Old Ones."

Jamie had to look at him twice. Once to see him. Once to understand what he was seeing.

He was human-sized, but he seemed bigger. He seemed to swallow up everything around him like a black hole in outer space. Jamie knew that he was looking at pure evil and that there was nothing more empty or more destructive in the universe. Chaos had no face. No features of any sort. With his every movement, he destroyed the area around him. He didn't just move. Without even trying, he cut his way through the world.

Jamie had no idea how long he had been standing on the hill. He felt rooted there. Time seemed to have stopped.

The two opposing armies faced each other. Just for a moment, everything was still. The knights stopped beating their shields and silence – somehow shocking – fell onto the battleground. There was a soft breeze. The grass bent and the banners fluttered. Somewhere, a horse snorted. There were about thirty metres between Matt and Flint and the forces they had come to fight.

Chaos had reached the front. He took out his sword. Jamie heard the metal grinding as it came out of its sheath. A moment later, he spoke – but he did so without opening his mouth. The sound seemed to come from him like water rushing out of a pipe, and although he had not raised his voice above a whisper, it echoed across the battlefield and reached them high up on the hill.

"The power of the Five has been defeated," he said. "One of you is trapped far from here and one of you has been killed. He died painfully. And now, you cannot win. Lay down your arms and I will be generous. I will give you a quick death. The rest of you I will allow to serve me. There is no need for this battle. You know it has already been won."

Matt said nothing. Jamie saw him reach down and draw his sword. That was his answer.

The King of the Old Ones nodded slowly. He said nothing more. Suddenly he raised his weapon, lifting it above his head. It was the signal. At once there was an explosion of screaming, cheering, laughing, shouting. A thunder of hooves. A crash that might have been thunder.

The black army surged forward.

The battle had begun.

THE FIRST CIRCLE

All too quickly, the killing started.

The army of the Old Ones came like a tidal wave rising up from a black and boiling sea. The slaves in the front line were the first to move, rushing forward with their axes and clubs as if they couldn't wait for their own, inevitable deaths. Behind them the knights marched, one pace at a time, relentless, swords raised. The heads of the unicorn horses were writhing as if in pain, the metal horns stabbing at anyone who came close. Then came the man-creatures, tumbling across the field, lashing out with claws and teeth. And finally there were the monster animals. To Jamie, watching from the hilltop, they looked unstoppable. They were so huge, surely they would have been able to win this battle on their own.

The giant monkey had leapt forward into the middle of the opposing ranks. In the next few seconds, dozens of men and women were thrown aside as it swatted them with its paws, dashing them to pieces. Horses reared in terror, throwing their riders. Metal clashed against metal and in an instant the grass was splattered with blood as the first casualties fell. Jamie

293

looked for Matt and Flint but already they had disappeared, folded into the confusion. For what had a few moments ago looked like a neat map, the forces lined up with mathematical precision, had now become a sprawling hideous mess.

Matt's forces had begun to fight back.

The archers, positioned behind the main body of the troops, fired one volley after another, the sky darkening as hundreds of silver arrows curved overhead and fell, finding their targets. Twenty or thirty of them hit the monkey and although, in comparison to its own huge size, they were little more than needles, they stung its face and blinded one of its eyes. The monkey howled in pain, baring its teeth, but held its ground. Then there was an explosion and a white glowing missile shot past it, just missing its head. Jamie turned to see where it had come from. He had thought the cannons had opened fire, but in fact the shot had come from one of the copper pipes that he had noticed before. The pipes were a crude type of bazooka which the men had hoisted onto their shoulders and which they were aiming into the enemy forces. Jamie saw another one go off, the white-hot missile streaking through the air on a trail of smoke. This one found its target. One of the knights had broken through Matt's lines. There was an explosion and he was gone, quite simply blown apart.

There was no way to tell where the line between the two armies had been drawn. It seemed as if both sides had abandoned any strategy as soon as the battle had begun and were now engaged in completely random, hand-to-hand combat.

Matt's soldiers were standing their ground, holding the man-creatures at bay. Yet the bodies were beginning to pile up. Medical teams were already rushing into the field with stretchers, somehow emerging again with the injured, carrying them to a makeshift hospital that had been set up among the tents. Even in these early stages, and as much as he hated to admit it, Jamie was sure he was on the losing side. The odds against them were too great.

And still Scar refused to move. Nobody had noticed her and her troops, high up on the hill overlooking the battlefield, partially concealed behind the pine trees. They were only a hundred strong – not enough to make any real difference. But Jamie couldn't bear just standing there. He felt wretched, a coward.

"We have to go down!" he exclaimed.

"No!" Scar was furious. Her eyes were fixed on what was happening down below and her whole body seemed to be frozen.

"Why not? We're not doing any good."

"This is the way Matt wanted it." Scar was clutching her sword so hard that her fist had turned white and Jamie wondered if she would even have attacked him if he had tried to advance. "They don't know we're here," she explained. "That's the whole point. They mustn't see us. And we have to wait."

"Wait for what?"

"You'll see!"

Jamie glanced at Finn as if he might say something different, but the big man shook his head slowly and continued to watch the progress of the battle. Jamie forced himself to look back at the field and at once the screams of the dying and the sickly smell of newly spilled blood rose up and consumed him. He had seen films. He had played computer games. But this was utterly different. There were no cameras, no artful arrangements. Here death was vicious, random, all around him.

And then the monkey fell. A great ball of orange flame had soared over the fighters. Once again, Jamie was unsure where it had come from. Then he saw an elaborate catapult, a strange construction of metal and wood, like something salvaged from a breakers' yard. It had been hidden among the tents and had just fired a blazing missile at the creature, hitting it square on the shoulder. The huge animal exploded in flames that spread in seconds across its fur, its whole upper body disappearing in a red inferno. Jamie saw it trying to beat out the fire with its hands but then its arms caught alight too. The monkey screeched once – a hideous, piteous sound. Finally it plunged backwards, crushing several of its own soldiers, and lay still.

But there was no time to celebrate this one small victory. The other giant animals were killing dozens of people, the condor and the hummingbird striking down again and again, the spider spitting poison or crushing its victims underfoot. The spiked knights were also continuing forward, more like robots than men, cutting down anyone who stood in their path. The cannons roared and two of the knights fell, their horses screaming as they came crashing down. The Old Ones had no heavy artillery – no cannons or catapults. But they didn't need them.

For the first time, Jamie noticed the thirteen horsemen who had accompanied Chaos. These had to be the fire riders that Scar had mentioned the day before. They were dressed in grey, like monks or friars, their faces completely hidden by hoods. And they were unarmed. But now he saw one of them lean forward and touch one of Matt's fighters almost gently, as if trying to get his attention. A single touch was death. The young man burst instantly into flame – turned into ashes before he could even scream. The fire rider straightened up then reached out and struck again. This time it was a woman, gone before she knew what had happened. The other horsemen were equally busy. It seemed to Jamie that Matt's army was rapidly dwindling and the fighting was moving ever closer towards him as his own side was overwhelmed.

They were losing. It was as simple as that. And although he had never met Matt, although he hadn't known anything about this world until now, he felt the bitterness of defeat and a sense of anger that it had been planned this way. Why had he and Scar been kept out of the fighting? As soon as they left the safety of the hilltop, they would die. But that didn't matter. Jamie thought of the boy called Flint, who was somewhere down there, perhaps already wounded or even dead. With all his heart he wished he could have met him, if only briefly, before the end.

Suddenly, Scar shouted and stretched out a hand. "There!" She had spotted something. Finn, too, was looking in the same direction.

At first Jamie couldn't see anything. Scar was pointing towards the very edge of the field, beyond the fighting, where the river of grass dipped down and disappeared. But there was something. The light seemed to be darkening. It was impossible, but the very clouds were being drawn together as if they had somehow become magnetized. Jamie felt a sudden heaviness, a thudding in his head that told him there was about to be a storm.

"It's them," Scar said and the next moment there was a great flash of lightning and a downpour so heavy that it was as if a screen had been drawn across the edge of the battlefield. The rain lashed down on the fighters. Thunder exploded above their heads. Jamie felt the water soaking through his clothes and running in rivulets down his skin. The change in the weather had been instantaneous – as if one of them had somehow controlled it.

"What's happening?" he demanded.

Scar didn't answer. She was gazing into the distance. Jamie followed her eyes and saw that a line of figures on horseback had appeared, riding at full gallop towards the edge of the battle. So far, nobody else had seen them. The rain had taken care of that. There were just six of them. Five men and a boy. It was difficult to make them out in the darkness and the confusion of the storm, but Jamie could just see the figure riding in the centre. Long dark hair. Dark skin. He too was carrying a shield. His was decorated with a blazing sun.

Inti had arrived.

And he wasn't alone. Behind him, more soldiers – perhaps fifty of them – appeared, rising up over the edge of the field. They looked nothing like any of the other fighters, wearing tunics with headdresses made out of feathers and beaten gold. They carried outlandish weapons – slingshots, bolas and very small curved bows that they fired while still galloping, taking out some of the man-creatures that had strayed too close. They carried a banner with the blue star.

One of the fire riders turned, sensing them for the first time. Jamie saw Inti lean forward in his saddle. He had unsheathed a sword with a blade shaped like a crescent moon. Now he swung it. The rider's head flew clear of its shoulders. The rest of the body fell to its knees and then toppled forward. Inti hadn't so much as hesitated. If anything, his horse had sped up, carrying him straight to the very heart of the battle.

"It's time!" Scar exclaimed. She turned to Finn. "Are you ready?"

"I've waited too long," Finn growled.

"Then let's finish it." She steadied her horse. For a moment she was very close to Jamie. "Use your power," she said. "Find Matt. That's all we have to do."

And at last Jamie understood Matt's strategy. Chaos had joined the battle in the belief that only three of the Gatekeepers – Matt, Flint and Scar – would take part. Inti was supposed to be pinned down somewhere far away, unable to reach them. Sapling was dead. At least, that was what the king had thought when he had tried to get his enemies to surrender. He was confident that the fight was already over, that this was nothing more than a last encounter before humanity was made extinct. But he had been tricked. Inti had managed to fight his way through. And though Sapling had gone, he – Jamie – was here.

Jamie felt a rush of excitement. More than that. It was as if there were an electric current surging through him. He knew what had to happen next.

The Five had to meet.

Scar also knew. She smiled briefly at Jamie, then drew her sword. Jamie did the same.

Scar called out. A single word. "Forward!"

And then, at once, they were chasing down the hill, heading right into the face of the enemy but completely unafraid, eager to join the fray. Jamie felt his horse almost flying beneath him but there was no chance of his falling – he and the horse were one. He had his shield in one hand and his sword in the other. Frost. When he had first taken hold of it, he had known that it had been made for him, forged to the very shape of his hand. Frost was more than a piece of inanimate metal. It was a friend.

The hillside was steep and his horse almost stumbled, but Jamie steadied it and raced on, round the tents, past the physicians with their bloody saws and bandages, between the archers, who parted to allow him through, cheering him as he went. The moment he had passed, they fired another volley to distract the enemy. Jamie saw the swarm of arrows take off, darkening the sky above his head, and gave his horse free rein as if he could leave the ground and fly with them. He felt the hooves hit soft earth. Seconds later, the battle had swallowed him.

On the hill he had been able to see the field in its entirety, to understand the lie of the land and the direction of the fighting. Now he became part of it. He couldn't see Scar or Inti. If he stopped even for a few seconds to look or to take his bearings, he knew he would be killed. Some instinct told him that the only way to survive was to keep moving. But ahead of him the way was blocked. He reined in his horse and almost at once one of the creatures lunged at him. Jamie saw a cobra's head, black eyes burning, a yellow fork spitting at him from a twisted mouth. At the same time, there was a crack and something flailed past, inches from his neck. The snake had a human body with human arms and legs – and it was holding a whip. It had attempted to knock him off his horse but Jamie had been lucky. It had missed. He swung his sword and severed the creature's neck, feeling no resistance as the blade cut through. Blood sprayed out. The whip fell aside. The body crumpled.

The noise here was deafening. Very little of the sound of warfare had carried up to the hill but now it was all around him. There were the screams of men and horses and it was hard to say which were the more heart-rending. Sword clanged against sword and there was the terrible ripping sound of metal entering flesh. A body, one of his own men, pitched into the ground and lay still. Another man, blinded, with blood streaking his face, cried out for help and was only silenced when one of the fire riders touched him and he was instantly vaporized.

Down!

The warning wasn't spoken. It was sent as a thought that slammed into Jamie, making him duck almost instinctively. A second spear, thrown by one of the knights, flew over his shoulder, missing him by inches. Somehow Flint had seen him. Flint was still alive and had been looking out for him in just the same way that Scott would have done. There was no sign of the other boy but now Jamie remembered what Scar had told him a few moments before. His power had returned to him. He had to use it.

The knight who had just tried to kill him had taken out a twin-bladed sword. He was already galloping forward, the horse aiming directly for him with its deadly spike slanting out of its head. Jamie didn't move. He simply sent out an instruction.

You cannot move. You cannot hurt me.

The knight was almost on top of him but didn't even try to

swing his sword. Nor did he flinch when Jamie lifted Frost and drove it straight into his chest. He was helpless. Jamie felt the sword cut through and recoiled in horror as the entire body fell apart, becoming in an instant a buzzing cloud of flies. The hesitation almost cost him his life. He saw a shadow out of the corner of his eye and turned just as another man-scorpion began its strike. Its tail and stinger were already slashing down and he thought he was finished. But they never completed their journey. In front of his eyes they seemed to separate themselves from the man-scorpion's body. The creature howled and died and Jamie saw Corian saluting him with his sword and realized that his life had just been saved for a second time.

Briefly, he caught sight of Scar – over to his left. She had disappeared but now she was back again, chopping and hacking with her own sword, keeping five or six half-human creatures at bay. Finn was close by. Jamie knew that the older man would never be far from her if he could help it. At the same moment he saw, with a jolt of alarm, that Finn had been wounded. There was a gaping wound in his shoulder that opened and closed like a bloody mouth as he moved: a blow from an axe that had almost taken off his arm. But he didn't seem to have noticed it. He had transferred his sword to his left hand and swung his blade. Another of the knights disintegrated into a swarm of black flies.

Something slammed into Jamie's shield and he looked down, afraid he might have been hit. It was an arrow, the tip laced with poison. He saw it just as it bounced off, leaving a slight dent in his shield. A man-alligator snatched up the arrow and twisted round, planning to drive it into Jamie's leg.

Into yourself...

Jamie thought the two words and watched in satisfaction as the creature turned the arrow on itself, driving the point into its own neck. The man-alligator howled in protest and crumpled to the ground.

Then something blotted out the light. He just had time to see Scar staring at him in horror. Perhaps she was trying to warn him. But she was already too late. An enormous shape was hurtling towards him. Jamie looked up just as the hummingbird dive-bombed him, plummeting down at fantastic speed. Had it picked on him because it recognized who he was? Jamie knew there was no time to defend himself. His sword would be useless. The bird would split him in two before he had time to move. There was only one thing to do. He let go of the reins and threw himself backwards, onto the ground. The world turned upside down and, for a moment, the armies were above him, all the fighting had become a swirling mass of noise and colour and he was drowning in it. Then his shoulders slammed into the earth, his sword left his hand and all the breath was knocked out of him.

If he had waited another second, he would have been killed. As it was, the pointed beak of the hummingbird slammed into his horse, impaling it. The horse cried out – a terrible, deafening scream. Then the hummingbird pulled away. Jamie could feel the air being blasted by its wings as it hovered over them. The bird was searching for him, hoping to strike again. But then Erin appeared from nowhere and slashed at the bird's face, using the five knives that were his thumb and fingers, aiming for its eyes. The bird reared back and flew off. The horse folded sideways and lay still.

Jamie had bitten his tongue when he fell and could taste his own blood in his mouth. Worse, he had lost his horse, his shield and his sword. He still wasn't scared – there was no time for fear – but suddenly he wanted this to be over. Scar had been right about one thing. He had no idea how long he had been fighting. A few minutes or several hours? Either way, he was worn out. He'd had enough.

But he knew he had to find Frost. He was lost without it. He looked around – and there it was, lying undamaged on the ground. But as he leant to retrieve it, a man-pig holding a wicked-looking curved dagger scurried towards him. Jamie dived underneath it, grabbed Frost, then lunged upwards. The sword buried itself in the creature's belly. Jamie jerked it out again, rolled over and got to his feet. There were bodies all around him. Men and creatures fighting. Knights and horse-men. Everything was a blur. His neck was hurting. He touched his fingers to it and saw red. The man-pig had managed to cut him but the wound couldn't be too bad – there wasn't enough blood. He let his hand fall. What now?

And right then it all became clear.

Ahead of him was an open space. It was as if the fighters

had deliberately parted to create a circular arena. And in the middle of it, two figures stood facing each other. One was Matt. The other was the King of the Old Ones, the creature that had been given the name Chaos. Matt had a sword, but he wasn't using it. Jamie could feel the power emanating from the first of the Five. Someone hurled a spear towards him but it never came anywhere near. The air shimmered around him. The spear shattered. The pieces were spun away.

"You cannot defeat me. Kneel before me and still I may let you live." Chaos did not speak. Instead the words radiated from him, ice cold and poisonous. He towered over Matt. Was it Jamie's imagination or had he grown since the fighting had begun, as if feeding on so much death?

Matt stood where he was. Jamie examined him properly for the first time. He was just a boy with square shoulders and short dark hair, but his face was much older than his fourteen years. He had the eyes of a man, full of wisdom and experience. He was dressed, like Jamie, in a coarsely woven grey shirt that hung down below his waist, crossed by a leather belt running diagonally across his chest. He had a sword in one hand and a shield in the other. The symbol that he had chosen was a fish.

Matt suddenly raised his hand, not attacking his opponent but pointing to the side. Two knights had been closing in but they were instantly thrown back, sent flying off their horses by an invisible force. Several humans – overlords and slaves –

were hurled into the air. Matt had created a corridor in the fighting and a second boy stepped into it. Jamie looked across the clearing and saw what could have been a mirror image of himself. Or it could have been Scott. But he knew that it was Flint. Flint was bruised and exhausted from the battle, his clothes torn and his shield broken, but still quite obviously his identical twin.

Flint walked forward and at the same time Scar made her appearance, bringing down a man twice her size, stabbing a second and leaping over a third with her sword angled up in front of her, her eyes fixed on Chaos as if she planned to attack him all on her own. Now there were three of them surrounding the motionless figure, the black space at the centre of the conflict.

The King of the Old Ones was amused by the new arrivals. "Three of the Five. But not enough. Still not enough!" The words vibrated in the air. They made Jamie's head ache. He felt sick.

He was about to step forward but before he could move, another boy ran past him, almost brushing his shoulder. It was Inti. He was soaking wet from the rainstorm and there was blood running from a wound on his cheek. He had lost his shield but he still had his sword.

"Four of you!" The words came hissing out of the darkness, full of contempt.

"Five," Jamie said, and joined the circle.

Flint saw him and nodded, his face filled with delight. Inti and Scar smiled. Matt gave nothing away. He unsheathed his sword.

And that was when the King of the Old Ones knew that he had been deceived. The boy who was dead was somehow alive again. Inti had arrived, unseen, on the battlefield. Chaos was surrounded by the Five, who had been born for this very moment and sent to defeat him. Four boys and a girl. Each of them armed. The battle, raging all around them, was almost forgotten.

"Go back where you came from," Matt said.

He took a single step forward and stabbed with all his strength, burying his blade in the creature's heart.

The others did the same. First Flint, then Inti. The King of the Old Ones writhed as each blade went into him. His shape was shimmering like ripples on a pool of water. But three blows was not enough to finish him. Scar went next, burying her own sword up to the hilt. And at last the creature cried out, feeling pain for the first time.

Jamie was the last to step forward. Gritting his teeth, he plunged his sword into the blackness in front of him. He felt his arm freeze and wondered if the blade had shattered. At the same moment, he was deafened by the terrible death scream of the defeated king.

The five points of the five swords had touched.

Chaos had never been a man and at that moment he lost the pretence. He seemed to explode outwards, completely losing his human shape, becoming nothing more than a huge shadow, a sort of living night that was at last being torn apart by the coming of the day. He screamed one last time and his servants knew, right then, that the battle was lost. The sound reached the furthest corners of the world and still it didn't stop. Every evil being in the universe heard it and knew that the end had come.

Jamie was paralysed. If Frost was still in his hand he couldn't move it. He could feel the power of the Five now that they were finally together and, although he had never been stronger, at the same time he was overwhelmed. The power was intensifying and he was sure that it would break him apart. It was more than he could bear. He tried to look for Finn or any of the others but it was as if nothing existed outside the circle they had formed. He was aware only of four faces. Matt, Flint, Inti, Scar. They were all strangely alike, all fixed in silent concentration and he knew that they were feeling exactly the same as he was.

The King of the Old Ones was no longer there. It was as if he had been turned into smoke that was already drifting away. The Five were standing in a circle, their blades still touching, but with an empty space between them. And nothing could reach them. Although the fighting still continued all around, it was as if they were inside a crystal jar. Swords flashed but the blades broke in mid-air. Spears and arrows rained down on them but bounced off uselessly. The condor plunged towards them in a last, desperate attempt to reach them but its out-stretched claws suddenly shattered and it was sent spinning away, a shapeless ball of feathers and blood.

Jamie wondered if he had been more badly hurt than he'd thought. Was he dying? All the sounds of the combat were very distant. There was a great rushing in his ears and a sense of something flowing through him. The Five were cocooned, completely safe, at the very centre of the battle but apart from it.

And now something even stranger was happening.

The five of them seemed to be moving, turning slowly as if on a merry-go-round. But it wasn't they who were moving. It was the world that was moving around them. The field and the forest and the hill were spinning faster and faster until they no longer existed. They had become a blur, nothing more than a streak of colour that swirled around them with no beginning and no end.

There was an ear-shattering crack. Jamie looked up.

The sky had opened. A chasm had appeared, the very fabric of the day peeling back to reveal a universe filled with stars. At the same time, the wind was howling. It had formed a tornado that was tearing up clumps of grass and pieces of earth. First, dead bodies and then living ones were being pulled into it and carried away through the vortex. With every second that passed, the process was becoming stronger and faster. One after another, the servants of the Old Ones were being taken, spinning helplessly as they were carried up. Jamie watched them as they were pulled into the void and knew that he was partly responsible for what was happening. It was his power that was doing this. He and the other four.

The remaining fire riders had gone, ripped off their horses and blown away like rags. The fly-soldiers had disintegrated. The spider and the hummingbird – all the giant animals – were no more than specks, spiralling ever further upwards. Finally, the dark shadow which was all that remained of Chaos was sucked in, following them into oblivion. And then at last it was over. The tunnel closed up behind them. The wind died down. There was a distant rumble of thunder and the sky rolled back, closing off the darkness, healing its own, self-inflicted wound.

The Five stood in silence.

"Sapling…" It was Flint who had spoken. But Matt raised a hand, holding him back. Not yet.

Scar stepped forward. She was staring at something high above her, shielding her eyes. Jamie looked up and saw that at last the clouds had parted and the sun had been allowed to show its face.

"So that's what it looks like," Scar muttered. "I always wondered." She turned to Matt. "What does it mean?" she asked.

"It means that it's over," Matt said. "We've won."

BENEATH THE STARS

They stood looking at each other, the five Gatekeepers: Scar, Inti, Flint, Matt and Jamie. None of them spoke. Too much had happened too quickly. Jamie only knew what Scar had told him, a very small part of the history that had brought them all here today. But he understood that a journey had just ended, and one that had taken their entire lives.

All around them, everything was changing. And it was happening with incredible speed. The Old Ones had brought the planet to the edge of destruction, polluting the water and darkening the sky. But now that they had gone, the world was restoring itself. The rain had stopped as quickly as it had started and the ground was already dry. The clouds had parted as surely as if they had been curtains waiting to be pulled and the sky on the other side was a dazzling blue, the sun already spreading its warmth over the ground. And with the coming of the sun, true colour had returned. The forest, which had seemed black and grey, was now many shades of green. The pine trees were somehow less threatening, the grass softer and more natural.

The three armies that had come together under the symbol of the blue star were only just realizing that the battle was over and the Old Ones had gone. They were still stunned, unable to take in what had happened. A hole in the universe had opened. The Old Ones had been sucked into it. The people were finally on their own, undefeated, and the world was theirs once again. Slowly they began to pick themselves up. Survivors found each other and embraced. Some people stood where they were and wept. Some threw down their weapons and laughed out loud. And many – the dead and the dying – lay where they were, scattered across the four corners of the field.

"Is it really over?" Scar asked. "Is this the end?"

"We've won the battle," Matt said. "And tonight we'll celebrate. But right now, there's a lot we have to do."

"There are many injured." Inti spoke for the first time. Although he used the same language as the others, he must have learned it only recently. He had a strange accent and had to search for the words.

Matt nodded. "You must go to them."

"I have been searching for you, Matteo. For many years. I am glad to have found you at last." Inti nodded at Matt and at the others. Then he turned and walked away.

He was the first to break the circle.

"I shouldn't have doubted you, Matt," Scar said. "You were right. It all worked out exactly the way you wanted."

"It wasn't my plan," Matt replied. "It was just the way it was meant to be."

Scar slid her sword back into its sheath. "I have to find Finn," she said. "He was hurt in the fighting and he's going to need looking after." She stood awkwardly, not wanting to leave but needing to find her friend. Then she hurried off.

Flint and Jamie found themselves face to face. The other boy was looking at him with a mixture of emotions.

Jamie wasn't sure how to react himself. "You're Flint ... I suppose," he said. "I mean ... of course you are." He noticed that Flint was carrying a sword that was identical to Frost. He wasn't surprised. Everything about them was the same. "You look like Scott," he said. "You sound like him too."

"Who is Scott?"

"My brother."

Flint nodded. "And you look and sound like Sapling."

Jamie tried to smile, but it was difficult. "Is anyone ever going to explain all this?" he asked.

Both boys turned to Matt.

"We can't talk now," he said. "I'm sorry ... but we have to make a start. There are people who need our help."

"When?" Flint demanded.

"Tonight."

Jamie looked around him. Only now was he aware of the scale of the battle he had just fought. It reminded him of what he had seen at Scathack Hill, only this was much worse. All over the field there were men and women with terrible injuries. They had begun to cry out in pain. Blood was every-where.

"Inti has the power to heal," Matt said. "But there's too much for him to do on his own. People will want food and water. The physicians will need help with the stretchers. The questions can wait."

Flint nodded. He took one last look at Jamie as if trying to work him out, then turned away.

Very quickly, the army had divided itself into different groups. Those who had not been hurt, or who had been hurt only a little, were helping those who had been less fortunate, carrying them to the field hospitals, bringing them water or just staying close by to comfort them. The dead were left where they had fallen. There was nothing that could be done for them: their one solace was that their suffering was over.

Jamie found work for himself, filling water bottles from a barrel that had been brought on a cart to the centre of the field, carrying them to those men and women who were unable to move and who had yet to receive help. The first person he came upon couldn't have been more than eighteen or nineteen, and it was clear that he wasn't going to live much longer. His chest had been torn open and his face was white. And yet when he saw Jamie he smiled. As Jamie trickled water between his lips, he held onto his arm and seemed completely at peace. It was as if he had wanted to meet Jamie all his life and now that he had, he was prepared to die.

It was the same, time and time again. Jamie noticed Matt walking among the wounded, stopping to clasp a hand or to kneel down and help someone drink. Everyone in the field seemed to know who they were – which was strange because Jamie wasn't sure he knew himself. He went back to get more water, wishing that the day was over and they could all sit down and talk.

On the next journey he found Scar and Finn.

By now, Jamie could tell almost at a glance who was going to live to talk about this day and who was not. He could see at once that Finn was dying. The big man was lying with his legs outstretched and his back against the stump of a tree. Scar was kneeling beside him and Inti was there too. Corian and Erin were also near by, watching anxiously. Jamie was relieved to see that neither of the brothers had been hurt.

Inti had been leaning forward with his hands resting on Finn's shoulders but as Jamie approached he straightened up and glanced at Scar, signalling that there was nothing more he could do. Jamie could see why. Whatever Inti's power, he had arrived too late. Finn had taken a terrible blow to the shoulder and lost too much blood. He was very close to the end.

Finn saw Jamie and managed to bend the fingers of one hand, gesturing at him to come closer. Jamie held out a water bottle but Finn shook his head. He no longer had the strength to swallow. Nor did he need to prolong what little life he had left.

"Sapling!" he said.

As Scar turned round and noticed him for the first time, Jamie saw that there were tears in her eyes.

"You did well." Finn coughed and a few specks of blood

flecked his lips. "I knew you would. Didn't I tell you?"

Jamie nodded but couldn't speak.

"Finn…" Scar began.

Finn took her hands in his. "You're not to cry, Scar," he whispered. "I've told you before. It's not fitting."

"How will I manage without you?" Scar exclaimed.

"Don't be foolish. You have your friends. The Five…" Finn patted her hand. It was all the movement he could manage. "But we had adventures together, you and I. People will remember them and talk of them one day, perhaps."

"Oh, Finn…" Scar couldn't hold back the tears any more.

"You're going to be on your own now. But you don't need me any more. I'm not sure you ever did." Finn reached up and gently stroked her hair one last time. "We won," he said. "That's all that matters." Finn looked adoringly at her. Then his head fell back and Jamie knew that he would never speak again.

He couldn't bear to see any more. He snatched up the water bottle and hurried away.

The day wore on, the sun set and at last all the activity began to wind down. The physicians had done what they could. The wounded were resting. And those that had been chosen to die had done so quietly and without complaint. Jamie was almost overwhelmed with tiredness. Part of it was the exhaustion of the fight and the long hours spent working once the battle was over. But he recognized that it was something more. It was a reaction to what he had been through –

so much happening so quickly, so many deaths. He was emotionally as well as physically worn out.

That was when Flint returned. Jamie had wondered what had become of his brother – for he couldn't think of him any other way – but suddenly Flint appeared riding on a horse-drawn wagon which was piled high with sacks and barrels. He had taken six men with him and they had all returned with similar wagons. They tore through the middle of the field and stopped. Flint leapt to his feet.

"We've found food!" he called out. "The overlords had a camp on the other side of the valley and of course they kept all the best supplies for themselves. We have bread and wine and cheese and dried meat and fruit. So light a fire. Tonight we're going to eat well."

About three hundred men, women and children had come through the battle unhurt. Hearing Flint's words, they broke into cheers. Jamie joined in. He knew that if Scott had been here, he would have found the food. That was how he had always been, scavenging for himself and Jamie whenever anything was needed. The more he thought about it, the more it seemed to him that Scott and Flint were one and the same – just as he and Sapling were more or less identical. It was impossible, of course. But then so was everything else.

The survivors must have been as weary as Jamie but somehow they found new strength. First they made a great bonfire out of scattered weapons, branches from the forest and their own catapult, which they dismantled and fed to the flames.

They spread out cloths and carpets in front of the tents. Then they unloaded the wagons and distributed the supplies, making sure the injured weren't forgotten. Soon what had been a field of death suddenly became the scene of a huge open-air banquet beneath a sky full of stars.

A makeshift table with five folding stools had been set up slightly to one side for himself and the other Gatekeepers. He went over to it. Matt was already standing there, deep in conversation with Inti, but the two of them stopped as Jamie approached. Matt poured Jamie a bowl of wine and passed it across. Inti held out a hand.

"It's good to be with you," he said.

Then Flint and Scar arrived. If Scar had been grieving for the loss of Finn, she didn't show it. She seemed to be in a bad mood. She plumped herself down on one of the stools, poured herself some wine, drank it, then poured some more.

Flint had sat next to Jamie. "Have you seen the stars?" he asked.

Jamie looked up. The whole universe was ablaze. "It's a beautiful night," he said.

"I've never seen the stars. All my life there have only been clouds." He craned his neck, gazing into the night. "People used to say that the sky could look like this. But I never believed them."

Matt sat down. He looked exhausted. Scar poured him a bowl of wine. It occurred to Jamie that the Five were together again. But for how long?

319

He had lost count of the number of people who had approached him during the day as he made his rounds with the water bottles, but as the feast began, the five of them were left alone. It was as if it had been decided that they should be allowed to rest and – Jamie reflected – they certainly deserved it. They drank more wine and ate soft cheese and some sort of meat with chunks of tough, chewy bread. Jamie was surprised to find he was ravenous.

In another part of the field someone began a tune, playing on a pipe, and a moment later two others joined in with a drum and some sort of single-stringed instrument. The flames from the bonfire leapt up, sparks twisting in the air.

Scar glanced at Matt. "So what happens now?" she asked. "And before you say anything, I'm sorry. I shouldn't have argued with you about Scathack Hill and the rest of it. But how was I to know? You're just a boy. Nobody even told me who put you in charge."

"It's too late to say very much tonight," Matt replied. "And anyway, I don't have all the answers – whatever you may think. But there is one thing you need to know right away. We've spent our whole lives searching for each other but very soon we will have to part."

"I had a feeling you were going to say that."

"The four of us have work to do. But Jamie isn't from our world. He has to return where he came from."

Jamie felt a jolt of sadness which he couldn't explain. He didn't belong here – he knew that. But nor did he want to leave.

There was a long silence, broken at last by Flint. "He's not Sapling then," he said simply.

"Sapling is dead," Matt replied. "He died at Scathack Hill."

"Then I killed him."

"No."

Flint slammed his fist down on the table, spilling his wine. "You told us to choose," he cried, and from his voice, Jamie could tell that he was close to tears. "You said one of us had to go and I let him volunteer."

"It was his choice." Matt remained calm. "You don't have to blame yourself."

"But if he isn't Sapling," Scar said, "who is he?"

Matt turned to Jamie.

"I've told you all along," Jamie said. "My name is Jamie Tyler. I live in Nevada, in America."

"Where is America?" Inti asked.

Matt stood up. "We have so much to talk about," he said. "Here we are, together at last. The Five. Today we did what we were born to do. We defeated the Old Ones and gave the world a new start. Flint, I promised you answers and you will have them. You too, Jamie. But right now I'm too tired. I'd like to spend the whole night with you, sitting at this table, but I can't do it. I need to sleep."

"I, too, am tired," Inti muttered.

"We won't be together for long," Matt continued. "But it isn't important. A year, an hour or even a minute ... all that mattered was that we met. Because in that instant our work was done. That was the end of it. That was the only reason we ever existed. And if we never see each other again, we need have no regret.

Scar stood up next to him and refilled all five bowls. "Whatever you think about fate and destiny and all the rest of it, I want to celebrate," she said. "I want to remember this moment for the rest of my life. You, me, Inti, Flint and Jamie. We did it together. We are the Five. Let's drink to that."

They raised their bowls.

"The Five," Scar said.

"The Five," they all chorused. They touched the bowls together, metal against metal, then drank silently.

Matt smiled. "Goodnight," he said. "We'll talk again when the sun is up."

He walked away.

"I go too." Inti yawned. "Forgive me. This feast may go on all the night … but I cannot. I travelled far today. I must sleep."

Jamie watched as he walked off a few paces behind Matt. They stopped at the first line of tents and spoke a few words before they parted company, each of them going their own way.

Scar finished her wine. "Matt never tells us anything," she said with a sigh. "And when he does, we don't understand it. But we've won the battle … and the war. So I suppose I'll go along with whatever he says." She held out a hand. "Good night, Jamie. I'm going off to find Erin and Corian. We're going to have a drink to the memory of Finn. And then we're going to keep drinking until we forget that he's gone. I'll see you in the morning."

She and Jamie clasped hands. At the same time, she leant forward and kissed him lightly on the cheek. Then she too left the table.

He and Flint were alone.

"I'm sorry," Jamie muttered. He didn't know what else to say.

"Don't be." Flint sounded worn out. "I'm glad you were here. I'm glad you were sent in Sapling's place."

"Me too." Jamie thought for a moment. He was so tired that he had to struggle to find the right words. "Let me tell you about Scott," he said. "He's smarter than me. He's looked after me all my life. But a week ago, these people came after him. He was kidnapped. I managed to get away. I can see now that it must be something to do with the Old Ones. That must be why they were looking for us. I don't know where Scott is right now. He may have been killed. I don't know. I've been trying to find him."

"Could he be here?"

"No. I don't even know where here is. But you heard what Matt said. This world hasn't got anything to do with Scott or me. I suppose I will have to go back home..."

Flint got unsteadily to his feet. All around them, the feast was still continuing. Inti had been right. It would go on until sunrise.

323

"I'm going to sleep," Flint said. "I'll see you in the morning."

"Goodnight, Flint."

"Goodnight, Jamie."

Jamie watched his twin walk away and disappear into one of the tents, knowing in his heart that this was more than goodnight and that the two of them would never see each other again.

THE RIVER

Jamie was woken from a deep sleep by someone shaking him. He opened his eyes and saw Matt, fully dressed, leaning over him. Dawn still hadn't quite broken. He could see the half-light through the gap in the tent.

"I'm sorry," Matt said. "But I have to wake you."

"Why? What is it?" Jamie was still groggy. He'd slept as if he were dead. There had been no dreams.

"We have to talk."

Jamie had slept in his clothes. He was beginning to get used to it. He'd been given a blanket and a sack full of straw as a pillow. Now he peeled himself away from them, picked up his sword and followed Matt out of the tent. It was going to be a beautiful day. There was a ripple of pink in a sky that was already soft shades of blue and grey, without a cloud in sight. The feast had finally ended. People had fallen asleep where they sat. There were sleeping bodies everywhere, a strange echo of the battle that had taken place the day before.

There was no sign of Flint, Scar or Inti. Matt was wearing a loose-fitting shirt over woollen trousers and leather boots. He had left his sword behind but Jamie was holding Frost. Why had he brought it? There was no enemy, no need to be afraid any more.

"Should I leave this?" he asked.

"No," Matt said. "Bring the sword with you."

"Where are we going?" Jamie asked.

"It's not far."

They made their way through the tents, following the line of the hill where Jamie and Scar had waited before beginning their attack. They were walking towards the edge of the field, the same direction as Inti had come from. As they left the tents behind them, Jamie heard the sound of rushing water and was surprised to come upon a wide river, rushing across the field in a deep gully. The water was an icy blue and looked fresh and clean. The world was regenerating itself – and it was all happening at an incredible speed.

The two of them found a flat rock and sat down, close to the water's edge.

"There are things I need to tell you before you go," Matt said.

"Am I going back where I came from?" Jamie asked.

"Yes."

"Then tell me about Nightrise. Tell me about Scott. What have they done with him?"

"I don't know, Jamie. I'm sorry. That's your world, not mine. But there are ways I can help you. I only wish I knew where to begin…"

Matt drew a deep breath. Then he spoke again.

"As I'm sure you realize by now, you've travelled from one world to another. But what you have to understand is, it's the same world. This is the past. You live in the future. Two civilizations separated by ten thousand years.

"I can't tell you very much about our world. It was very beautiful once, a long time ago. I think we were peaceful. By and large, people just got on with their lives without hurting anyone else.

"But then something bad happened. The Old Ones. I don't know where they came from or how they got here, but as soon as they arrived everything changed. They had only one aim and that was to break us down. Somehow they turned humanity against itself and after that, things got worse and worse. It was obvious that they weren't going to stop until there was nothing left. But it had to be as slow as possible. That's the whole point, Jamie. That's their nature. They feed on misery. It's the whole reason for their existence.

"You've already seen a small part of what they've done here. Scathack Hill and the City of Canals. They tore apart anything that was beautiful or useful – homes and temples, gardens and terraces, villages and towns. Anyone who stood in their way was either killed or made into slaves. And even that wasn't enough for them. You have no idea how powerful they were. They managed to change the atmosphere on the entire planet. They cut down our forests and killed all the animals that had once lived there. They poisoned the rivers and even clogged up the seas and by the end it was almost impossible to find water to drink. They melted the ice fields in the north and took away the barriers that had been put around the earth to protect us. They couldn't destroy the sun or the stars but they covered them in cloud so that nobody would see them again.

"All of this began before I was born and continued while I was still very young. The reason why Scar and I and the others don't know any different is that for us the world was always like this. I'm fourteen years old … I think. I'm probably the same age as you. In fact, it's quite likely that all five of us were born at exactly the same moment. None of us ever knew our parents. And we were all special. We had powers…"

Jamie nodded. He had seen Matt sweeping the enemy aside just by waving his hand. He and Flint had been able to read each other's minds. Inti was a healer. And what of Scar? If she had a power, she hadn't displayed it. Jamie wanted to ask about her but Matt had already gone on.

"We were sent into the world to lead the fight against the Old Ones. But we soon realized that we wouldn't be strong enough: not each of us on our own. It's what I said last night. The whole point was, we had to come together. We had to find each other, and then … well, you saw for yourself. All we had to do was meet.

"But that wasn't as easy as you might think. For a start, we were in different lands. And life was already horrible and dangerous when we were born. Scar was forced to work in the

328

mines. Inti started telling me yesterday how his people hid him in the mountains. Because that was the other thing. The Old Ones knew about us and they were looking for us from the start. They tried to kill me many times. I spent a year as their prisoner.

"We found each other through our dreams and this is where it gets a bit complicated, Jamie. I've talked about the two worlds – the past and the future – but there's a sort of third world which is a bit like a tunnel between the two. It has a great sea and an island…"

"I've been there!" Jamie exclaimed.

"Yes. It exists in your time and in mine."

"I saw you in a boat made of straw. I think Inti was with you."

"And I saw you."

"Tell me about the dream world."

"There's a wilderness with a woman who lives there on her own. And there's also a library. One day, maybe, you'll find it. But I'm not going to tell you about that now. What you need to know is that the dream world has been created for the five of us. We can meet there and talk to each other – and it doesn't even matter if we don't speak the same language. It seems frightening sometimes when we travel there. But the dreams help us. Never forget that.

"And now I'm going to try to explain how you got here and why you can't stay. This is the most difficult part of all and I'll probably make a mess of it – but I'll do my best."

Matt paused for breath. There was nobody else around. The water was rushing past, sparkling in the early morning light.

"I've talked about the past and the future," he began. "And when we think of time, we usually think of a straight line. A week is just seven days in a row. A century is a long line of years – one hundred of them. Your life also seems to only go one way. You're born, you grow up, you get old and then you die.

"But suppose time wasn't like that. Suppose time was actually circular. Think what that would mean."

"There would be no beginning," Jamie said. "And no end."

"Well … the end and the beginning would be the same." Matt raised a hand. "It would be a bit like a clock. Most clocks are circular and when you get to midnight you've reached the end of one day but you've also come to the start of the next. In other words, just for a fraction of a second, the beginning and the end of the day both exist at the same time.

"The same is true about us. The beginning and the end. They've sort of met in the middle and that is exactly where we were born."

He shook his head and sighed, annoyed with himself.

"This isn't going right," he said. "Let me start again."

He thought for a moment, then continued.

"Yesterday, four boys and a girl finished a long war against the Old Ones."

"That was us."

330

"Yes. We beat them and managed to send them into another dimension. And that's where we are now. If you like, you could say that we're at twelve o'clock and a new day is about to begin. We've trapped the Old Ones on the other side of a gate and right now it seems there's no way that they'll ever be able to return."

"So what will happen next?"

"The world will change. There's not very much of humanity left, Jamie. It came very close to total annihilation. There are a few thousand people scattered across the planet, but what happened here – the battle and the five of us – will soon be almost completely forgotten. And as the years go by, the world will change. The ice hasn't finished melting in the north and new continents are forming. We are entering a dark period: a time – if you like – for civilization to catch its breath. But then, slowly, the wheel of time will turn and new cities will rise, new cultures will flourish. It will all begin again.

"And then, one day, you and your brother will be born. Ten thousand years from now! Your world will look very different from ours and although a few names and places may echo faintly across the centuries, very few people will know what they really signified. The Old Ones. The Five. The building of the first gate.

"You'll think that you live in a safe and comfortable place, but I'm afraid you'll be wrong. Because the whole thing will begin again. The Old Ones will somehow break out of the prison we've made for them and what will follow will be exactly the same as what happened here. They will grow in strength and power and they will finish off what they began."

"They'll destroy our world," Jamie said.

"Yes."

"Nightrise. They're part of it."

"The Old Ones don't actually show themselves for as long as they can help it. They find people who are greedy or mean or full of hate and give them power. These people think they're going to get rich. They think they'll be rewarded with anything they want. And it's only at the very end that they realize that the Old Ones have lied to them and they're doomed too. There will be no survivors. The entire planet has to die.

"So what is happening in your world is exactly the same as what happened in mine. Yesterday the cycle ended and the last battle was won. For you, the same cycle is about to begin. The Old Ones will grow in strength. The world will be torn apart. And you will have to face them a second time."

"On my own?"

"No, Jamie. In your world, there are also four boys and one girl who have to come together. Five Gatekeepers. There's a Matt and an Inti and a Scar just as there is in mine."

"But are we the same or are we different?"

"We're the same but we're living in a different time."

"I don't understand!"

Matt sighed. "Don't try to unravel it. Just think about how it actually works. That's all that matters.

"Five Gatekeepers in the past. The same five, born again,

332

and fighting in the future. Sometimes, we meet..."

"In the dream world."

"Yes. Otherwise we're separated."

"Then how did I get here? What am I doing here now?" Jamie didn't understand everything Matt was saying but it was clear to him that he had somehow jumped from one world to another and that he didn't belong here.

"This is the one thing that the Old Ones never understood," Matt replied. "I can explain it to you now but they never realized it and that was how I was able to deceive them.

"This is how it works. Somewhere, in your world, there is a boy called Matt. And if he were killed, I would instantly replace him ... so there would still be five Gatekeepers. And if I had been killed, the future Matt would have been called to replace me. Do you see? It's as if each of us has two lives. To kill us properly, the Old Ones have to kill us twice."

"Sapling was killed."

"Yes." Matt bowed his head for a moment and when he spoke, his voice was low. "There was never anything for Sapling to find at Scathack Hill. I sent him because I knew he would die there. And he knew it too. I told him. Flint blames himself but the truth is that Sapling sacrificed himself for the rest of us.

"You see, I had to let the Old Ones kill one of us. They had to think that the circle had been broken, that the Five would never meet and that they had won. That would make them careless. They saw Sapling die but they didn't realize that you would be sent to take his place and that there would be five of us after all. And that's exactly what happened. They allowed Inti to slip through their lines. And when you and Scar rode down into the battle – that was it. We beat them by a trick."

"But if I'm not Sapling, how come I can speak his language?" Jamie was still aware that the words he was using would have made no sense in twenty-first-century Nevada. "How come I can ride a horse? And this…" He picked up Frost. "I feel this sword was made for me. I'd never killed anyone in my life but as soon as I had it in my hand…" He stopped, preferring not to remember the slaughter of the day before.

"One day you will fight another battle," Matt said. "And by that time you will be equally skilled. The past learns from the future and the future learns from the past. I've already told you. We are always the same Five."

"But we have different names."

Matt nodded. "It's true. But where do names come from? We don't choose them. They are given to us."

Jamie thought for a moment. He had been called Jamie because it was the name of the doctor who had examined him when he was found abandoned as a baby. Scott had been christened after a box of grass seed. Those weren't their true names. They were just something to put on a form.

"In this world, Inti was named after the sun," Matt went on. "But in the future he will be called Pedro. It doesn't matter. The names make no difference to who we really are."

"What is your real name?" Jamie asked.

Matt fell silent. "I prefer to use my name from your world," he said. "I'm just Matt."

Jamie had pins and needles in his leg. He wondered how long they had been sitting here. The sun was rising higher all the time. "There's not much more to add," Matt continued. "But you might like to know where you are. Ten thousand years from now, this country will look very different. It will have formed into a small island. Its name will be England. The forest will have been replanted and there will be a village about a mile from where we're sitting now. The village will be called Lesser Malling, and although the people there will have forgotten all about the Old Ones and the battle that we've just fought and won, they will have faint memories that something important happened here. There will be a stone circle, built around the very place where you and I, Inti, Scar and Flint finally met. That circle will come to be known as Raven's Gate."

Matt smiled to himself and pointed down.

"You see this river where we're sitting? One day, it will save my life. Well, not exactly mine." He pointed upstream. "The other Matt will swim from over there and he'll come up spluttering and half drowned right at this spot. And when he drags himself out, he won't know anything about me. Because, you see, he belongs to the future. And I'm here in the past."

"What happens now?" Jamie asked. "You're going to send me back."

"Yes. You have to find your brother. I have to warn you, Jamie, if Scott has been taken by the Old Ones, you must prepare yourself for the worst. They'll hurt him. They may try to change him. If you do find him, he may not be the same."

"He wasn't at Silent Creek," Jamie said. He suddenly felt miserable. With everything that had happened in this other world, he had forgotten how he had failed in his own. Scott had been at the prison but he had gone. The search had to begin all over again. "Where do I look for him?"

"Use your dreams. The dream world that we visit acts in a strange way. Sometimes it sends us messages in the form of pictures or symbols. Always remember what you see there. It may mean something."

Matt stood up.

"I have to go," he said. "There's still a lot of work to do. And in a few days' time I'm going to travel with Inti to his country. There's a weak spot there and we have to construct a second gate to make sure the Old Ones can't break back in. Inti has a brilliant idea for a sort of lock, but on a huge scale. We're going to design it together so that it can be built into the desert floor—"

"But what's the point?" Jamie interrupted. "You've already told me that the Old Ones are going to come back again."

"Well, that's an entirely different argument. Just because we know they're coming back, doesn't mean we can't try to stop them. And the longer we keep them out, the more time the world has to restore itself."

"Do you really have no idea where I can find Scott?"

"I'm sorry. But he must still be alive. If he'd been killed, Flint would have replaced him and he would have somehow managed to find you."

There was a loud screeching sound and something swooped out of the sky, landing on the outstretched branch of an oak tree on the other side of the river. Jamie started up, alarmed – but it was only an eagle. He wondered where it had come from. It wasn't moving now and seemed to be staring right at him.

Matt had noticed the bird and Jamie had the impression that it meant something to him. "There's one more thing I can tell you that might help," he said.

"What's that?"

"There are two gates that exist in my world and yours. We made the first of them ourselves today. Inti and I will design the second very soon. But there's something else that you need to know about. There are also twenty-five doorways."

"What do you mean?"

"How do you think we've travelled these great distances to find each other? Inti has come from the other side of the world and I can assure you he didn't take a boat! The doorways are short cuts. You go in one door and you come out another a thousand miles away. There are doorways in your world too."

"Where?"

"They are all in sacred places – or places that have become

337

sacred mainly because the doors were there. Places of worship. Buildings of one sort and another but also caves, burial chambers, even hills. They're marked with the same five-pointed star that we carried on our banners. It's the symbol of the power of Five. You're going to need to find them. All of you."

"How do we do that?"

"There's a map. It was drawn by a man called Joseph of Cordoba. He was a monk but they made him into a saint. He was one of the very few men who knew about us and our war with the Old Ones. He put the map in his diary and it shows all twenty-five doorways. Find the diary and it will give you the secret paths around your entire world."

"How do I get back to my world?" Jamie asked.

"That's easy. Someone has sent a guide for you."

Jamie looked across the river. "The eagle?"

Matt nodded.

"What do I do?"

"Follow the eagle. He'll show you where to go." Matt got to his feet.

The two boys stood looking at each other.

"Goodbye, Jamie," Matt said. "You and I will meet again."

"I'm glad I was able to fight alongside you, Matt. Say goodbye to Inti and Scar for me. And to Flint." Jamie unsheathed his sword one last time. He held it for a moment, not wanting to let it go, but he knew he couldn't take it with him. He handed it over. "Look after Frost," he said. "I only had it for a little while but it served me well."

The two of them looked at each other one last time. Then, leaving Jamie beside the river, Matt turned round and walked back towards the camp.

Jamie glanced at the eagle, which stirred slightly, ruffling its feathers. "Which way?" he called out.

The eagle flew the short distance to the next tree, then a little further to one set back from the river. Its message was clear. Jamie was expected to swim across. He wasn't sure he liked the idea. The river was deep and cold and the water was flowing very fast. But it seemed he wasn't going to be given a choice.

"Whatever you say…" He climbed down the gully and waded in.

He was halfway across and well out of his depth when he realized that the current was too strong and he wasn't going to make it. The river had him in its grip and it was carrying him downstream, sweeping him along between banks which rose up ever higher, blocking out the light. Worse still, his clothes were weighing him down, threatening to drag him beneath the surface. Jamie began to panic. He turned round, wondering if he could call out to Matt for help. But Matt was far away by now and the moment he opened his mouth he found himself swallowing water. Desperately, he thrashed around. If he couldn't reach the bank or catch hold of something, he was going to get pulled under. It was crazy. Had he come through so much simply to drown?

The eagle was still watching him, perched in another tree. Jamie caught one glimpse of it and guessed that what had happened had been quite deliberate. He had been invited into a trap and like a fool he had walked into it. The water – freezing cold – churned and foamed all around him. He went under. Gasping, using all his strength, he broke through the surface and breathed again. Ahead of him he saw a cave, a jagged hole in the rock. The water was rushing into it and Jamie was being dragged along too.

He managed to scream once and then he was sucked into utter blackness. He was pulled under again – and this time there would be no coming back up. Water flooded into his nose and mouth. He was spinning round and round. How had he allowed this to happen? He was certain that this was death.

And then nothing.

Jamie opened his eyes.

He was lying on his side, wrapped in a blanket. He was in the Mojave Desert and it was dusk. There was a small fire in front of him and he could feel a burning pain between his shoulders. Joe Feather was leaning over him. The Intake Officer was smiling, his face filled with relief.

He was back.

BACK TO RENO

"How long have I been here?" Jamie asked.

"Two nights and two days," Joe Feather replied.

"And where exactly are we?"

"We're south of Boulder City. In the mountains. Nobody's going to find us here."

Jamie made a quick calculation. His time unconscious in this world seemed to equate with his time fighting and surviving in the other. He watched as Joe poked a stick into the campfire, making the sparks leap up. The sun was setting and soon the evening would grow cool, but the fire was really there to boil water, to cook their meal and to provide them with a little light once the night came. There was no sign of Daniel. He was asleep in the tepee.

"There are things I need to ask you," Jamie said.

"Are you well enough to talk?"

Jamie moved his shoulder blade. The moment he had returned to his own world, the wound had come back. He could feel where the bullet had hit him. He would probably feel it for years to come. But it wasn't hurting too much now.

"We had to cut you open," Joe said. "We took the bullet out and dressed the wound with willow bark." Jamie looked puzzled. "It's traditional. But it also makes sense. Willow bark contains salicylic acid – it's a natural painkiller."

"Who did it, Joe?"

"Me and a friend."

Jamie nodded. "Well, thanks…" He certainly wasn't going to complain. He'd seen much worse injuries in the last two days.

"Here…" Joe lifted a kettle from the fire and poured boiling water into two tin mugs. Whoever had driven them here had left them with plenty of supplies. Joe had made a rose-coloured tea that tasted slightly bitter. "Meg gel tea," he explained. "It purifies your blood. Maybe it'll push some of the toxins out of the wound."

"Thank you." Jamie took the steaming liquid but he didn't drink. "Are you sure we're safe?"

"Yes. The authorities won't be looking for you here and if they are they won't find us. My people are Washoe. We know how to hide."

"You're Washoe too."

"Yes. Like you and your brother."

"You knew about the Five." Jamie remembered what Joe had said when he came to the isolation cell. "Do you know about the Old Ones?"

Joe fell silent for a moment. "That is not what we call them," he said. "Each tribe has a different name for them. The

Navajo call them the *Anasazi*. That means ancient enemy. We speak of them as the people eaters. They are the same."

"How did you know who I was?"

"I had been waiting for you." Joe sipped his tea, inviting Jamie to do the same. "How do I begin to tell you everything you want to know?" he said. "Perhaps I should ask you how much you know about the Washoe – and about other Native Americans."

"I don't know very much," Jamie admitted. "We talked about Indians at school. About what happened to them."

"Then you must begin by understanding that my people were destroyed," Joe said. He spoke the words as a matter of fact and without rancour. "The Washoe was a mountain tribe and we learned how to hide. But even so there are only a few hundred of us left today and we have almost nothing. Of course we were not alone. All the native people in America suffered the same way. The white people took our past from us and we grew up with little hope of a future. Many of our parents turned to alcohol to try to forget what had been done to us. Many of our young people have turned to drugs for the same reason.

"But there are some of us who walk two worlds. We work in modern America – in the hotels or casinos or, like me, in the prisons. But we have not forgotten our history. And we still tell the story of a great battle that took place at the beginning of time and of two heroes – twins – who helped to win it."

"Flint and Sapling."

"Those are not the names we use. Those names are Iroquois, I think. But it doesn't matter. There was a time when all the tribes were one tribe. And anyway, the stories have never been written down. They change with the passing of time.

"But even today we still tell stories of twin heroes. The Apache, the Kiowa, the Navajo and many others. The twins are always boys of your age. In many of the stories, Flint is evil. He causes the death of his brother, Sapling."

"He wasn't evil," Jamie said. "Sapling wanted to die."

"We were always told that the twin heroes would return at a time of great need and that we should watch out for them. There was one way we would be able to recognize them." Joe reached out and touched his own shoulder. "They would carry a mark. Here…"

"A tattoo…"

"You call it that, but it was not something injected into you. I saw that at once. It is something you were born with."

"What does it mean?"

"Indian symbols have many meanings. But the spiral is a symbol of human life. Every human being has a spiral on their body – look at your fingerprints or the hair on the crown of your head – and to us these parts have always been sacred. A spiral is circular and never ends, so it can also mean immortality. As for the line, dividing it in two, that could signify many things. Night and day. Good and evil…"

"Twins."

"Yes. I saw the mark when you were in the shower and guessed at once who you must be. But you confused me. You lied to me. You said you had no brother."

"I couldn't tell you. I couldn't tell anyone."

Joe nodded. "If I had known, I might have acted sooner. Even so, I made contact with my friends. That was not easy. I had to contact them by satellite phone and all the calls at Silent Creek were monitored. But I made them understand and they agreed to gather. Then Max Koring found out who you were. He told me your real name and said that you had a twin. That was when I knew you were in great danger."

"So you raided the prison."

"Yes."

"Where are your friends now? I never even got a chance to thank them."

"They don't need your thanks. They were honoured to be able to help you. Most of them have now returned to their homes. A couple of them were wounded. None of them were killed."

There was a movement and Daniel appeared, crawling bleary-eyed out of the tepee. He had nodded off during the afternoon but now he blinked and smiled, pleased to see Jamie. "You're awake!" he said.

"Danny... I need to talk to you." Jamie struggled to raise himself up. It hurt his back but eventually he managed to position himself, sitting cross-legged in front of the fire. Both of them were still wearing their prison trousers but someone had supplied them with new T-shirts. Danny's shirt was advertising engine oil.

"I thought they'd killed you," Danny said. "This old woman came – and I mean *really* old. She spent ages looking after you. They wouldn't let me watch. I don't know what she did but this morning she packed up her horse and left. I figured you were dead." He shrugged. "I'm glad you're not."

Joe got to his feet. "I'll leave you two together," he said. "I must prepare the meal." He disappeared behind the tepee.

Jamie looked around him. They were in a sort of cleft in the mountains, surrounded on all sides. Unless a helicopter flew directly overhead there was no chance of their being seen – and, as Joe had said, why would anyone be looking for them here? He examined the tepee where Daniel had been sleeping. It looked like the genuine article, made out of animal skin with a simple pattern of interlocking lines around the base. The sun was low in the sky, making the mountains glow a deep red. Nothing moved apart from the fingers of flame, licking at the dead wood and the trickle of smoke, folding in on itself as it climbed up.

He glanced at Daniel. "How are you?"

"I'm good." Daniel sighed. "But I'd like to go home now. Joe has a cell phone but there's no reception here. I haven't even been able to phone my mum."

"Can you tell me about Silent Creek?" Jamie asked. He paused. "Can you tell me about Scott?"

"There's not much to tell." Daniel sat down on the other side of the camp fire. "They grabbed me when I was on my way home from school and they took me there. There were sixteen of us in the Block. I was the youngest. There were four girls. The rest were boys." He thought for a moment. "The first month was the worst. They did these experiments. They had this idea that I had some sort of power. That was what they were interested in. They were looking for kids with powers."

"You saw into the future."

"Did my mum tell you that?"

Jamie nodded.

"It only ever happened a couple of times and it wasn't like seeing the future. It was more like having a bad feeling. There was a bus that crashed and I sort of knew it was going to happen. Maybe that's how they found out about me, because it got into the newspapers. Anyway, they tried to make me do it again and when I couldn't, they hurt me. They had a special room. They said that was the only place in Silent Creek where my power would work, but it didn't make any difference because there was nothing I could do and after a bit they lost interest in me."

That at least explained one thing that Jamie hadn't understood – why he had been unable to force Max Koring to do what he wanted. He had thought his power had failed. But it was the position of the prison that was to blame. A natural phenomenon – perhaps some sort of natural magnetism – had neutralized him. Nightrise had left nothing to chance.

"They were searching for the Five," Jamie muttered. It was suddenly obvious to him.

"They called it the Psi project," Daniel went on. "The other kids were from all over America. It was the same for all of us. They did the tests. They hurt us. Then they left us alone. After that, we were just kept in prison, which sucked because we hadn't done anything wrong. Billy was afraid they would kill us one day – if they didn't need us any more."

"Who was Billy?"

"He was my friend. I'm sorry we had to leave him behind. I hope he's OK."

"Tell me about Scott."

"Scott was the last to arrive. That must have been a couple of weeks ago. He had the cell next to mine and I saw him before they began on him." Daniel saw Jamie flinch. "I'm sorry…" he muttered.

"How badly did they hurt him?"

"Well, they took him away and I know they must have done a lot of bad things because after a few days he wouldn't talk to me any more. He wouldn't talk to anyone. The bald man was working on him … Mr Banes." Daniel paused. "We knew Scott was important to them because this woman arrived. She was thin and scrawny with grey hair and a face like a sort of rotten fruit. We'd only ever seen her once before. Everyone was scared of her."

"Do you know her name?"

Daniel shook his head. "She never said who she was."

There was one more thing Jamie wanted to know, although he almost dreaded putting it into words. "What happened to Scott?" he asked. "What did they do with him?"

"I don't know, Jamie. I'm sorry. One minute he was there, the next he was gone. Nobody knew where they took him."

So that was it.

It was the same as Joe had told him. Jamie felt a wave of black despair but he forced it away. He wasn't going to give in. He remembered everything that Matt had said. He had led an army and fought in a war … even if it had been in another world at another time. The strange thing was, there wasn't a single part of him that believed it hadn't happened, or that the whole experience had been some sort of fantasy, imagined while he lay unconscious. He knew it was real. And Joe recognized him for what he was. One of the Five. Whatever happened, he would find Scott – no matter how long it took.

"When can we leave?" Daniel asked.

The boy was eleven years old. He had been kidnapped in broad daylight, separated from his mother, kept prisoner for seven months. Jamie understood how he must be feeling.

Then Joe appeared, carrying a saucepan.

"When can we leave?" Jamie repeated the question.

"Where do you want to go?" Joe asked.

"We have to get back to Reno. Danny's mother is waiting for him there."

Joe considered. "Another twenty-four hours," he said. "The nearest road is seven miles away and we'll have to move at night. I have friends waiting for us. They'll drive you wherever you want to go."

"Can we really leave tomorrow?" Daniel said.

"If Jamie is ready."

"Don't worry, Danny," Jamie said. He took a sip of the tea. "I'll be ready."

They left the following evening, Jamie supporting himself on a staff that Joe had brought for him. He knew he wasn't really ready for the journey. His shoulder and left arm were on fire and he was still weak from loss of blood. But he couldn't keep Daniel waiting any longer. It was a perfect night with a full moon and perhaps a million stars guiding them on their way. They came slowly down the mountains, but once the ground had levelled out they made better progress. Joe knew exactly where they were going and never hesitated once. Jamie imagined that he had been born with these skills, something handed down instinctively from generations ago.

Soon he was exhausted and wishing he had waited longer before setting out. Every step seemed to take the pain and amplify it, sending it shuddering through his body. He found himself leaning on Daniel for support. But he refused to complain and although they stopped a couple of times for water, he never asked for a rest.

He didn't actually see the road until they reached it. One moment his foot was on sand, the next it had come down on

350

tarmac. He looked to the right and there it was, a straight line cutting into the far distance. There were no buildings anywhere around but a line of telegraph poles followed the road, the wires looping between them. Daniel let out an exclamation of delight. Telephone wires meant contact with his mother. It was all he wanted.

They had walked down the road for about a hundred yards when Jamie saw headlights moving towards them. He was immediately nervous but then he glanced at Joe, who nodded slowly. This was what he had been expecting. A few moments later, a beaten-up minibus pulled out with an Indian driver behind the wheel. Jamie wasn't sure how he had found them. Had he been patrolling the road every night, waiting for them to show up? But that didn't matter now. He was just grateful to get off his feet, glad to be finally on his way.

Joe spoke a few words with the driver and they all climbed in. At once they set off. Daniel must have been more tired than he thought because he fell asleep almost immediately. Jamie sat, slumped against the window, watching the landscape – dark and empty – flash by.

An hour later they stopped on the edge of a small town. Jamie saw electric lights in the distance and the bulky shadows of houses. He had no idea where they were.

"I leave you here," Joe announced.

"Thank you." Jamie wasn't sure what to say. "What will happen to you now, Joe?" he asked. "The police will be look-

351

ing for you. And you haven't got a job."

"My people will look after me. You don't need to worry. And if you need us again, we will come."

Jamie knew that was true. He had no way of contacting them but somehow they would look out for him. If the need arose, they would be there. Joe leant over and the two of them shook hands. Then the Indian climbed out of the minibus and the three of them set off, leaving him standing alone.

After that, Jamie slept.

The next time he opened his eyes, he knew at once where he was: right back where it had all started, in the city of Reno. The familiar landmarks were all around him. The Hilton Hotel in the distance. The great black glass block of the City Hall, towering over the city centre. The casinos and the pawn shops. The rushing water of the Truckee River. In a way it was the last place he had wanted to be, but he and Alicia had agreed that it made sense. She wanted to be close to him while he was in Nevada – but not too close. Alicia could rent a place in Reno and be just a few hours away from the prison. She had decided she would wait for him here.

"Where do I take you?" the driver asked. Jamie knew nothing about him – not even his name.

"There's a place called Paso Tiempo," Jamie said. "It's near the airport."

Paso Tiempo was a mobile home park just round the corner from the motel where Alicia had stayed the last time she was in Reno. It was a long strip of road with houses that were little more than boxes on wheels parked alongside each other in a neat row. They slowed down and stopped outside one of the homes: number twenty-three. It was the prettiest one in the park, surrounded by flowers. Alicia had rented it for a month.

The minibus stopped. Jamie nudged Daniel. "Wake up," he muttered. And at that moment the door of the trailer opened and there was Alicia, standing on the top step. She must have heard them arrive. Perhaps she opened the door whenever any car pulled up. Daniel saw her and was wide awake instantly, his entire face filled with an expression of joy. He scrambled past Jamie, almost falling out of the minibus, and ran to her. Then the two of them were in each other's arms, not wanting to separate ever again.

Jamie got out more slowly. He was in a lot of pain. He could barely move his neck or his right arm and he was limping. At that moment he felt many things. He was glad he had brought Daniel back. Of course he was happy for the two of them. But, looking at them, he was also aware of something else: a deep sadness that cut into him even more than the wound in his back. He had no mother. Nobody had ever held him like that and nobody ever would. He was ashamed of himself. It was wrong of him. But he knew that he had come to the end of a road. Alicia and Daniel had each other. There was nothing more they could do for him.

Alicia looked up and saw him.

"Jamie," she said. "You brought him back."

Jamie nodded.

"How can I thank you? How can I ever thank you enough?" Then she realized. "What about Scott?"

"Scott wasn't there."

She heard the heavy words and went over to him, taking Daniel with her. For a moment the two of them faced each other and she reached out, wanting to draw him into her embrace. But he stepped back. "You're hurt," she said.

"I'll be all right." Jamie looked past her. "Do you mind if I go in? I need to lie down."

"Of course. You must tell me…" She stopped herself. "I'm so sorry … about Scott."

But Jamie had already walked past her. Somehow he dragged himself up the steps and went into the trailer. It was cool and clean with a little kitchen and a sofa and a table. He sat down. The mother and her son remained on their own, outside.

NATIVE SON

They did nothing at all the next day. Jamie needed to rest and Alicia and Daniel were glad to have time alone with each other. They felt safe in the trailer park. People came and went and nobody asked too many questions. Jamie hadn't been seen. They could have been a family trying to sort themselves out or they could have been on the run from the law – to the other inhabitants, it made no difference.

Alicia was worried about Jamie. She had brought him lunch and changed the dressing on his wound. They had spoken a little, but most of the time he wanted to be by himself. He had been gone only a week, but now that he had come back he was completely changed. Of course, he had been shot. He had nearly died. And she could sense his disappointment at not finding Scott. But it was something more – even more than all that. He had aged. He was looking at the world with different eyes.

The next day was a Saturday and Jamie woke late. The trailer only had one bedroom, which Alicia was sharing with Daniel, and Jamie had a sofa bed in the main room. They all knew that they couldn't stay here much longer. They were wasting their time in Reno. There were still things they had to do.

When Alicia came through, Jamie was sitting up. She was glad to see that a lot of his colour had returned and he seemed to be moving more easily.

"Coffee?" she asked.

"Thanks." He looked around him. "Where's Danny?"

"Still asleep."

Alicia went into the kitchen area and boiled the kettle. "How are you feeling?" she asked.

"I'm tired, Alicia. But I'm going to be all right. I just need to start looking for Scott." Jamie hesitated but there was something he had to know. "When are you and Danny going back to Washington?" he asked. "You've got your work to go back to. There must be a lot of stuff you have to do."

Alicia brought the coffee over to the bed. "You can get one thing out of your head," she said. "I'm not going to leave until we've found Scott. I told you that from the start. We're in this together … and Danny agrees. We're going to stick with you."

Jamie nodded his thanks. "I don't have any idea where to start," he said.

"But I do." Alicia sat down next to him on the edge of the bed. "A lot has happened in the last few days," she explained. "Starting with the fact that the Feds took over Silent Creek while you and Danny were hiding out in the mountains."

"They went in…?"

"It was John Trelawny. He's been desperately worried about you. He called the authorities."

"I thought he couldn't do that."

"Something changed. He wants to speak to you urgently. I'd have called him yesterday only he was travelling from the East Coast – and anyway you were out of it."

"So what happened to Silent Creek? Did they find the Block?"

Alicia nodded. "All the prisoners – the ones they called the Specials – have been released and the other kids are going to be transferred to state facilities. I spoke to Patrick. Do you remember him?"

Jamie thought back to the silver-haired man they had met at the hotel in Los Angeles. He had been the senator's California campaign chairman.

"He told me as much as he could, which actually wasn't very much. For the moment, nobody's talking. Of course, Nightrise is denying any knowledge of the kidnappings or anything to do with them. They're trying to claim that it was all down to Colton Banes, that he was running some sort of independent operation – and since he's dead, he's not going to argue."

"Has there been anything in the newspapers?"

"Not yet. The story is so huge and nobody quite understands what's been going on. For the time being, they're keeping it quiet."

357

Jamie understood. He knew there would be a cover-up. There were too many questions that were not only unanswered but unanswerable. He didn't care. He was just glad that Daniel's friend – Billy – and the other kids would be returned to their families. And it was good news for Baltimore, Green Eyes and the other prisoners too. They'd be better off with the Nevada authorities looking after them. Maybe they'd even earn an early release.

"It's all good news," Alicia said, and Jamie could tell that she wasn't just trying to cheer him up. "The Feds are in control. They arrested a man called Max Koring and they seized all the paperwork in the administration block. They're going through it now. There must be some record of what happened to Scott. Someone must know where he is. They'll find something. I'm sure of it."

Jamie wanted to share her optimism. But he wasn't so sure. It seemed to him that Nightrise was bigger and more powerful than any of them suspected. But then he had seen the Old Ones. The shape-changers. The fire riders. The mutilated humans. So much death, delivered without a second thought. Sitting here in this trailer on the edge of Reno airport, Alicia thought the world was safe. Jamie knew how wrong she might be.

"Why does Senator Trelawny want to see me?" he asked.

"He didn't say. He just said that he had new information and there was someone you had to meet. He thought they'd find you at the prison. The people who went in ... their first

358

job was to get you out and bring you to him. We'll see him tomorrow."

"Where is he now?"

"Not all that far from here. He's just over the state line in California … in the High Sierra. Have you heard of a place called Auburn?"

Jamie shook his head.

"It's an old mining town. It got big in the gold rush days. John was born there and today it's his fiftieth birthday, so they're giving him a parade." There was a television in the room, on the kitchen counter, and a remote control next to the bed. Alicia reached out and picked it up. "There should be something on the news," she said.

She switched on the TV.

It was already tuned to a twenty-four-hour news channel. The anchor man was talking about the result of a trial following some big financial scandal. Then there were advertisements. Then a story about a basketball player charged with murder.

"We'll meet the senator in Los Angeles," Alicia said.

"Are the police still looking for me?" Jamie asked. It suddenly dawned on him how ridiculous his situation had become. He had committed no crime but he was still wanted for the murders of Don White and Marcie Kelsey. And as Jeremy Rabb, he was presumably wanted for various drug offences and for escaping from Silent Creek. How had he got himself into this mess?

But Alicia never got a chance to answer the question.

"...and in Auburn, California, last-minute preparations for a very special birthday party. John Trelawny, the man most people believe will win the November election, is returning to his home town, where he was born fifty years ago. These are the streets where, in just a few hours' time, five thousand people are expected to gather to welcome the senator..."

The story they had been waiting for came onto the screen. Glancing at the picture, Jamie froze. It was as if a chasm had opened up underneath him and he had been sucked into it. He found himself grabbing hold of the bed as if to steady himself. His eyes were fixed on the TV.

He had seen a face he recognized. Not John Trelawny. It was the last face he had expected to see. It wasn't anyone he had met in the real world. It wasn't a real person at all.

It was a statue.

A grey stone face. Skin like putty. Hollowed-out eyes. The figure was wearing a shirt with the sleeves rolled up and a cowboy hat. It was resting on one knee, holding a bowl. There was some sort of metal bridge in the background and a few pieces of old mine works around.

"What is it?" Alicia demanded. She had seen the look on his face.

The camera had only lingered on it for a moment but Jamie had heard the words of the commentary, "...looking for gold, the town was first founded in the nineteenth century..." And suddenly he understood what this man was ... the man he had first seen kneeling by the water in his dreams.

Not a cowboy. A gold prospector.

Why?

"Jamie...?" Alicia was becoming alarmed.

"Did you see? Just now..."

"What?"

"On the screen!"

It was too late. The picture had changed. Now it was showing old footage of John Trelawny waving to the crowd at another rally.

"There was a man on the screen just now. Not a man. A statue. I've seen it before and ... I don't know why, but it means something. It's important."

"In Auburn?"

"Yes. I think so."

Alicia slid off the bed. She had a laptop with her and she opened it, powering it up and connecting it to the Internet. Meanwhile, Jamie was thinking furiously. He knew he had been sent a sign and that it was up to him, and him alone, to make sense of it.

The statue of a gold prospector in Auburn. A grey giant kneeling on a beach. They were one and the same – Jamie was sure of it. He remembered what Matt had told him. The dream world was there to help them. But sometimes it sent them messages in strange ways. What had the grey man told him?

"He's gonna kill him. And it's your job to stop him."

Was Scott going to be killed in Auburn? Was that what he had meant?

"His name is Claude Chana," Alicia said. She had accessed an Auburn website on her computer and was looking at a picture of the statue now. "He found gold in the Auburn ravine in 1848 and that led to the establishment of a mining camp which later became the town. There's a statue of him down by the old firehouse."

"He's gonna kill him."

"You mean ... Scott?"

"No, boy. You don't understand—"

But suddenly, with horrible clarity, Jamie *did* understand. There were two men fighting to become president: John Trelawny and Charles Baker. Nightrise supported Baker. But Trelawny was winning.

So Nightrise were going to assassinate him.

And they were going to use Scott.

"He's gonna kill him." The "he" was Scott. The "him" was Trelawny. It was as simple as that.

"You have to call the senator," Jamie said, and it almost sounded to him as if it was someone else who was talking. "You have to warn him."

"What...?"

"They're going to try to kill him."

Alicia stared at him. "What are you saying? How can you know that?"

362

"Please, Alicia. Don't argue with me. I can't explain it to you but they're going to kill Senator Trelawny in Auburn today and you have to get him on the phone and stop him going there."

Alicia hesitated only a few seconds more. Then she grabbed her cell phone and speed-dialled a number. Jamie waited as the number was connected. He saw her face fall.

"Senator..." she said, and he could tell she was leaving a message. "This is Alicia McGuire. I've been talking to Jamie and he says you're in danger, that you mustn't go to Auburn. Please call me back."

She snapped the phone shut.

"He wasn't there," Jamie said.

"I only have his personal cell phone number," Alicia explained. "He wanted me to be able to call him directly. But he may have left his own phone behind. He may have switched it off. I don't know how to reach him."

"How far is it to Auburn?"

"I don't know. It's the other side of Lake Tahoe."

"How long would it take us to get there?"

Alicia's face brightened. "Not that long. A couple of hours."

"And when does the parade start?"

"Midday." She looked at her watch. It was a few minutes after ten o'clock. She made a decision. "We can make it," she said. "Get dressed. I'll wake Daniel. It's going to be tight, but we can get there..."

*   *   *

363

The crowds had started arriving early for the birthday parade and by eleven o'clock there must have been two thousand people lining the pavements, with more spilling out of their cars every minute. There were dozens of police officers on special duty. The secret service had gone in the night before and cordoned off the area where the parade would take place. While the local residents slept, they had discreetly swept the entire town, using dogs to sniff out any trace of high explosives, installing security cameras, identifying the rooftops and the second-floor windows that might provide a marksman with cover.

There were two quite separate parts of Auburn. The modern section was unremarkable, a couple of streets that met at an angle with the usual assortment of shops and offices. But the Old Town, as everyone called it, had been almost perfectly preserved, a living echo of the nineteenth century and the gold rush that had created it.

It stood – or nestled, rather – at the bottom of a hill. The main street swept down and then split into two, each side curving round like the two halves of a horseshoe with an open area, like a town square, in the middle. Shops and houses ran all the way along the edges, most of them brick or timber-framed. But it was the buildings in the middle of the square that were the town's pride and joy. One was an old post office, the other a firehouse, which looked like an oversized toy with its pointed roof and red and white stripes.

Auburn had its own courthouse that stood high above the

town, its great dome glinting in the sunlight. In the summer months, the heat could be almost too much to bear and the town would resemble not so much a horseshoe as a frying pan. But someone, a long time ago, had planted a cedar tree behind the firehouse and its branches had spread in every direction, the dark green leaves providing at least some shelter from the sun.

The statue of Claude Chana stood next to the cedar tree. This was where the Old Town came to an abrupt end, with Highway 80 carrying six lanes of traffic, roaring past east and west. There were two filling stations facing each other and a railway bridge behind. This was what Jamie had seen on the TV.

It was going to be a hot day.

The sky was almost cloudless and the sun dazzled as it bounced off the tarmac and the shop windows. The entire town had been dressed up for the parade, with a row of bleachers, six high, constructed in front of the post office and facing back up the hill. The parade would come this way. It would turn off past the main shopping parade and make a complete circle behind the cedar tree before stopping once again at the bleachers. There was a platform, a row of microphones, an area for the press. The mayor would make a speech welcoming John Trelawny. John Trelawny would make a speech thanking the mayor. Then everyone would have lunch.

There were flags everywhere. Hundreds of them. Flags on

365

lampposts and street corners, attached to cars, bikes and prams, fluttering from the dome of the courthouse. A great banner had been erected above the bleachers so that everyone would see it as they came down the hill.

```
╔══════════════════════════════════════╗
║   AUBURN WELCOMES SENATOR TRELAWNY    ║
║       HAPPY BIRTHDAY, JOHN!           ║
╚══════════════════════════════════════╝
```

And although the shops had been closed for the day, their windows were filled with messages of support.

VAL'S LIQUOR SUPPORTS
JOHN TRELAWNY FOR PRESIDENT

PLACER COUNTY BANK WELCOMES
JOHN TRELAWNY – NATIVE SON

The local dignitaries were already taking their places on the bleachers. The mayor's wife was there, sitting next to Grace Trelawny and her two sons. The chief of police and the fire chief, both in uniform, had taken seats in the front row. The town's founding families and its most prominent businessmen had been invited, as had many of the people who had known John Trelawny when he was growing up: his principal, his teachers, the local minister, the football coach. By quarter to twelve, every seat had been taken apart from two, right in the middle. They had both been marked with RESERVED signs.

Barriers had been erected for crowd control and by now people were lining the pavements, five or six rows deep. The local police were patrolling the edge of the street, occasionally barking out orders through their bullhorns – even though there was no need for it and nobody was listening. The atmosphere was light-hearted. It was obvious that everyone in Auburn supported John Trelawny and, if there were any protestors, they had been wise enough to stay away.

At midday exactly the parade began.

First up was the local high school marching band: the trumpets and trombones glinting brilliantly, the music blasting out. Among them was a tiny boy with a huge drum and a huge boy with a triangle. Two baton twirlers led the way and they were followed by a drill team: a dozen girls in sparkling silver, going through a series of tightly rehearsed steps. Someone threw a switch and a rap song burst out, fighting with the music from the band. But it didn't matter. The jumble of noise and colour was what it was all about.

Then came the vehicles: open-top Cadillacs and sports cars. The president of the Chamber of Commerce, waving and looking pleased with himself. Miss Auburn and two other beauty queens with their sequins and sashes. A single fire truck with half a dozen firefighters (they got the biggest cheer from the crowd). War veterans, some of them in wheelchairs. Then dozens more children walking behind. Boy scouts, girl scouts, cub scouts. And flag bearers – all dressed identically in silver and blue – spinning flags over their heads and around their shoulders, perfectly in step.

As the procession made its way down the hill, two late-comers slipped through the seated dignitaries on the bleachers. One was a middle-aged woman with short grey hair, a thin neck and glasses that were slightly too big for her face. The other was a teenage boy, rather strangely dressed in a black suit with a white shirt, open at the collar. The clothes didn't look right on him, as if someone had chosen them for him against his wishes. The boy was very pale. His eyes were empty. He had no expression on his face at all.

The woman muttered her apologies as the two of them took their places in their reserved seats. Susan Mortlake and Scott Tyler had arrived. Now they sat and waited for the man they had come to kill.

"We're not going to make it," Jamie said.

"This car won't go any faster," Alicia muttered. "I'm doing the best I can…"

But it was already twelve fifteen and although they had seen signs for Auburn along Highway 80, the town refused to come into sight. There were three of them in the car. Jamie was next to Alicia. Daniel was sitting in the back, leaning over them both.

Jamie hadn't been able to explain how he had worked it out but he knew, with cold certainty, that he was right. He had seen photographs of Charles Baker when he was in the Nightrise offices in Los Angeles and Senator Trelawny had explained how the corporation was bankrolling his rival's campaign. Perhaps this was why they had wanted Scott and Jamie in the first place. Scott could order Trelawny to throw himself under a car. He could tell him to stop breathing and the senator would suffocate then and there. The two boys had always tried to keep their powers hidden. They had learned, from bitter experience, what they were capable of. If Scott had been turned into a weapon, he would be unstoppable.

Scott. That was the other thought racing through Jamie's mind. Of course he wanted to save the senator's life. But if they got to Auburn in time, he would see his brother again and that mattered to him more.

"We're here!" Alicia spoke the words and a moment later veered off the highway, taking an exit that sloped up to a bridge and over to the other side. As they turned, Jamie saw the statue of Claude Chana crouching below. Was this really the same figure that had haunted him, repeatedly, in his dreams? There could be no doubt of it. The statue might look harmless now. It wasn't a giant or a monster. But somehow it had been sent to bring him a warning. Jamie glanced at the clock on the dashboard. Twenty-five past twelve! He wondered if he was already too late.

They reached the other side of the bridge. Now Jamie saw some of the crowds spilling over the pavements and heard the music of the marching bands. There was a policeman ahead, signalling them to move forward. But that was the wrong way.

The road would lead them past the courthouse and up to the new town. Alicia needed to turn right – but that way had been blocked off. From this position, there was no sight of the bleachers, the post office, the stage where Trelawny would speak. But one thing was certain. There was nowhere to park, no way they could drive into the crowd.

The policeman was waving at them, more angrily now.

"Mum…?" Daniel muttered from the back seat.

"Hold on," Alicia said.

She spun the wheel to the right and slammed her foot down on the accelerator. The tyres screamed. The car shot forward and down the hill towards the crowd.

John Trelawny was in the back of a vintage 1960s Cadillac. The mayor of Auburn was next to him. As usual there was a secret-service man driving. Warren Cornfield was in the front passenger seat, his eyes completely hidden behind a pair of solid black wraparound sunglasses. There were two more secret-service men walking with the car, one on each side. They had followed Trelawny all the way down the street and the strange thing was that, despite the heat, they had barely broken into a sweat.

Trelawny could see his wife sitting in the bleachers next to another woman, whom he had met earlier that morning – she was married to the mayor. His two sons were sitting there too and he knew that they wouldn't be enjoying this. Both of them felt shy about being out in public. His car had almost completed its circuit around the bleachers and any minute now it would stop and he and the mayor would get out. The speeches would begin. It seemed so strange to be here. Trelawny remembered playing in these streets as a child. And now here he was, fifty years old, and all these people had turned out on account of him. He wished his parents were alive to see this moment. He also hoped the speeches wouldn't go on too long.

The car slowed down and stopped. Warren Cornfield was the first out, his hand resting on the car door, his head swivelling to take in the crowds.

About fifteen metres away, in the middle of the bleachers, Susan Mortlake leant over and rested her hand on Scott's arm.

"All right, my dear," she whispered. "It's time. Do it now."

There was a filling station at the bottom of the slope and it was the one thing in the town that hadn't closed. Alicia drove off the ramp and into the forecourt, skidding to a halt beside the pumps. She and Jamie left the car. Daniel scrambled out after them.

"Hey!" The garage attendant had come out of his office. "You can't leave that here!"

But they were already on their way, abandoning the car, pushing their way through the crowds. Alicia knew that they were in danger. The policeman on the bridge must have seen what they had done and he would have put out a radio alert. There was a presidential candidate in the area and anyone behaving strangely would have to be brought down quickly. In other words, shoot first – ask questions later. She wished now that she had left Daniel behind.

"How are we going to find him?" Jamie shouted.

He couldn't absorb it all: the people in their thousands, the bands still playing, the welcoming banners, the sunlight, the flags flying red, white and blue. He felt he was being stifled. The wound in his shoulder was throbbing badly. For a moment he lost sight of Alicia.

"Watch where you're going!" He had barged into a family. The father was a fat man, wearing a Homer Simpson T-shirt. He was scowling at him.

Alicia was a little way behind, clinging tightly onto Daniel. "Use your power!" she called to him. "You can find Scott. You don't have to look for him."

Jamie understood. He didn't need to look. He could think. If Scott was anywhere near, surely he would be able to sense him. He turned his head…

And saw his brother.

Scott! He was there!

At first, Jamie didn't recognize him. Scott was sitting so still. And he was pale, as if the life had been sucked out of him. His hair had been cut short in a style that didn't suit him and he was too smartly dressed in a black jacket, black trousers and a shirt that was a brilliant white. It was Scott but it wasn't him. Jamie had never seen him like this before and he was suddenly afraid.

He noticed the woman sitting next to him and knew her instantly, even though he had only ever seen her once – and then very briefly. She was part of Nightrise. She had come out of the Los Angeles office when he was there. Her eyes, behind the oversized glasses, were fixed on Scott. She was like a mother who was overly proud of her son, but – Jamie could see it in her face – this was a son who was about to do something horrible.

"Jamie!" Alicia had called out a warning. The policeman who had seen them drive down the ramp was searching for them. He was in front of the filling station – and would have spotted them if it hadn't been for the crush of people between them. There were three more policemen with him.

"Ladies and gentlemen. It is my very great honour to welcome a fine politician and a fine man back to his home town on this … his big day!"

The mayor was speaking. His voice was being amplified by speakers positioned all the way up the street. Jamie saw him, standing on a platform in front of a bank of microphones. Senator Trelawny was next to him.

The crowd burst into applause.

Scott was staring at something, deep in concentration. Jamie couldn't run over to him. He would have to push his way through four lines of people, climb over the barrier and cross the road. He would never even get close. There was only one thing he could do.

Scott…! He projected his thoughts over the crowd, directly into his brother's head.

And reeled back, stunned.

It was as if he had run into a brick wall. He actually felt it, a physical blow. His head snapped back. He tasted blood.

"Jamie? What are you doing?" Alicia had managed to reach him. Daniel was with her. But Jamie couldn't explain it to her. Not now.

"Fifty years old today – and before he's fifty-one, he'll be the next president of the United States." The mayor grinned and put an arm around Senator Trelawny. The crowd applauded again.

Scott! It's me! Jamie tried again. Once again, he was rocked backwards. His brother had built a sort of force field around himself. It had never happened before. Scott wasn't letting him in.

"Mum…!" Daniel pointed. The policemen had seen them.

What was Scott doing? His eyes seemed to be fixed on the senator. No. It was the big fair-haired man next to him. The security chief. What was his name?

Warren Cornfield removed his sunglasses. Jamie saw him drop them on the ground as if he no longer cared about them. Then he took out his gun.

Jamie understood exactly what was happening. He could see it in the eyes of the grey-haired woman, her expectant smile. This was her doing. It was all happening exactly as she had planned.

A presidential candidate may feel safe, but he is always surrounded by men with guns – and one of those men had just been turned against him. Scott's powers must have grown stronger than ever. He was giving orders tele-pathically, without opening his mouth. Jamie could see it happening now.

He was ordering Warren Cornfield to assassinate his boss.

And standing next to him, Susan Mortlake felt the power flow and almost wanted to laugh out loud. How ironic it was that it should be one of the Five who should be instrumental in creating the new world – one that would have President Charles Baker in the driving seat. It was perfect. The blond-haired man would kill Trelawny. There would be two thousand witnesses. Nothing would connect him with Nightrise. Later on, they would assume he had gone mad. And she and the boy would slip quietly away. It was almost too easy. And this was just the beginning…

Jamie was sweating. There was nothing he could do. He couldn't break through the crowd. He couldn't connect with Scott. But now he could see the gun in Warren Cornfield's hand. The security man was staring into space, unable to stop himself. Nobody else had seen him. Everyone was watching Trelawny and the mayor.

"Ma'am – I want you to come with us…" The policemen had reached them, the crowd parting to let them through. The officer who had seen them on the bridge was leading them. He was short and plump with brown-tinted glasses and a moustache. Alicia turned to argue with him.

Warren Cornfield aimed his gun at Trelawny.

Jamie was still fighting, trying to reach Scott. But the wall was solid. There was no way through.

It was over.

No.

There was another way…

Jamie turned away from his brother and focused all his mental energy on Cornfield. He sent his thoughts across the street, through all the noise and the confusion, the cheering and the applause, and immediately it was as if he had broken into a private room and Scott was there with him, inside the security man's head. Jamie heard him giving the orders that were forcing Cornfield to commit murder. At the same moment, he felt the gun in his hand, his finger tightening on the trigger and knew that it was already too late, that he couldn't stop the man firing.

The secret-service men closest to the platform saw the gun.

Somebody screamed. The policeman had taken hold of Alicia but now he turned to see what had happened.

Jamie did the only thing he could do. He knew he was about to make the most terrible decision of his life but he could see no other option.

He gave the order.

Not Trelawny. The woman!

Warren Cornfield fired.

But at the very last moment, he swivelled round and shot directly into the bleachers. His bullet hit Susan Mortlake in the centre of her forehead. She was thrown backwards. And at once everything changed as the crowd went crazy, screaming and struggling to get away, and the entire parade exploded into chaos.

The secret-service people had acted too late but now they moved fast. Two of them threw themselves on top of Trelawny, dragging him to the ground. Two more dealt with Warren Cornfield. If there hadn't been so many people around, he would have been shot and killed. Instead, they tackled him, knocking him down and disarming him. He didn't even try to resist. All the life had gone out of his eyes. He didn't seem to know where he was or what he had just done.

The policeman let go of Alicia. He suspected that she was part of what had just happened but he couldn't be sure, and his job right now was to try to bring the crowd under control before anyone else was killed. There were people running everywhere, screaming, trying to protect their children. The barriers were being knocked over. The bands had abandoned their instruments and were trying to get out of sight, afraid that there might be more shots. As Jamie watched, Senator Trelawny was led away and thrown into a car as if it was his turn now to be kidnapped. But of course his safety was the first priority. His wife and children were also being bundled out of their seats. The whole family had to be removed from the scene before any more shots were fired.

And what about Scott? He was sitting in the same place and looked dazed, as if he couldn't quite understand what had happened. Susan Mortlake was next to him, her head flung back, her legs apart. She was quite spectacularly dead. Jamie took advantage of all the confusion around him. The way ahead was clear. He ran forward, leapt over a barrier and crossed the road. A moment later, he was climbing up the bleachers. There was a doctor crouching next to the mayor's wife, who was screaming, in hysterics. A few people were still in their seats, traumatized, blood-splattered. Jamie ignored them.

Finally he had reached his brother.

"Scott!"

Scott turned but didn't recognize him and that was when Jamie knew how much had been done to him, how badly he had been hurt.

He didn't know what to do. He felt a burning in his throat. He had dreamed of the moment when he would find his brother again but he had never expected it to be like this.

And then a woman he didn't know came up to him. Jamie glanced at her only briefly, taking in her dark red hair and expensive clothes. But she seemed to know him. "Are you Jamie Tyler?" she asked.

He didn't know what to say. He just wanted her to leave him alone.

"You don't know me, but I'm a friend of John Trelawny." She had to shout to make herself heard above all the confusion. "My name is Nathalie Johnson. I was here today as his guest but I've been looking for you. For both of you…"

"My brother…" Jamie could only think of Scott.

378

The woman nodded. "Please. Trust me. I can help you. We have to get you both away."

On the other side of the street, the policeman who had been about to arrest Alicia was making connections. He had worked out that he knew the boy from the car. He was the boy who was wanted in Nevada – the one who had shot his uncle. And there he was on the bleachers, talking to someone, right next to the woman who had been shot.

The policeman didn't understand what was going on. There was too much going on to understand. But one thing was certain. The boy was a wanted felon.

He picked up his radio and began to talk.

CAVE ROCK

There was no time to think and there was so much they needed to do. Nearly everyone had left the bleachers by now, desperate to get away from the sprawled-out corpse of the woman who had been shot. At the same time, police and paramedics had arrived and taken charge. They had no interest in Scott, who was still sitting there, staring ahead of him. There were some spots of bright red blood on his white shirt.

"Was he with her?" one of the paramedics asked. The boy looked as though he was in shock. Maybe it was his mother who had been killed.

"No," Nathalie replied. "He's with me." She turned to Jamie. "We have to get him out of here," she said.

"Scott!" Jamie crouched beside his brother. Scott had blocked him out before but if he saw him, if he heard his voice, maybe it would be different. "It's me … Jamie. It's all right now. Nightrise is finished. They've closed Silent Creek. I've been looking all over the place for you but I'm here. Everything's going to be OK."

Something passed very briefly through Scott's eyes – perhaps a flicker of recognition. He opened his mouth and tried to speak but no words came. Jamie turned to Nathalie Johnson and there were tears in his eyes. "What have they done to him?" he cried. "What have they done?"

Between them they helped Scott to his feet and carried him with them. He moved like a sleepwalker, not resisting but seemingly unaware of where he was going. Alicia was waiting for them at the bottom of the bleachers, with Daniel. She hadn't been able to come any closer. She couldn't expose her eleven-year-old son to the sight of the dead woman.

"Jamie! Scott!" She didn't know what to say.

"Are you Alicia McGuire?" Nathalie asked.

"Yes."

"It's all right. I'm a friend. John told me about you."

"Who are you?" Alicia asked.

Nathalie looked around her. The streets were emptying rapidly, people scattering in all directions. Soon there would only be policemen left. "We can't talk here," she said. "We have to get these boys on their way."

"On their way where?"

"Alicia...!" It was already too late. Jamie pointed. The policeman with the moustache was striding purposefully towards them. He had unfastened his holster and his hand was on his gun.

"Tyler." The single word was an accusation. The policeman

stood with his legs slightly apart, like a cowboy in an old film. "Jamie Tyler. Right?"

"No." Jamie looked him straight in the eyes and pushed. "Jamie Tyler was here but he's gone. You've missed him. And now you've got to help all these people. You're not interested in us."

The policeman frowned as if he hadn't quite heard what Jamie had said. Then he relaxed. "You're right. I've got to help these people." He turned round and walked away.

Nathalie Johnson stared, not sure what she had seen. But Alicia understood. Jamie had done the same thing when they were trapped in Don White's house in Sparks. Even so, she shivered. She couldn't imagine what it must be like for a fourteen-year-old to have so much power.

She turned to Nathalie. "Listen to me," she said. "We're not going anywhere until we know who you are."

"I'm Nathalie Johnson."

The name meant something. Alicia had seen it in the news. "Computers?" she asked. "Are you that Nathalie Johnson?"

"Yes."

"You helped the senator. You did a couple of fundraisers last year…"

"Yes. But that's not why I'm here." Nathalie stopped. The policeman with the moustache had disappeared but she had no doubt that others would soon arrive. They had been lucky that he had decided to make the arrest on his own – but he would surely have put out an alert before he moved in. "I have a car very near here," she said. "Will you come with me at least that far? I'll tell you the rest once we're on the way."

Alicia nodded. She couldn't take her own car. The police would surely be guarding it, waiting for her to return. And anyway, they would have circulated its number.

They hurried round behind the bleachers and down towards the statue. Nathalie first. Then Jamie and Alicia, guiding Scott between them. Finally Daniel. As they went past, Jamie glanced one last time at the statue. He felt a strange mixture of emotions, looking at the craggy face, doomed to kneel for ever with the dusty highway in front of him. The prospector had travelled a long way to deliver his warning. At least Jamie hadn't let him down.

Nathalie's car – a blue Mercedes – was parked near by in a spot reserved for VIPs. Normally she would have had a chauffeur, but today she had decided to drive herself.

"You can take my car," she said. She handed Alicia the keys. "The best way I can help you is to make some calls."

"Where am I meant to go?" Alicia asked.

"Give me a minute. You need to get to an airport. I'm just trying to think which one."

"An airport?"

Nathalie sighed. "I know this is difficult for you but you have to understand. I know what's been happening … or some of it anyway. You see, I belong to a group of people, an organization, that exists solely to help Jamie and Scott and the other Gatekeepers."

Gatekeepers.

Jamie stared. Had this woman really said that?

"What do you mean?" Alicia demanded.

"It's all right, Alicia," Jamie cut in. He looked at Nathalie. "You know about the Gatekeepers," he said.

"Yes, Jamie. The Gatekeepers. The Five." She paused. "I know Matt Freeman."

"Where did you meet him?"

"In England. I met him there twice. But he's not there now. He's in Peru. A place called Nazca, just south of Lima. And that's where you have to go."

"Peru...?" Alicia couldn't believe what she was hearing.

"It's OK." Jamie hadn't told Alicia anything about the time after he was shot. He had decided it was too much to explain. He hadn't even wanted to try. "Why is Matt in Peru?" he asked.

"There was a second gate. It opened. Matt tried to stop it but he was hurt. Pedro is with him now. Pedro may be able to help your brother. That's another reason why you have to be there."

"What about Scar?"

Nathalie shook her head. "I don't know any Scar."

Jamie had made his decision. Everything that Nathalie had said had made him think that she was telling the truth, and the mention of Pedro clinched it. That was Inti's other name. Matt had told him. And Inti had the power to heal. The sooner Scott was with him, the better.

"How do we get there?" he demanded.

Nathalie let out a deep breath. She had been afraid that she would be unable to persuade them – but somehow Jamie had found out who and what he was. One day she would ask him how that had happened. But for now, she had to think straight. They were in Auburn. The police were still looking for them. Nightrise might be looking for them too. How to get them away…

"Lake Tahoe Airport," she said. She glanced at Alicia. "It's just off the 89. Right down at the south end of the lake."

"I've passed it," Alicia said. "But Sacramento is nearer."

"If the police are looking for you, they'll close off all the airports. Lake Tahoe is tiny. And there are no main roads. It's the last place anyone will think of looking."

"What happens when we get there? I just buy the boys a single ticket to Lima?"

"I can arrange a private jet. I can have it in the air within fifteen minutes. It'll fly out from San Francisco and it should be there waiting for you when you arrive."

"And you're just going to give us your car?"

"The car doesn't matter. Nothing matters. Just get them there." She rested a hand on Jamie's arm. "I'll call Matt and tell him you're coming," she said. "And one day you and I will meet properly and you can tell me everything that's happened." They heard the squawk of a radio on the other side of the bleachers. The police were sealing off the entire area. It was time to go.

Alicia didn't even try to argue. She unlocked the doors. Daniel got into the front. Jamie helped Scott into the back and was about to follow him. But then he remembered something. He straightened up, facing Nathalie.

"The security man," he said. "Warren Cornfield…"

"You made him do that." So she had guessed what had happened.

"I couldn't do anything else. Will you be able to help him?"

"I'll do what I can, Jamie. I promise."

Then another policeman appeared, walking towards them. Jamie got into the car. Alicia didn't even wait for him to close the door.

She started the engine. They sped off.

Nobody said anything for the first few miles. They were heading south towards Placerville, another gold-mining town. From here they would pick up the 50 heading east back to Nevada. Scott seemed to be neither awake nor asleep but somewhere between the two. He was sitting slumped against the window. Jamie was next to him, watching the scenery go past without taking any of it in. He was thinking about Matt. Of course, it wouldn't be the same Matt that he had spoken to after the battle, at the river's edge. For a start, this Matt would never have met him or Scott. But they wer still the Five. The same … but in a different time. That was how Matt had explained it. Perhaps when they were all together in Peru it would make sense.

Peru. Jamie didn't even know where it was. Somewhere in South America? Even now, a private jet should have been taking off to collect them. The very thought of it made his head spin. He had never flown in his life.

Alicia glanced round. "How's Scott?"

"I don't know." Jamie had examined his brother. He could see no sign of any external injury, but in a way that made his condition even more disturbing.

"We'll be there in a couple of hours. Maybe you should try to get some sleep."

But they never made it to Lake Tahoe Airport.

They had just passed through the Eldorado National Forest and some of the most beautiful countryside in California and were heading north towards the lake itself. They came to a sign pointing to the airport and Alicia turned off, following a narrow leafy road. Nathalie had certainly been right. Nobody would think of coming here.

But the police must have decided to cover every airport in the surrounding area. It was always possible that they weren't working alone. Perhaps Nightrise had been influencing and advising them. Either way, the road was blocked. There was a single police car parked across with two young officers checking every car that came their way. They were looking bored. There couldn't have been more than half a dozen cars in the last few hours.

Alicia pulled in and waited with the engine ticking over.

What now?

"Is there another way?" Daniel asked.

Alicia bit her lip. "I don't think so, Danny. I didn't see any other signs."

Jamie was sitting up in the back seat. He was feeling sick. They were so near. It didn't seem fair that they should be stopped at the very end. "Can you drive round?" he muttered.

"There's no point," Alicia said. "I could get past them – but suppose the plane hasn't arrived? They'd just follow us into the airport and that would be the end of it. And even if the plane's there, we'd never reach it in time."

"We could try on foot…"

"Scott won't make it. And anyway, it's too late."

She was right. The two police officers had noticed them. They were already muttering to each other, staring at them suspiciously. It was always possible that the details of Nathalie's number plate had been sent out. It didn't really matter. A car had been driving towards them. Now it had stopped. Something was obviously wrong.

Alicia made a decision. It was probably the wrong one but she couldn't think of anything else to do. She slammed the car into reverse, spun the wheel and sped off.

"What are you doing?" Daniel demanded.

"We can't get past them. The road to the airport's closed. The only thing to do is to get back to Reno. We can hide out at the trailer park. Nobody knows we're there. The senator will help us. Maybe that's what we should have done from the start."

388

The two police officers had seen them leave. Without a moment's hesitation, they ran back to their car and set off in pursuit. One of them was already on the radio calling for assistance from every town in the area. Four suspects heading east towards Carson City. A blue Mercedes, registration number NATHAL3. There were few roads in this part of the country and the distances were huge. There was no chance they were going to get away.

The Mercedes was doing almost a hundred miles an hour. Alicia was gripping the wheel, her eyes fixed on the road. She already knew that she had made a mistake, trying to break away. She had turned herself into a target. Any minute now she expected to see more cars blocking the road. Maybe a helicopter would come swooping out of the sky. She had lost sight of the police car but she could hear it. The officers had turned on their siren. It was less than a mile behind.

They flashed through a commercial centre with supermarkets and shops selling boat equipment and ski gear. That was the thing about Lake Tahoe. Skiing in the winter, boating in the summer, beautiful all the year round. Now they caught occasional glimpses of the lake on their left, the icy, deep blue water shimmering on the other side of the pine trees that covered the banks. They were still speeding, putting more space between themselves and the pursuing police car, which seemed to have dropped back a bit in the distance. Certainly its siren seemed fainter. Alicia wondered if she should come off the road – but there was no turning, nowhere to hide.

On one side there was the lake. On the other, the ground rose up steeply with a rough sandy rock face and above it more trees that seemed to continue all the way to the sky.

They were trapped on the road and Jamie had come to the same conclusion as Alicia. They weren't going to get away. What would happen if they were arrested by the police? John Trelawny would help them – but would he be able to reach them in time? It only took one policeman, paid the right amount of money, to make sure that none of them were ever seen again.

They shot through a tunnel that had been bored through a huge mass of rock. Ahead of them the road twisted to the right.

And then Jamie heard it. A whisper in his head.

Stop the car...

Three words. But he hadn't heard them. Nor had he imagined them. With a thrill of excitement, he realized what had happened. Scott had sent them. He had finally made contact.

"Stop!" he shouted.

Alicia carried on driving.

"Alicia! Stop the car! Now!"

The urgency in his voice made itself felt. Daniel was already twisting round, looking at him as if he was mad, but Alicia slammed her foot on the brake and the car sliced across the road and skidded to a halt in a lay-by. The engine stalled. Somewhere behind them, the scream of the siren filled the air.

"Jamie..." Alicia began.

She was on the edge of tears, blaming herself for what had happened. But looking around him, Jamie realized something.

He knew where he was. He had been here before.

Five or six years ago. Before Don and Marcie. Even before Ed and Leanne. Derry, their social worker, had brought them to this exact spot because she had wanted to show them where they had been found. It was this lay-by, right here. This was where the two babies had been abandoned in a box intended for garden seeds.

And she had told them something about the area. According to Derry, the Washoe Indian tribe had been living here as long ago as ten thousand years. It was the main reason she had assumed that Scott and Jamie were Washoe themselves. Lake Tahoe was the very centre of their universe and somewhere below them there was a cave that was so sacred that tourists weren't allowed anywhere near it. Even the *shamans* wouldn't go there.

The Washoe called this place *de'ek wadapush*. In English, that translated as Cave Rock.

"We're getting out," Jamie said.

"Jamie…" Alicia knew from his voice that there was no point arguing. They had only seconds left. The police car was still out of sight but it would be thundering towards them.

"I think this is goodbye, Alicia." Jamie didn't know how he knew. He just did. "Thank you for helping me. Thank you for everything."

"You did it all, Jamie. Not me…"

"Goodbye, Danny." Jamie reached forward and shook hands with Alicia's son, then opened the door. He slid out, then waited for Scott to follow. Alicia had also got out. They had no time. She seized hold of Jamie and kissed him briefly on the cheek, then pressed something into his hand. The scream of the police siren had disappeared. For a brief instant she thought it might have gone a different way or even broken down – but her hopes were dashed almost at once. The car had simply entered the tunnel and the bulk of the mountains was blocking any sound. As she looked up the road, it burst out. Worse still, a second police car had joined it. Both cars were racing towards them.

A sandy track ran through the fir trees and past a series of boulders. Jamie and Scott had broken into a run, heading away from the road and down towards the lake. The ground tumbled unevenly all the way to the water's edge. A wooden platform had been built for tourists and the view was certainly awesome, with the lake a dazzling blue in the afternoon sun and a range of mountains, some of them snow-peaked even now, spread out on the other side. There was nobody else around. Jamie leapt over a fence and breathed a sigh of relief as his brother did the same.

Scott – are you with me? He sent the thought without opening his mouth.

I'm with you. The words were indistinct, as if transmitted by a faulty radio. But Jamie heard them and felt a surge of hope that carried him on. He had no real idea why he was doing this. He wasn't even sure what he was doing. The very fact that they were here at all was surely some sort of crazy coincidence. But at the same time he knew that it was meant. They were doing the right thing.

"This is the police! Stay where you are! If you don't stop, we'll open fire!"

The words rang out, amplified through a bullhorn. Jamie almost laughed. They weren't going to stop now. Did the police think that having come so far they would turn round and give themselves up? But the smile was wiped off his face a second later. There was a gunshot and a bullet ricocheted off one of the boulders just a few yards away. A warning shot? Or were the police really prepared to shoot them in the back?

He didn't intend to find out. They were climbing down. The ground had fallen away so steeply that they had to use their hands and feet to guide them. The road was high up above them and unless the police followed them over the fence, they would be out of sight. With Jamie leading the way, they scrambled down the last few yards, using the lower branches of the fir trees to stop themselves falling. At last their feet hit shingle. They had reached the edge of the lake. The water spread out in front of them, millions and millions of gallons. And despite everything that had happened and the exertion of the descent, Jamie felt strangely at peace. It was as if he had come home. He still didn't know for certain that he would find what he expected to find, but he was glad he was here.

He turned round – and there it was, just as Derry had said.

A path of pure, white sand led to an opening in the rock. The cave was very dark and twisted back underneath the road. There was a design scratched into the surface, just above the entrance, so faint that he might not have noticed it unless he had been looking for it. A five-pointed star. Anyone else might think it had been carved recently but Jamie knew differently. It had been put there a long, long time ago.

Someone shouted, high above. One of the policemen. Jamie took a deep breath. It was finally over. It was time for him to go.

He took hold of his brother. The two of them walked up the path and together they went into the cave.

The police never found them. They climbed down and searched along the shoreline. They even looked inside the cave although they had heard of the Washoe traditions and knew they had no right to be there. By the time the sun began to set there were more than a dozen officers in the area. But if Scott and Jamie Tyler had ever been there, they had now completely disappeared. Had they walked into the lake and drowned? It seemed impossible. They would surely have been seen from above, and anyway there was no sign of the bodies.

Alicia was admitting nothing. In fact she and Danny denied that the two boys had ever been in the car. She demanded to speak to Senator Trelawny.

And while the police were calling off the search and discussing what to do next, many thousands of miles away, a

394

door in a church had opened and two boys were stepping out into a strange and unfamiliar world. A few tourists glanced at them curiously. A priest, who had seen them emerge, scratched his head in puzzlement. The door had been kept locked for as long as he could remember and he was sure that there was nothing more than an empty storeroom on the other side.

It took Scott and Jamie half an hour to find a tour guide who spoke English and from her they learnt that they had arrived in Peru, even if they had managed to wind up in quite the wrong part of the country. They were in the city of Cuzco, high up in the Andes. The church was called Santo Domingo and had been built by the Spanish on top of another sacred site ... Coricancha, the temple of gold, once a place of worship for the ancient Incas.

They were far away from California and although everything – including the language – was very alien to them, they knew they were safe. That night, they stayed in a hotel. At the very last moment, acting on impulse, Alicia had pressed a hundred dollars into Jamie's hand. The money would pay for a room and a meal. The next morning they would use it to buy two bus tickets to a little town on the western coast. A place called Nazca.

In fact, the journey took them more than thirty hours. Scott still wasn't talking – he wasn't even sending any thoughts – and at night, when he was asleep, he would mutter and cry out and his body would twitch as if it was being prodded or given electric shocks. Jamie forced himself not to worry. Pedro was waiting. The healer. Scott would see him and he would be all right.

Three days later, they arrived. A taxi dropped them at an attractive whitewashed house set in a large garden with fountains playing and llamas wandering across the lawn. As they walked through the gate, the front door of the house opened and a boy emerged. Jamie recognized him at once. Dark hair cut short. Broad shoulders. Blue eyes.

It was Matt.

Another boy stepped out behind him and again Jamie knew at once who he was. Pedro. It seemed strange to think that the last time they had met, they had been drinking wine together in a field just hours after finishing a war. He wondered how he would ever explain it all. Where would he even begin?

Matt stepped forward. Although he was trying not to show it, it was obvious that he was in pain. So that made three of them. Scott needed help. And Jamie still had a large hole in his shoulder. He wondered how many of them would be hurt, how many of them would have to die before this was all over.

At last they stood facing each other.

"Jamie," Matt said. "And Scott."

He reached out a hand. Jamie took it.

Four of the Five had come together. The circle was almost complete.

DEPARTURES

The girl in the business-class lounge at Heathrow Airport was dressed in a short white jacket, a pink T-shirt and trousers cut off above the ankle. She had a backpack on the seat beside her and a book open on her lap, although she hadn't read any of it in the thirty minutes she had been there. There was a glass of Coke on the table in front of her but she hadn't touched that either.

It was the second week in November and the weather had suddenly turned nasty, blustery showers hitting London and sending the commuters running behind umbrellas and clutched hats. Even now the rain was rattling against the windows of the lounge, dripping off the wings of the waiting planes. The runways looked even greyer than usual. Most of the flights had been delayed.

The girl carried a British passport but her features were anything but. Her looks were very striking, partly Chinese with long black hair tied at the back and eyes that were an unusual shade of green. She was small and thin but there was a confidence about her, a sense that she could look after herself. She was making the flight as a Skyflyer Solo – that was what the airline called her – and they had given her a plastic label to wear around her neck. She had pulled it off the moment she had sat down.

Her name was Scarlett Adams and she was fifteen years old.

She wasn't usually a nervous flyer but she was nervous today. She still didn't know why she was making this journey. Only the day before she had been at the expensive private school in Dulwich where she had been sent when she was thirteen. St Genevieve's was an all-girls school, housed in a rather grand Victorian building with ivy growing up the walls and extensive grounds at the back. Although the school did have a boarding wing, she was a day girl. Her parents lived abroad but they had a house five minutes away and a housekeeper who looked after her during term time.

Yesterday, just before lunch, the headmistress had asked to see her in her study. As Scarlett had climbed the stairs to the waiting area, which everyone called the graveyard because there were so many portraits of dead teachers, she had wondered what sort of trouble she might be in. Was it that argument with Miss Wilson, the geography teacher? Or the physics homework she had "left on the bus"? Or the fight in the computer block – even if it hadn't been her who'd started it?

But when she was shown in to the cosy room with its gas fire and view over the front drive, it was the last thing she had expected to hear.

"Scarlett, I'm afraid you're going to be leaving us for a few weeks." The headmistress didn't look at all pleased. "I've just had a phone call from your father. He was very mysterious, if you want the truth. But it seems that some sort of crisis has arisen. He's well – but he needs you with him. He's already arranged the flight."

"When am I leaving?"

"Tomorrow. I have to say, it's very inconvenient. You've got your GCSEs to consider and we're going to have to recast the Christmas play. But he was insistent. He said he'd talk to you tonight."

Scarlett had spoken to her father when she got home but he hadn't added much more to what the headmistress had already said. He needed her to come out for a week or two. He would explain why when she got there. The housekeeper – a dark and rather sour-looking Scottish woman – was already packing. It seemed that there was nothing to discuss. Scarlett had spent the rest of the evening emailing and texting her friends and went to bed in a bad mood.

And she wasn't feeling much better now, waiting for her flight to be called. She looked around her. There was the usual collection of business people, some of them hitting the free alcohol, others catching up with the day's news. A plasma TV stood in one corner of the lounge and she glanced at the screen.

"Today, the new president-elect of the United States issued a statement ..."

They were going on about the election again. For the past week, the news had been full of little else. Scarlett watched as Charles Baker appeared behind the rostrum, facing the press corps.

"The defeat of Senator John Trelawny sent shockwaves among his friends and supporters," the report continued. "The final vote, with Baker taking just over fifty-two per cent of the nationwide ballot and the electoral college, took everyone by surprise and has led to increasingly bitter accusations of electoral fraud."

Now Baker was speaking. He was smartly dressed and looked relaxed. He would have been handsome except that there was something wrong with his eyes. It was as if they weren't quite able to focus.

"I hate to accuse Senator Trelawny of sour grapes," he said. "But these accusations are completely ridiculous and I see no reason for an official enquiry."

The image changed. There were shots of people protesting outside the White House. They were carrying banners, walking in angry silence.

"At issue are the computer systems used to count the votes," the report went on. "Almost seventy per cent of votes in a US election are counted by machines and critics point out that no fewer than three of the main vote-counting companies have strong links with the Nightrise Corporation – which backed Charles Baker throughout the campaign."

Scarlett had been about to stop watching. She had no

interest in politics. But one word had caught her attention.

Nightrise.

How strange.

That was the company her father worked for in Hong Kong, and that was exactly where she was heading now. Could they really have been involved in some sort of fraud? It seemed very unlikely. Her father was a lawyer and she couldn't imagine him ever doing anything wrong.

A young woman in a British Airways uniform had come into the lounge. She walked over to Scarlett. "Are you ready?" she asked. "We need to go back through departures. They've begun boarding."

Scarlett gathered her things and stood up. The report on the television had finished. She smiled and the two of them left together, on their way to the waiting plane.

ACKNOWLEDGEMENTS

There are some books I just couldn't write without help – and this was one of them. So let me start with Crystal Main, Social Services Chief in Carson City, Nevada, who opened so many doors for me. She arranged for me to visit the Jan Evans Juvenile Hall in Reno and the Summit View Youth Correctional Centre outside Las Vegas. I have borrowed elements from both in writing this, but Silent Creek is entirely my own invention. I'd also like to thank Audrey Fetters, the superintendent at Summit View ... particularly for providing me with some ingenious escape plans! I was very fortunate to meet Lynda Shoshone and Keith Daniel Wyatt, both elders of the Washoe Indian tribe; they told me much about their culture and history. I also owe a debt of thanks to Robert Wilkins, who first suggested Auburn to me as a location. The town – right down to the statue of Claude Chana – is exactly as I describe it in the book. My assistant, Cat Taylor, arranged the research trip for me and my editor, Chris Kloet, has helped knock the book into shape. Finally, my son Cassian read the manuscript and gave me some great ideas.

THE POWER OF FIVE

BOOK FOUR

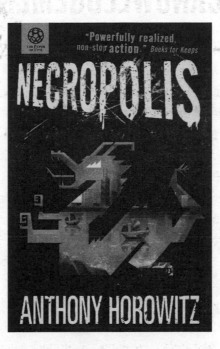

An ancient evil is unleashed.
Five have the power to defeat it.
But one of them has been taken.

Turn the page to read a short taster...

ROAD SENSE

The girl didn't look before crossing the road.

That was what the driver said later. She didn't look left or right. She'd seen a friend on the opposite pavement and she simply walked across to join him, not noticing that the lights had turned green, forgetting that this was always a busy junction and that this was four o'clock in the afternoon when people were trying to get their work finished, hurrying on their way home. The girl just set off without thinking. She didn't so much as glimpse the white van heading towards her at fifty miles an hour.

But that was typical of Scarlett Adams. She always was a bit of a dreamer, the sort of person who'd act first and then think about what she'd done only when it was far too late. The hockey ball that she had tried to thwack over the school roof, but which had instead gone straight through the headmistress's window. The groundsman she had pushed, fully clothed, into the swimming pool. It might have been a good idea to check first that he could swim. The twenty-metre tree she'd climbed up, only to realize that there was no possible way back down.

Fortunately, her school made allowances. It helped that Scarlett was generally popular, was liked by most of the teachers and even if she was never top of the class, managed to be never too near the bottom. Where she really excelled was at sports. She was captain of the hockey team (despite the occasional misfires), a strong tennis player and an all-round winner when it came to summer athletics. No school will give too much trouble to someone who brings home the trophies and Scarlett was responsible for a whole clutch of them.

The school was called St Genevieve's and from the outside it could have been a stately home or perhaps a private hospital for the very rich. It stood in its own grounds, set back from the road, with ivy growing up the walls, sash windows and a bell tower perched on top of the roof. The uniform, it was generally agreed, was the most hideous in England: a mauve dress, a yellow jersey and, in summer months, a straw hat. Everyone hated the straw hats. In fact it was a tradition for every girl to set the wretched thing on fire on their last day.

St Genevieve's was a private school, one of many that were clustered together in the centre of Dulwich, in South London. It was a strange part of the world and everyone who lived there knew it. To the west there was Streatham and to the east Sydenham, both areas with high-rise flats, drugs and knife crime. But in Dulwich, everything was green. There were old-fashioned tea shops, the sort that spelled themselves "shoppes", and flower baskets hanging off the lampposts. Most of the cars seemed to be four-by-fours and the mothers who drove them were all on first-name terms. Dulwich College, Dulwich Preparatory School, Alleyn's, St Genevieve's ... they were only a stone's throw away from each other, but of course nobody threw stones at each other. Not in this part of town.

It was obvious from her appearance that Scarlett hadn't been born in England. Her parents might be Mr and Mrs Typical-Dulwich – her mother tall, blonde and elegant, her father looking like the lawyer he always had been, with greying hair, a round face and glasses – but she looked nothing like them. Scarlett had long black hair, strange hazel-green eyes and the soft brown skin of a girl born in China, Hong Kong or some other part of Central Asia. She was slim and small with a dazzling smile that had got her out of trouble on many occasions. She wasn't their real daughter. Everyone knew that. She had known it herself from the earliest age.

She had been adopted. Paul and Vanessa Adams were unable to have children of their own and they had found her in an orphanage in Jakarta. Nobody knew how she had got there. The identity of her birth mother was a mystery. Scarlett tried not to think about her past, where she had come from, but she often wondered what would have happened if the couple who had come all the way from London had chosen the baby in cot seven or nine rather than cot eight. Might she have ended up planting rice somewhere in Indonesia or sewing Nike trainers in some city sweatshop? It was enough to make her shudder ... the thought alone.

Instead of which, she found herself living with her parents in a quiet street, just round the corner from North Dulwich station which was in turn about a fifteen-minute walk from her school. Her father, Paul Adams, specialized in international business law. Her mother, Vanessa, ran a holiday company that put together packages in China and the Far East. The two of them were so busy that they seldom had time for Scarlett – or indeed, for each other. From the time Scarlett had been five, they had employed a full-time housekeeper to look after all of them. Christina Murdoch was short, dark-haired and seemed to have no sense of humour at all. She had come to London from Glasgow and her father was a vicar. Apart from that, Scarlett knew little about her. The two of them got on well enough, but they had both agreed without actually saying it that they were never going to be friends.

One of the good things about living in Dulwich was that Scarlett did have plenty of friends and they all lived very nearby. There were two girls from her class in the same street and there was also a boy – Aidan Ravitch – just five minutes away. It was Aidan who had prompted her to cross the road.

Aidan was in his second year at The Hall, yet another local private school, and had come to London from Los Angeles. He was tall for his age and good-looking in a relaxed, awkward sort of way, with shaggy hair and slightly crumpled features. There was no uniform at his school and he wore the same hoodie, jeans and trainers day in day out. Aidan didn't understand the English. He claimed to be completely mystified by such things as football, tea and *Dr Who*. English policemen in particular baffled him. "Why do they have to wear those stupid hats?" He was Scarlett's closest friend, although both of them knew that Aidan's father worked for an American bank and could be transferred back home any day. Meanwhile, they spent as much time together as they could.

The accident happened on a warm, summer afternoon. Scarlett was thirteen at the time.

It was a little after four and Scarlett was on her way home from school. The very fact that she was allowed to walk home on her own meant a lot to her. It was only on her last birthday that her parents had finally relented ... until then, they had insisted that Mrs Murdoch should meet her at the school gates every day, even though there were far younger girls who were allowed to face the perils of Dulwich High Street without an armed escort. She had never been quite sure what they were so worried about. There was no chance of her getting lost. Her route took her past a flower shop, an organic grocer's and a pub – The Crown and Greyhound – where she might spot a few old men, sitting in the sun with their lemonade shandies. There were no drug dealers, no child snatchers or crazed killers in the immediate area. And she was hardly on her own anyway. From half past three onwards, the streets were crowded with boys and girls streaming in every direction, on their way home.

She had reached the traffic lights on the other side of the village – where five roads met with shops on one side, a primary school on the other – when she noticed him. Aidan was on his own, listening to music. She could see the familiar white wires trailing down from his ears. He saw her, smiled, and called out her name. Without thinking, she began to walk towards him.

The van was being driven by a twenty-five-year-old delivery man called Michael Logue. He would have to give all his details to the police later on. He was delivering spare parts to a sewing machine factory in Bickley and, thanks to the London traffic, he was late. He was almost certainly speeding as he approached the junction. But on the other hand, the lights were definitely green.

Scarlett was about half-way across when she saw him and by that time it was far too late. She saw Aidan's eyes widen in shock and that made her turn her head, wanting to know what it was that he had seen. She froze. The van was almost on top of her.

She could see the driver, staring at her from behind the wheel, his face filled with horror, knowing what was about to happen, unable to do anything about it. The van seemed to be getting bigger and bigger as it drew closer. Even as she watched, it completely filled her vision.

And then everything happened at once.

Aidan shouted out. The driver frantically spun the wheel. The van tilted. And Scarlett found herself being thrown forward, out of the way, as something – or someone – smashed into her back with incredible force. She wanted to cry out but her breath caught in her throat and her knees buckled underneath her. Somewhere in her mind she was aware that a passer-by had leapt off the pavement and that he was trying to save her. His arm was around her waist, his shoulder and head pressed into the small of her back. But how had he managed to get to her so fast? Even if he had seen the van coming and sprinted towards her immediately, he surely wouldn't have reached her in time. He seemed to know what was going to happen almost before it did.

The van shot past, missing her by inches. She actually felt the warm breeze slap her face and smelled the petrol fumes. There had been two books in her hand: a French dictionary and a maths exercise book ... an hour and a half's homework for the evening ahead. As she was carried forward, her hand and arm jerked, out of control, and the books were hurled into the air, landing on the road and sliding across the tarmac as if she had deliberately thrown them away. Scarlett followed them. With the man still grabbing hold of her, she came crashing down. There was a moment of sharp pain as she hit the ground and all the skin was taken off one knee. Behind her, there was the screech of tyres, a blast of a horn and then the ominous sound of metal hitting metal. A car alarm went off. Scarlett lay still.

For what felt like a whole minute, nobody did anything. It was as if someone had taken a photograph and framed it with a sign reading ACCIDENT IN DULWICH. Then Scarlett sat up and twisted round. The man who had saved her was lying stretched out in the road and she was only aware that he was Chinese, in his twenties, with black hair, and that he was wearing jeans and a loose-fitting jacket. She looked past him. The white van had swerved round a traffic island, mounted the pavement and smashed into a car parked in front of the primary school. It was this car's alarm that had gone off. The driver of the van was slumped over the wheel, his head covered in broken glass.

She turned back. A crowd had already formed – perhaps it had been there from the start – and people were hurrying towards her, rushing past Aidan, who seemed to be rooted to the spot. He was shaking his head as if denying that he had been to blame. There were twenty or thirty school kids, some of them already taking photographs with their mobile phones. A policeman had appeared so quickly that he could have popped out of a trapdoor in the pavement. He was the first to reach Scarlett.

"Are you all right? Don't try to move…"

Scarlett ignored him. She put out a hand for support and eased herself back onto her feet. Her knee was on fire and her shoulder felt as if it had been beaten with an iron club, but she was already fairly sure that she hadn't been seriously hurt.

She looked at Aidan, then at the white van. A few people were already helping the driver out, laying him on the pavement. Steam was rising out of the crumpled bonnet. Next to her, the policeman was speaking urgently into his shoulder mike, doing all the stuff with Delta Bravo Oscar Charlie, summoning help.

Finally, Aidan made it over to her. "Scarl...?" That was his name for her. "Are you OK?"

She nodded, suddenly tearful without knowing why. Maybe it was just the shock, the knowledge of what could have been. She wiped her face with the back of her hand, noticing that her nails were grimy and all her knuckles were grazed. Her dress was torn. She realized she must look a wreck.

"You were nearly killed...!" Why was Aidan telling her that? She had more or less worked it out for herself.

Even so, his words reminded her of the man who had saved her. She looked down and was surprised to see that he was no longer there. For a moment she thought that it was a conjuring trick, that he had simply vanished into thin air. Then she saw him, already on the far side of the road – the side that she had been heading towards – hurrying past the shops. He reached a hair salon on the corner, where a woman with hair that was too blonde to be true had just come out. He pushed past her and then he was gone.

Why? He hadn't even stayed long enough to be thanked.

After that, things unravelled more slowly. An ambulance arrived and although Scarlett didn't need it, the van driver had to be put on a stretcher and carried away. Scarlett herself was examined but nothing was broken and in the end she was allowed to go home. Aidan went with her. A WPC accompan-ied them both. Scarlett wondered how that would go down with Mrs Murdoch. Somehow she knew it wasn't going to mean laughter and back-slapping at bedtime.

In fact, the accident had several consequences.

Paul and Vanessa Adams were told what had happened when they got home that night and as soon as they had got over the shock, the knowledge of how close they had come to losing their only child, they began to argue about whose fault it was: their own for allowing Scarlett too much freedom, Aidan for distracting her, or Scarlett for showing so little road sense, even at the age of thirteen. In the end, they decided that in future Mrs Murdoch would take up her old position at the school gates. It would be another nine months before Scarlett was allowed to walk home on her own again.

The identity of the man who had saved her remained a mystery. Where had he come from? How had he seen what was about to happen? Why had he been in such a hurry to get away? Mrs Murdoch decided that he must be an illegal immigrant, that he had taken off at the sight of the approaching policeman. For her part, Scarlett was just sorry that she hadn't been able to thank him. And if he was in some sort of trouble, she would have liked to have helped him.

That was the night she had her first dream.

Scarlett had never been one for vivid dreams. Normally she got home, ate, did her homework, spent forty minutes on her PlayStation 3 and then plunged into a deep, empty sleep that would be ended all too quickly by Mrs Murdoch, shaking her awake for the start of another school day. But this dream was more than vivid. It was so realistic, so detailed that it was almost like being inside a film. And there was something else that was strange about it. As far as she could see, it had no connection to her life or to anything that had happened during the day.

She dreamed that she was in a grey-lit world that might be another planet ... the moon perhaps. In the distance, she could see a vast ocean stretching out to the horizon and beyond – but there were no waves. The surface of the water could have been a single sheet of metal. Everything was dead. She was surrounded by sand-dunes – at least, that was what she thought they were, but they were actually made of dust. They had somehow blown there and – like the dust on the moon – it would stay the same forever. She walked forward. But she left no footprints.

There were four boys standing together, a short distance away.

The boys were searching for her. If she listened carefully, she could actually hear them calling her name. She tried to call back, but although there was no wind, not even a breeze, something snatched the words away.

The boys weren't real. They couldn't be... Scarlett had never seen them before. And yet somehow she was sure that she knew their names.

Scott. Jamie. Pedro. And Matt.

She knew them from somewhere. They had met before.

That was the first time, but over the next two years she had the same dream again and again. And gradually, it began to change. It seemed to her that every time she saw the boys, they were a little further away until finally she had to get used to the fact that she was completely on her own. Every time she went to sleep, she found herself hoping she would see them. More than that. She needed to meet them.

She never spoke about her dreams, not even to Aidan. But somewhere in the back of her mind she knew that finding the four boys had become the single most important thing in her life.

THE BESTSELLING ALEX RIDER SERIES

Alex Rider – you're
never too young
to die…

High in the Alps,
death waits for
Alex Rider…

Sharks. Assassins.
Nuclear bombs.
Alex Rider's in
deep water.

Alex Rider has
90 minutes to save
the world.

Once stung,
twice as deadly.
Alex Rider wants
revenge.

He's back –
and this time there
are no limits.

Alex Rider
bites back…

Alex Rider –
in the jaws
of death…

One bullet.
One life.
The end starts here.

ANTHONY HOROWITZ

RUSSIAN ROULETTE
THE DEADLY PREQUEL TO THE
BESTSELLING ALEX RIDER SERIES

OCTOBER 2013

Become an Alex Rider insider...

www.alexrider.com   www.facebook.com/alexrideruk   www.youtube.com/alexriderinsider

Author photo by Des Willie

ANTHONY HOROWITZ is the author of the number one bestselling Alex Rider books and The Power of Five series. He has enjoyed huge success as a writer for both children and adults, most recently with his highly acclaimed Sherlock Holmes novel, *The House of Silk*.

He has won numerous awards, including the Bookseller Association/Nielsen Author of the Year Award, the Children's Book of the Year Award at the British Book Awards, and the Red House Children's Book Award.

Anthony has also created and written many major television series, including *Injustice*, *Collision* and the award-winning *Foyle's War*.

You can find out more about Anthony and his work at:
www.anthonyhorowitz.com